Cover illustration by Noah Stacey.

This 1st edition: September 2012

Part One

SOUTHERN COMFORT

BALAZS PATAKI

Prologue

Zone of Alienation – somewhere in the former USSR, 3 June 2011, 07:14:10 East European Standard Time/EEST

The pale light of early dawn filters through the reeds and across a foul swamp. Mist lingers in the air, slowly evaporating in the wind that moves a weather-worn sign hanging on rusted barbed wire. The inscription is in Russian: *Опасная зона. Посторонним вход воспрещен* with the biohazard sign in between the lines.

A man is running, wearing a suit half combat fatigue, half urban explorer gear. He is obviously trying to escape something or someone. His face is hidden under the hood of his anorak. Mud spots spoil the battered, Russian-made automatic carbine in his hand.

Commands are barked from afar. The running man speeds up his pace. Shots are fired. He turns back, frantically fires a burst from his weapon, then continues running. Through the fading mist, about a hundred meters ahead of him, an abandoned farmstead looms.

The running man throws himself in cover behind a log hut. He is fighting for breath. The shouts come from closer. He fires his weapon in the direction of his pursuers, realizes the magazine is empty and quickly slaps a new magazine into the carbine. He fires a short burst to the direction of the shouts, then continues to run.

A derelict tractor stands among the ruins. It is a rudimentary machine that must be decades old. The fugitive takes cover behind it. By now the hunters' shouts are very close. He fires. So do the hunters. Bullets whizz and ricochet from the tractor wreck. The fugitive jumps up and runs, stumbles in a rusted metal object, his rifle falls from his hand. On all fours in the mud, he grasps after it, then freezes.

Dread is written all over the fugitive's face as he looks up to the soldier towering above him, wearing heavy body armor and pointing an AK assault rifle at him. The helmet and its lowered visor leave only the soldier's strong jaw visible. A name patch on his assault vest has the name ЛАЗАРОВ standing on it in Cyrillic, with LAZAROV written below in smaller Latin characters.

The soldier looks down at the fugitive at his feet.

"You are trespassing in an ecological disaster zone." The soldier sounds calm as he speaks but keeps his finger on the rifle's trigger. He kicks the fugitive's carbine away.

The fugitive takes the anorak's hood off his head in a sign of surrender, submission even.

"Please! Don't shoot me, Lieutenant!" he exclaims.

"That wouldn't be my style," Lieutenant Lazarov replies. "You know that, Sasha."

More soldiers appear and surround Sasha. Lieutenant Lazarov shoulders his rifle.

"Check his gear," he commands.

The fugitive called Sasha tries to protest. "I don't have anything!"

"Is that so?" Lazarov asks almost amusedly.

"It was a bad raid! I didn't find anything, I swear!"

One of his soldiers pats down the fugitive's gear. Then he takes a device that looks like a miniature version of hand-held metal detectors used at airports and holds it close to Sasha's rucksack. Immediately, the device emits a sharp beeping sound.

The soldier takes a half step back. "Seventy-five thousand millirems!"

"What the hell, Sasha?" Lazarov asks. "Carrying a nuclear reactor around or what?"

"It's just background radiation, Lieutenant, I swear it! Your army-issue detector is shit! It's not reading properly!"

"Unless the sergeant has farted, the detector indicates you carry something you are not supposed to carry. Would you

6

accuse Sergeant Bobrov of farting in my presence, Sasha? I thought not. Now let me see your rucksack."

Sergeant Bobrov points his assault rifle at Sasha. "Don't try to pull any tricks, Stalker, or I blow your head off."

Lazarov unpockets and dons a pair of heavy gloves. He cautiously opens the rucksack. After a minute of rummaging he takes out a small container.

"Sasha, Sasha," Lazarov says with a smile as he removes a shiny, metallic object from the container. "You're the dumbest Stalker I've ever had the misfortune to catch. You've been carrying this relic all the time and didn't notice it?"

A yellow, unearthly light illuminates Lazarov's black gloves as he studies the object. The soldiers look at it as if mesmerized.

"It's just a Guppy," Sasha says. "Ain't worth shit, man."

"People like you mustn't remove even shit from the Zone," Lazarov replies, cautiously placing the relic back to the container. "You are a trespasser and thief, Sasha, and a stupid one too if you don't know what this relic is worth. Bobrov, call in the helicopter. Tell Perimeter Base we have caught a Stalker with a relic."

"Aren't we supposed to shoot him, sir?"

Lazarov shrugs.

"If we shoot him, we have to continue our foot patrol for another three days. If we take him in as prisoner, we can call a helicopter to take us back to base where he will be interrogated. Any questions?"

The sergeant grins and shakes his head. The rest of Lazarov's soldiers too exchange relieved looks.

Suddenly a howl comes from the misty reeds. Sasha gasps with fear. The soldiers immediately hold their weapons ready to fire, except Lazarov who leisurely lights up a cigarette.

"Make that call quickly, sergeant. We better don't tarry here too long."

"What made that noise?" Sasha asks worriedly.

7

"Maybe you better ask *who*," Lazarov calmly replies. "One can never know in these parts."

He looks down at his prisoner with an almost friendly, patronizing smile.

"The helo will be here in about twenty minutes," Sergeant Bobrov reports. Lazarov acknowledges it with a nod.

"How much is that relic worth?" a soldier asks.

"At the research facility, Professor Korolev might pay fifteen thousand for it," Lazarov replies. "If Sasha had managed to smuggle it to the Big Land, he could have sold it for two or even three times that."

The soldier makes a low whistle. "Good God... fifteen thousand!" He shakes his head. "But dollars or rubles?"

"Your guess," Lazarov answers with a quiet laugh. "Now you better gather the men and set up a perimeter... just to distract you from any illicit thoughts you might have about that thing."

Perimeter Base, military headquarters, 3 June 2011, 08:50:36 EEST

The confinement room is lit by a weak lamp of outdated design on the table and a small window above. It looks like a basement, the walls are of bare bricks and everything says that it's a makeshift facility in some building that was abandoned a long time ago; it could have been a factory or a farm once. Sasha, who is sitting at a roughly hewn table with his hands cuffed, nervously looks up when the door goes open and Lazarov appears.

"Please, let me go!"

Ignoring Sasha, Lazarov steps to the window and removes his helmet. His face would be handsome if the brown eyes set deep didn't tell of combat fatigue and mental exhaustion. He rubs his temples and eyes, as if trying to get rid of his weariness. Then he lights up a cigarette.

"Someone's got a nasty habit here," Sasha remarks.

"How many times did we already catch you trying to sneak into the Zone, Sasha?" asks Lazarov with condescending authority, still with his back to the Stalker.

"Three, I guess."

Lazarov exhales the smoke.

"I remember differently."

"My last raid doesn't count! I made it to the greenhorn camp then. I was already inside!"

"Even one attempt makes it a criminal act."

Lazarov sighs and finally turns to Sasha.

"Anyway, I'm glad it was you who caught me", the Stalker says. "They say you're the best of the army's scouts. Ain't any shame to be caught by you. You don't shoot Stalkers like me on sight either."

"Maybe I should," Lazarov says as he steps closer to the table. He knocks off the ashes, ignoring the Stalker's look that seems to be begging for a cigarette. "It would save trespassers like you from what's deeper inside the Zone."

"Yes, Lieutenant, you should. Because I won't give up until I'll get to the center one day — "

" — or die trying," cuts in Lazarov. "Sasha, there's nothing there. Trust me."

"Yeah, you army guys are supposed to say that. But everybody knows of the relics all those experiments have created!"

Lazarov's voice sounds tired. Maybe he himself doesn't believe what he says.

"Urban legends, Sasha, spread by people with too much imagination. Only the dangers are for real."

"You have orders to kill on sight. Why so if there's nothing to hide, huh?"

"Those orders are not coming from me."

"But you bend them like the Zone bends the laws of physics, don't you?"

A faint smile appears on Lazarov's face. He drops the cigarette to the concrete floor and crushes it with his boot. "That's why you're still alive."

"No, Lieutenant! It's not up to you!" shouts Sasha and as he continues, his expression becomes more and more that of a religious fanatic. "No, no! You are one of us. You hear her calling just like we do! You wouldn't shoot your brothers, would you? No!"

Lazarov bluntly shouts him down. "That's enough! You will be transferred to a place far away where 'bend over bitch' will be the only calling you hear. If you're lucky, you'll be out in a few months. But I warn you — do not try to test my patience one more time. Go, get a life and forget about the Zone of Alienation."

"I never will!" Sasha defiantly shouts back.

"How old are you, Stalker?"

"Nineteen."

"And you still believe in fairytales? Let me tell you this: next time I see you, it will be game over for you. This is the Zone of Alienation, *my* Zone and I don't have to account for the fate of trespassers like you!"

Sasha grins even broader. "Cut the crap!" he shouts in a startling voice. "You do know it. I know it. The Zone knows it! She has chosen you! That's why you are still alive!"

Lazarov looks to the window and takes a deep breath. *She has chosen you! That's why YOU are still alive!* The words echo in his head, like a deep sinister drone coming from the darkest parts of his soul. He is about to light up another cigarette to calm himself when the door swings full open and a brawny officer enters. Lazarov immediately stands at attention.

"Major Voronov, sir!"

"What the hell is going on here?" The base commander's grey eyes pierce into the Stalker's. Sasha bites his lips and turns his look elsewhere. "Why is this jerkface still alive?"

Lazarov thickly swallows. "I am interrogating the prisoner, *komandir*."

"You didn't get the question, Lazarov. What is this trespasser doing here?" Without waiting for the lieutenant's reply, Voronov continues his rant. "Don't you know standing orders?"

"He was unarmed when we caught him," Lazarov says. He is not lying—after all, by the time the greenhorn Stalker stumbled into the trap set by Lazarov, he no longer had his weapon on him. "I don't find shooting unarmed trespassers appropriate."

"You don't find it appropriate? The army doesn't give a damn about what a lieutenant finds appropriate. *I* don't give a damn about what you find appropriate either."

"He could tell us about their infiltration points," Lazarov patiently explains. "Matter of fact, the Perimeter is so porous that it can be infiltrated almost anywhere. We need to know the latest—"

Lazarov cuts his sentence when he sees Major Voronov unholster his Tokarev pistol. Before Lazarov could utter any words of protest, Voronov points the pistol straight at Sasha's head and pulls the trigger apparently without any second thought. The shot sounds deafening in the confined space. Blood and brain splash to the moldy brick wall.

"Where's the relic he had on him?" Voronov asks holstering his still smoking pistol.

"It's… under guard, in the armory," Lazarov says with a painfully dry throat.

"Good. I will, uhm, oversee it being transported to the Big Land." Lazarov is not sure but he believes he sees the shimmer of greed appearing in the base commander's hawkish eyes. "Assemble a patrol and move out to the north-west approaches leading to Black Defile. A heavily armed squad of the Intruders has been sighted there a few hours ago. They are to be eliminated."

"Sir!"

Voronov gives him an angry look. "You better carry this mission out with extreme prejudice, Lieutenant. Your attitude has been rather forgiving lately and I cannot forgive that. Last chance. Got it?"

Without returning Lazarov's salute, Major Voronov opens the door. "Clean up that mess," he says pointing at the dead Stalker. "It's high time for you to get your hands dirty!"

The door slams shut, leaving Lieutenant Lazarov alone with the body; though it is his own dark thoughts that suddenly make the gloomy room appear creepy and suffocating.

Three years later

"I love being in the army, *komandir*. Where else could I get a chopper flight over the Zone?"

Major Mikhail Lazarov doesn't return the young lieutenant's cheery grin, instead choosing to spend the last minutes being lost in his thoughts. Seen from above, through the tiny windows of the Mi-24 gunship flying them to their mission, the marshy frontiers of the Zone look peaceful like a national park: golden brown fields of reed bowing in the wind, the low September sun reflected in the waterways, the wooden shells of abandoned houses peering out of a shred of mist, anomalous fields in the distance glowing with eerie green. Lazarov is glad that the distance spares him the details: the Geiger counter's constant clicking, the rotten stench, the sight of decomposing corpses fallen to mutants, radioactivity and anomalous traps.

"Save your high spirits for the underground, Ivanchuk," he glumly replies. But his second in command seems to be in a talkative mood.

"How come it's in this mess today? That hellhole under the marshaling yard was supposed to be sealed off ages ago."

"Some Stalkers made it into the Hideout. We're going in to seal it for good."

"Piece of cake!"

Lazarov can't see the lieutenant's eyes under the helmet's dark visor but he's sure his second in command is not just swaggering. *Today you will be tested, Lieutenant.* He looks at the two other troopers huddled up in the cramped compartment, flanking a technician who carries welding equipment. Kolesnik and Shumenko had been veteran Stalkers until they signed up to the army, motivated more by their need to escape debt collectors than fulfilling patriotic duty. They were made sergeants to let them know their place in the military's food chain. Although not cast from the mold of legendary Stalkers, they were at least good team-players. For Lazarov, now commander of army's Zone scouts, this is more important than individual abilities. He looks at the lieutenant's fingers nervously drumming on his AKSU-74 assault carbine.

"By the way, lieutenant... what's that duct tape on your magazine? Is it falling apart or what?"

"I taped two mags together, so that I can change them with a flip of my hand!"

"Do you see that on my rifle? No? And can you think why?"

"Because I'm stupid and you are smart, *komandir!*"

Lazarov laughs out loud. His grumpy mood vanishes in an instant. From the corner of his eye, he can even see two hard-boiled sergeants grin.

"What to do? That's a fact," he shrugs and gives a pat on the lieutenant's Kevlar helmet. "Hand me that duct tape if you still have it on you."

The lieutenant pats down his pockets and hands him a roll of blue duct tape. Lazarov takes out a spare magazine from the pockets on Ivanchuk's body armor.

"If you keep the mags like that," he explains, "your *avtomat*[1] will feel much heavier than it is."

He whips the tape around the magazine, leaving free an inch-long flap. "Look. If you grab it by this flap, you can draw it much quicker from the pocket and win a second if you're in a firefight. Then there's that carabineer on your assault vest. When you remove the empty magazine, just fasten it there with the duct flap. See? Like this... It will win you another second. Once the party is over, you can put the magazine back into to the vest pocket."

---

[1] Automatic assault rifle

14

"Two minutes to touchdown," the pilot reports, "I have a visual on Fortress One."

"All right people, here we go," says Lazarov fastening the strap of his helmet, "check your gear and ammo. Finger off the trigger until you're on the ground."

He detaches the magazine from his silenced SA Val rifle and pushes the first cartridge down to make sure no cartridge is stuck inside. The steely clack of the weapon cocking is like music to his ears.

"One minute to touchdown," sounds the intercom. "Landing zone is clear."

Lazarov has landed more times in a helicopter than he can count but he still can't shake off the slight sickness he feels during the sudden descent. He grabs his weapon and opens the hatch. Giving each man an encouraging pat on the shoulder while they exit, he waits until everyone is out. He signals to the pilots with his thumb up and follows his soldiers. The gunship immediately takes to the air and sets out on a circling path over the abandoned buildings to watch over the environment. Its turbine engines are still too loud for Lazarov to address the squad leader without shouting.

"Any developments, Lieutenant Nabokov?"

"We saw a pack of mutants not far from here but the helicopter's noise scared them away."

"Keep your eyes peeled, just in case something nasty comes out of this hole. Are the Stalkers still inside?"

"I've been standing by with Fortress One since zero-six-hundred. No one has left through here, sir, and Fortress Two didn't report any earlier contacts either."

"Good. Chumak, come over here!"

The technician—a haggard civilian who usually tends to the vehicles at the base and now looks helpless in the bulletproof vest he's wearing for the first time—doesn't appear too happy over being sent on this mission. Lazarov gives him his pistol.

"You know how to handle a Strizh?"

"Yes, *komandir!*"

"Then let me see you preparing it for firing. Hey! Keep it pointed to the ground, will you?"

"Uhm… where is the cock?"

"What cock?"

"That thing I need to move with my thumb and then it makes that clicking sound."

Lazarov exchanges a grin with Lieutenant Ivanchuk. "So that's how you know how to handle it. Very well then. You want a clicking sound like in the movies, yes? Hold it tight. Pull back the slide. Yes, with your free hand. Allow the slide to spring forward. There's your clicking sound."

"That's all?"

"Nope," Ivanchuk says. "It has a built-in safety system. If you ever point it at any of us, it will backfire and blow your head off. You hear me?"

"But, but…" Chumak points at Lazarov's rifle. "I'd rather have a machine gun like that."

The sergeants and Ivanchuk laugh but Lazarov remains patient.

"If you ever find you need to fire a bigger weapon, pick up any of our rifles because that would mean me and the soldiers are dead."

"We'll be all dead if he fires just any weapon," Ivanchuk adds still chuckling.

With his squad following behind, Lazarov walks to the manhole over the tunnel entrance.

"Chumak, on me. Kolesnik, Shumenko, move forward. Ivanchuk, you look out for our six. Our mission is simple: we go in, seal the shaft to the Hideout and get out."

"Rules of engagement?"

"Like always in the undergrounds, Lieutenant: shoot at everything that moves. Watch out for ricochets, those damned tunnels are narrow. Keep a little distance from the walls."

"If we find any relics, can we retrieve and sell them?"

"Not if I find them first, sergeant. Anything else?"

"Major, sir!"

"Spill the beans, Shumenko."

"Permission to take a leak before we go in."

"Do it quickly and make sure you don't put your *yalda* into an anomaly."

"Shumenko's dick needs not fear any anomalies on the ground" says Kolesnik with a grin.

The lieutenant is quick to reply. "He's only pissing to let the mutants know his territory!"

Lazarov sighs with impatience, but he has given up cutting such casual manners long ago. Even if this squad was improvised just an hour ago, at least he could count on these men should things go wrong. He knows this could happen. His men know it too. And Kolesnik's joke wasn't that bad for a man who is about to descend into a mutant-infested tunnel system where anything that can move will move in for the kill.

"Feeling much better."

"All right... now that Sergeant Shumenko has gracefully marked his territory, let's get moving. Switch to your breathing system. Check night vision and intercom."

"Ivanchuk here. Always ready."

"Kolesnik ready."

"Shumenko here. Locked and loaded."

"Uhm... can I ask you something?"

"Ask it quickly, Chumak."

"Will we survive this?"

"You mean you want to live a long and happy life?"

"Of course, *komandir!*"

"Then just keep breathing and we'll take care about the rest. Let's move!"

Tunnel system, 09:28:00 EEST

Before Lazarov descends into the narrow shaft leading to the tunnels, he switches the channel on his radio. "Perimeter

Base, this is Condor One. Condor Squad moving in. Over and out."

The sergeants climb down through the narrow shaft. As soon as they arrive at the bottom of the ladder, they kneel and assume a firing position.

"Clear," Shumenko reports.

Lazarov notices a disapproving look on the technician's face. He ignores it, but Ivanchuk jumps at the opportunity to lecture him.

"What are you looking at, Chumak? Command elements take point only in war movies. If there's an ambush down there and the *komandir* gets shot first, the mission is compromised."

His comrades descend one by one. Lazarov can hear their panting. With his left hand, he signals them to proceed. The tunnel reeks of rot, dampness and corrosion. Above, a lonely red light flashes and casts its eerie light across the walls, like the reminder of a long-forgotten alarm when these catacombs were still part of a secret laboratory. All is quiet but for the shrieking noise of the rotating flashlight and moisture dripping from the ceiling.

Suddenly, something moves on the ground with a noise that sounds like a thunder.

"Sorry, Major," whispers Chumak, "I stumbled on something."

"Why don't you just shout 'hey we have just arrived!'?"

"I'm sorry!"

"Shut up, Chumak" comes Ivanchuk's voice.

Lazarov hears something like footsteps approaching. He raises his left fist, ordering the others to stop. He aims his weapon and a shadow moves into the red dot sight of his rifle. As the emergency light's orange beam flashes for a second in its direction, a human silhouette emerges from the darkness. Without hesitation, he fires two short, noise-suppressed bursts. Lazarov hears the man gasping and pulls the trigger again. The man emits a shout, intended as swearing but ending in a gasp of pain. His rifle fires a burst into the ground as death spasms his fingers. At last he falls. Two seconds have passed since he appeared, maybe three. *Strange,* Lazarov thinks. *That fellow was pretty heavily armored for a Stalker.*

Staying in cover, Lazarov peeks around the corner. The hall below is dimly lit by another faint emergency light. Lazarov can't see them but knows that a few railway carriages are still there from the time when this place was a more sinister version of the ordinary marshaling yard above — a bomb-proof facility where nuclear warheads had been loaded to underground trains that carried them to storage vaults and missile silos before something went horribly wrong decades ago. A thick concrete column blocks his view, but he senses no movement. He waves to Kolesnik.

"Grenade."

The sergeant loads a 40mm high-explosive incendiary grenade into the launcher attached to his AK-74, aims for a heartbeat and releases it. After a split second the projectile explodes into a blinding ball of fire. Desperate screams mix with the thundering detonation. Lazarov shouts *forward!* and jumps down the stairs into the hall. His Geiger counter starts ticking frantically. Two bodies lie on the ground but Lazarov ignores them as he scans the next room, once an elevator station, for further targets. His night vision is too weak to light up the corners and he doesn't want to switch on his headlight. It would turn him into an illuminated target for hostiles wanting to practice headshots.

"All clear," he says, "let's move on."

But Chumak, who is in the underground for the first time, stands in front of two pools of a glowing substance. The substance is moving, looking like boiling blue water in slow-motion. He is about to touch it when Ivanchuk pulls him back.

"That's a Bloop-Bloop, rookie. An anomalous trap. One step closer and the acid will consume your *yalda* in a second."

19

"There's more of that shit here in the underground than mushrooms in a forest," Kolesnik remarks. Lazarov is about to tell them to keep quiet when the other sergeant shouts out.

"Enemies detected!"

Shumenko doesn't wait for the major's order and releases a long burst into the elevator chamber. Now it's the major's turn to throw a grenade. Another deafening explosion sounds but the enemy keeps firing. The lieutenant leaps forward, firing his AKSU-74 assault carbine. Silence falls. Lazarov points to the round chamber in front of them, with a massive pillar in the middle.

"Ivanchuk, you and Kolesnik to the left. Shumenko, on me. Chumak, stay behind me."

Slowly and with weapons ready, they enter the chamber. Below their feet, rusty iron grates cover corroded pipes, disappearing into the ground. A lever stands in the middle, the turning wheel having fallen off. Above them, the metal tubes of a ventilation system follow the curve of the walls, here and there lacking a few cover pieces.

"All clear. Coming through."

Lazarov lowers his Val when he sees the lieutenant appearing from the other side. In front of them, a staircase leads to the level below.

"Shall we?" Ivanchuk asks. Lazarov shakes his head.

"Watch the stairs. Keep your eyes peeled, Lieutenant. I want to check out those bodies before we go below."

Now that the area is cleared of enemies and with the only exit under watch, Lazarov switches off his night vision and turns on the headlight. He approaches the Stalker shot by the lieutenant.

"Good shot," he says, loud enough for the sergeants to hear it as well. The corpse lying in the light circle before him is wearing a tactical helmet with an integrated gas mask, its tube attached to his body armor's breathing system. His bulletproof vest has been penetrated by five armor-piercing rounds from Ivanchuk's carbine. Even in his death, he holds his modern, German-made assault rifle tight.

"Shumenko, take over the guard. Lieutenant, come over here." Lazarov points at the corpse. "This was no Stalker but a mercenary. Our intel was bad like usual." The lieutenant nods and kneels down to remove the gas mask from the corpse. "Don't. I'd rather not see his face."

"And if it was a pretty woman?"

"You're one sick son of a bitch, Lieutenant. Better find something that the FSB[1] guys could use... maybe they'll do a better job next time."

"But if it's a woman and I find a lipstick, can I keep it? My girlfriend —"

"Cut your stupid jokes, for God's sake. You're not even remotely funny."

Lazarov searches the other bodies. They all wear the same gear, meaning they indeed belonged to the group of mercenaries who occasionally appear in the Zone of Alienation. Unlike Stalkers, they not only hunt for relics but for the occasional human target as well, be it a Stalker carrying a special relic or one who didn't deliver on time what he was supposed to. And, being far better equipped and trained than ordinary Stalkers, they also cause headaches for the army when they appeared close to the strictly no-go areas like the marshaling yard.

"Nothing useful here," Ivanchuk reports.

"After all, no mercenary would be stupid enough to carry his mission orders with him. Damn... A band of them in our territory is the last thing we need."

"I suggest we report this to the base, *komandir*."

---

[1] FSB - Federal Security Service of the Russian Federation (Russian: ФСБ, Федеральная служба безопасности Российской Федерации); the main domestic security agency of the Russian Federation and the main successor agency of the KGB.

Lazarov checks his radio. "No signal. Anyway, we still have something else to do. Let's go below."

It gets darker with each step as they carefully descend the winding metal staircase. The ground below is dotted with bubbling anomalies, illuminating the tunnel with bluish glow. Now Lazarov can even hear their noise: a sizzle echoing like a chorus of monsters in the darkness, as if communicating with each other in a deep, foreboding whisper. His Geiger counter ticks faster.

"Turn off the headlamps," he orders. The anomalies glow strong enough to illuminate their surroundings. On the far end of the tunnel, an emergency light shows the direction. Lazarov can only hope that if there are any enemies here, they will make a clear silhouette against the dim beam of light.

"Stick to the wall. Skirt the traps," he whispers to Chumak.

He looks down for a second as the technician stumbles over a fallen pipe. Immediately, he feels a steel fist hitting his chest. Then he hears the rifle shot. He wobbles to the wall, his hand instinctively touching the spot where he was hit. Shumenko fires a long burst with Kolesnik's rifle joining in.

"Shit," somebody shouts, "he came out of nowhere!"

"Major, are you hit?"

"I'm fine, Lieutenant," Lazarov replies as he stands up with a groan. He is glad that the visor of his tactical helmet hides the pain on his face. His heavy armor caught the bullet, but the impact was strong like the hit of a hammer. His chest is left bruised and sore. *Thank God for body armor.*

"Let's keep moving!"

Their shooter must have been guarding the exit of the tunnel, which leads into the big research hall. As they enter it, they see huge metal containers behind a dilapidated iron fence and more pipelines disappearing into nowhere through holes in the concrete walls. Another emergency lamp casts its maddening light. Through cracks and holes, air moves with a deep howl.

They have to cross the wide shadow of a concrete pillar. Lazarov reaches to his helmet to switch on his headlight. The shrieking noise of the revolving light hurts his ears like a dentist's drill but what makes his blood curl is a howling roar from the darkness.

"Fire forward, fire all you have!"

He tosses the technician to the ground and throws himself down too, biting his tongue, ignoring the sharp pain and frantically firing towards the pair of glowing eyes that are reflecting the light of their headlamps and getting closer at inhuman speed. The howl turns into a beastly rattle, regardless of the fire directed at its source from the three assault rifles. The major runs out of ammo but as he desperately reaches for a spare magazine the rattle ceases and, with a loud hump, something heavy falls to the ground just a meter away from him.

"That was a close shave," he hears the lieutenant's voice.

Lazarov gets back to his feet. A humanoid figure lies in the light circle ahead of him. It has longer arms and legs than humans, but the biggest visible difference is the mouth wide open, where behind a row of razor-sharp fangs two smaller mouths are revealed, both flashing smaller, but not less sharp teeth. Shumenko steps closer and empties the rest of his ammunition into the dead mutant's head before replacing the magazine.

"Wh-what was that?" Chumak's whole body is shaking.

"An upyr[1]," Lazarov replies reloading his rifle, "and a male one, judged by what's left of it... the female is probably waiting for him to come home with fresh meat. Usually they stick together, so let's keep our eyes open."

"I... I refuse to go on... I just can't," the technician stammers. He is close to crying. "I want to get out of here!"

"Pull yourself together, Chumak," Lazarov says and offers him his hand. "Come on, man!"

---

[1] Vampire (Russian)

"No!"

The major glances at the two sergeants. They cross to the whining technician and pull him up to his feet. Without any emotions on his face, Lazarov points his rifle at Chumak's forehead.

"Let's go," he says, but the technician only shakes his head.

"All right, we'll take your gear and leave you." Lazarov lowers his weapon and aims now at Chumak's legs. "But first I'll shoot you in the knee. Mama upyr will be pissed off when papa doesn't return and they can smell human blood from far away."

Chumak looks at Ivanchuk. The lieutenant nods. "Female or not, you don't want to have a blowjob from those lips. I mean, well, it's up to you."

The technician eventually grabs his gear and falls in. Without saying any more, Lazarov moves on. He is nervous about every dark corner but no other mutants come into sight. *Or maybe it is us not being in the mutants' sight.*

Soon, a corridor branches off to the right. Lazarov has been there before: it is one of the long tunnels running between the marshaling yard and a nearby factory. They have to turn left but would expose their right flank. If they threw a grenade to clear the way, anyone waiting for them in ambush would know of their approach. He signals the men to stop, peeks out to the left, and gives a sign to Ivanchuk to proceed. As he turns to the left, he sees the stationary beam of a headlight. The mercenary hasn't seen them yet. Lazarov aims carefully. His shots hit his target's body armor but have no killing effect. By the time he can fire another shot, the mercenary disappears.

"Dammit," he swears as he hears barking commands ahead. "Kolesnik, drop a frag! Twenty meters ahead!"

The grenade falls a little short but hits the mercenary just at the moment when he is reckless enough to peer out from his cover.

Weapon fixed on the door in case more enemies emerge, Lazarov rushes forward. A silhouette appears in the visor, the head right behind the scope's red dot. He fires.

"Left! Watch your left!" he shouts taking a grenade and throwing it through the door. It was too quick. One second after the detonation, another enemy pops out from around the corner. Lazarov's rifle falls silent after one shot. He ducks for cover to reload. An AKSU-74 rings out over his head.

"He's down," Kolesnik says.

They wait for a minute. Only the wind howls in the tunnels, with the occasional rummaging noise from the long-forgotten levels far below. Maybe a room collapsed. Maybe a upyr is fighting for his life with a pack of rabids, perfect camouflage versus ten meter long jumps and knife-sharp canine teeth. Maybe it's the soldiers' fear echoing in their mind.

Stepping over a dead enemy whose head and chest was dreadfully blasted by the grenade, Lazarov moves his squad into the room. From there, another corridor opens to the left. A few meters further down, a round ventilation shaft opens into the wall. Wooden crates stand below, as if used as stairs to gain access to it. Once it housed a ventilator and the remains of the iron grater that once covered it are still lying on the ground. Now a man could comfortably crawl into the opening. There's even a metal ladder leading up the shaft.

"Welcome to the Hideout, Chumak," Lazarov says and pats the technician on the shoulder, "you made it. Now it's time for your big performance."

"Thank God," the technician sighs with relief, "so, what am I supposed to do?"

"Remove a few pieces of that ladder. Weld its parts as a grid to prevent anyone from climbing in."

"Are you sure there's nothing inside, *komandir*?"

"I don't mind giving you a little tour... We all deserve a rest anyway." Lazarov turns to the soldiers. "Keep your guard up while I show this greenhorn around. That corridor will be our exit route. It's full of garbage for cover, so keep your eyes peeled. Chumak, follow me."

Wary of booby-traps, he cannot shake off an uneasy feeling as they climb up the ladder. Cautiously, Lazarov peeks inside. Seeing no danger waiting for them he descends into a small chamber.

The Hideout, 09:59:07 EEST

"What is this place?" the technician asks. Lazarov scans the walls with his headlamp. They are covered with Stalker graffiti in several languages.

The Intruders were here. Dumbass Guardians you're all gay.
Wie sagt man auf Russisch: Hände hoch oder ich schiesse dir die Birne weg?
Прыгни в аномалию, очистить зону от сосунков.
Want yourself a tailor-made chemical suit? Message me. Beacon, Zone fashion designer.
Uշտ այստեղ էր.
Don't bring mutants' balls to the trader. Eat'em they taste good. T.S.
Stalkeri italiani, in avanti! Darimar
Need a miracle to keep your M16 from jamming? I can work one. Magician, next to Ranger's Den, Wormwood Forest.

Save for a few crates and other junk, the chamber is empty.

"I'm more into shooting than all that scientific mumbo-jumbo, but since you're here with us I suppose you have the right to know what we're up against."

Fear casts a shadow on the technician's face, very much to Lazarov's liking.

"What is this place?"

"A particularly badass guy once used to keep his stash here. Nowadays Stalkers come here to prove they've got balls and leave all kinds of stupid graffiti behind."

"That's why the mercenaries we ran into were here?"

"I doubt it. They prefer spraying the walls with our blood, not paint. What concerns us now is that the son of some big fish in Moscow died during an attempt to get here. We were ordered to make the place inaccessible."

"I understand."

"No, you don't. What we do here makes no difference... it's an uphill battle all the time. Sometimes I wish I'd be a free Stalker, with nothing in my mind but relics and how to spend money once I get rich by selling them. Then an order comes like today and makes me forget about such thoughts."

Lazarov climbs to his feet but the technician persists in questioning him.

"I know about the Stalkers. But the guys in the base told me something about factions called the Intruders and Guardians, too."

"It's two sides of the same coin. The Intruders claim that the whole world has a right to study the Zone. As if anyone believed that! They are sponsored by Western powers who want to have their share of relics, but the Zone is ours only. Am I not right? Hence some government hardliners set up a group, half black-ops half militia, to help the army eliminate those Western-sponsored anarchists. They call themselves Guardians."

"Truth be told, even if the Intruders are criminals they do have balls to mess with the army and the militia."

"Well said," Lazarov admits. "I'd never say the Intruders are cowards. No one *can* be a coward who approaches the Zone on his own will. That's why I respect even the greenest of Stalkers."

Lazarov hesitates for a moment before continuing. Then he decides that speaking his mind would mean no harm. Back at their base, no soldier takes Chumak seriously enough to believe what the technician says, should he ever become chatty about what he is about to tell him now.

"You know… years ago, when I arrived here as a lieutenant, I believed that the Zone's resources should be exploited for the benefit of our country. After all, it is us who suffer from it most. It would be just fair for use to take whatever benefits the Zone has, scientific or else. Later on, when I saw that our generals have nothing else in mind than getting rich from selling relics on the black market, I was more and more wishing the Zone would disappear, either by force or a miracle. It corrupts people as much as it corrupts nature. It brings out the best and worst of human nature, but the worst a little more."

Lazarov looks around in the chamber, taken over by a feeling of hopelessness. He envies Raider, the legendary Stalker who was once hiding here during his deep raids into the heart of the Zone.

"It was different then…," he silently continues. "There was still reason to be here. Now we know everything about the Zone except what she is, and this we will never find out. We're stuck with her, like a child who takes a bite too big and can neither swallow nor spit it out. I wish I could move on with it, but I'm trapped here. There's no way for me to live outside of the Zone, even if there's nothing but corruption inside. You'll understand if you stay here long enough… but that's enough chit-chatting."

"But what is the Zone after all?" Chumak asks. "How was it created? By the A-bomb tests? Secret experiments? Or perhaps by… aliens?"

"You want a scientific explanation?"

"Is there one?"

Lazarov smiles. "Sure. Listen: the Zone is a bad day of the universe. That's that. Now come, let's get this job done."

"Yes, *komandir*, but tell me… I mean, I'm sorry for snapping after that upyr attacked us… but you were kidding when you pointed your shooter at me, weren't you?"

"That's not a shooter," Lazarov replies patting off the dust from his leggings, "it's called an assault rifle with integrated silencer."

Once back to the tunnel, Chumak ignites the torch of his portable welding kit and starts working with quick, accurate movements. He appears to be in his element now. In a few minutes, the ladder lies in pieces. He takes the longer parts and skillfully welds them to the iron trunks. When he switches off the blue light, the shaft is barred by a strong new grid. The bitter smell of freshly welded steel mixes with the stale underground air.

"*Molodets,*" Lazarov says and gives Chumak a look of approval, "and now let's get the hell out of here. Shumenko, take point."

"Why always me," the sergeant sighs but assumes the leading position at once.

"Maybe the *komandir* overheard you last night bragging about your balls being bullet-proof," Kolesnik grumbles from behind.

"That's why I still have them, unlike you," Shumenko snorts.

Lazarov is about to cut in when, to his satisfaction, the young lieutenant at last says the word.

"Shut the hell up at last!"

Tunnel system, 10:15:03 EEST

After twenty meters another chamber opens to their left. On Lazarov's sign, Ivanchuk moves over and keeps his weapon aimed into the room until the others pass by. Then he assumes his place on the rear, keeping a cautious eye on the far end of the tunnel.

They barely proceed a few meters when the sergeant raises his fist. Two anomalies block their way but judging by the distance between them, Lazarov finds they could pass through safely.

"Form a line. Watch your step," he orders his men.

"There's something in that anomaly, sir."

Lazarov takes his detector device and turns towards the anomaly. Shumenko's eyes might have been misled by wishful thinking but the detector proves him right. The display lights up and indicates a small green dot, just a meter away. Cautiously stepping closer, he investigates the substance. A tiny object levitates an inch above the green acidic goo, as if it was weightless.

He cautiously picks it up, avoiding any contact with the acidic substance beneath. It would burn through his protective gloves in a moment. "Look at this little fellow," he says as if talking about a puppy, "Hello, Porcupine!"

Holding the relic, the major feels his skin become tougher. It looks like a small hedgehog with long, crystallized quills protruding from its dark purple core. The pointed crystals retract on his touch as if the Porcupine was a living, sensitive creature.

"*Komandir*," says the sergeant, "With all due respect, I saw it first."

"Duly noted," Lazarov replies, as he carefully lets the relic slide into a container on his armored suit. "Ever heard about chain of command?"

The sergeant seems disgruntled but Lazarov ignores him. It would be fair to divide the price with his men if he decides to sell the relic. The traders nestled in the villages along the Perimeter pay generous amounts for any relic, though the scientists in their facilities near Lake Diamond pay even better. That would however mean a long and dangerous trek. He will worry about it later.

The squad slowly proceeds between the anomalies towards the tunnel end, where an iron ladder leads upwards.

However, as they approach it Lazarov sees even more traps ahead. He signals a stop and takes a pistol magazine from his vest. The spring inside the magazine pushes the shells upwards and he only has to direct them into the anomaly with his thumb. Landing in the sizzling substance, they immediately dissolve with a sharp, hissing sound.

"No way through this one," he says with frustration. "I had a feeling that we wouldn't get out so easily."

"Maybe we can neutralize the trap if we ask Shumenko to piss into it."

"Ha, ha, ha, Lieutenant," replies the sergeant with a fake laugh. "If you want to know, ever since I visited that bitch you talked about my piss is burning so much that I could blast a hole in the wall with it."

"Did you at least manage to blast her hole?"

"Keep your mouths shut, for God's sake," Lazarov hisses. "We've got to backtrack and find another way out."

"Shit," swears Ivanchuk. The major responds with a grin.

"You still like this job, Lieutenant?"

"I do, *komandir*… I was just mentioning that I dislike visiting places I've already been to."

"That's the spirit. Now, if we are lucky, our mercenary friends tried to retreat and ran directly into Fortress One. If not… we kick more ass. Let's move."

Either because they killed everyone on their way in or because the mercenaries were indeed ambushed upon trying to leave the catacombs, the squad makes its way back into the laboratory undisturbed. Chumak carefully skirts around the dead upyr, as if it could jump up any second. As he passes the dead mutant by, Kolesnik shoots it again.

"Just to make sure, *komandir*."

"Don't waste your ammunition. Move!" Lazarov nervously says. He knows this is the worst time. All missions become most dangerous when they are almost over. Men tend to lose patience and caution with disastrous results.

In a minute, they are back to the first tunnel they traversed, with the ladder leading up to the shaft and out of the underground. He notices that the lieutenant has his headlamp switched on. *Damn, does he want to get a headshot?*

"Switch off your headlamp, Lieutenant!"

"It's just that the night vision makes my eyes pop from their sockets... and now this headache..."

Lazarov suddenly also feels pain creeping into his skull.

"What is that?" Chumak asks and steps forward, emboldened by the proximity of the exit shaft. Before Lazarov can order him back he hears a faint, sharp noise, rapidly strengthening into a deep howl rolling through the darkness.

"What the fuck is that?" Shumenko screams in horror.

A loud *bang* hits Lazarov's eardrums. It's not transmitted through his ears—the sound is already echoing inside his head, as if his brain was exploding. But it's Ivanchuk who falls to his knees as Chumak strikes his pistol and shoots the lieutenant in the face.

"Get into cover!" Lazarov desperately yells. Bullets whizz towards the dark end of the tunnel where a shadow looms, seemingly absorbing the frantic gunfire. Pulling his remaining willpower together he charges forward. *It's not fair,* flashes through his painful mind, *so close to the end, it's just not fair!* He sees the silhouette against the red flashes of the last emergency light. Having finished off the soldiers, it now tries to take hold of his mind. Desperation and rage seize the muscles of its soon-to-be prey. In two seconds, Lazarov reaches the mutant and empties the whole magazine into its torso. The apparition tries to step back. Lazarov senses its aggression vanish, as if he himself had absorbed it while he smashes the mutant's head again and again with the butt of his rifle until the weapon breaks.

Suddenly the tight, fiery ring that gripped his skull recedes then disappears. The *bang-bang* is gone. His panting sounds deafening in the sudden silence.

Blood flows from Lazarov's nose and ears. He switches on his headlamp. The floor, where the dead enemy should be, is empty.

Kolesnik gets up from the ground, groaning. Then Shumenko rises, holding his head that must still be in pain. Chumak kneels above Ivanchuk's body. He has torn the gas mask off his face. From his eyes, still maddened by horror, tears are flowing.

"I didn't— I didn't want—"

"No." Lazarov's voice is hoarse and trembling. He takes the pistol from the technician. "Your mind has been... taken over."

He looks at the lieutenant's body.

Of all the wounds a bullet can inflict, he most hates the sight of a headshot. It's bad enough to realize how thin the layers of muscle, body tissues and skin are that make the difference between a pile of organs and a human form. But a face, distorted into a dreadful yawn by a last traction of the muscles and the scattered brain protruding from a cracked skull, still emanating body warmth into the chilly air, is something else.

Lazarov feels the urge to vomit but pulls himself together. Kolesnik is weaker. He leans against the wall and throws up. Only Shumenko remains on his feet, expecting Lazarov to say something. The major clears his throat.

"Take this," he says, reaching to his belt and handing the relic to Shumenko.

"I'm fine, sir. I know it speeds up healing but... I'm fine, really."

"Take it. Tomorrow, you and Kolesnik will go on a patrol to Diamond Lake."

"I understand," the sergeant quietly replies. "I'll send the lieutenant's share to his family. What about yours?"

"You know, Shumenko, you are just a damned Stalker. Your uniform didn't change anything about that. You barely escaped death but you're thinking about loot and money already."

Shumenko faintly smiles. "Is that good or bad?"

Lazarov pats him on the shoulder. "Let's get out of here."

Together, they help Chumak to his feet. Kolesnik joins their effort. His armor is darkened by stains of vomit. Lazarov steps to the ladder and reaches for his radio transmitter.

"Fortress One, this is Condor One."

The reply crackles but comes through audible enough.

"This is Fortress One, over."

"Mission accomplished. We are at the shaft. We got a KIA. Send down a harness. Over."

"Wilco. Out."

By the time the lifting harness is lowered from above, Lazarov has already attached a gas mask to Ivanchuk's face — no need for the soldiers above to see a comrade like that. Carefully, they fasten the harness around the body. Shumenko, already out of the shaft, waves to the pilot and Lieutenant Ivanchuk's body sets out on its journey to a cemetery somewhere in a godforsaken village in Siberia. He waves to his remaining men.

"Let's get to the chopper!"

When Lazarov finally emerges from the shaft, his knees tremble to such an extent that he has to sit down in the grass. Like always, once the danger is over, all the fear and excitement his mind kept at bay under duress unloads in a heavy, almost nauseating wave. Lieutenant Nabokov offers him a cigarette. Lazarov can't resist.

"Was it bad?" Nabokov asks.

The major doesn't reply immediately. He removes his blood-smeared gloves and watches his fingers tremble.

"I'll need a new rifle," he says. "That thing will need a new head."

Nabokov does not bother him with any more questions.

Marshaling yard, 10:35:26 EEST

Before climbing into the helicopter, Lazarov and his two sergeants form a small circle, holding each other's shoulder

34

like they usually do after a successful mission. They emit a loud shout to release the adrenaline still circulating in their blood, but with the lieutenant's body inside the helicopter their shout falls short of victorious. Then the gunship pulls up and passing over the ruins, flies off towards the south east. Lazarov glances at his watch. He can barely believe that only one hour has passed since they descended into the underground.

Probably he will spend the rest of the day doing paperwork, including the drafting of a letter to Ivanchuk's next of kin. The thought depresses him.

Flying over along the tree-lined road where wrecked trucks rust away, the helicopter slowly gains altitude. To distract his thoughts from the body travelling with them, Lazarov keeps looking out of the window, wishing he could clean the rotten smell of the underground and stinging gunpowder residue off his nostrils with the fresh air outside.

The Zone of Alienation would still be beautiful for a wilderness, if one disregarded the abandoned vehicles and tanks, the dilapidated farms and ruined industrial buildings. He wishes he could exchange the helicopter's deafening noise for the Zone's silence. In the Zone, no songbirds ever sing, only ravens croak. No critter moves in the bushes, only mutants roam. Whatever noise the wind is bringing from afar, it's about a sound of death: a rifle burst; a mutant's growl; a human scream. And occasionally the roaring thunder of a storm, painting the sky in deep purple, flashing lightning and engulfing everything with darkness before bursting out in a gigantic display of flame-like rifts in the sky that resemble the Northern Lights. These mysterious supercells would be a spectacular sight if it weren't lethal to stay in the open and watch.

During the years he had spent here, Lazarov not only learned how to survive in the Zone of Alienation, he also learned how to love it; although he loved it more when there had still been secrets to explore. Sometimes he wished the

Zone was even bigger, but wasn't sure anymore if this was his own desire or that of the Zone herself. No protective suit, no armor could prevent the power of the Zone from creeping into his consciousness. The daily fear, the short moments of joy over a mission well done, the grief over fallen comrades, the mysteries he witnessed formed an ever-growing layer around his mind. With each beat of his heart, there was more and more of the Zone in his blood, and as time passed by, he unwillingly assumed the Stalkers' manner of speak of referring to the Zone as a *she*.

When the helicopter reaches a train station with the abandoned engines on the rusting railway tracks, a slow rain has set in.

"Condor One, this is Perimeter Base," comes through the radio. *"Do you copy? Over."*

"Loud and clear, Perimeter Base. Over."

"Colonel Goryunov is here to see you. Over."

Lazarov glances at his watch. "We'll be there in ten. Over and out."

"Roger. Perimeter Base out."

Lazarov suddenly feels as if a stone is weighing down his stomach. Ever since they met during the aftermath of a mission that went awfully wrong, he'd known Goryunov as one of the few officers not tainted by corruption. They'd become friends, as far as an agent and a Spetsnaz officer could be friends among the rivalry between the security service and the army. He often joined Lazarov on patrols deep into the Zone. Nothing ties men together than the memory of nights spent side by side in lonely look-out posts, fighting off mutants until daybreak.

Lazarov also knew that the FSB considered Goryunov more of a Stalker than an agent, just like his own fellow officers took him for an oddball because he didn't partake of their pleasures: bullying the lower ranks and shooting Stalkers for sport. For a moment it occurs to him that Goryunov might have arrived for another foray, but he doubts his own optimism. His friend appeared less and less frequently. There was not much left to explore in the Zone after all. They had been to every territory, explored every cave, bunker and catacomb, and Lazarov couldn't blame Goryunov for finding the Zone smaller and smaller after each raid.

The base is close now. Lazarov hears the pilot reporting in.

"Perimeter Base, this is Osprey One. We are inbound."

"We have a visual on you, Osprey One. Welcome home."

Perimeter - military base, 11:15:27 EEST

Lazarov is surprised to see a KA-60 on the helipad, a modern helicopter usually used for VIP transports and liaison duties. It has FSB written all over it despite its civilian color scheme. When Lazarov climbs out of the gunship's hatch, Goryunov and a lieutenant in Spetsnaz fatigue rush to greet him.

"Major Lazarov, this is Lieutenant Volna," Goryunov shouts over the engine noise after exchanging salutes. "He will debrief your men. You and me, we need to talk. Let's go to the command room."

"Good to see you too, Andrei," Lazarov shouts back.

Inside the dingy command room overlooking the gate, they give each other a hug.

"You still have blood on your face," Goryunov says as they sit down at Lazarov's desk, facing each other, and unpockets a pack of tissues.

"We met a... never mind," replies Lazarov. He moves to wipe his face with the back of his gloves, but seeing they are bloody too he accepts the paper tissue offered. Compared to Lazarov, who is still wearing his blood-stained, bullet-riddled armored suit, the colonel's impeccably clean and neatly ironed uniform makes him look like a visitor from another planet.

"I hope I didn't spoil your uniform."

"Come on, Misha. It's damn good to see you're alive and healthy."

"I wish you could say as much to Lieutenant Ivanchuk."

"Yes, I heard the dispatch on my way here... pity. He was a good man."

"He could have grown into an even better one." Lazarov looks up to the wall with its faded green paint. Next to the large drawing board with patrol orders and watch rosters, a upyr's file photograph is fastened to the wall with scotch tape. Someone has skillfully covered the mutant's head with the portrait of a very top-level politician. He didn't ask but knows that it's Ivanchuk's artwork. Once Goryunov is gone, he'd better remove it. "I suppose you're not here to write the letter to his next of kin for me?"

"No." Goryunov leans back in the chair and pulls out a hip flask from his pocket with two little shot cups. "But before we talk—*davay vipyem!*[1]"

"To Ivanchuk," Lazarov says raising his cup, "he was a good soldier."

The vodka, still cold from the chilly weather outside, slowly creeps down Lazarov's stomach and turns into comforting warmth. It does not dissolve his concerns about Goryunov's visit, however.

"If the FSB sent you to investigate this incident today," he says, "they were either very quick or knew beforehand that it was going to be messy."

"Those were not Stalkers down there, were they?" Goryunov asks as he puts his heavy suitcase onto the desk.

"They were mercenaries," Lazarov replies, "I've never met mercenaries so close to the Perimeter. I hope it was a one-time incursion, otherwise things will get really shitty for us here. We have barely enough men to keep the southern approach to Black Defile secure."

---

[1] Let's have a drink.

"If it's of any comfort to you, the Guardians are having troubles too. A few months ago, their quartermaster sold a whole shipment of weapons to the free Stalkers."

"Hear hear. Even the Guardians are becoming corrupted?"

"They tried to track the culprit down but he disappeared into thin air. Probably he has left the Zone altogether."

"The Guardians' problems don't make my life easier. On the contrary, we'd be screwed for good long ago without them." Lazarov looks out of the window to the dilapidated buildings. "Last week I had to literally beg general staff to provide us with fuel for the chopper. We got none. One more flight and we'll run dry."

"I know." Goryunov sounds concerned. "I have asked for more resources on your behalf but still get stonewalled by your brass. It's as if they don't care about you grunts here at all."

"Tell me something I don't know yet."

"This is exactly why I came here," Goryunov says, raising his eyebrows. "You don't have to worry about those mercs anymore… or about the Zone of Alienation itself, for that matter. It's Volna's job now."

Lazarov swallows hard, thinking: *Could it be that the army wants to get rid of me?*

"Are we so low on resources that the brass sends a lieutenant to replace me?" he asks. Lazarov's innocent enough question can't hide his concern. His friend seems to read his thoughts because a smile appears on Goryunov's face, even if it's not a very reassuring one.

"Volna is a capable officer. And as for you — I have good news and bad news. First of all, you are relieved of your duties as local commander. I don't know if this is good or bad news for you, actually."

"Depends on why my command is terminated." Lazarov turns his face away and looks out through the window. "Am I to leave the Zone of Alienation?"

"Well... we have a problem, and you will be the solution." Goryunov takes a deep breath before continuing. "I suppose you've already heard about the developments in Afghanistan."

"What? Afghanistan?" shouts Lazarov in surprise, so loud that a guard by the gate glances up with a concerned look on his face. Lazarov points his fingers to his eyes and then towards the Zone, reminding the soldier of the direction he is supposed to watch. Then, still perplexed, he turns back to his friend. "I mean, yes, I heard about strange things happening there after the nukes went up a few years ago... Stalkers talk about a Klondike of relics."

"To cut a long story short: looks like a new Zone has happened there."

"Is it true then? A *new* Zone? Anomalous traps, relics, mutants and all?"

"Kind of."

For a long minute, Lazarov looks his friend in the eye. "I think I need more vodka."

Goryunov fills his cup. "We believed we'd done a good job here, with all the Stalker activity in decline. I know what you think... well, it's declining according to statistics and that's what the generals want to see. Don't give me that look, please. Anyway, then we realized that the central regions in Afghanistan, which were not directly hit by the blasts, have become the new attraction for Stalkers. The Americans can't keep anything secret... You know what? I'm glad we have no Freedom of Information Act."

"I still don't get it," says Lazarov looking at his cup. "The nukes? How come? Even the greenest of Stalkers knows that the Zone wasn't created by radiation." He finishes his second shot.

"You want to leave some vodka for the end, brother. We have been studying things there for a while, having exactly the same question in mind. How could a new Zone happen there? An expedition was sent, similar to those in the Zone. The name of Professor Korolev should ring a bell."

Lazarov scratches his head. "If I recall correctly, he was the FSB's, uhm, pulse artillery expert? "

"No, that was Professor Dubinin. Korolev was responsible for the psychotropic research. Anyway, his team was digging up something in a place called Shahr-i-Gholghola until we lost communications." Goryunov takes a thick envelope from his suitcase and gives it to Lazarov. "Here's the detail. In short: you will go there, find them and get them out. But most importantly, you will secure any research results you find. That's your top priority. Misha, are you still with me?"

"The City of Screams..." Lazarov murmurs, lost in his thoughts.

"Exactly. That's what that Gholghola thing means. You've heard of it?"

"My father mentioned it in one of his letters to my mother, yes."

Lazarov regrets his words as soon as they are spoken. Colonel Goryunov's smile remains on his lips but it is not jovial anymore. It more resembles the grin of a predator, ready to jump at its prey.

"I understand," he says leaning closer.

"I don't want to talk about this," Lazarov protests. "For me, one of the few good things about the Zone is that it made me forget certain things."

"He died there without seeing his boy grow up, is that correct?" asks Goryunov, looking at the major with narrowed eyes.

"Yes. He died in Afghanistan when I was two years old. So what? You know my file!"

"I do. I also know that you were born in the year the Zone of Alienation happened," Goryunov pushes on. "Looks like you have a score to settle with both shadows of our past."

"My father's memory is none of your damned business!"

For a long moment, the seasoned soldier and the shrewd agent lock their eyes. In the end it is Goryunov who looks away. "Do you have a cigarette?"

"No. I'm trying to quit. And for God's sake, Andrei, stop being a spook for a minute. Go and try your mind-games on a mutant, not me. *Kruto?*"

"Yes, okay, okay... sorry again. Curiosity is my occupational disease."

"And that's what killed the cat, remember that. Anyway, what about the good news?"

Goryunov is now eager to change the subject. "First, that envelope contains a pretty amount in US dollars. Would you sign this proof of receipt, please? Stalkers love money, so use this to bribe them for any information if necessary. In the worst case, feel free to buy any resources if it comes down to that."

"At least I won't have to play their 'I'll tell you what you need if you get me what I need' game."

"Exactly. Second, this will be no lone wolf mission. You will have two squads of the 104th Regiment, 76th Airborne Division, at your command. All professionals, not the *srochniki*[1] you get to kick around here."

Lazarov nods approval. "*Nikto krome nas*[2]. I love their motto. But whatever they've been through in Chechnya and the South Caucasus won't help them much if they run into mutants and traps."

"Agreed. That's why you will be their command element." Goryunov smiles as he continues. "You'll be surprised but to some extent, I do envy you."

Goryunov looks out of the window to the concrete barrier, where the road to the inner part of the Zone begins. Flanked by tall poplars, the decaying tarmac looks like any ordinary road in the vast Russian countryside; yet it leads through

---

[1] Conscripts
[2] *Nobody but us*

areas soaked with blood, right up to the far heart of the Zone of Alienation. "You remember the old days, Misha? We have turned every stone and been everywhere. You name it. I wish there were new places to discover. I wouldn't even mind if the Zone got bigger."

Lazarov nods. "I hear you. But keeping it from spreading is part of our job... at least on paper."

Goryunov turns away from the window. "We failed. Whatever power had created the Zone has outsmarted us and it has happened again. You will look at the new Zone with fresh eyes... like we did here at the beginning."

"Andrei, Andrei," Lazarov replies and slowly shakes his head with a bitter smile. "You know how you sound? Like a pimp, tempting a married man to cheat on his wife with a whore."

"That's exactly how I wanted to sound," Goryunov laughs.

"And what exactly was a psychotropic weapon's expert digging up there?"

"That's classified." Before Lazarov could press on, the colonel changes the subject. "I managed to get you a few gadgets."

"I could use a new Val rifle."

"What, did you lose your weapon?"

"How to say... the Val's a fine rifle but not designed for beating a mutant's head into pulp."

"Oh you." Goryunov switches on his shockproof, heavy-duty laptop. "Damn, I left the charger in Moscow... hope there's still a little juice left in the battery. Come on, boot up, boot up..."

"Now you see why I stick to my palmtop."

"But you don't have minesweeper on that! At last... now look at this. It's the latest DARPA exoskeleton. The Americans treat it as a secret weapon, but certain generals must have good connections overseas. Unfortunately, we only have three. One for you and each platoon leader."

Leaning over the desk, Lazarov curiously watches the heavy armored suit appearing on the screen. "Impressive. Can I at last scratch my butt in this one?"

"Now don't be so unimaginative. It has Neovision night sights with infrared scanning, an integrated tourniquet — you only have to pull it here, you see? —, a wound healing system using hemostats and tissue-repairing collagens, carrying capacity more than eighty kilograms, Dragon Skin plates capable of stopping an armor-piercing bullet, full NBC protection... I tell you, it's the Armani of all protective suits. We have added a built-in anomaly detector and a few relic containers too. They block radiation of course. And yes, you can even scratch your butt in this."

"What about the troopers?"

"Upgraded body armor and standard kit." Goryunov switches his computer to map mode. "Now... let me recap Operation Haystack. First of all, this mission is classified — if..."

With a bitter smile, Lazarov cuts into the operator's words. "If I succeed, I'll get a pat on my back. If I screw it up, you spooks will deny to have ever heard of me. I know the drill."

"That's the way it goes, *bratan*[1], especially since we vowed never to go back there again. You will keep your call sign — Condor. Your gadgets are waiting for you at Termez Air Base, which will be referred to as Whiskey. There you will catch up with the paratroopers. Your teams will be known as Sparrow One and Two."

"Is that a subtle message?"

"Come again?"

"Why are my squads named after birds poking their beaks into shit?"

Goryunov makes big eyes. "I think you need to get laid, Misha."

"I do, but... never mind."

---

[1] brother

"You will be flown from Termez to the old air base at Bagram, or what's left of it now. Here. Your flight team will consist of two helicopters: a Mi-24VP, designated as Dragonfly One, which will blast away anything that blocks your path. A Mi-8 will transport your gear and supplies, call sign Dragonfly Two."

"What about radiation?"

"The mountain ranges north of Kabul have protected your area of operations from the worst. Radiation should be no stronger than here at the Perimeter. Once your forward base is established, preferably in this grid north-west of Bagram, you will proceed westwards to the last known position of the scientists, referred to as Needle. You will move along the old Bamyan road using low-profile recon tactics. Dragonfly One will stand by to provide close air support. Dragonfly Two will keep you supplied. Once you locate and secure Needle, Dragonfly team will bring you home. That's all."

"Can't we fly to Gholghola directly?" Lazarov asks studying the digital map. "The forward base seems to be pretty far from the target zone."

"I'm only passing on the orders to you."

Lazarov frowns. "Uh-hum... I knew there would be a catch."

"What catch?"

"Close air support, two full squads, state of the art kit, clearly defined mission objectives... all this sounds too good to be true. Is there anything more I need to know?"

Goryunov pauses for a moment. As Lazarov studies his face, his friend seems to be concerned regarding how much information he can disclose.

"Damn it, Misha, you're not supposed to know but probably you need to. We already lost a team. And it wasn't due to anomalous traps or radiation fallout."

"What then? A pulse rifle?"

"Apart from the fact that such weapons officially do not exist, it takes more than a pulse rifle to shoot down a gunship. It wasn't AA-missiles either."

"Who would still linger around there with heavy weapons?"

"We don't know," Goryunov shrugs. "We know of Stalkers, of course, and maybe what's left of the *dushmans...* you know, the Taliban. In one of their last dispatches the scientists did mention something about mercenaries too, probably hunting for relics. They were few and lightly armed, though, and they left the egg-heads alone. However..." The agent leans closer and lowers his voice. "The strangest intel we have is about rogue *pindosi.*"

Lazarov's eyes open wide in disbelief. "Rogue Americans?"

"A weird bunch of renegades calling themselves the 'Tribe'. Probably ISAF deserters or black-ops who have gone off the radar before the nukes. Only thing we know about them for sure is that they are led by a renegade American officer gone insane. "

"Is that so?" Lazarov curiously asks.

"He considers himself the reincarnation of Genghis Khan. Would you believe that?" Before Lazarov could say no, Goryunov carries on. "Bottom line is, we have no idea who brought down our bird or how. If you find any clues it's all for the better, but that's not your priority." Goryunov halts before continuing to give his next words more weight. "We do not have plans to get involved there."

"Sounds like an interesting place down south." Lazarov looks out at the hills, wishing he would be out there in the wilderness. "What about mutants and anomalies?"

"Some animals have mutated in similar ways to the Zone. Look at these pictures... We have reports saying that they have not only outstanding motoric capabilities like those in the Zone, but surprising intelligence too. Unfortunately it's still impossible to reason with them, so you won't have the chance to return with a pet mutant."

"These beasts look like rabids to me," Lazarov says looking at the picture displayed on the screen. "You know, those canine mutants."

"It's jackals. The reports also say that unlike mutants we know, who more or less follow normal animal patterns, hunting for food and so on, the species down there seem to kill for the joy of it."

"If so, maybe one day they'll evolve into human beings."

"I hope you can keep your philosophical attitude when the jackals bite off your hands first to prevent you from shooting them, or an upyr sneaks up behind you instead of running up with a roar that can be heard from afar."

"*Gospodi*. Are they learning?"

"Maybe, but at least they don't use weapons... yet."

Lazarov can't explain why, but Goryunov's last words sound strangely sinister to him. Knowing how secretive the colonel can be, he decides not to press him on this.

"Now, about physical and chemical anomalies: their presence is confirmed. Relics as well. We are still evaluating the scientists' early reports. Give me your palmtop, I'll transfer the most important intel. You will have ample time to study the rest during your flight to Termez."

"I hope it will be you coordinating this mission, Andrei?"

"I'll be in contact as Kilo One until you reach Afghan airspace." Goryunov clears his throat. "From then, Colonel Zarubin will take over tactical coordination."

"Oh no! That bastard Voronov's drinking buddy? You've got to be kidding me!" Lazarov's voice trembles with sudden anger. "When I took over the Perimeter after my promotion, it was a complete mess. Zarubin and Voronov degraded our base into a pig sty!"

"I know that, but—"

"Listen Andrei, I swallowed my pride when I saw them buying a career with relics looted from dead Stalkers. But being led by such an asshole in unknown and hostile territory... Call sign Whiskey, huh? Why not Bravo for bastards?"

Goryunov bites his lips. "Once on the ground, you'll be practically free to do as you see fit. Just say 'yes, sir' a lot."

"Please, don't tell me Voronov is involved in this too."

Goryunov shrugs. "Last time I met him was a year ago. I don't know where he is, actually. Maybe they made him a military attaché in Mongolia or something like that."

"The farther away he is the better."

"Couldn't agree more."

"Rules of engagement?"

"If possible, bypass any Stalkers you meet. If not, gather any information you can. That's what you've got the money for. But you have permission to return fire if attacked. Anything else?"

"I'll go through the details and contact you if necessary."

"Good. Let's finish that vodka. *Na zdarovye... za udachi!*[1]"

"Like I give a damn about your luck," Lazarov replies, sending the last shot down his throat.

Goryunov raises his glass, laughing. Their habitual toast upon departure, always seeming rude to others, evokes the memory of raids long ago.

"I almost forgot to give you Raider's regards."

"Does he know his old hideout has become a tourist attraction?"

"I'm not sure if that old wolf would approve of that," Goryunov says while he stands up and closes his laptop. "All right then. You'll have the night for leave, so the sooner we get to Moscow the better for you."

"Wait a minute, Andrei... you didn't even tell me when the mission starts."

"I thought that was obvious," Goryunov replies with an impish grin. "Now!"

---

[1] To health and to success.

#Kilo One, this is Diver calling. Do you copy?#
#[static]#
#Kilo One, this is Diver calling. Do you copy?#
#Diver to Kilo One. Loud and clear. I have approached their base as close as I could. The listening device is in position. The source is in range. Stand by for voice transmission.#
#Kilo One. Standing by.#
#[static]#
#Sir, I have just debriefed Lieutenant Bauer. #
#I hope she made it back safely. That area is crawling with mutants. I would have crushed Bauer's skull with my own hands if he allowed her to be harmed. He was supposed to protect her with his life. No swag is worth such a risk, no matter what she needs it for. #
#She is fine, sir. I wouldn't worry about her. #
#You don't need to sing her praises. We all know what she is capable of.#
It's us that I'm worried about, sir. Bauer's scouts report that the diggers have made progress.#
#You have been with me there... in the depths. You, my most senior warrior, should know that the intruders will never get deep enough. Not even with the help of their new friends.#
#The danger is... #
Acceptable.#
Do you want us to remain inactive? The men are eager to strike.#
Let the idiots clean up the mess they've made. We will remain inactive.#
Inactive, sir? That's hardly worthy of us.#
#It's not just inactivity but masterly inactivity. Let them dig and let them fail... or do you doubt the power of the Spirit?#
#With all due respect, sir: hell no!#
#Let her come to me now. The horror... the pain... it will never end. I need her help, Top.#
#[static]#

#Kilo One to Diver, we have too much noise, adjust transmission.#
#Diver. Relocating.#
#Continue transmission.#
#Negative. Must commence exfil. Shit! I see them coming. How could they have spotted me? Oh God, they must be using thermal scopes!#
#Report back when you've reached a safe spot.#
#Don't know who you'll send in as bait but he better be damn good. Diver out.#
#[static]#

The old apartment blocks look depressingly gray in the heavy rain. A Lada Niva SUV with the FSB crest on its doors drives along Kirovogradskaya Street, its windscreen wipers fighting a losing battle with the thick raindrops. It stops in front of an apartment block. Lazarov, wearing a water-proof raincoat over his leave uniform and carrying a suitcase, gets out. He waves to the driver and hurries towards the entrance where a lonely boy wearing a blue and red T-shirt plays with a ball. The ball shoots out into the rain after an ill-directed kick. Lazarov skillfully kicks it back to him.

"Thank you, officer," the boy says catching the ball and curiously studying the medal ribbons on Lazarov's uniform. "Do you fire real weapons in the army?"

"We do."

"And did you ever kill someone?"

"No."

"I guessed so," the boy laughs. "My parents keep telling me that our army is no good."

"You mustn't talk like that," Lazarov sternly replies. "Don't you know about the Great Patriotic War?"

"That was seventy years ago," the boy replies. "I don't like history anyway."

"And what *do* you like?"

"FC Barcelona", the boy proudly replies and pats his T-shirt. Then he starts kicking his ball against the wall again.

Lazarov hides his bitter smile and leaves the boy to his game. Stepping inside, he doesn't mind the smell of garbage and pesticides. It was like that even back in his childhood. Just like the elevator, still operational after five decades without any apparent maintenance. A short, silver-haired woman opens the door, plumped up by age, with only her deep blue eyes telling of her former beauty.

51

"Misha! What a surprise," she cries out as she embraces Lazarov. He returns her hug.

"Good to see you, mother."

"Please tell me you are on leave, *sinok*," his mother says helping him out of his raincoat. "It's been ages since I saw you last, my son."

"Five months and three weeks, to be exact."

"Yes. Are you well?"

"I'm... *normalno*[1]."

Throughout the trip from the air base, Lazarov had been trying to find the proper words to greet her with. His feelings were mixed: the grief and exhaustion of the last mission, the happiness and relief of being home again, the concern and anxiety about his new task – it is too much for him to put into a few words. Eventually, he says exactly what is on his mind.

"Is there beer in the fridge?"

His mother rushes into the kitchen. "I wasn't expecting you. Why didn't you call? I don't have any decent food for you and you must be ravenous. Such a shame on me!" Lazarov takes off his shoes and makes himself comfortable in a chair in the living room. Only now does he start to realize that he is actually home. His mother arrives with a glass and a bottle of Baltika beer. "I still have a few *galushki* from yesterday... do you want some? Of course you do..."

"Uh-hum," replies Lazarov gulping the chilled, bitter drink. The rather ordinary lager tastes so good it's as if he had never had beer before.

"I see you were thirsty." His mother looks down at him, radiating happiness. "Tell me, how are things in Sverdlovsk?"

"Boring," Lazarov replies, wiping the excess foam from his lips.

"But what have you been doing there all the time?"

---

[1] Russians never say *I'm fine* but *I'm normal*. Probably things are already fine if going the normal way.

"I told you many times before, mother. We're a logistics division, repairing trucks."

"Couldn't you at least come home more often? You are an officer after all."

"That's why I can't... you know how it goes. While the cat's away, the mice will play." Lazarov admits to himself that what he just said does actually fit his situation in the Zone.

His mother turns to the TV. "I heard Baskov and Fedorova are getting married," she says.

"I don't really care about celebrities, mother."

"But I do love their songs. By the way... will you meet Tanya while you are home?"

"No. She wrote me one of those letters a few weeks ago."

"What letters?"

"You know, mother," Lazarov explains patiently, "a letter beginning with 'my dearest' and ending with 'I hope we can still be friends'."

"Is that so?" His mother sounds disappointed. "I'm sorry to hear that. I took her for such a decent woman."

"Maybe she got impatient."

"My mother waited four years for your grandfather. I don't understand..."

"Girls are different nowadays. Tanya wrote she joined a dating site on the internet. Just for fun, of course. Then she hooked up with a dentist from London and fell in love with him. How romantic! Can I have another beer?"

"Such a *negodnitsa*[1]... I'm sure you will find another one."

"Why, you don't keep them in the fridge?"

"I meant another girl. You are still young, and have a safe job in the army," his mother says as she follows him into the kitchen. "They do keep you safe, don't they?"

"Oh yes," Lazarov reassuringly says and opens the fridge. "The only danger is of being bored to death."

"Mishka, my son..."

---

[1] Useless woman

"Where's the bottle opener?"

"On the table." She eagerly gets it for him. "You know, when Fedorova and Baskov were on TV last night, I prayed for your happiness…"

Lazarov cuts into her words. "Mother, I'm home for a single night and I have to leave early in the morning. Could you do me a favor and switch off that damned TV?"

"The army is a bad influence on you… you were such a sweet boy before." Shaking her head, his mother goes back to the living room and picks up the remote. "You never used to use such profanities."

Lazarov cannot resist laughing, but suddenly feels compassion for his mother living alone in a sea of concrete buildings, having only television and the neighbor's gossip for company and above all else believing that her only son tends to trucks in a dull garrison.

"Mother," he says as softly as he can, "please, could I have some coffee?"

"But of course, why…"

Lazarov walks back to the living room and finishes his second beer. With the TV switched off, he can hear the rain rapping on the window. He steps to the big cupboard where his mother's memories are neatly lined up in a china cabinet: cheap souvenirs from trade union holidays in the Crimea, faded postcards and other trinkets from the long-gone Soviet world that formed the backdrop to his parents' lives.

The exhilarating smell of freshly boiled coffee comes from the kitchen. Lazarov takes one of his mother's cigarettes that lie on the table and lights it up. The smoke twists and curls on the window glass. Outside, beyond the grey curtain of rain, lies a park that stretches into the distance.

This is how it must have been before.

With the ghost towns of the Zone in his mind he feels the Zone creeping back into him. He wishes he could be back there now; he wishes Goryunov hadn't come today.

"I love the bracelet you gave me for last Christmas," he hears his mother saying from the kitchen. "The elevator was out of order last week and I had to climb the stairs, but imagine, I didn't feel tired at all… That amulet seems to really work. Much better than all those pills and balms the doctors prescribe. Did you really get it from a UN observer from India?"

A smile comes to Lazarov's face. The bracelet has a piece from a Spirit relic inside, renown throughout the Zone for its beneficial effects on human catabolism and hence stamina.

"Yes," he replies loudly.

"I only wish it was a bit lighter, *sinok*… lead is not very elegant."

Too bad, mother. The thing emits radiation.

"You better not tamper with it," he shouts back. "It will lose its healing power if you remove it from the lead bracelet. That Indian guy told me himself."

China jangles as his mother arrives from the kitchen, bringing with her the smell of freshly boiled coffee.

"I didn't make your coffee too strong," she says. "If you need to leave early tomorrow, you better have a good night's sleep. I switched on the heater in the bathroom. You'll have hot water in twenty minutes. I will prepare a few *pirozhki*[1] for you."

"Thank you. I love your *pirozhki*, you know."

His mother sits down with a satisfied sigh and stirs the sugar in her coffee. "Why do you have to leave so soon?"

Returning her glance, Lazarov feels sadness and regret over the lies he has to tell her. But for once, he can tell the truth.

"I have some unfinished business down there… in the south."

---

[1] Baked or fried buns stuffed with a variety of fillings, preferably minced meat

55

Then he switches on the TV so as to direct his mother's attention to a Brazilian soap opera with Russian voice-over, before she can ask more questions that could only lead to him telling more lies. He joins her on the sofa and stares at the screen, sipping the hot coffee and trying to switch off his exhausted mind.

Alejandro, eu não quero mais viver assim!
Alekhandro, ja bolshe ne mogu tak zhit.

Too many melodramatic exclamations sound from the TV. They are made even worse by the male speaker emotionlessly dubbing the actress' theatrical sighs. Frustrated, Lazarov gets up, takes his suitcase and walks into his room, closing the door.

He steps to the shelves, moving his fingers along the rows of books with a movement that is almost a caress. It occurs to him to take a book for the long flight but a half-empty bottle of vodka draws his attention. It still stands on the table, just as he left it when he was here almost half a year ago. He opens it and takes a swig. Lazarov looks around in the cramped room holding the memories of a life he has almost forgotten by now. In the corner a guitar stands, which he never learned how to play. He moves his fingers across the transparent plastic boxes holding his compact discs. To his surprise, they are not dusty — his mother must keep the room neat and clean, maybe waiting for the day when he comes back for good. Aside the big pile of old, yellowed issues of *Guns Magazine*, an outdated desktop computer stands on the table. Next to it, another plastic box holds more compact disks.

Dammit, he thinks, *I wouldn't mind playing Doom for old times' sake, if I wasn't so tired. Or Baldur's Gate... Goryunov doesn't know but that's how I learned English... translating all those endless dialogues with a dictionary. And* Guns Magazine.

A cartridge casing lies besides the keyboard. Lazarov takes and studies it with a sad smile. It is all that remains of the first live cartridge he ever fired.

It's been a long way, old friend.

Holding the olive-green shell in his hand, the boy's words come to his mind. What he said about the army was exactly what he had felt when arriving at the Zone, three years ago, as a lieutenant. He had developed a liking for clandestine missions — there were enough corpses bearing a faction's characteristic armor, from hand-made Stalker suits to the Intruders' more sophisticated body armor and army-surplus tactical suits worn by the Guardians. It was not the thrill of sneaking he liked but the relief of moving around freely, without unnecessary kills. He realized soon enough that the worst enemy was not the humans who tried to survive in the Zone, but the creatures who had once been human but hadn't survived as such.

His first assassination brought him a promotion and with it the first doubts about who his real enemy was. What he already knew by then about Major Voronov's shady dealings, achieved through the blood of soldiers and Stalkers alike, caused the first cracks to appear in his hitherto unshakeable sense of duty.

The military wanted to have its share of the Zone's riches. Voronov had bought himself a step up in ranks and was replaced by Major Zarubin, but neither of them was in the cramped compartments of the helicopters and BTR personnel carriers that were sent into the gloomy mist surrounding the center of the Zone. As always, it was the grunts that had to remove the obstacles between the generals and anything that would make them rich — relics, information, whatever. And just like always, most of them died. By then, Lazarov had become a squad leader. His men survived the onslaught. In the aftermath of the operation, Zarubin became rich; soldiers were obliged to hand over any relics they found, and the deeper they penetrated the Zone, the more they found. Lazarov was made captain; an empty pat on the back for services rendered.

For the army, obtaining control over the center was like candle light to a moth. The Holy Grail of the generals. Again, an operation was launched and again it failed. Holed up in a ghost town and prepared to make a last stand against mutants and mercenaries, help came from where the beset Spetsnaz had least expected: Goryunov had turned up with a rag-tag band of Stalkers, whom Lazarov almost opened fire upon when they ran into his patrol team. When he was rewarded and promoted to major after that operation, Lazarov couldn't care less if that was for bravery under enemy fire or for just surviving. All that counted was that he got a week's leave.

And then it happened that I met her, he thinks looking at a photograph pinned to the wall. He puts the shell back into its place.

The photograph, not of very good quality and obviously taken with a mobile phone in a mirror, shows a pretty, blonde woman with blue eyes and full lips.

"You sent me one single photograph and even on that, you were making that stupid duck face," Lazarov grumbles to the photograph. He tears it from the wall, then crumples and tosses it under the neatly made bed. "Bitch... I prefer brunettes anyway."

Everything looks to him as if he would be trespassing in a stranger's room. He might have survived everything that the Zone threw at him, but the young man who once dreamed and loved here did not.

Lazarov opens his suitcase and takes out the palmtop. Waiting for it to start up, he takes his old school map from the shelf. It opens up almost on its own at the two-page map of the USSR. One line, drawn by a faded pen stroke, connects Moscow with a place in Afghanistan, still marked on the outdated map as 'Democratic Republic of Afghanistan'. In the margin, distances and names of places in childish handwriting remind him of a childish plan to go there.

I wanted to hitch-hike but didn't get past the first militiaman.

When he turns the pages to find a closer map of the area, a black and white photograph falls out.

Picking it up from the floor and looking at it, Lazarov's sight becomes hazy. It shows three young soldiers in ragged fatigue leggings, wearing stone-age flak vests over their striped T-shirts. With a broad smile that flashes bad teeth, they lean against an armored vehicle. The soldier in the middle, wearing a tank driver's black headwear, looks like a younger version of himself: a lean face with sunken cheeks and dark, fiery eyes. Only the moustache and curly hair tells how long ago the picture was taken.

He turns the photograph over to read the few words on the back, the handwriting looking oddly old-fashioned: *With love from Kunduz, October 1987. Yuriy and the gang.*

"That damned spook," he murmurs to himself, putting the photograph in his pocket. "He mentioned my father to motivate me into this insane mission."

With a muted beep, his palmtop signals its readiness. Lazarov opens the map, switches to 3D mode and scrolls all the way from Moscow to Afghanistan. A smile comes to his face when he compares the capabilities of his palmtop to the yellowed school map. The state of the art combat gear waiting for him in Termez comes to Lazarov's mind, and his smile hardens.

Things will be different now. And I swear by God — I'll make the dushmans suffer!

He hears his mother knocking on the door.

"Misha! Come, dinner is ready!"

"I'm coming," he reluctantly replies. "Just a minute!"

"I hope you didn't start playing video games again... you will never change, *sinok!*[1]"

---

[1] My little boy

Termez Air Base, Uzbekistan, 20 September 2014 06:00:00 UZT

Termez... Shit. I'm still only in Termez... Every time I think I'll wake up back in the Zone.

Lazarov's inner clock hasn't adjusted itself yet. Switching off the alarm on his palmtop, he glumly reckons that he has to go on a mission today.

Covered in sweat, he rises from his bunk bed. Colonel Zarubin assigned him one of the dozen or so metal containers where officers unfortunate enough to miss out on a place in the cooler quarters could sleep. The air conditioning had gone off in the middle of the night. Now, yawning and naked, Lazarov feels like he is sitting in a steam bath. To awake his muscles, Lazarov performs a few *Systema* movements: kicking, punching, throwing imagined enemies, crushing imagined skulls, grasping imagined hands and suffocating imagined throats. By the time he finishes the close-combat exercise, a healthy amount of adrenaline is rushing through his veins.

Colonel Zarubin had been waiting for him by the landing strip when Lazarov arrived on the previous afternoon. Zarubin even tried to be decent, concealing his disdain, except during the mission briefing when he presented Lazarov as a plain paratrooper officer "with some experience in hostile environments". This understatement was obviously intended as a punch below the belt. The soldiers seemed self-confident enough, bolstered by their previous missions in Chechnya, but most of them had no idea of what they were up against now.

If he was concerned about his troopers, the new exoskeleton proved perfect. His backpack carrying first-aid kits, bandages, personal hygiene kit, socks, tee-shirts, underwear, combat meal packs, anti-radiation drugs, his ammunition web holding spare magazines, fragmentation grenades, smoke grenades and the combat belt with the army-issue palmtop, first aid kit, combat knife and side arm seemed almost weightless once supported by the titanium-alloy bodyframe. Even his new Val assault rifle, strapped over the armor plate covering his shoulder, felt as light as a plastic toy.

But now, after cleaning himself up in a shared shower facility nearby and finishing a ration of oat meals for breakfast, he is less eager to get into the suit. He knows it will feel hotter than a Flame anomaly in there.

War is hell, Lazarov thinks with a sigh and grins over his own sarcasm whilst preparing the exoskeleton.

Ten minutes later he reports for duty in the operation room. Colonel Zarubin doesn't care to return his salute. Instead he looks down at Lazarov's exoskeleton, his eyes wide as if he finds something funny.

"Do you think Termez is about to be overrun by mutants?" Zarubin says by way of greeting. "Remove that suit at once. There's nothing but mosquitoes and butterflies around here. What the hell are you afraid of?"

"I thought I was going on a mission," Lazarov replies, unsuccessfully trying to suppress his resentment with a tone of formality. "And with your permission, Colonel, I would like to inspect the men now."

"No need for that, Major. I inspected them already and made all arrangements while you were still sleeping. Let's go."

Zarubin's voice is full of mockery, as if Lazarov had not shown up punctually to the second. He also talks loud enough for everyone in the operation room to detect the disdain in his words and tone. The only thing going for Lazarov is that there is no alcohol on Zarubin's breath.

Could it be that he takes his duty seriously after all, and his remarks about my exo were just because he's got too used to the safety here?

"What are you, deaf?" Zarubin snaps impatiently. A few computer operators look up from their screens, but quickly drop their heads again. "Move!"

"Yes, sir." Baffled, Lazarov walks down to the runway with Zarubin.

"Doesn't that shrieking noise from your gear drive you mad?"

"With all due respect, sir, I don't hear my exo making any noise."

"Maybe you still have Zone dirt in your ears. The metal joints shriek like a dentist's drill. You better remove it and have it fixed before you go into battle."

Lazarov cannot understand. The exoskeleton does not make any noise apart from the buzz of its kinetic motors, and that is so faint that only its wearer could hear it.

The two helicopters are already prepared for take-off. The two squads stand in front of them, neatly lined up in formation. Lazarov doesn't believe his eyes: the soldiers are not wearing their exoskeletons, bullet-proof suits, or helmets, only their summer fatigue and berets. He feels embarrassed in his exoskeleton as if overdressed for a party.

"Summer fatigues?" he asks gripping the Zarubin's arm. "Do you think they are going to the Victory Day parade?"

"Calm down, Major," Zarubin coldly replies, freeing his arm from Lazarov's grasp. "First: the mission will be a piece of cake. Second: it's goddamn hot. They will have enough time to slip into their gear later."

"I can't believe this. You must order them into their battle gear!"

"The hell I will. And now I'm going to hold a nice speech." Zarubin glances at his Rolex. "You are already three minutes behind schedule. Now shut up or I'll report your insubordination."

"Don't forget that I will also file a report," hisses Lazarov but Zarubin ignores him and starts addressing the men.

"At ease, at ease... Soldiers, you are about to set out on a dangerous mission. Many of you might have looked forward to this day but I assure you, it won't be anything like you have experienced before. Remember your training. Keep your weapons clean. Follow your orders. You set out to save the lives of fellow citizens who have been performing important scientific tasks!"

The colonel's speech would impress Lazarov if he didn't already know it by heart. It is one of the standard motivational speeches taught at the military academy. One only needs to exchange the place and mission objectives. He finds it pathetic to use this randomized text for soldiers embarking on a mission like this.

"…by successfully completing this mission, you will bring great honor to your unit and our motherland. And now your new commander also has something to say. I suppose it will be about how hot he feels in that boiler."

Lazarov sees the grins on a few soldiers' faces. Quickly, he prays for an opportunity to lead Zarubin deep into the Zone and throw him into an anomaly.

He thinks for a second. Then he shouts out.

"Desantniki! Smirna!"

Heavy boots thud on the ground as the paratroopers stand at attention. Instead of improvising a speech, the major walks up to the soldiers and inspects their ranks with slow steps, looking each man into the eyes. He is an impressive sight in full combat gear, but it is not his martial appearance that impresses the paratroopers. Lazarov is unaware of how much the Zone has marked him. He only sees that as he passes them by, the soldiers' faces harden with respect — even fear. No one dares to return his gaze, except Sparrow One's hardened warrant officer who will be his second in command. The soldier with a thick grey moustache is the last in the row. When their eyes meet, Lazarov bows his head in a barely noticeable nod. Already standing at full attention, the soldier squares his broad shoulders even more, a relaxed, jovial smile still lurking in his steel-blue eyes.

"Well," Lazarov asks quietly, glancing down at the nametag on the uniform, "are you ready, Zotkin?"

"Ready to go, *komandir.*"

Zotkin's reply is quiet but Lazarov immediately knows that if treated with respect, or at least asked politely, this man will follow him into hell. The other squad leader, a young and nervous-looking master sergeant, doesn't impress him much.

Walking back to Zarubin, he cannot refrain from darting a murderous glance in the colonel's direction. Zarubin avoids his eyes. Lazarov turns back towards the ranks and shouts out again.

"*Desantniki!* Who but us?"

"Nobody, *komandir!*" reply the soldiers in a steely choir of confidence.

"Into the helicopters! Let's go!"

While the squads hurry to the helicopters, Lazarov turns to the colonel.

"I hope you know what you're doing, Zarubin."

"Much better than you would believe. Now you better go before you miss your flight, Major," the colonel says contemptuously, pronouncing 'major' like a swear-word. "Impressive speech you gave, by the way."

"It comes from doing an officer's job. One day you should try it, Colonel."

Leaving him without saluting, Lazarov hurries to the gunship. It's hot inside with the helicopter having baked in the sun the whole morning.

"Switch on that ventilator," he barks taking his place on the grey bench. "I can't believe Zarubin let you embark like this. You don't even have your bloody helmets with you!"

"He thought it appropriate—" Zotkin explains but his last words are suppressed by the Mi-24's howling turbines. Lazarov signals for him to switch over to the intercom.

"I said, he ordered Dragonfly Two to carry the armored suits!"

"I hear you now, Zotkin, you don't need to shout."

"It's a bad idea to me too, sir, but he insisted."

"At least the troopers are carrying their rifles with them… but where are the machine gunner and the sniper?"

"All aboard!"

"Then why don't I see their weapons?"

"Dragonfly Two carries all our heavy gear. The Colonel's orders—"

Hearing this, all that Lazarov can do is to burst out in a stream of profanities. Most of it is directed at Zarubin, the rest at the army brass as a whole. Zotkin grins in approval.

The ventilator might ease the heat for the soldiers but Lazarov is bathed in sweat under his exoskeleton. Its kinetic motors are supposed to load the batteries powering the cooling pads but he hasn't moved enough to fully charge them yet. He switches off the system to save power for their arrival. He knows that one thing that not even the nukes have changed in Afghanistan is the heat. A signal beeps in his intercom.

"Condor, this is Kilo One, do you copy?" Lazarov is delighted to hear Goryunov's voice. He touches the speaker's button on his neck and replies: "This is Condor. Copy you loud and clear."

"In five, you will be in Afghan airspace. Give me a sit-rep."

"All well, but according to Whiskey we're going to a parade ground."

"Say again, Condor?"

"Listen up," shouts Lazarov losing his patience, "I'm moving into a god damn Zone in god damn Afghanistan with my men wearing nothing but their god damn uniforms!"

"Two minutes to Afghan airspace," reports the pilot.

"Listen, Condor... all you can do now is consolidating your gear as soon as you touch down. Our satellites indicate your landing zone as clear. Whiskey will give you updates from now. You are good to go," Goryunov reports. "Good luck on your raid. Kilo One clearing out."

"That river below is the Amu-Darya, Major" the pilot observes, "you can see the Friendship Bridge to our left... and the refugee camps."

All that Lazarov sees is a huge square below, once probably consisting of neatly arranged army-issue tents, now turned into a colorful mess, like an oriental carpet, by ten times as many people living there as the camp was laid out for, using every square meter to carve out a space for living.

"Bloody Afghans," Lazarov hears Zotkin's voice. "They still hate our guts. I hope I'll never have to see these refugees appear in *my* country."

The helicopter flies over the Amu-Darya, a silver band crossing the ochre-colored plains.

"Here we go," comes the voice of the pilot. "We're flying over Afghanistan now."

Lazarov looks out of the tiny window. The endless plains below look the same all over.

According to his watch they still have forty minutes to their landing zone. He unfastens his safety belt and moves closer to the window. The two helicopters are flying over undulating terrain, the color reminding him of milky coffee. The sand dunes appear like wrinkles on the palm of a hand, even though they might be several meters high.

"I never thought we'd ever be back here again," Zotkin says. "Never."

"We aren't, at least officially," Lazarov replies.

Lazarov's second in command narrows his eyes, as if checking if his words could make an impression on the major.

"We can't change what happened, can we?"

"No, but we can have our revenge. Can't we, Zotkin?"

"I don't care about revenge, *komandir!*"

"You didn't lose anyone from the family there? Your brother, father, a friend? Because it's pay-back time!"

Zotkin frowns. "After two tours of duty in '87 and '88, I was hoping to never see that cursed land again!"

Lazarov leans closer to the soldier, as if that would make a difference in the helicopter's roar while they talk through the intercom. "What? You've been there?"

"As a private, then a sergeant with the blue berets. Airborne. Got a hang of it. Had to lie about my age, but who cared?"

"How come you're still just a warrant officer?"

"Best rank in the army, *komandir*. Lieutenants listen to me, captains ask for my advice."

"I'll do both, because I've a feeling that we'll make a hell of a team!"

"It would be a privilege," Zotkin replies with a smile, then turns his attention to one of the soldiers who is nervously drumming his fingers on his AKSU-74. "Stop fondling that rifle, son! If it goes off I'll throw you out of the chopper!"

After a few minutes they reach a hilly region. According to Lazarov's map, the wide and flat Shamali valley lies beyond it, still invisible in the haze.

"It's the Salang Range" the pilot says as if he were a tour guide, "there's a pass and a long tunnel beneath. It was our main supply route back in those times… you know."

Their altitude is low enough to make some hills tower over them, appearing close enough for the rotor blades to strike. Only the helicopters' tiny shadows show how far up they actually are. The jagged, rough mountains around them fill him with awe. Suddenly, Lazarov sees a gleam on a ridge, seconds later another one. He puts on his helmet and zooms in with the built-in binocular.

"Can we get any closer to that ridge at forty-five degrees?" he asks the pilot.

"That's off of our flight path," comes the reluctant reply.

Lazarov's curiosity prevails and he ignores his gut feelings telling him he might be about to make a mistake. "Turn right and lower the altitude."

For a moment, the pilot remains silent before acknowledging. "Yes, sir. Adjusting course by zero-four-five."

The gleam appears again for a split second. Now it is Zarubin in his earphones.

"Dragonfly One, we noticed an unauthorized deviation from your flight path. I want you to—"

Before the sentence finishes, the other helicopter's pilot's scream pierces into Lazarov's earphone.

"Dragonfly One, this is Dragonfly Two, we've been hit, I repeat—"

Lazarov's pilot shouts *"pull up, pull up"* but the only reply is fragmented swearing, getting thinner until it becomes static. The gunship is making a desperate, almost vertical ascent. Lazarov's stomach seems to drop as he frantically tries to reach for his safety belt. He knows the pilot's drill: climb over and disappear behind the nearest ridge to make any anti-aircraft weapon lose its target, unless it was a missile. He grasps a handle but the weight of his exoskeleton pulls him down. His head smashes against the cabin wall. The helmet softens the impact but he feels blood gushing from his mouth. A sizzling thunder suppresses the soldiers' agonizing screams. The turbines howl like wounded animals fighting for their lives. Blue electric sparks splutter everywhere, as if the gunship had been hit by a hundred thousand volts of electricity. The earphones transmit the pilot's desperate scream of *"Brace for impact!"* before falling silent. Consciousness dims and blacks out, then darkness engulfs Lazarov's sight.

***Encrypted digital VOP transmission. Central Afghanistan, 20
September 2014, 16:44:08 AFT***

*#You were not supposed to shoot down those choppers, you trigger-
happy bastards.#*

*#Next time make sure they stick to their flight path. They were
approaching our positions. When are you sending us the next
exoskeleton delivery?#*

*#There will be no more deliveries, shithead. Can't you understand
this one was carrying three exoskeletons, not to mention the regular
suits? You don't expect us to suck more American cock to get them,
do you?#*

*#You already received half the money in advance. Make sure you
deserve the second part. A deal is a deal.#*

*#You can get one exo from the Hind. The rest were on the transport
chopper.#*

*#We'll send a team to the first crash site. We know its location. But
we need the whole shipment.#*

*#Then go and get your damned delivery from the transport
chopper's carcass.#*

#Negative. That's your area. We must keep a low profile.#

#So what do you expect me to do?#

*#If you want to stay in business, get those other suits like you did
last time. Out.#*

Hindu Kush range, New Zone, 17:04:56 AFT

Being dead is not so bad at all... save for the nausea.

Lazarov's nose and lungs are filled with the reek of burning flesh. Blinding light pierces into his brain with weird reflections. He doesn't dare to open his eyes.

I am dead and must be in hell.

Slowly his brain starts working again. He realizes his eyes are open. The light comes from above. It's the empty sky, with the sunrays refracted by his helmet's broken visor. He wants to sit up but cannot move.

Oh God my spine is broken.

He tries to move his fingers and toes. To his relief, none of his bones feel as though they are broken. He can even raise his left hand now.

But why can't I move my body?

Then he grasps that it's the exoskeleton holding him. It must have saved his life but now, shattered and deformed by the impact, it keeps him down as if he's tied by its metal tubes. Groaning, he reaches for the combat knife fastened to his belt and cuts through the straps attaching his backpack to the metal frame. With his shoulders free, he leans forward to release his legs. Finally he rises to his knees and, after gathering his strength for a long moment, he stands.

Instinctively, Lazarov's first thing to do is to draw his Strizh pistol; luckily for him it was fastened strong enough in its holster. Then he pulls his rugged, military-issue palmtop from a pocket on his assault vest. It's still in one piece but doesn't function.

Damn it... where in the hell am I?

The gunship's smoking wreck is a few steps away. The impact threw the crew compartment hatch open and the noxious stench comes from inside. His helmet's integrated breathing system should keep it out, but when he checks the filter he finds it hanging loose of its casing, rendered completely useless.

I can't believe this is happening to me.

Checking his exoskeleton's built-in instruments, he finds that only the Geiger counter remains operational. It ticks dangerously close to the yellow zone. He removes his helmet. It won't help him anymore.

He limps to the wreck. Initially, he manages to fight his nausea but as he peeks inside the compartment and sees the burnt corpses of his comrades, Lazarov turns around and retches. He needs several minutes to pull himself together. Covering his nose and mouth with his hand, he climbs inside. Sparks still sizzle among the broken instruments and torn cables. Most of the corpses sit where they were during the flight, fastened to their bench with their safety straps, still in their very last posture as they tried to protect themselves from the impact. They look like grey, smoke-blackened statues. Among them, with his neck broken beneath his half-burnt skull, lies the *praporshchik*. Zotkin's remaining steel-blue eye is staring at him and Lazarov turns his head away. It's not the sight that disturbs him so much as the feeling that the dead man is looking at him reproachfully; a reproach made more terrible because Lazarov knows that it is just.

His weapon lies in the compartment, but with the butt stock broken the rifle is now nothing more than a piece of junk. It could probably be repaired, if only he had the tools. Lazarov throws it away in frustration. Checking his backpack he despairs to see it is burnt and ripped open. Apart from the grenades, only a few anti-radiation drugs and bandages, three packs of army rations and a first aid kit is all that he can still use. Neither has he any use of the spare magazines now that his rifle is beyond repair. His frantic search still yields a few pairs of spare socks, always a blessing for soldiers in the field, and his toothbrush. Holding it in his hand, he bursts out in hysterical laughter.

Oh God! A short time ago, I was a high-tech warrior riding in an assault chopper. Now I'm standing here with a damned toothbrush in my hand!

It seems to the major as if the New Zone had wanted to show its power, outwitting and forcing him to make his first steps here alone, even more poorly equipped than the greenest of rookies.

The paratroopers' rifles didn't fare much better than his own but eventually he finds an AKSU-74 that looks more or less intact. Lazarov fires a few shots to check if it works properly. Satisfied, he slings it over his shoulder.

The pilots were spared electrocution in their heavily protected cockpit, but as Lazarov judges by the splashes of blood inside the plexiglass, the impact killed them in a perhaps even crueler way. They wear light armored suits, designed to keep them protected from the worst only until rescue comes. But even if hardly suitable for combat, the light, olive-green suits would still be more protective than his ruined exoskeleton.

"Sorry comrade, but you don't need this any longer," Lazarov murmurs as he cuts the straps that fasten one of the bodies into its seat before dragging it out of the cockpit. He changes the exoskeleton for the dead pilot's protective suit. Inside it he finds a torchlight and a small survival kit: a ration pack, one more first aid kit, a compass, a field flask filled with water and two flares.

Now that he can act like a soldier again, duty to the squad comes to Lazarov's mind.

I could at least bury them, he thinks. But the ground is hard and rocky, so instead he takes the pilot's body and moves it into the trooper's compartment, where it will be safe from animals and worse.

Had that bastard let them wear their protective suits they'd be still alive. I should have insisted, damn it. It was my fault after all.

Lazarov doesn't let himself look for excuses. He cannot deny himself that it was his recklessness that led them into disaster. Properly protected, especially the squad leader in his exoskeleton, they would have had a better chance. But this is irrelevant. He was not supposed to change the flight path.

I will be court-martialed for that alone… if I ever get out of here at all.

Lazarov finds it strange that he does not see any entry point on the helicopter. *If Dragonfly One was brought down by hostile fire, which those gleams* must *have surely been, it must have hit us somewhere.* But pondering through the few impressions he remembers from the crash, and finding no hole or explosion trace on the wreck, it all looks to him as if the helicopter had been hit by an enormously strong electrical impulse that had instantly electrocuted almost everyone inside and fried the on-board systems.

Suddenly his ears detect the faint noise of a helicopter.

Could it be the rescue?

Listening more carefully to the approaching noise, his feeling of relief proves short-lived.

It doesn't sound like one of ours.

Something inside tells him to hide, but he couldn't make it up the hills quickly enough and the barren valley does not offer any hide-outs. Finally he dashes up a knoll and hides behind the sparse bushes.

Soon, a double-engine helicopter appears over the valley and lands at the crash site, swirling up a huge cloud of dust. Lazarov sees five or six figures jumping off, all wearing thick body armor with tactical helmets and holding modern-looking weapons. They start inspecting the wreck. One of them, wearing a bulky backpack, looks inside. To Lazarov's horror he steps away and sends a stream of liquid fire into the compartment. Immediately, the wreck goes up in orange and white flames.

Oh Gospodi![1] They have a flamethrower. They came to make sure everyone is dead.

---

[1] Oh my god!

One of them stumbles upon his exoskeleton. The others gather round. Lazarov cannot hear anything they say but it seems to him as if the men are arguing. The first, apparently the leader among them, orders two others to recover the remains of the armor and load it into their helicopter.

What the hell is happening there?

He wishes he still had his binoculars. There are no marks or call signs on the helicopter. It is painted entirely black. The visitors look around, scanning the area. One of them starts walking up the knoll on which he is hiding. Cautiously, Lazarov prepares his AKSU-74.

He is lucky, however. The leader orders his men back to the helicopter and in a few moments only the wild fire in the wreck is left as a reminder of their visit. After a few minutes, the helicopter's noise fades away.

Lazarov sighs in relief but waits a few moments before leaving cover. Then, safe at last, he reconsiders his options.

First, I have to establish contact with Whiskey. Probably Zarubin would want me to check out Dragonfly Two's fate first, and now I have no means of communication anyway.

Allowing himself a little wishful thinking, he hopes that the transport helicopter fared better than the gunship.

He looks at his watch. Dusk will soon fall, and with the sun already low it is getting dark in the narrow valley. Lazarov knows the drill: he should stay close to the crash site if he wants any rescuers to find him. But if there was going to be a rescue, it should have arrived long ago. Three hours have passed since they got shot down and Termez is just forty minutes away.

Maybe they'll come later, perhaps tomorrow morning.

But the mysterious visitors could also soon be back in greater numbers. Not even darkness could hide him if they brought thermal imaging equipment with them, and as he had observed from their gear, they certainly wouldn't lack for state-of-the-art equipment if it was needed.

Lazarov decides to climb up the ridge to get an overview of the area, hoping to see rising smoke or anything that could give him an idea of Dragonfly Two's whereabouts. As he toils up the steep hillside, the thought that the visitors might have also found the other helicopter occurs to him. He finds the prospect frightening.

That would leave me completely alone.

But then, as he arrives on top of the ridge after a rigorous climb, what he sees shatters all his false hopes.

What looked from below like a high ridge is all but a small hill compared to the ragged peaks beyond. He removes the tiny compass from the survival kit and takes a bearing.

To the west lies a circle-shaped valley with a tarn in its middle, its dark blue hue reflecting the brown mountains and the patches of grey snow on their fells. But as Lazarov strains his eyes he sees the water itself is swelling with mounds of water, slowly moving up and down, as if a sudden chill had frozen its waves in a storm.

It's a trap.

Looking at the far, snowy peaks on the red horizon, he feels lonelier than anywhere in the Zone.

If this is the New Zone, it will take a hundred years to explore just the half of it.

All of a sudden he understands why the black chopper left in such a hurry. To the south, where his original destination lies, a curtain of darkness falls, lit up for split seconds by flashes of thunderbolts. Even from far away, Lazarov can see it moving closer as it engulfs the lower hills.

I don't care if this is just a storm or a new kind of super cell. I must find shelter, and I must find it right now!

Below, where the slope meets the tarn, he sees a cave. He unshoulders his weapon from his shoulder and runs down the ridge. It is much farther away than he thought. Finally, gasping for air, he reaches it just as the storm strikes, making everything disappear in a howling, suffocating cloud of dust. His Geiger counter shrieks beyond extreme values. The tiny particles drift through his helmet's air filters and soon he feels as if a myriad of needles are picking at his throat and trachea.

Coughing and with eyes full of tears, Lazarov lights a flare and enters the cave. The red light casts ghostly shadows on the rock wall. Holding his weapon at the ready, he moves deeper into the cave to escape the radioactive dust. With each step he takes, the ticking of his Geiger counter lowers until the usual ticking cycle sets in, signaling a more survivable level. The *click-click* and the muted howl from outside is all he can hear.

The ground is covered in inches of thick dust. His steps make no noise. After a minute, he can hear his own heartbeat.

The cave widens. A thick cable lies on the ground. Lazarov raises the flare to see more. A hiss comes from the shadows. His blood curls as he sees the cable moving. In a second, it darts up and to Lazarov's horror, he sees the flare light reflected in the glowing red eyes of a snake, its body as thick as a man's limb. Greenish, phosphorescent patterns glow upon its skin, either to scare him away or root him to the spot with fear. He screams and stumbles. It is instinct rather than willpower that moves his finger, trigging the AKSU-74 to pump a dozen steel core cartridges into the mutant's flesh, puncturing skin, ripping through muscles and shattering bones even before the thundering *bang-bang-bang* can reach his eardrums.

"*Fuck!*" he swears, gasping.

Exhausted and with his heart still pounding hard, he picks up the fallen flare and sits up. The nauseating smell of burnt gunpowder pervades the cave. He opens his flask and takes a deep gulp of water. As his senses are clearing up, he can clearly smell the stench of rotting flesh.

Maybe it was a sick snake, he thinks getting to his feet and warily kicking the carcass to make sure it's dead. The flare burns out. He switches to torchlight. Penetrating the shadow, the tiny circle of light suddenly falls upon a body.

It was eating them, bit by bit.

Normally he would not do such a thing, but now it is clear to Lazarov that normality ended in the moment when he left the Zone. Eager to see if the corpse has anything useful on it, he overcomes his nausea and steps closer to it. The prey was a Stalker, leastwise the kit looks identical to the attire of more experienced Stalkers: army surplus leggings and assault vest, a light, loose-fitting long coat and a canvas shoulder bag holding a gas mask. A brown shemagh still covers the victims's head, sparing Lazarov the sight of the dead man's face. A small camelback water bag is attached to the patrol pack laying a step away from the body.

This kit seems well adapted to this place, but didn't save this hapless fellow.

In the dim light of the torch, Lazarov's search proves fruitful. The pouches and patrol pack produce an AK magazine, an outdated anomaly detector, a pair of binoculars and a few anti-radiation drugs. He quickly applies one of them, hoping that it won't make him more nauseous than he already is from the stench. Lazarov wants to stand up and move away from the corpse but keeps sitting with his back to the wall, his face buried in his hands and body tortured by hunger, pain and exhaustion.

#Where have you been? We tried to call you several times.#

#I was hanging on my satellite phone all night, trying to talk them out of sending a rescue mission. Well, they won't bother. Did you find the exo at the crash site?#

#Positive. But it was in very bad condition. We can't use it.#

#That's not my problem. It was in a perfect state when leaving Termez. What about its owner?#

#There was no body inside.#

#Strange. Any survivors?#

#One crew member might have gotten away.#

#Shit! Are you imbeciles at least tracking him?#

#We tried to search the area around the crash site but a dust storm was approaching. It probably killed him. In any case, we deployed several drones to scan the whole map grid.#

#You better find him quick. If he gets into the tunnel, and probably that's where he will go, you will lose him for good.#

#We know. We've already sent several squads to intercept the fugitive.#

#They better do. I cannot do everything by myself, do you understand? Now try to be effective for once.#

#[static noise]#

#I didn't copy that. Anyway – go to hell, you amateurish morons. You will ruin this whole thing. Out. #

When he returned to the crash site at dawn, Lazarov had hoped that he would find a rescue helicopter and squad of soldiers there, but as he stands next to the smoldering wreck again, his hopes vanish for good.

Good-bye, comrades. It was my fault but I'll redeem this mistake. Forgive me.

Lazarov salutes the wreck that is now the grave of his soldiers. Then he heads towards the south. He had ample time on the long flight to Termez to study the map and now, even with his palmtop broken, he knows that the nearby road leads to a tunnel traversing the Salang Range.

Setting out southwards in the barren, mountainous landscape, Lazarov can't shake a feeling of déjà vu. Rusty, abandoned vehicles litter the road here and there, many of them the KAMAZ and ZIL trucks that sit rusting in the Zone he knows. Occasionally, he finds the wreck of an age-old BTR-70 too, probably a relic of the Soviet war. The potholes and cracks in the decaying tarmac, the barriers and abandoned guard posts are so much the same to him that if it wasn't for the mountains he would believe himself to still be in the Zone. It's all so familiar, right down to the routine of stopping and scanning the area ahead for anomalies, all accompanied by the Geiger counter's unceasing clicking.

Sensing danger, Lazarov quickly kneels down next to an abandoned tank and goes into cover behind its iron mass, ignoring the Geiger counter's intensifying noise. Looking through the binoculars he sees a deer walking cautiously beside the road. Or rather, something like a deer, because this animal's antlers are unlike anyone he has seen before—they bend and twine like a ball of thick, bony strings.

Another animal appears among the rocks, at first resembling something between a fox and a wolf. On closer inspection, however, Lazarov can see the two long, curved ngs in its snout and he realizes that it's a mutant jackal. He'd ,een a picture on Goryunov's computer screen, back on that day that was only three nights ago but now feels like a thousand years past.

Another jackal's head appears, and another one, then the whole pack of a half dozen furry mutants. The deer senses their presence. It raises its head, smells the wind and runs. But the pack is already closing in for the kill. They outrun and accurately encircle the deer, as if following a master's call or training, until the strongest performs an incredible leap and thrusts its fangs into the neck of the prey.

If he had a better rifle and ammo to waste, Lazarov would help the deer and pick off the jackals one by one. Now he can only watch as the beasts tear it apart. As sorry as he feels for the deer, he has to admit that these jackals are the best hunters he has ever seen among mutants. Watching the carnage through his binoculars, he whistles in awe — and immediately realizes that this was a big mistake.

The biggest mutant turns its head in his direction, emitting a sharp bark and leading the pack towards him at breathtaking speed. Lazarov's blood curdles as he sees them leave the carcass of their prey almost untouched. Goryunov's words flash through his mind: *they kill for the joy of it.*
Seeing their speed and how far they can leap, he realizes in a split second that climbing up the tank wouldn't help him like when facing the canine predators in the Zone. Gripping his weapon firmly, he kneels down with his back against the wreck to prevent any mutant jumping at him from behind and carefully aims at the nearest jackal. A short burst from the AKSU brings it down, then the second one. For a moment, the jackals seem to be confused, allowing him to take down another two. His aim gets more erratic and his bursts longer as they get closer and closer.

Still ten rounds inside. You are one with the rifle. Don't think. Shoot.

Now there's only the pack leader and one other left. A lucky shot hits the second animal in the head and the mutant whines, rolling over as it tumbles down the hillside. Lazarov turns the rifle's ironsight towards the pack leader, its mouth drooling blood and saliva. He pulls the trigger. The weapon jams.

He has only moments left to watch the jackal covering the last meters. He sees the muscles of its back legs stretching as they project the heavy body in a long, deadly leap towards his face. He closes his eyes so as not to see it coming.

That was a really short raid.

The smell of blood is strong as the jackal lands upon him, but there is no attack. Lazarov opens his eyes to see the air fill with a pale red haze as the jackal's head is almost ripped off by a bullet. A split second later he hears a loud *bang* that is still echoing along the valley as he throws the carcass off him and frantically changes his magazine. But when he sees a rifleman emerge from behind a rocky outcrop, he lowers the rifle. Even if need should be, he could never hit him at the distance of several hundred meters.

A long, wide cloak flutters from the stranger's shoulders as he approaches. It's a sniper's ghillie suit, except this one does not resemble thick foliage but has shreds of earth-colored fabric fastened to its net. The different shades of brown make the camouflage almost indistinguishable from the rocky slope. The sniper keeps his rifle upright to show he has no hostile intentions. In reply, Lazarov raises the hand holding the rifle. Now he can even recognize the type of rifle that had just saved his life: a Dragunov SVD. The Stalker's face remains hidden by a black balaclava save for his pair of ice cold, blue eyes and mouth that arches into a grin as he walks closer.

"Impressive fight you've put up," the sniper greets him. "Have a good one. Name's Crow."

"It jammed," Lazarov replies, showing his rifle. His heart is still beating hard from the adrenaline rush. Before introducing himself, he decides that for now it will be better if he doesn't out himself as an army officer. Most Stalkers use call signs or nicknames, not their real ones, and having no better idea on the spot, he decides to use his usual call sign.

"Call me Condor," he finally says.

"That was a big one," the Stalker says inspecting the pack leader's carcass. "These beasts are smart enough to let the smaller ones take the lead. The alpha only moves in to finish the kill."

Lazarov has seen enough loners to recognize one and addresses Crow in the familiar way of Stalkers.

"You really helped me out, *bratan*."

"Don't mention, it, brother. But let's get out of here. This place might hide worse things than jackals."

Lazarov is not sure if they are much safer behind the tipped-over trailer truck where they sit down, but at least it hides them from any spying eyes. Crow pats his pockets and emits a frustrated sigh.

"You happen to have any smokes? No? Dammit... anyway, where did you come from?"

Lazarov hesitates for a moment. "Rostov."

"I'm from Ryazan, myself. Any news from the Big Land?"

Lazarov had always been too preoccupied with the Zone to pay attention to happenings in the outside world, politically or otherwise. Only one thing comes to his mind. "Nikolay Baskov is banging Oksana Fedorova."

"Still, or again?"

"What?"

"I thought that's news from yesterday."

"Honestly? I couldn't care less."

"What are you up to here, anyway? And where did you get that suit from? You're twice its size."

"Actually, I arrived recently... I'm on my way to Bagram. And the suit... my own got a little worn and I found this at a crash site, not far from here."

Crow studies him with a look full of doubt. Lazarov avoids his stare.

He doesn't seem easy to fool.

"One more chopper? Looks like the army wants to stir up trouble. I saw another one yesterday while I was crossing the Salang Pass."

Lazarov's heart starts beating faster. "You mean there's another crash site? Was there any... loot?"

"The chopper was damaged for sure but as I watched it, it seemed to make it to the plains. By now it should be a treasure trove for the brothers down there..." Crow frowns. "Don't tell me you were one of the pilots and bailed out accidentally."

Lazarov sighs. The Stalker has saved his life and he doesn't want to repay it by dumping a lie on him. He decides to partly reveal his identity. Although Crow has an AN-94 rifle on his back and a silenced Glock-17 pistol loosely holstered on his armor webbing, with the AKSU-74 ready he would hold the advantage if his rescuer turned aggressive.

"All right... Truth is, I was with the army chopper that went down. I made it through. My own gear was busted, so I took the suit from the chopper's dead gunner. I spent the night in a cave when the storm hit. Now I'm trying to get to Bagram, but I swear on my mother's life it's not about you Stalkers."

"On your mother's life? You sons of bitches from the army aren't supposed to have mothers!"

Looking at Lazarov's carbine pointed at him, the friendly expression disappears from Crow's face.

"Listen up, 'brother'," he says looking Lazarov in the eye, "I don't care much about who you are and what you do, but you will not be welcomed in Bagram."

"Let that be my problem."

"And where was your crash site, anyway?"

"A few kilometers up north, but there's not much left of it."

"You lie. The wrecks around Bagram had been looted for years. You have no idea how much useful stuff a helicopter's wreck can yield."

"This one was blasted by a bunch of gunmen, well-trained and armed to the teeth. They came by a chopper."

Crow scowls. "A black one? Big, two-engined?"

"Exactly."

"Okay, Condor, or whatever your name is — we better get out of here right now. Normally I wouldn't even bother saving your ass but you seem to be cool at close quarters. And I could use a sidekick because the Tunnel is not exactly a sniper's heaven."

"Are you going to Bagram?"

"No. After the Tunnel, we part ways. You can try to get through alone and die, or you can join me and still die. But together we stand a better chance. Make up your mind, I haven't got all day."

Lazarov reflects over his options for a moment. *A rescue mission could still be coming. But then this is no time for wishful thinking.*

"All right," he says slinging the carbine over his shoulder, "I'll follow you. Let's go."

"Let's."

Moving quickly, they head down the slope into the valley.

Lazarov soon admits to himself that the Stalker is a good guide. Instead of walking down the road, Crow leads him up the mountainside where the rocks and shallow chasms offer cover at every step, following tracks invisible to Lazarov even from a few meters' distance. With the sun still shining from the east, Crow sticks close to the shadows cast by the massive rock walls towering above them, occasionally looking up to the sky as if expecting something foreboding from above.

Before leaving the cover of an overshadowed cliff, the Stalker stops and points forward.

"Look… that's the northern entrance."

Through his binoculars, Lazarov sees the road curving before disappearing under the mountain through a huge arch. Beyond the road, a field of anomalies gleams with silver sparks amid a cluster of ruined buildings.

"We rest here for a few minutes," Crow says. "It's time to eat something."

While sharing a can of luncheon meat, Lazarov dismantles his weapon to clean its components. He also removes the cartridges from his remaining magazines and cleans them one by one before loading them back. Fingers moving in swift and skillful movements, he reassembles his AKSU-74.

"Do you have duct tape?" he asks the Stalker.

Crow nods and silently hands him a roll. Lazarov tapes the torchlight to the rifle. Handing the tape back to the sniper, Lazarov catches an appreciative look in the Stalker's eyes.

"It's good to have one who knows about weapons watching my back," Crow remarks.

"And you're one hell of a marksman."

"I know."

"Hunting must be easy with such an upgraded SVD."

"Not exactly… good sniper rounds are hard to come by, so I don't waste them. If it's game I'm after, the *avtomat* is good enough. But tell me, have you been to the Zone?"

Crow sounds curious. Lazarov hesitates before answering. He already knows that being a soldier is not the best pedigree here, especially coming from the Zone where Stalkers and military had hated each other's guts for a long time.

"I've been there once in a while, delivering supplies."

"Is that so?" Crow grins. "What's it like? I've never been there, you know."

"Similar to here, except there are no mountains and it's not so barren. Mutants are a little dumber too."

"There's a wide plain east of Bagram. It was all orchards and potato fields before the nukes but it's become a forest now. Lots of lush decay there."

Lazarov nods, considering. "And what's your story, Stalker?"

"I was a wildlife photographer and was sent by National Geographic to shoot photos of mutants. But I soon realized that shooting them with a sniper rifle is much more fun."

Lazarov smiles as if he believed him. "That's the most pathetic thing I ever heard," he says sarcastically.

Crow bursts out in muted laughter. "Whatever, bro… maybe later we'll have time for proper introduction. The only thing that matters now is getting through that damned tunnel. The question is how do we get through a tunnel full of anomalies and hostiles and stay alive in the process?"

"Bound and overwatch," Lazarov says after a minute of quick thinking. He is eager to function again as an officer. "You take a protected position. I move forward, let's say fifty meters. You watch over my advance with the Dragunov. Once I have reached the forward position, I'll cover you until you join up. Then we play the same game until we get through the tunnel."

Crow gives him a skeptical grin. "Is that a grunt from the supply train talking? Let's go… And put your gas mask on. It's horribly dusty inside."

They proceed along a narrow dirt track beneath the steep mountainside, keeping an eye on the tarmac road to their right and the ruins beyond. Before getting close to the entrance, the Stalker signals him to halt. He takes an army-issue box from his backpack. With careful hands, he removes a night scope from inside and fixes it to his rifle. "I hope the battery will last until we get through," he says removing the scope's lens cover. "What's that unhappy look on your face, Condor?"

Lazarov almost says something about the state-of-the-art equipment that was at his disposal just twenty-four hours ago. The pilot suit, not designed for the rigors of combat, barely offers him any protection and his helmet has no night vision. He bites his tongue. "Hope this piece of crap won't let me down," he says cocking the battered carbine.

"We better be more concerned about the two pillboxes at the entrance. Check them out."

Peering over the corner, Lazarov sees two small concrete shelters, more like guards posts than pillboxes. They seem empty. He gives a signal to the Stalker to move up and switches on the torch taped to the rifle barrel.

"Climb up there, Stalker, and keep your eyes peeled." He waits until Crow assumes a firing position on the bed of a pick-up, resting his rifle on the cabin's roof.

"Good to go!"

Cautiously, Lazarov moves forward. It is pitch dark inside and full of wrecked vehicles – trucks, jeeps, pick-ups, buses, as if a huge traffic jam had blocked the cavernous tunnel. He has barely covered a few dozen meters when he sees the first anomaly. A net of thin blue lightning swipes the ground, emitting a buzz that can rapidly grow into a deafening discharge of electricity. Signaling Crow to follow up, he reaches into his pocket. *Damn it. No bolts, no nuts, no nothing.*

"Do you have bolts?" Lazarov ask as Crow arrives.

The Stalker gives him three rusty bolts. "That's all I have."

Lazarov aims cautiously before throwing the bolt into the anomaly. The blue lightning flashes into a burst of energy as the bolt falls into it, casting dire blue light into the tunnel for a second. Then it disappears from the ground for two seconds. Lazarov tosses the second bolt and dashes through. Hoping that the Stalker will not mess up his timing, he lets the anomaly discharge with the last bolt. Crow leaps through dexterously. As soon as he arrives at Lazarov's side, the anomaly again starts its deadly dance over the ground.

"I hate such traps," Crow whispers, "but at least one can see these damned sizzlers."

Upon seeing the Stalker take a detector out to search for any relics in the anomaly, Lazarov fails to hide his impatience.

"We don't have time for that. Let's move on."

"I'm coming, I'm coming... wait! Did you hear that?" They freeze for a moment. Crow shrugs. "Must be hearing things."

"Stick to the wall. Cover me."

As he moves forward in the narrow space between the wrecks and the tunnel's wall, blackened from the exhaust fumes that the concrete had absorbed for decades, an uneasy feeling passes over Lazarov. There's something sinister about the Stalker that makes him concerned about being shot in his back. But the forbidding darkness that is absorbing the weak light of his torchlight gives him more concerns. The tunnel runs straight over a long distance and a truck occasionally blocks their way, making them climb over it. Their steps on the metal echo in the darkness and his Geiger counter's signal speeds up every time they get close to a vehicle. Lazarov feels the taste of metal in his mouth.

Bending to spit the nauseating saliva saves his life as a bullet hits the wall where he was standing just a second ago. Crow's Dragunov fires in response, its echo rolling through the caverns like thunder.

"Hostiles at twelve o'clock," the Stalker shouts, "fifty meters!"

By now the muzzle flash of their rifles has betrayed the enemies' position. Lazarov quickly skirts the old truck behind which Crow's sniper fire keeps their opponents pinned down. The AKSU-74's hard-hitting bullets get the black-clad gunmen in their flank. One falls, three more swiftly move back behind the nearest wreck with well-trained movements. Crow hits one more as they retreat.

"I can't see them!"

Lazarov leaps to the truck, jumps up to the flat-bed and opens fire at the enemy ducking below. The echo of his last shot is still rolling up the tunnel when the last hostile falls, cursing in a language he can't understand.

"Clear!"

He is not surprised when he sees the corpses wearing the same black body armor as the squad at the crash site. Eager to find any useful information about them, he goes through their pockets, but his search is in vain.

"They were good," he tells Crow when the sniper catches up with him. "Any idea who they might be?"

The Stalker shakes his head and Lazarov checks the weapon lying beside one of the bodies. He never laid his hands on this mule of an assault rifle: it appears to have been shoveled together from the best and worst weapon designs he knows.

"I admit the Chinese know a thing or two about weapons," he says shaking his head in disdain, "they managed to produce something that's even uglier than a Groza rifle."

"Frankly, I couldn't care less about the design of the rifle that's being fired at me."

"That's a good point... but anyway, here's a joke. Do you know why the Chinese call this scrap Qing Buqiang Zidong?"

"Please do tell."

"They can't spell the 'r' in Groza."

"Ha, ha, ha," Crow clasps his hands in mock amusement, "as if you wouldn't give one arm to have one with you now. Why don't you just take that Chinese rifle? It's way better than your carbine."

"At least I know where this one fires the bullets." Lazarov bitterly grins looking at his rifle. Seeing at what Crow is up to, he frowns. "What are you doing?"

"I want to see that bastard's face."

"I wouldn't do that. It brings bad luck."

Crow leaves the tactical helmet on the corpse. "It's just because I rarely come that close to the baddies I shoot."

"I know. That's what I could never understand about snipers... I mean, you lay hidden, see a head close in the reticule from hundreds of meters and then blow it to pieces. Do you at least feel something when you see them dying?"

"Yes," Crow says as he reloads his Dragunov, listening to the bolt clicking back to position as if it was a sophisticated musical instrument. "I do feel something."

"And what would that be?"

"Concern over one less bullet remaining."

Lazarov shrugs and turns back to the bodies. He's never liked scavenging from dead enemies but, being low on resources, the hand grenades and bandages he finds will come in useful. After a moment of hesitation, he removes the bullet-

89

proof tactical vest from the corpse and puts it over the light pilot suit.

It didn't save its previous owner… but still could save me.

"I'll move on. Stay here and wait for my sign to proceed."

"Roger, Condor."

Suspecting that the small party they have run into was only a vanguard, Lazarov remains cautious as he sneaks from cover to cover. After a few minutes, he is relieved to see light appearing in the distance. "Looks like we're almost through!"

"That's a stretch covered by a concrete roof, with openings to the side. It was an open road once but got covered after the traffic was regularly hit by avalanches."

"Shit. I was hoping it's the other end already."

"Only two more kilometers to go."

The light falling in from the opening in the concrete wall takes a toll on his eyes, already accustomed to the darkness. Lazarov closes his right eye to keep it accustomed to the darkness. He passes the stretch concerned about their flanks open to any danger coming from outside. His instincts prove right when the *thud-thud* of rotor blades sounds above them.

"Run!"

Lazarov doesn't need Crow's warning to dash forward as quickly as he can, hoping that no enemies lie in wait where the row of casements end and darkness continues. Arriving at the first wreck offering cover, he looks around for Crow but the Stalker has disappeared. Hiding behind the burnt-out frame of a bus, he can hear the helicopter hovering directly above.

He proceeds only a few meters further into the darkness to a car that might once have been a Humvee when a voice makes him freeze.

"*Stoi!* Lay down your weapon!" The words echoing in the tunnel ahead are Russian, but spoken with a strangely soft accent. "You are surrounded!"

His memories from last night's encounter with the snake-like mutant still alive, Lazarov recoils as he sees a thick cable descend from one of the wall openings behind him. His distress gives way to fear as three commandos slide down the rope and take cover behind the wrecked bus, moving swiftly like cats without even giving him a chance to aim his rifle.

"Surrender!"

Lazarov takes his chance and leaps into cover behind the wrecked Humvee. Automatic rifle fire starts ringing out from behind the bus. He throws himself to the ground. A hail of bullets hit the Humvee's massive steel frame.

Where in the hell is that damned sniper?

Even betrayal comes to his mind when a familiar rifle barks up. Crow runs up to him, panting but with a victorious grin on his face.

"At last! We're sitting ducks here," shouts Lazarov amid the rifle fire. "They've blocked the tunnel ahead!"

"Sorry bro! I had to switch the scope."

"Give suppressing fire from the left!"

Crow stays in cover while firing a long burst, holding his rifle over his head and what was once the vehicle's engine compartment. At the same time, Lazarov rolls to his right, jumps up and rushes forward, firing his AKSU-74 into the enemies appearing in the beam of the torchlight.

"Forward," he screams, "forward!"

His limb hits against something hard as he moves in to finish the ambushers. He can hear someone barking commands but the crossfire coming from left and right cuts them short. One enemy tries to drag himself away. Lazarov grabs and turns him onto his back.

"Who are you?" he asks him in a commanding voice. All he gets in reply is a scornful grin that doesn't vanish even as he points his rifle at the enemy's face. It turns into a grimace when Lazarov fires his weapon. Stepping closer, the Stalker looks down at the body.

"Damned mercenaries... I tried to loosen up their tongue more than once. But they wouldn't talk."

"Check him for loot if you want," Lazarov curtly replies. While the Stalker busies himself with checking the bodies, Lazarov keeps his weapon aiming towards the tunnel stretch where the mercenaries descended, though the helicopter's noise has now receded into the distance.

"I found a pack of smokes," Crow joyfully reports. "You want one?"

Thick dust swirls in the light of Lazarov's headlight but the temptation to remove his gas mask is too strong. "Quadruples the dose of daily radiation," he grumbles, "and fills your lungs with polonium…"

"Correct, but that was not my question."

"All right… give me one."

The Stalker removes his gas mask and sits down on the body of a dead mercenary as if it was a cushion. He lights up his cigarette, then offers the pack and his lighter to Lazarov. "I'm trying to quit, you know. But there are moments when I could kill for a smoke."

"You just did," Lazarov replies removing a cigarette from the box.

"Yeah… bad habits die hard. Maybe if I stick to my bad habits, I'll also die hard."

Lazarov carefully studies the Stalker. Crow's combat skills seem too good for a Loner Stalker, for whom battle was more about satisfying trigger-happy fingers and surpassing each other with cocky battle cries than following coordinated tactics.

"You've got a good sense for teamwork, you know?" he observes.

"Heard that before. Take it, buddy… don't let anyone say that Crow didn't share his smokes." The Stalker puts the still burning cigarette butt into the mouth of the corpse he was sitting on and gently pats its face. "*Molodets.* You no longer need to care about lung cancer, do you?"

As they move on with Lazarov taking the lead, he soon halts in his tracks when his torchlight illuminates a huge bulk of fangs and muscles, its fur scorched by fire. The air surrounding it still smells of burnt flesh.

"At least the mercs took care of this one," Crow remarks as they pass by the dead mutant.

"What the hell was that?"

"I'd have thought you have bears in the northern Zone. Don't you?"

"Bears? No. Especially not like this, with claws longer than a hand's span and a row of spiky bones along its spine."

"If I ever have kids, I'll take them to the Zone one day. It must be like a petting zoo."

After hours in the darkness and suffocating dust, Lazarov feels relief wash over him when, at last, daylight glimmers at the far end of the tunnel. He has to force patience and caution on himself as he moves from the wrecks to wall niches, still concerned about more gunmen waiting to ambush them. When they reach the exit, Lazarov exchanges a glance with the Stalker. Crow nods and they exit the tunnel at the same moment, Lazarov aiming his weapon and scanning the area for any hostiles, while Crow does the same to his left.

"Clear," Lazarov says lowering his AKSU-74.

"Looks like we made it, *bratan*," Crow replies with a sigh.

The Geiger counter clicks steadily at normal level, meaning that Lazarov can at last remove his gas mask and take a deep breath, enjoying the fresh and cool air streaming into his lungs. After the dark and narrow tunnel, his senses struggle to perceive the awe-inspiring scenery.

He raises his binoculars. Flanked by snow-capped peaks, the valley descends steeply towards the south where a wide plain opens up, covered by lush forest. Clouds of mist drift over the dark green foliage that stretches towards the horizon. Low clouds cover the view beyond the far hills that bite into the steel-blue sky like giant teeth. Deep in the forest, the hugest anomaly he has ever seen looms, having carved a gigantic archway leading into the hills beyond it. The glint of purple fire flashes in its middle. An exhilarating sense of freedom overcomes Lazarov.

"Welcome to the New Zone," Crow says behind him.

Lazarov turns to share his excitement but freezes at the sight of the silenced Glock that Crow is holding in a steady aim, his eyes narrowed and not promising anything good.

"*Ruki ver,*" the Stalker coldly says, "drop that weapon, *boyevoychik*[1]."

Lazarov lets go off his rifle and raises his hands as commanded.

"Lock your fingers behind your head. Get down on your knees...good so. Who are you and what was in that chopper?"

"We didn't come here to harass the Stalkers! Didn't I tell you already?"

"I don't care about the Stalkers. I want to know what was in that chopper. Especially in the Mi-8 that made it through."

"We were escorting a scientific expedition—"

"That's bullshit."

Lazarov sighs, knowing there is no way he can bluff his way out. His only hope is to be convincing enough for Crow to let him live, yet also be skillful enough to omit what little he knows of the scientists' mission.

"I am Major Mikhail Lazarov. We are on a search and rescue operation..."

Crow listens carefully to his story, without showing any emotion. Only when Lazarov describes the commandos destroying the helicopter does he narrow his eyes.

"They took an exoskeleton? That actually explains a thing or two." The Stalker holsters his weapon. "Okay. You're not a hunter. You're *being* hunted."

"Does that make two of us?" Lazarov asks, still unsure whether Crow is an ally or not.

"Let's move into that hut over there," the Stalker replies looking around.

---

[1] Hands up; *boyevoychik* – "soldier boy"

Crow leads him into a half-ruined brick building that still has POLICE CHECK POINT painted on it in faded letters. A recent campfire is still smoldering inside, emanating pleasant warmth after the chilly wind.

"We're in Stalker country now," the sniper says sitting down by the fire. "A few brothers must have been here recently. Probably the mercs had interrupted their breakfast."

"I don't see any bodies around."

"They obviously didn't feel like taking on a whole squad of mercs and dusted off. Wise decision." Crow takes a box of canned meat from his backpack. He opens it with his combat knife. "You want some *havchik*?"

"Gladly," Lazarov says taking the chunk of greasy meat that Crow offers him on the tip of his knife. "To be honest, you scared the shit out of me."

"I wasn't out to scare you. I meant it. But we're more or less in the same shoes... Condor. At least you have a fitting name for a Spetsnaz."

"So, are we running from the same enemy?"

"I am not running, Condor. I am on the trail of a bizarre arm smuggling enterprise. It's none of your business for whom I do this errand. Don't even ask. At first I believed you might be involved," Crow explains, "but I couldn't understand why anyone would blast your chopper if it was supposed to be carrying a precious load. Besides... never mind, it doesn't add up."

"Those people from the crash site and the tunnel? Who are they?"

Crow shrugs and spits on the ground. "I don't know. Gunmen, henchmen... Now they're dead men."

"And dead men don't talk."

"If I knew who had sent them, I would have collected my reward already. Some people in Bagram might have great interest in state of the art equipment like your exoskeletons."

"Tell me about that place."

"It's run by a weird character calling himself Captain Bone. He would never remove his curtain helmet, even if it makes him look like a crazy astronaut. Then there's an old Stalker medic called Placebo, tending to those who ran out of luck. Then there's a junkie called Sammy. He runs a gun shop and bar and trades in everything. There's his buddy, Grouch, a gun nut. And of course all sorts of Stalkers, rookies to veterans. Bagram's like a Klondike built from war debris."

"Youe ever heard of the Tribe?"

"Worst sons of bitches I've ever seen," the Stalker scowls. "Take the skills of highly trained soldiers, add the cruelty of Genghis Khan's warriors, top it up with excellent American gear and you have the Tribe."

"Maybe it was them who shot us down?"

"It's a possibility, although the people we've run into were definitely not of Tribe." Crow spits out a mouthful of canned meat. "Shit, what do they make this from?... Anyway, I've never seen them using choppers. Instead, they ride around in Humvees."

Goryunov's words about rogue Americans come to Lazarov's mind. "Maybe the *pindosi* are back?"

"Well... if their rules of engagement now include torturing prisoners, keeping tribal women as birth machines and decorating their vehicles with skulls and bones, then yes, one could say they are back." Crow apparently balances every word he says, making Lazarov wonder how much the sniper really knows. "Back to Bagram I heard that the Tribe was already here when the first Stalkers arrived. Don't worry about them, though. Usually they keep to themselves unless one gets too close to them."

All this sounds too far-fetched to Lazarov's ears to be true. Only one thing attracts his interest. "They have women?"

"Probably got to them before the nukes went off... You better not have any high hopes, brother. Most Afghans who were still alive after the nukes sought refuge in Iran, Uzbekistan, Pakistan... This sandbox is empty now."

"I saw one of the refugee camps close to Termez." Lazarov looks into the small fire which is about burning itself out. Seeing that the Stalker is preparing to leave, he asks him one more question. "You mentioned the Taliban. I never thought they would be still around."

"Dushmans are like cockroaches, almost impossible to exterminate. You'll run into them soon enough."

"Maybe we could contact each other from time to time. Share information. What do you think?" Lazarov suggests.

"Maybe," Crow shrugs. "Now, I have to do some business of my own but let's hook up in Bagram. I'll be there in a few days. Until then, a word of advice: that place is messier than it seems. Do not trust anyone."

North of the Shamali Plains, 2014, 16:11:35 AFT

After his mysterious companion has disappeared into the wilderness, Lazarov takes his binoculars and scans the horizon. He can't see any trace of Dragonfly Two's crash site; no fire, no smoke column, nothing. To the south, he can make out the cluster of buildings and grey landing strip that must be Bagram. Below his position, the road turns to the west and continues in an almost straight line to where the hills and forest meet, passing through ruined settlements along the way. The stream from the valley he and Crow had been following broadens and runs directly south.

The road appears easy going which means it's dangerous. The river bed seems safer but it's probably crawling with mutants.

His watch tells him he has four hours till nightfall. Still in doubt over which route provides the better option, Lazarov leaves the road and starts walking towards the forest.

Upon entering it, he is gripped by a feeling of familiarity. The dense undergrowth, the darkness beneath the thick foliage, the low, ruined walls here and there — all serve to remind him of the lush decay of the Zone in Russia. So does the eerie silence.

But it is also different here. The trees grow taller, their intertwining foliage casting a suffocating darkness over the muddy ground that seems to suck at Lazarov's feet as he makes his way through the mud and rotting undergrowth. The deeper he moves, the darker it gets, with tree trunks appearing like silent monsters in the beams of light falling through the foliage. Noxious vapors emanate from the muddy ground. The Geiger-counter's crackle is the only noise, sounding in his ears like an echo of his quickening heartbeat whenever he sees a weirdly deformed tree reaching out with rotten branches as if to suffocate him, or dense bushes that might hide a mutant preparing for the killing leap before feasting on his remains.

The major stops and shakes his head, as if to rid himself of a headache. A glimpse at the Geiger counter tells him that radiation levels are slightly above normal, but still below the dangerous level.

Lazarov removes his gas mask to allow him to breath with more ease. The sickening odor of rotting earth immediately assails his nostrils, making him grimace with disgust.

Whenever he pauses the forest seems to want to suck him in, to make him part of it. Trees, bushes, stones, water — all around is dead.

As he sneaks from cover to cover, his weapon held ready, the brown mass of an abandoned armored vehicle looms ahead of him. Moving closer, Lazarov sees it is the first of three. It might have been a convoy, but he doesn't recognize the type of vehicles. The only thing he is sure of is that they are not from the Soviet war. Looking at the holes in their hulls, it is also clear to him that they were ambushed.

Curious, he opens the hatch of the first one and peers inside. His heart almost stops beating when he hears a hiss and senses rather than sees the movement inside. He just manages to duck aside as a snake's mouth darts towards his face. But now he has better options than in the cave. He throws a grenade inside before frantically slamming the hatch closed. Jumping off the vehicle, his feet have barely touched the ground before a muted explosion shakes the wreck. The smell of burnt flesh and putrid decay rises from inside when he opens the hatch again.

Inside, among bloody shreds of snake flesh and the rotting remains of a small mutant that looks like a jackal pup to Lazarov, he sees hundreds of cartridge casings.

Whoever was inside here must have put up a desperate fight, he thinks, unaware of the grimace on his face.

He picks up a pocketful of shells, thinking that they'll come in handy if or when he encounters another anomaly, and has almost closed the hatch again when he notices something among the shells. Picking it up and wiping off the grime reveals it to be an old-fashioned mobile phone. Unsure of whether it can be of any use or if it might at least offer a clue about the convoy's fate, the major puts it into his pocket.

Here and there the gloomy undergrowth is pierced by a ray of light, making the dust visible. But the shadows deepen as the sunlight fades. Lazarov anxiously sees that, judging by the distance to the mountains, he has barely covered one third of the distance to Bagram.

I hope I don't get lost. Spending the night here would not be pleasant at all.

His thoughts are interrupted by a howl, followed by a deep, aggressive growling. More howls join in, forming a chorus. He takes a few steps in the direction of the sound. Cautiously peering through a bush, he sees a clearing in the woods and a pack of jackals running toward him. He raises his rifle but by the time he takes aim, the jackals have reached his position—and to his surprise run on, ignoring him. Lazarov has no time for relief because after a few moments, a huge, lumbering shadow emerges from the undergrowth. It is the biggest mutant he has ever seen: its furry head resembling that of a bear but the mouth open stretching down to its neck, showing a double row of bloodied teeth. Its side is covered with deep wounds, but the mutant seems to ignore them as it turns toward Lazarov with a blood-curdling growl. He is not sure if he can kill this beast with the ammo he has loaded, or if he had time at all to change the magazine once it is empty, so he does the only thing he can. He runs.

He would have no chance in the open, but here among the dense woods he moves with more agility than his lumbering adversary and jumps over a low mud wall into what might have been an orchard in the past. After a few meters, he looks back, thinking that the bear-like mutant had been unable to follow him. Then a brick crumbles, then more, and Lazarov sees with horror that the mutant simply broke through the wall. He runs on, out of breath, with a stinging pain in his kidneys. The growling behind him draws closer with every step. Suddenly he sees a large pool of mud, with stains of reddish water oozing a fiery vapor. He can't dodge it and besides, even with the meager protection his suit offers, he has more chance of surviving an anomaly than the assault of the raging mutant.

Lazarov holds his breath and jumps. Rolling on the ground, burning pain bites into his sizzling skin. Moaning, he manages to raise himself into a kneeling position, ready to fire, knowing he's no longer able to run.

The old Stalker trick of running towards an anomaly, evading it at the last moment and then watching the mutants running headlong into the trap had saved him many times back in the Zone. But now, to his horror Lazarov sees that the mutant stops and walks up and down in front of the anomalies, as if debating whether if it could jump over to finish the hunt. Then, to Lazarov's even greater shock, it stretches its dreadful head forward and starts sniffing around the anomalies, until it finds a path through the sizzling substance.

Damn! This wretched beast is smart, Lazarov thinks as he desperately crawls backwards.

Halfway through the anomalies, the mutant rears up on its legs, unleashing a deafening roar. It is probably intended to paralyze its prey, leaving them wide-eyed and defenseless with horror, but Lazarov still has enough control over his body to raise his weapon and empty the magazine into the mutant's torso. But as he fires his last cartridge, the shooting doesn't stop. Perplexed, Lazarov sees heavy bullets still pouring into the mutant's flesh until it emits a pain-filled yelp and falls right into the anomaly. Its fur catches fire immediately and Lazarov, gasping for air, watches it being consumed by acidic flames.

I'm getting tired of others saving me.

Still oblivious of where the shots came from, he looks around.

"Don't move," a Russian voice commands. "Stay right where you are!"

"I couldn't move even if I wanted to," Lazarov shouts back.

Then, to his unspeakable relief, two paratroopers emerge from the woods. Wounded men, even if only lightly. One of them, a stout, blond soldier with blue eyes thick set in his round face, is holding a PKM machine gun. To Lazarov's astonishment, he wears no armor, only the standard issue white and blue striped tee-shirt and a green bandana. *This guy must be either a tough bastard or totally crazy,* he thinks.

"Sparrow Two?" he cries out.

"*Komandir?*" one of the soldiers asks incredulously.

Lazarov nods and the two soldiers quickly pull him away from the anomaly. For a moment, Lazarov's joy over finding the lost squad makes him forget about his badly burnt legs.

"Thanks to that damned mutant," he groans, "it chased me right into your arms!"

"It's great to see you alive, *komandir*," the machine gunner says. "Where are the others?"

"It's just me. Give me a first aid kit and bandages... my legs are burnt."

With quick, well-trained hands, the other soldier cuts through the burnt rags of Lazarov's leggings and pours water from his canteen over the wounds.

"Lucky for us, our medic made it through," the soldier says as he applies antiseptics and fixes a silicone bandage. "He'll take care of the rest. This should do till we get back to the crash site."

"Tell me what happened to you, while I brace myself up."

"Yes, Major," the machine gunner says. "We were hit... or whatever, because it was no projectile... Suddenly all the electrical systems went dead, at least almost all, though the pilot managed to keep the chopper in the air for a few minutes. We were incredibly lucky not to smash into the mountains, but then the engine died and the chopper started to spin, and we crash-landed into this forest. Eight of us survived, with three others badly wounded."

"Who is in command now?"

"Senior Sergeant Zlenko. It was probably him who saved our life, because as soon as we took off he ordered us into our armored suits."

"That was a wise choice. And where is *your* kit, soldier?"

"Err... I got a serious case of armor chafe and removed it. It's because of my size. Even the biggest one is too small for me, sir!"

Lazarov decides not to flak him for the moment, although he suspects that the machine gunner has used armor chafe as an excuse to flaunt the many tattoos on his robust arms.

I got it, he thinks. *He's crazy.*

"What happened to the other squad, sir?"

Staring at the ground, Lazarov shakes his head.

"Not even Zotkin?" the soldier with the first aid kit asks.

"Not even him."

"How did you survive?"

"I was wearing my exoskeleton, remember? It saved my life but was destroyed. I hope you have a spare armor suit."

"We do, sir. Actually, we have too many spare suits."

102

"Help me up and let's get to the squad. I hope you established a defensive perimeter?"

"Certainly, sir," the machine gunner says cutting down two boughs from a tree with a combat knife. "But there is this shit all around us. Nothing gets through, but in exchange, we can't leave the perimeter either. Sit on this, sir. Kamensky, hold the branches from the other side, will you?"

Lazarov hates the idea of arriving at the crash site like an invalid, but when he tries standing on his feet he realizes that he actually *is* one. Swearing, he reluctantly lets the two soldiers carry him.

"Don't worry, sir," the chatty machine gunner says. "Making it here alive was feat enough in itself. All the boys will agree with that. There's nothing bad about being carried for a few meters. Besides, it's better to have a little burnt skin than your head ripped off by that beast. Wouldn't you agree, Major?"

Lazarov scowls, his face still distorted by pain. "What's your name, trooper?"

"Private Nikolai Ilchenko, sir. Friends call me Ilch. And that's Private Kamensky to your left."

"Good. And now, Private Ilchenko: hold your mouth! You talk more than a salesman."

"As ordered, sir," the soldier grins.

"It's good to have an officer around again," Kamensky whispers, flashing a gloating glance at Ilchenko.

The two troopers arrive at the crash site as proudly as if they were carrying some large and noble prey. Their comrades, most of them with arms and heads wrapped in bloody bandages, cheer when they see them carrying their commander. Ilchenko loudly tells everyone what had happened. Lazarov doesn't mind; at least it's not him who has to tell the squad about their ill-fated comrades. For him, it's the first moment since the crash when he thinks that maybe the mission has not failed altogether. However, his relief is overshadowed by the sight of four bodies covered with waterproof canvas. If not for his reckless decision to change the flight path, those men would still be alive. Or maybe they would still have died but in an ambush or a firefight, something that offered a more dignified death.

Even with their heavy losses, the survivors have preserved their cohesion as a unit, having set up a small perimeter around the badly damaged helicopter with the squad's grenade launcher positioned to cover the area where the woods open up. They have also erected a small tent where the medic, a very young but smart-faced soldier, tends to the wounded.

"Dragonfly Two carried fourteen men, including the pilots," the squad's senior sergeant reports. He wears a blood-soaked bandage around his head. "We lost two troopers and the pilots in the crash. Now we have four heavily wounded and four men combat ready."

"Thank you, Sergeant Zlenko," Lazarov replies while the medic is treating the burns on his legs. "Do we have communications?"

"The radio is busted, sir."

"What do you have that still works?"

"Since our flight carried all the equipment, we have enough ammo, food and medical supplies to last a while. The two exoskeletons are in their crates. " A smile appears on the young non-com's concerned face. "They would have been useful for hauling all those heavy crates from the wreck but we don't needed them with Ilchenko around. What we don't have is a way out of this hellhole."

"Worry about that later. Why aren't you wearing the exoskeleton assigned to you?"

"If my men don't have them, I don't want to have one either."

Lazarov begins to look at the non-com with different eyes. "That's very noble of you, Zlenko, but I prefer you staying alive to being noble."

"Understood. I'll have them fetched for the two of us, sir."

104

Lazarov looks into the forest where darkness is growing like thick, black fog. Attempting a night march through the unknown wilderness would be reckless, even with full forces. With half of the survivors barely able to walk, including himself, it would be utter suicide. He also needs to find a way through the anomaly field.

"Matter of fact, we can put them to better use. Let two wounded of your choice wear the exos. It should make walking easier for them." Hearing Lazarov's words, Zlenko nods his agreement. "We move out at daybreak."

"Where to, sir?"

"Bagram. It makes no sense to establish a forward operations base with half of the men down."

"No rescue mission, then?"

"Looks like we have to get out on our feet or die here."

"Will we be able to get through those fire traps?"

"All right, listen up. I'll need to explain to you a few things. Gather the men."

Lazarov explains the basics about mutants and anomalous traps to the survivors, adding his latest experiences with the jackals, the snake and the bear. As he talks, the forest around them seems to come alive. Growls, grunts, roars and howls penetrate the darkness, causing the soldiers to exchange anxious glances.

"Make a bonfire," Lazarov orders, "and be prepared for another long night."

"Are you sure the fire will keep the beasts at bay?" the medic asks. Fear looms in his eyes behind the thin spectacles.

"No."

"But then... why?"

"Because it's cozy."

"Lobov has a point, sir," the sergeant interjects. "What if hostiles see it?"

"The hostiles we should be concerned about don't need a campfire to see us."

"If you say so, Major... I'll go and see to that fire."

Lazarov nods in approval and leans against the helicopter's wreck to rest his aching body. Soon, a bonfire casts its relaxing light over the perimeter. The warm flames, together with the soldiers' quiet chatter, remind him of nights in the Zone. This familiarity eases his nerves; he feels safe at last, but still doesn't let his rifle out of his reach.

A trooper comes and offers him a loaf of bread. It's still fresh and must be from the rations they got in Termez. Lazarov gladly accepts it. His stomach is rumbling almost as loudly as the mutants growl in the gloomy night.

Shamali Plains, 22 September 2014, 07:10:15 AFT

The dawn brings rain, turning the already muddy forest ground into a veritable swamp. Lazarov orders the squad to move out at first light, or better when first light should have appeared according to his watch. He observes the slowly moving column of soaked soldiers, all of them carrying as much extra equipment from the crashed Mi-8's load as they can bear.

Sweat and rain blend on his face as he moves on, keeping his eyes on Ilchenko who walks in front of him. Like a gray ghost shrouded in a veil of rain, Sergeant Zlenko follows them at the tail of the column. With the mud sticking to his boots and making every step twice as difficult for his wounded legs, Lazarov is content with the slow pace.

It is not only the heavy rain that slows them down. When Lazarov tries to find a path through the anomalous field surrounding the crash site, he makes an unpleasant discovery: unlike in the Zone of Alienation, where such traps more or less stay in one place, their southern counterparts move, making it difficult to navigate through them. It is like walking through a minefield where the mines are shifting position, making Lazarov realize again that, no matter concerning its similarities with the northern Zone, this is a more evil place where he has to learn the local ways as if he were a greenhorn once again.

After burying the fallen in the morning, Lazarov exchanged his battered AKSU-74 to an AKM rifle. He also finally got rid of the ragged pilot's outfit in favor of a heavier armored suit. He'd ordered the soldiers to carry as much of the weapons and supplies as they could and had had the helicopter's wreck blown up before leaving. Once the medic pumped him full of painkillers to get him on his feet again, he was able to walk and lead the squad, albeit with a heavy limp.

As he stands and watches over the troopers passing by, the sergeant turns up at his side.

"Permission to speak freely, *komandir*?"

"If you've got something to say, Zlenko, say it."

"Perhaps it wouldn't be too shameful to abandon the mission, given our condition."

Lazarov looks at a trooper with a badly wounded arm. He'd watched the medic changing the bandages that morning, but he can see blood oozing through again already. Another soldier is wearing an exoskeleton, its kinetic motors making walking easier, though he still has to be helped along by one of his comrades. Two other soldiers carry a third on a field stretcher.

No, he thinks, *it wouldn't be shameful to abandon the mission.*

For him, it would be more than that. It would be disgraceful and being court-martialed with Zarubin in charge would mean not only the end of his military career but probably many years in prison also, all for one mistake.

On the other hand, the soldiers seem tough and resilient. Recent events have left a bitter taste: he, who made it to the rank of major and commander of the Perimeter, had been forced to run from a mutant and had also been carried by two grunts to the crash site like a wimp. Lazarov's pride is perhaps even more deeply hurt than his legs and, whatever happened, he had to show his new squad that he hadn't put in charge for nothing.

He frowns as he looks into the eyes of his second-in-command. "Honestly, Sergeant, from the very beginning this mission, with close air support and two good squads seemed to be too good to be true."

Zlenko doesn't reply, but keeps looking at Lazarov in anticipation.

"If we can make it to Bagram, we can properly patch up the wounded. We can wait a few days until they gather enough strength and maybe even contact Whiskey to get new instructions. Then we continue our mission. After all, we are here to find those scientists, not to conquer this cursed land."

"So we will press on, with half of the men incapacitated?"

Lazarov likes the sergeant's attitude. Zlenko might be ready to follow orders but his sense of duty is apparently less important to him than the state of his soldiers.

"Sergeant Zlenko — what's your given name, anyway?"

"Viktor, sir."

"So, Viktor, if I give the order to continue, are the men with me? Are you?"

"When we landed in this hellhole with all those anomalies, as you called them, around us, the only thing we hoped for was a rescue mission. But your appearance boosted morale. Now they think that if you could make it through alone, they too can make through together."

"And what do *you* think?"

"I think the same way."

"Good," Lazarov replies laconically, "then you better go back to the rear. Make sure no one tails away."

"*Tak tochno, komandir.*"

"One more thing. Keep in mind that Stalkers will be neutral towards us at the best. If we encounter them, we must not provoke any hostile action."

"I'll pass the order not to shoot first. And if we are attacked?"

"We blast them."

With a satisfied grin all over his lean face, Zlenko hurries back to the soldiers. Lazarov takes a gulp from his canteen and follows him. He can already hear Zlenko translating his orders into language the grunts can understand.

"Keep moving that stretcher, Bondarchuk, it ain't time to relax yet... Ilchenko, keep moving your chubby ass! Finger off the trigger until we are being shot at!"

Shamali Plains, 09:22:06 AFT

Passing by the odd ruined farm and vehicle wreck, the column soon arrives at the riverbed. Lazarov decides to allow them a short break before continuing southwards. The rain has stopped and, with the sun appearing again, the swampy ground seems to be steaming in the sudden heat. Flies buzz around Lazarov's sweating face in the close air.

Removing his heavy backpack, he stretches his shoulders and is about to reach for his canteen when he hears rifle fire. He immediately orders the soldiers to take cover and, with Zlenko at his side, climbs up onto a rock for a better view.

"Look," he whispers handing the binoculars to the sergeant. "Stalkers."

"As I see it, soon to be dead Stalkers."

Not far from them, four Stalkers are fighting off two huge bears, similar to the one that had chased Lazarov the day before. However, here the mutants have the advantage. The Stalkers kept trying to climb up the steep sides of the riverbed in desperation. One of them, obviously already wounded, stumbles and falls. Lazarov puckers his lips in disgust as he sees one of the mutants start tearing the luckless Stalker to pieces.

"Should we intervene, sir?"

"It's time to earn some Stalker goodwill. Too far for our rifles, though... Get the sniper and Ilchenko with the PKM."

"As ordered, sir. Hey, Ilchenko, drag your ass over here! Kravchuk, where are you when I need you?"

The soldiers arrive quickly. Lazarov points to the fight.

"See those mutants?"

"Clearly."

"Kill them."

"With pleasure!"

Lazarov now forgives the machine gunner for his garrulity. Making the best use of his advantageous prone position, Ilchenko displays remarkable marksmanship with his otherwise inaccurate weapon, while the sniper joins in the carnage with his SVD. The sergeant watches the scene through his binoculars.

"Kravchuk, can't you hit that fucking mutant from three hundred meters? It's bigger than your aunt's ass, goddammit!"

The young sniper looks at Lazarov from the corner of his eye, his face red with shame.

"No wonder, Private," Lazarov says without turning to the sniper. "If you keep looking at me you'll never hit them."

But it is no longer necessary for the sniper to continue shooting. The two mutants lay motionless on the other side of the riverbed.

"Am I good or am I good?" Ilchenko theatrically blows the smoke from the machine gun's barrel like a cowboy in a western and grins, apparently pleased with himself. Lazarov can't blame him. For two of the Stalkers their intervention came too late, but the remaining two seem unscathed.

"Let's collect our reward," Lazarov says cheerily as he jumps down from the rock. No sooner has he landed on the ground, however, than a bullet whizzes by his head. He drops on his belly. Fearing the worst, Lazarov looks up — and notices that the Stalkers hadn't been shooting at him, and his squad isn't firing at the Stalkers.

"Hostiles!" Zlenko screams. "Close ambush from our nine!"

The major quickly realizes that it would be unwise to climb back and thereby offer a clear target to whoever is shooting from the shadows. With a loud thump, Kravchuk lands at his side.

"Who the hell ordered you down from your position?" Lazarov shouts at him.

"I had no visual on the enemy from there, *komandir*, and thought you might need some backup!"

"Listen up," bellows Lazarov amidst the gunfight, "you see that slope over there? Let's make a run for it!" Then he shouts up to the sergeant, "Zlenko!"

"Here!"

"Keep this position! In two minutes exactly, give suppressing fire with everything you got! Kravchuk, let's move, now!"

They dash to the slope about fifty meters away. Reaching it, Lazarov signals the soldier to crouch. Silently moving into the trees, Lazarov proceeds for a hundred meters before turning towards the north. In this moment all hell breaks loose as the squad lays down suppressing fire.

"Cover our left," Lazarov barks to the sniper, then, moving fast from tree to tree, he advances.

He doesn't have to look long before he spots the enemy: about two dozen men with AK rifles, all seeking cover from the paratroopers' bullets. To his relief, their opponents are not the highly trained commandos of yesterday. And, judging by the light armored vests they are wearing over long linen cloaks, they must be either be suicidal or very much adapted to this environment — or maybe both.

"Here we go!"

Their enemy clearly hadn't expected a flanking attack and several of them fall before they see the pair of soldiers or hear their fire. One, however, better armed than the rest, unleashes a terrible scream and dashes toward Lazarov, firing his light machine gun from his hip.

Lazarov remains calm and aims his rifle, only to hear a faint *clack* from the empty weapon when he pulls the trigger. Temporarily disarmed and cursing himself for such an oversight, the major throws himself to the ground. His assailant is so close now that his bullets will find their target even if fired from the hip. As he rolls to the side, releasing and switching the magazine, enemy bullets throw up dirt from the ground, missing him by a hairspan. Still rolling in the mud, Lazarov gets the magazine home and cocks the weapon, knowing it might already be too late but only hoping that his armored suit will save him from the worst.

Abruptly, the hostile fighter's head jerks back, his skull spurting bone and blood. Looking up, Lazarov sees the sniper kneeling over him, the Dragunov slung over his shoulder and his pistol still at aim.

"Thanks, Kravchuk," Lazarov says as he gets up to his feet.

Suddenly, someone shouts *"Nobody but us!"* A roaming *hurrah* follows from the squad's direction.

"Hold your fire," he tells the sniper, "that... Zlenko has just ordered a bayonet charge!"

Lazarov had almost said: *that idiot*, and thinks, *How could he order a bayonet charge with four men?*

But by now he can already see the paratroopers approaching, firing their rifles from the hip and finishing off the few remaining hostiles. Their faces are full of excitement. The swiftest one catches up with a running enemy and stabs him with a triumphant yell. He recognizes the victorious soldier as Kamensky.

"Hold your fire," he shouts at the paratroopers. "We're coming through!"

Still unsure if he should reprimand Zlenko in front of the troopers or have a very serious talk with him afterwards, Lazarov walks up to the sergeant.

"I can't believe what I've just seen, Sergeant."

"That makes two of us, sir. Your flanking trick was brilliant!"

"I know." Lazarov cuts into his words and takes a deep breath before continuing but Zlenko, still running on adrenalin, keeps on talking.

"Major, when I saw those bastards on the run I let the men move in by force. There was something about them that had to be unleashed... I apologize if I did something wrong."

Lazarov looks at the dead hostiles and the soldiers searching the bodies. They are as elated as if they had just won the biggest battle of their lives. To the sergeant's luck, all appear unscathed. Lazarov looks deep into Zlenko's brown eyes.

"How old are you, Viktor?"

"Twenty-five, sir."

"How many battles have you been in?"

"None, sir. This was my first."

Lazarov sighs. He knows he should reprimand Zlenko for his reckless attack. After all he, Lazarov, knows only too well how disastrous hotheadedness can be. But then, it comes to his mind that enthusiasm is a rare treasure among a squad of wounded and emaciated soldiers, left to fend for themselves in a terrain far from home with dangers they have barely come to know.

"Be proud of yourself. There are many generals who never had the chance to order a bayonet charge."

Zlenko is smart enough to understand that he made a mistake. "Do you think that I took an unnecessary risk, *komandir*?" he anxiously asks.

Lazarov gives him a grim smile. "Keep it up, Viktor... but next time you give such an order without asking me, I'll rip your buttocks so far apart that you'll be able to shout *fix bayonets!* through your asshole. Is that clear?"

"Yes, sir. I apologize."

"Don't. Now go and check the bodies for anything useful. I'll catch up with those Stalkers before they disappear."

"*Yest, komandir!*"

Sergeant Zlenko's salute is as perfectly presented as if they were on a parade ground.

Lazarov hurries towards the riverbed. He slows down after a few steps, where the two remaining Stalkers appear in the woods, their weapons unholstered. The taller one wears a raggedy camouflage suit that must, judged by the tiny German flag on the sleeve, come from Bundeswehr surplus. Lazarov can see the obvious patches where the jacket has been improved with Kevlar plates. Half of his face is covered by a black and white shemagh but his blue eyes look shrewd and cheerful. The other Stalker looks like rookieness incarnate with his less than impressive hunting rifle. The ordinary anorak he is wearing barely gives him any protection from the dangers around.

"Thanks for helping us out, bro," the rookie says by way of greeting. "We wanted to help you deal with them zombies, but—oh no, you're goddamn *boyevoychiks!*"

He raises his beat-up rifle but the other Stalker pushes the weapon back down.

"Shut up, Danya, they've just saved our skins!" Turning towards Lazarov and shouldering his MP-5 submachine gun, he continues with a grateful tone in his voice. His Russian is impeccable, yet the way he speaks betrays that it's not his native tongue. "You were the last ones we expected here, man... military or not, we will not forget your help anytime soon! Drop by Bagram and we'll show you our gratitude!"

Lazarov grins and looks at the Stalkers. "Why not right now?"

The smarter-looking Stalker returns his smirk. "Well, we could offer you a few pistol mags or a can of meat, perhaps a half-empty first aid kit but—"

"Keep it."

"Yes, I knew you'd like this better." He rummages in his side bag and holds a small relic to Lazarov. "It's called an Emerald. Keeps you running for a while when you're out of breath. Please, accept it as a token of our gratitude."

"If you insist."

Satisfied, Lazarov takes the relic that looks like a dull pebble with a pale green core. The one who named it 'Emerald' must have had a vivid imagination, but as he lets it slide into the relic container on his belt he feels as if the ugly little thing has sucked all fatigue from his limbs.

"I hope you haven't depleted your stocks of gratitude yet. We were on our way to Bagram. Could you lead us there?" Seeing the Stalkers' concerned faces, he tries to calm them. "We are up to no trouble. Our chopper crashed and we need a safe place where we can pull ourselves together. We'll leave again in two or three days. That's a promise."

The Stalkers look at each other. "It's not up to us, actually," the rookie says, "it will be up to Captain Bone to decide if you can stay."

"That might be so, but first we have to get there so that he can make up his mind."

The Stalker who gave him the relic looks at Lazarov and the grim-looking soldiers now lining up at his side. "Ooo-kay... it's your lucky day, man. Call me Squirrel. I am a guide and a very good one too! "

"This guy is looking like a pot-head to me," Zlenko says under his breath. Lazarov nods agreement. *Oh God,* he thinks, *am I really to trust a junkie from the Intruders, even if he's obviously a loner now? It can't get lower than that.*

"Come, on, man! Don't look at me like that. Believe me, I can lead you there straight as the crow flies, avoiding zombies and all that shit," he says licking his lips. "Our raid is blown anyway with Misha and Vitka dead."

He was directing his last words more to his fellow Stalker than to Lazarov. But his mate resists.

"Are you out of your mind, Squirrel? Guiding the military to Bagram? For *free*? You charged me eight hundred rubles for the trip to Hellgate!"

"See, Danya, first you didn't save my life. Second, they have half a dozen weapons pointed at us which puts them into a pretty good bargaining position. Why not be friendly with them? Chill out, man!"

"My stomach turns at the thought of getting involved with the army's business!"

"Ask Lobov for something that helps you with your nausea," Lazarov jerks his thumb in the medic's direction. "Don't worry about guiding us. You will only assist us carrying the stretchers."

Then the major remembers Goryunov's words about making friends on their way. He pats the rookie on the back. "It's all right," he tells him with a wide smile. "We will protect *you* from this place, not the other way round."

The Stalker returns his friendly look with a scowl. "Damned *boyevoychik*... you have the smile of a jackal. I'd prefer you bitching at me." But Lazarov doesn't have to comply with his wish as the young Stalker reluctantly falls in line.

With the rookie giving the stretcher-bearers a helping hand, they proceed much quicker through barely trodden paths and shortcuts through the forest. Either because the intensive fighting scared them away or because they are less active during daytime, no mutants harass them.

"Those were zombies, you said?" Lazarov asks the guide called Squirrel, who is marching at point.

"Nah, just a manner of speaking. I call them zombies because they've got no brains. Imagine, you are peacefully enjoying the scenery or looking for relics and then they come at you out of nowhere, shouting *allaaaaah* and crazy stuff like that. One can shut them up with bullets only."

"They are Taliban then?"

"Call them whatever you want... we just call them dushmans, for old times' sake, if you follow my meaning."

"I do," Lazarov nods.

"For us, they are just another kind of mutant. And they look like mutants too. You've seen their faces?"

"I did and they weren't pretty. They looked like they had a serious case of radiation sickness. No surprise, with the pajamas they wore for armor."

"Well seen, man. They don't value their own lives too much. The problem is, neither do they value *our* lives."

"Are there many of them around here?"

"One can never know… their den seems to be somewhere to the south, down the road to Kabul."

"So Kabul still exists?"

"In a way. See, instead of Kabul I should have said Kaboom, because that's what happened there. Anyway, sometimes they make it up to Bagram but we have an Outpost to keep an eye on the road. It's a funny place."

"How come?"

"Well, Captain Bone is an asshole but he values discipline. If a Stalker is caught stealing or something like that, he is sent to the Outpost for a few days. If he survives, he can come back and stay with us. If not—good riddance."

"This Captain Bone… is he with the Guardians?"

"Dunno, maybe he was. But with all us former Intruder guys around, he won't turn the place into a barracks. No way we will be doing morning drills, man!"

"Why are there so many Intruders here?"

The Stalker laughs. "*Bhango,* man."

"What's that?"

"Try to think harder. What has always been the Afghan delight?"

"Weed and opium, or so I've heard."

"You're super-duper smart for a *boyevoychik*. Now, tell me what happened to plants in the Old Zone?"

"Certain plants grew to unbelievable proportions."

"Polyploidy, yes. And you still don't get it? Oh, you guys really miss all the fun in life…"

Despite the pain in his chapped lips, Lazarov has to smile as he imagines drug-addicted Intruders flocking to the New

Zone to smoke weed made from marijuana buds as big as a fist.

"Now you got my meaning, man. Give it a try in Bagram because you obviously need to get high."

"Thanks, but no thanks. You know, in the army we stick to *bum-bum*," Lazarov replies, adding an explanation when the Stalker gives him a curious look. "You take brake fluid, add some raisins and sugar, then let it ferment for a few days in the sun. Gives a pretty good kick."

"That explains why there were no usable vehicles in the Old Zone... Hey, wait a minute! Where are you going? I'll need to save this recipe in my palmtop!"

Lazarov, who was about to check the column's rear, turns back to the guide. "Wait a minute. After your comrades died I guess you stripped them naked, huh?"

Squirrel shrugs the question off. "Once dead, a Stalker doesn't need his kit anymore, does he?"

"I could use their palmtops."

"Difficult, man," Squirrel replies scratching his head, "difficult. Sammy pays a good price for used palmtops. They're always in demand."

"Indeed they are. Give one of them to me and the other to Sergeant Zlenko. Tell him to provide you with one of our rifles and a few mags in exchange."

"That's robbery!"

"No. It's charity. Think about it: you get a mint condition *Kalash*[1] for two lousy palmtops."

The guide sighs and looks at his submachine gun. "Actually, I wouldn't mind a weapon with more punch... all right." Squirrel draws the devices from a pouch on his ammunition vest. "Which one you want?"

Switching on the devices, Lazarov finds that all data has been deleted from the memory units. It could have been done out of respect for a dead man's privacy, but the major rather

---

[1] Russian slang for AK, *avtomat Kalashnikova*

118

suspects that Squirrel wanted to keep the location of any personal stash for himself. However, Lazarov only cares about the map mode. The palmtop is not as tough and sophisticated as his own army-issue device had been but the digital map seems accurate enough.

"The map works but no voice coms or messaging beyond a ten-kilometer radius around Bagram," the guide explains. "Only Bone has gear that covers the whole area. He's the only one with access to the outside world too."

"Damn!"

"I agree, man. But about your end of the bargain— where's that sergeant?"

"Keeping his eyes on our rear. And when you give him the palmtop, don't forget to tell him how to use it, all right?"

Southern Shamali Plains, 2014, 16:56:21 AFT

Lazarov and his squad might have saved the two Stalkers from death, but as the sun starts setting beyond the snow-capped mountains, he admits to himself that they saved his squad from getting completely lost in the forest in return. Squirrel has led them through the wilderness on pathways only known to him, until they now emerge onto a road littered with vehicle wrecks. They have left the forest behind and a wide, sandy plain opens up in front of them. Electric anomalies fizz around ruined utility towers that look like the steel skeletons of fallen giants. Exercising a little caution sees them through. After another half hour's march, at last Bagram appears.

Or what's left of it, Lazarov muses.

Goryunov's words come to his mind as he scans the ruins through his binoc, taking in the sight of steel containers thrown across the mass of concrete and sand that must have once been the runway, the broken masts from which no ensign flies and the gutted airplanes and helicopters – most of them dating from the Soviet war, others left behind by the Western allies when they too had abandoned the country – like enormous bugs that had survived every cataclysm to hit this land.

"It's a sad sight, Major," Zlenko remarks.

"I didn't take you for an emotional man, Viktor," Lazarov replies.

"I don't mean shedding tears, but... imagine, it's 1986 and you've been drafted to the army from Kiev or Minsk or wherever and deployed here. Then you hear the news about what happened at the Chernobyl. And you still have to fight that senseless shit of a war without knowing what happened to your kin at home."

"They didn't know about it. Remember, Moscow tried to keep it secret. The folks in Pripyat learned about it last. Those bastards didn't even tell them what happened when the KGB was already out on the streets taking radiation measurements in full protective suits. Listen, Dynamo Kiev thrashed Atletico Madrid when the disaster happened and our football players learned about it from Spanish journalists! But one more thing..." Lazarov points at a junk yard full of wrecked, Soviet-made helicopters and airplanes. "You see those wrecks?"

"Looks as if we left half our air force behind!"

"Bagram was the base of our best helicopter pilots. When Chernobyl happened, they called them back to take measurements, kill the flames and drop chemicals to block the discharge of radioactivity from the reactor... no other pilots could do that. They took off from the very same spot where we stand now. It is a place where our two fatal disasters meet: Chernobyl and the Afghan war."

The sergeant frowns. "Honestly, *komandir*, sometimes I felt sad about the USSR collapsing... nostalgic even. But now, seeing those wasted helicopters over there, I get your point."

Lazarov is surprised at the change in the young sergeant's expression. His lean, handsome face has become like a cold piece of metal in an instant.

"I can guess the rest of the story, Major. Once the job was done, they were given a medal and sent back here to die."

"In fact, our last two men to die in a combat operation were a Hind crew."

"You want to know what I feel right now?"

"Sadness?"

"Anger. If you don't mind me saying so, sir—fuck the USSR."

The major has seen many people change in the Zone. Usually it was terror turning their hair grey after a night spent in the underground laboratories. Sometimes, it was rage over a fallen friend that caused the change. Other times, greed over a relic that was supposed to make one a millionaire outside took over. But he never saw anyone slaughtering his own illusions so palpably like this young soldier right in front of him, and it leaves him at a loss, not knowing how to reply. Suddenly, the photograph comes to his mind: *Yuriy and the Gang.*

"No, I don't mind at all," he finally replies. "Whatever lies in the past, here we go again. This is our little war now and this time we're not here to lose it. What's the name of that trooper carrying the grenade launcher?"

"Vasilyev."

"Give Vasilyev a hand. He can barely keep it on his shoulders." Lazarov looks at Zlenko who is still staring at the ruins. "Come on... Let's move, son."

Shamali Plains, 17:20:15 AFT

Among the bushes spawning from cracks in the asphalt where heavy airplanes had once landed and the rows of ruined buildings that seemed to stretch endlessly along the former runway, the Stalkers lead them towards a veritable bastion erected from steel shipping containers with sandbags on top. One bullet-riddled container blocks the entrance, the word

MAERSK still visible in faded white letters. A loudspeaker crackles from inside.

"*Stalkers! Veterans and rookies from the far north! If you've had enough of dust storms, mutants and dushmans, come to the Antonov. We have all comforts the New Zone has to offer!*"

The invitation comes from tantalizingly close by.

Two huge chains run up from the container blocking the entrance and disappear into holes in the metal rampart above. A sentry rises to his feet and emerges from under a shady camouflage mat, casually turning a fixed machine gun towards them.

"Halt! Who goes there?" he shouts down.

"Yo, Grisha! It's us, Squirrel and Danya!" the guide shouts back waving his hand. "Try not to shoot us, fellas!"

"And those dirty zombies you have in tow?"

"Huh… they look like military, but that's only a birth defect! They are cool, I swear it!"

"What? You brought the military here? Are you out of your fucking mind?"

"They saved us from two bears! And then we routed a squad of freaks together!"

The sentry hesitates. "I need to ask Bone," he replies and disappears behind the sand bags. Squirrel sighs and looks at Lazarov with doubt written all over his face.

"*Stalkers! Visit the Antonov! Chilled vodka, deer steak salted with potassodium iodide and all kinds of shiny new weapons await!*"

"If he mentions chilled vodka one more time, I'll take this damned place by storm," Ilchenko moans. "I swear it."

Lazarov has a queasy feeling in his guts. Back in the northern Zone, he did everything he could to ensure a fragile coexistence between his soldiers and the Stalkers, and the military had always been on good terms with the Guardians. But that might as well have been on a different planet.

"Do you think they will let us in?" Zlenko asks with concern.

"I couldn't blame them if they don't. It was not so long ago in the Zone of Alienation that we had orders to shoot Stalkers on sight."

Dark clouds gather on the southern horizon but the sun still shines down mercilessly on the exhausted soldiers. At last they hear a generator starting up and the MAERSK container is pulled up by the heavy chains. As the gate opens, a dozen Stalkers step forward from the swirling dust, all wearing heavy armor with an exoskeleton-clad figure in the middle. Their Russian-made Groza assault rifles are aimed at the soldiers.

Lazarov frowns. *Veteran Guardians. We wouldn't stand a chance against them… not in this condition.*

"No fooling around, men," he tells his soldiers and raises his arms to signal his peaceful intentions.

"Now look at this miserable bunch of *boyevoychiks*," the Stalker leader says with a mocking laugh. Then he turns to Lazarov. "What the hell are you here for?"

Lazarov is sure he has heard the same disdainful tone before. However, the exoskeleton's curtain helmet hides the leader's face and the voice, distorted by the face mask, is not recognizable.

"Captain Bone, I presume," he replies. "I was hoping to receive a slightly warmer welcome from a Guardian. I am Major Lazarov from the Armed Forces of the Russian Federation. We have no hostile intentions and need your help."

"I would sooner put my dick into a snake's mouth than help you." Bone looks at his gunmen. "This is not the Zone of Alienation and we are not bound to the Guardians or their alliance to the military. We are our own masters here."

"We're not here to bother your business. Our wounded need medical assistance. Let us rest for one day, then we'll leave you in peace and never come back."

"You have dust in your ears? You are not welcome here. Go and get eaten by mutants, I don't care a damn."

"Stalkers! Enjoy..."

Lazarov considers his less than favorable options and is about to order his men to charge down the arrogant captain and his troopers, choosing to die a soldier's death when the looped message in the loudspeaker is interrupted by a cheerful voice.

"Yo, Captain! Why dontcha let'em in? They must be thirsty like a upyr with no necks around to bite. It would be good for me business!"

"Sammy, you bozo," Bone snorts into his intercom, "stay out of this. It's adults talking here."

A trooper with telecommunications gear on his back comes up running to Bone and holds a speaker to his commander. "Call from the Outpost, Captain."

Bone listens to the message and orders his men to lower their weapons.

"A solution has just come up. We have a few men stationed to the south. They are about to be attacked by dushmans. You take your men and help them defend their position. Survivors will be permitted to enter our base."

Lazarov gives Bone a scornful grin and then darts a freezing glance at Zlenko who is about to shout something back, his face burning with anger.

"Captain, I understand that the Guardians need assistance from us professionals, but with half of my men barely able to walk we wouldn't be of much use now. I heard you have a doctor in the base. Have him patch up our wounded and maybe we'll give you a leg up."

"You overestimate your bargaining position, Major." Arrogance still lingers in Bone's voice but he seems less sure of his ground. "All right, here's the deal. Your wounded can stay. Those who are still able to lift a rifle go to the Outpost at Hill 1865." Lazarov wants to interrupt but Bone has not finished yet. "Of course, you'll leave those exoskeletons here, together with half your remaining ammo. Don't look so angry,

Major. You're making a valuable contribution to the future defense of Bagram!"

Lazarov bites his lips. What he just heard is equal to a death sentence. *If I ever get back to the north, I'll lead a strike force against the Guardians' headquarters and burn it to the ground. I swear it.*

"You bastard. Why don't you shoot us right here, right now? A damned big victory for you, with half of my men wounded!"

"Ah yes, that's the cocky Spetsnaz speaking now. To answer you properly: first, we save our ammo for mutants and dushmans and don't waste it on microbes like you. Second, I am actually being generous. You *can* survive at the Outpost after all. Your chances are a hundred to one. Go for it!"

"Even a brainless Guardian should see that we won't get there in time!"

"You won't have to walk on your stinkers," Bone replies and turns to one of his troopers. "Get the truck."

Barely able to swallow his anger, Lazarov turns to the sergeant. "Collect half the ammo from the men. Line up those still capable to fight."

"But—"

"Do as you were ordered." Lazarov's eyes flash like a lightning as he glares at the young sergeant. Then he adds in a more forgiving voice: "We don't have much of a choice here, do we? I've been concerned that one way or the other, we'd have to win over the Stalkers' hearts and minds anyway. Don't worry."

Zlenko looks at him with a mixture of anxiety and trust. "It's their hearts and minds, but our blood and guts... but we'll do as ordered."

Squirrel has been watching over their conversation without a word, but now sounds genuinely scared. "And what about me and Danya, captain?"

"You and your buddy made a mistake by leading these bastards to our base. Both of you will join your new friends."

"But we belong here! You can't do this to us!"

Bone ignores the guide's desperate pleas. A heavy engine starts up behind the wall and a huge URAL truck appears. Thick armor plates cover the driver's compartment and manned by two of Bone's guards, a double-barreled anti-aircraft gun rotates on the vehicle's back as it slowly rolls out through the gate.

"It will take you to the Outpost and if you're lucky, back here tomorrow morning," Bone laughs. "What happens in between is not my concern. Get onto that truck and leave my base."

"I'll see you again, Bone."

"Forget that attitude, Spetsnaz. Remember, your wounded are now with me!"

Climbing up to the truck, the only thing Lazarov can think about is if he hasn't made another mistake by calling at Bagram.

My men are worn out, I have no contact with Termez or Goryunov... What the hell was I supposed to do?

Still thinking about what a difference one more night of fighting could make, he looks out at the desert and the arid mountains behind. All of his soldiers have exhaustion etched on their faces, with the exception of Ilchenko who is doing his best to clean his machine gun as the rocking truck jostles along the bumpy road.

Despite his dar thoughts, the wide, open space around him and the clear sky, shining with a deep blue he has never seen before, fill Lazarov with exhilaration.

"You seem happy," Zlenko says, trying to make himself heard over the laboring engine and the wind.

Lazarov frowns, realizing that the sergeant has a point. His strange exhilaration is similar to what he had felt when arriving back in the Zone of Alienation after a leave, like feeling the familiar smell of one's home or the perfume of a

126

lover not seen for a long time. He feels sorry for his soldiers who have never experienced that place but, looking over the vast plain, Lazarov wonders if the New Zone doesn't offer much more than his old turf. And with this thought, he realizes that his exhilaration comes from just this expectation — the promise of new secrets awaiting discovery. But all this would need too much explanation, and Lazarov decides to direct Zlenko's attention elsewhere.

"Tonight, we will teach the dushmans a lesson!" he replies. "It is payback time!"

"Sure! But I hope one day we'll also get that bastard Captain Bone by his balls!"

"Maybe, if the mission is complete. We're supposed to be a rescue team, not assassins."

He can't hear Zlenko's reply over the truck's roaring engine noise and squeaking suspension as it speeds down the uneven road, but he sees the expression on the other man's face. It's enough to tell him what Zlenko's thoughts are. The major turns away and, taking his binoculars from their case, studies the hill in front of them.

The rise is slightly lower than the ridge on the other side of the road but still offers a perfect view over the area and the narrow pass where the road enters the plains leading to the ruins of Kabul. His Geiger counter, ticking at survivable values around Bagram, now climbs up to more dangerous levels. The truck rolls on, along a broken road that crosses over undulating sand riddled with vehicle wrecks and shell craters before it starts to climb up the hill, spiraling all the way to the top.

Hill 1865, 19:50:47 AFT

The truck eventually arrives at the small fortification perched on the hill and halts, the engine still idling. Lazarov watches his soldiers as they get off. Sergeant Zlenko, Kamensky and

Bondarchuk with AKMs; Lobov the medic with an AKSU-74; Kravchuk with his Dragunov; Ilchenko with his PKM; Vasilyev carries only a pistol, all he can manage since he is loaded down with the heavy AGS-17 grenade launcher.

They are quite well equipped. Even so, he can only hope it will be enough. He jumps out of the truck and looks around.

The hilltop position looks well-fortified at first sight, but Lazarov's heart sinks when he sees the two dozen rag-tag Stalkers, some of them having no better weapons than obsolete shotguns.

This will be a tough battle, he reflects with a sigh.

Lazarov had hoped that at least the truck would stay with them to give support from its massive anti-aircraft gun, but Captain Bone's driver had barely given his men enough time to dismount before turning the vehicle heading back to towards the Stalker base.

"Looks like this place has seen many battles before," Zlenko says surveying the hilltop.

Lazarov nods in agreement. The Outpost would be easy to defend if he had more men. Surrounded to the north and south with trenches shaped in the form of two semi-circles, a bunker stands in the middle of the perimeter. No windows or vents can be seen on the low concrete walls, but its top is fortified with sandbags, just like the smaller trench running between the bunker and the outer defenses.

He climbs up to its top. Looking around he can well understand how strategic this position is. The view is breathtaking: through his binoculars, Lazarov can still make out the hazy mountains around the Salang Pass to the north and the scattered ruins of Bagram. Just like after reaching the exit of the Salang tunnel where he first saw the dreadful beauty of this wilderness, the vastness fills him with awe. In his exhilaration, Lazarov even ignores the gloomy horizon to the south where flashes of lightning appear, their thunder rolling over the flat landscape like a foreboding echo under a sky turning to violent shades of red and purple. Beyond the far hills that screen the ruins of Kabul, gloomy clouds cover the sky like frozen waves of an eternal storm. The road runs below, between the hill and a higher mountain to the southwest, before it enters the sandy plains and disappears in the haze and swirling clouds of sand.

"All right, let's get down to business," he says, clapping his hands and turning to Zlenko. "Let the sniper and the grenade launcher set up here. Tell them to keep their heads low. I'll be damned if we don't receive sniper fire from that mountain beyond the road. We'll need as many soldiers as possible in the trenches. I'll get a Stalker to give Vasilyev a hand with the AGS."

"*Yest, komandir!*" Zlenko gives a sharp whistle and waves his hand to the two soldiers to join him.

Lazarov finds Squirrel sitting on a sandbag. The Stalker guide has his face buried in his hands and looks resigned in despair.

"Hey brother," Lazarov tells him. "Cheer up. You can whine when you're dead."

"I already am! I told you what this place is about. And I curse the fucking moment when I ran into you!"

"So you preferred being mutant food?"

"Whatever, man. I'm a Stalker, not a soldier. I know about mutants and traps but don't have the stuff for making last stands on godforsaken hills like this!"

"Nobody says it will be a last stand," Lazarov says, comfortingly. "I'm sorry that you've been punished for helping us. Listen, Squirrel, all I can do in exchange now is to offer you a relatively safe place. Join that soldier on the bunker and help him handle the grenade launcher. Stay low and you'll be fine."

Zlenko appears. "Vasilyev and Kravchuk are in position."

"Good. I want Ilchenko and the riflemen help the Stalkers in holding the line. Damn it, how I wish I had enough men to deploy into the forward trenches!"

They make their way towards the group of Stalkers who stand around what had once been a field gun, but now is almost falling apart from rust and wear. The Stalkers stop chatting and give the soldiers distrustful looks as they approach. The smell of marijuana lingers in the air around them.

"Stalkers, have any of you been to the Zone of Alienation?" Lazarov asks.

Almost all of them nod.

"Yes, we have," says a Stalker wearing an oversized trench coat made of black leather, covered with a thick layer of brown dust. His face his half-hidden by a hood. To Lazarov's surprise, as the Stalker steps forward and his trench coat opens, he recognizes below it the suit worn by the Guardians. The Stalker takes his battered AK from his shoulder, but seeing Ilchenko's machine gun he doesn't dare to assume a threatening stance. "That's why we prefer that you stay away from us."

"What's wrong with you?" Zlenko steps forward but Lazarov halts him with a movement of his hand.

He looks at the Stalkers. Now, closer in, he can guess their origins by the half-ruined armor suits they are wearing: rookies in army-surplus camo jackets; here and there the ravaged light armor with the Bundeswehr-issue *Tarnfleck* camouflage that is preferred by fighters of the Intruders. A few of them wear the more experienced Stalkers' grey-brown protective suits. Finally, his eyes return to the Stalker wearing the half-hidden Guardian suit.

"Listen up, brothers," he starts addressing the Stalkers. "I know you are here as a punishment. So are we — for all the things the army did to Stalkers back in the Zone of Alienation, even if neither I nor any of my men was part of that. But I say: fighting dushmans is not a punishment. We are here to teach them a lesson they will not forget. We can't avenge any wrongs from the past, but we do still have unfinished business with the dushmans."

Lazarov sees a sparkle flashing up in the eyes of older Stalkers. The younger ones, too, perk up their ears to what he is saying.

"I see loners, Intruders and even a Guardian here. You have fought each other back in the 'Old' Zone, as you say, and we soldiers have fought you all. Now we are all new to this place but face an old enemy. They might have beaten our father's generation, but now it is us they will be up against. And I tell you, they will be in for a surprise." Lazarov clears his throat. Mentioning his father turned his throat strangely dry. Looking at the Stalkers who now listen to him closely, he decides to ask them a question.

"You, rookie in that brown Kevlar jacket! Where are you from?"

"Moscow."

"And you, with that AK-47?"

"Katowice. Poland."

"You, in that *Flecktarn* jacket?"

"Irkutsk. I hated the cold there."

The Stalkers start replying one by one.

"Uruguay. You wouldn't guess where it is but I'm here and ready."

"Scotland the brave!"

"Sankt-Petersburg. No need to tell more."

"Belgrade. Serbia."

"Australia. Guess you don't know where Brisbane is but I do know how to fire a shotgun!"

"Yekaterinburg, and I know what you mean, officer. In all of Russia, we have the most beautiful memorial to those fallen in that war."

"From Krasnodar, just around the corner."

"A canuck here from Montreal."

"Hajmáskér. Hungary."

"Is that so, Mente?" The Russian Stalker from Moscow asks with surprise. "My uncle was stationed there in Soviet times with a tank battalion!"

"You're my friend, Moskvitch, but for us it was a relief to get rid of your uncle and his tanks," the Eastern European Stalker grumbles, staring at his sawn-off shotgun. The Stalker called Moskvitch just shrugs and gives his comrade a friendly pat on the shoulder.

"We seem to have all kinds of Stalkers here from around the globe," Lazarov concludes. "Our homes might be different but our blood has the same color. Don't have any illusions: it will be shed tonight. Let it be the sign of our union, because today we all fight together and will be victorious together. Our chances are not good, there's no doubt about that. But if the toughest sons of the Zones will keep together—who can stand against us, brothers?"

"We are not your damned brothers, *officer*," the tough-looking Guardian says, making the last word sound like a curse. He was one of the few Stalkers who kept their origin to themselves.

Lazarov keeps his temper. "So you want me to call you sister, or what?"

The Guardian's face flushes with anger when a few former Intruders start laughing. Feeling his momentum, Lazarov turns towards them.

"You listen up too, you pathetic bunch of no-good dope-smoking miserable anarchists! We're all together in this. A deep shit situation! There's not enough of us to use the forward trenches, so we'll make our stand right here. These riflemen and the machine gunner will be strengthening your line. Ilchenko, you'll take position here. You, Stalker with the woodland camo suit and you with that AK-47, take up positions to cover his flanks. The rest of you follow me. We better set up our defense now before night falls."

"Wait a minute," the Guardian says. "What the hell puts you in charge anyway?"

"Three assault rifles and one machine gun being pointed at you."

From the corner of his eye, Lazarov sees an ear to ear grin appear on Ilchenko's face. The Stalker reluctantly shoulders his weapon.

"That's what I call an argument," he grumbles. "All right, let's work together... for now. My name is Skinner. I had a different name back at the Old Zone but that's of no importance anymore."

Lazarov doesn't show it but feels great relief over the Guardian's decision to cooperate. "I am glad to see a Guardian here. It's good to have at least one Stalker around who has ever heard of discipline."

Skinner gives him a grin. "Sorry to bust your bubble but I'm a deserter."

"Is that so?"

"This is the land of plenty here. But I can't hunt for relics if I'm dead, can I? So, if you grunts will help me to survive, I don't give a damn how many Stalkers you've had mowed down at the Perimeter. I might even listen to your orders."

"Neither do I give a damn if you'll survive, Skinner. But I do care about you trying and killing as many enemies in the process as possible."

"Sounds like a deal to me."

Lazarov now turns to Zlenko. "Set up defensive position with the riflemen along the perimeter. Concentrate fire towards the south and that mountain. Makes sure there's one of us with every three or four Stalkers."

The sergeant nods and hurries off with the paratroopers, leaving Lazarov to turn back to the cocky Stalker.

"Bone told me the attack is imminent. Tell me more about what we'll have to face."

Surprise flashes in Skinner's dark eyes. "I didn't tell him it was imminent," he says. "I only told Bone that we saw a group of dushmans approaching from the plains. We fired a few shots at them and they disappeared."

"That's odd. Bone seemed to be sure that you'd need reinforcements, and soon."

It dawns now on Lazarov that the Captain might have just wanted to get rid of them by sending them into a hopeless battle and let the Stalkers' enemies do the dirty job. *One more reason to make it through alive*, he thinks.

"That whoreson could be right after all," replies Skinner pointing towards the south. "It might have been an advance party to check if they can catch us with our pants down. Maybe they will come back in full force after nightfall. To spice up the soup we're boiling in... did you see those clouds on the horizon?"

"Looks gloomy."

"Smells like a dust storm gathering."

"That should keep the dushmans away."

"You think so? Major, you might have been a big shot in the Old Zone but you're still a rookie here," Skinner grimly replies.

Lazarov frowns but can't find any mockery in the Stalker's words. Swallowing his pride, he even admits to himself that Skinner has a point: not even 48 hours have passed since he arrived.

"So, we expect some charming company tonight. But why do they want to take this godforsaken place?"

"It's not the Outpost they are after. It's Bagram. When the nukes went off, the mountains north of Kabul got the worst of the fallout. The devastation is pretty bad there. That's why they want to break through to the north. Anyway, when the storm will hit, we'll lock ourselves in that bunker because we stick to our life. The dushmans don't. Unless we beat them before the storm arrives, they will crawl up to the bunker, blow down the door and fry us inside, no matter how many of them get martyred in the process."

"*Oh Gospodi,*" sighs Lazarov.

"I agree. Praying never harms." Skinner takes a necklace with a small silver cross from under his armored suit and kisses it. "Still eager to make a gallant stand?"

"I am."

"I didn't take you for such a badass. Maybe Bone was right in sending you here... we won't give up without a fight, even if we're a bunch of thieves and murderers."

"And which of those things are you?"

"Not a thief, that's for sure," the Stalker says, turning away and raising his binoculars to scan the dusty plains. But Lazarov has one more question for him.

"How come Bone put you up with Intruders and free Stalkers? Guardians prefer formal court-martials, as far as I know."

Without removing the binoculars from his eyes, Skinner spits to the ground. "Do you play cards, Major?"

"Occasionally. Why?"

"Because the old deck of cards has been reshuffled. Here, none of us belongs to where he used to. Bone is not with the Guardians anymore, neither are his henchmen. Sometimes I wonder if they ever were. The one I killed certainly was not."

"How do you know?" Lazarov curiously asks.

"No self-respecting Guardian would try taking a free Stalker's relics by aiming a rifle at him. And neither would one beg for his life, not even with a free Stalker's knife at his throat."

Lazarov leaves him alone and looks back at Ilchenko who is positioning his machine gun among the sand bags. He notices with satisfaction that the soldier has picked a perfect position: protected, but still covering a wide angle towards the slope.

"Mow them down when they come, Ilchenko."

The soldier grins back at him, flashing impeccable teeth in his round face. "I will, sir. You know how it goes... *On Kazbek the clouds are meeting, like the mountain eagle-flock, Up to them, along the rock, dash the wild Uzdens retreating,/ Onward faster, faster fleeting, routed by the Russian brood,/ Foameth all their track with blood.*"

135

Lazarov's jaw almost drops in surprise. Reciting a poem was the last thing he expected from the tattooed machine gunner. "That's by Bestuzhev!"

"That's correct, sir." Ilchenko almost bursts with self-satisfaction. "I have a degree in literature but signed up with the army to see the world and all."

"You are a man of many talents, Ilchenko."

"Thank you, sir!"

"Let's see if digging is one of them. Grab that shovel and dig in deeper, if you don't want this shithole to be the last you see of the world!"

"As ordered, but—"

"And make it deep enough!" Lazarov shouts. "It will save us time when we have to bury you if you got shot because you were thinking about poetry instead of mowing down those *baystrukh*[1]*i*. They don't give a damn about Pushkin and Bestuzhev but do know Kalashnikov's name very well!"

Still shaking his head, Lazarov makes his way back to the bunker where Vasilyev is giving Squirrel a crash course in how to handle the grenade launcher.

"It handles like a dream if the blowback mechanism doesn't jam. But that's not your concern. Get those ammunition boxes closer. There's a belt with thirty high-explosive grenades in each of them. The box marked red contains VOG-30 grenades. They take more punch and have a longer range than regular rounds. Those are our life insurance. Do not feed them until I tell you to do so. Is that clear?"

"Yes, sir."

"Call me 'sir' again and I put a grenade up your butthole! Take two belts and load them into the metal drum magazines. We have two of them. As soon as one is empty, you remove and replace it with the reserve drum. While I keep firing, you load the next belt into the empty drum. Then you change it again if needed."

---

[1] bastards

"Keep your eyes on what Vasilyev is showing you, Squirrel," Lazarov remarks when he sees the Stalker sending concerned glances to the south. "Rest assured, the dushmans will come without you watching out for them."

Under his watch, the old *zastava* slowly gains the shape of a well-organized fire base. But from the top position he can also see how thinly stretched their defenses are. Defending such positions was among the basics in officer training but Lazarov has never faced such a task before.

Clearing the underground labs. Patrolling the Perimeter. Saving a lost recon squad from mutants. That was my job, not pitched battles. I am a Spetsnaz, a Zone scout, not infantry. Skinner was right about praying. But I don't believe in God. Not one that would help if asked nicely, anyway.

Vasilyev curses when Squirrel fails to properly fix the ammunition drum on his third attempt.

"Don't be too hard on the Stalker, Vasilyev," Lazarov advises as he helps Zlenko off the ladder.

"We're set, sir," the sergeant reports, still catching his breath. "We are stretched very thin, but we've got the southern and western slopes covered with the PKM and the automatic rifles we have. The Stalker's shotguns might come in handy if the enemy gets too close."

"I also saw a couple of them with submachine guns and carbines. We need to tell those guys to hold their fire until the enemy gets into range."

"I already gave that order."

"Good initiative. Now all we can do is to wait." Lazarov sits down and opens an army ration pack.

"May I join you, sir?"

He motions to the sergeant to sit down. "I hope we make it through." Lazarov lets the ration's wrapper fly off in the wind. "It would be a shame if these miserable biscuits were my last supper."

The sergeant smiles. "The Stalkers told me there's a bar in Bagram, set up in an old airplane."

"They have a special skill when it comes to turning every piece of junk into a bar... Stalkers would probably find a cozy place on the North Pole too, should a Zone pop up there."

"I guess so... but actually, what's on my mind is that this place seems strangely familiar to me."

"To me as well. It's a Soviet-built *zastava*."

"Not only that... the whole situation." The sergeant seems to be lost in his thoughts as he looks out to the plains where the mountains cast long shadows in the setting sun.

"We'll make it through, sergeant."

"What makes you so confident?"

"We built hundreds of small outposts like this in the Eighties. The enemy harassed and attacked them all the time, but we never lost a single one to them. Never ever, sergeant. If it happened now, it was a shame I wouldn't want to live with."

"Couldn't agree more."

"Did you lose someone during that war?"

"No, thank God. My father was posted to the DDR. East Germany. He cried when they had to leave and was quite upset when I signed up to join the army. He relaxed a little when I first sent money home. And what about—"

Zlenko bites his tongue but Lazarov knows what he wanted to ask. His father's photograph is hidden in his wallet, beneath the armored west, but he touches the place as if he could reach it.

"I did."

"I understand, sir... is that what motivates you? Apologies if I'm asking too many questions."

"We have orders and no one cares about our motivations to follow them. We will make it through tonight, trust me. Then we continue with our mission."

"Fair enough."

"No, it's not even remotely fair." Lazarov gives the sergeant a bitter smile. "The scientists were sent here to find out how all these mutants and anomalies were created."

"I thought it's from radiation. The fall-out and all."

Lazarov sighs. "That only plays a minor role, if at all... the Old Zone was created by an entity powerful enough to bend the laws of physics. If that happened here too that's bad enough, but things here are... meaner than in the Zone I know. Moscow wants to know how this happened. That's why securing the scientists' research results is our priority. And as I know the FSB colonel who briefed me, he would expect us to do the scientists' homework if they have failed."

"We can worry about that once we survive this night, I guess."

"Agreed. And to finally answer your question: yes, for me this battle, or whenever we meet those half-mutant sons of bitches — it will be personal."

"A fitting description for the dushmans," Zlenko says. "I also have to say that I admire your attitude."

"What attitude?"

"You almost seem happy over being here."

"You see... I have explored every square meter of the Old Zone. I have been to every secret laboratory, every dark corner. I fought every faction and mutant. Being here is like a new beginning, just like for the Stalkers around here. It's like... How can I say it? When I was home, I wanted to be back to the Zone, and when I was there, all I could think of was getting back home. Being here now feels like a divorce from a woman I still love but who has nothing new to say, after living together so long that I partly became her, in the way I function, think and speak. I'm here now, waiting for what will happen, like a recently divorced man waits for his first new date. Yes, Sergeant, I am happy... kind of."

"I wish I could see the Zone of Alienation one day."

"By the way, I just witnessed something miraculous." Lazarov tries to enjoy the bland taste of the rations before he continues. "A tattooed machine gunner reciting poetry."

To his disappointment, Zlenko does not look surprised.

"I guess Ilchenko was bragging again about his teacher's degree," he replies with a yawn.

"Are there any more such smartasses in the squad?"

"Lobov had to quit medical school because of drug problems, but he is reliable. The rest is just normal boys from the neighborhood who couldn't find a better way out of unemployment."

"And you?"

The sergeant sadly smiles. "I wanted to become a famous guitar player but my band flopped."

"That's not a disaster big enough to chase one into the army's arms."

"Yes, but having purchased a six-string Fender American Standard Stratocaster on rates and not being able to repay it to a loan shark definitely is."

He has barely finished the sentence when a rifle fires a burst. Jumping to his feet, Lazarov peers over the sand bags. All seems quiet.

"Just a bloody jackal," Skinner shouts in the trenches.

Lazarov swears nervously. "We better go and buck those trigger-happy Stalkers."

"Let me do that. I wanted to check the perimeter anyway."

Lazarov is eager to rest for a few minutes and close his eyes, which are already burning from exhaustion and fine dust. Night is about to fall and he knows neither he nor his men will be able to get any rest during the coming hours.

"I would appreciate that," he smiles, leaning against the stone-hard sandbags and trying to relax his overstrained nerves without falling asleep. He jerks upright again and looks around his men. "Kravchuk, keep your eyes on the ridge to the west. And switch off that headlamp. You are supposed to dish out the headshots, not get one yourself."

A bright flash.

For a second, Lazarov thinks he has slept until morning and it is the rising sun casting light onto his face. Then he realizes the true cause: a flare is hovering over the Outpost. He can hear the Stalkers shouting as he jumps to his feet.

"They're coming!"

"Major!" Zlenko shouts, excitement and fear mingling in his voice. "This is it! They're moving up from the south!"

Lazarov doesn't need the sergeant's directions to know where the attack is coming from. A long howl sounds through the chilly night, barely distinguishable from that of a blood-thirsty animal, but a hundred human – or at least human-like – voices join in. Then a hail of bullets hits the defenders. To Lazarov's horror, it comes from all around their position.

"Fire!" Squirrel screams. "Fire that shit!"

"I'll open fire when I'm ordered to!" Vasilyev shouts back, his eyes fixed upon his officer.

"Zlenko, into the trenches, now! Don't fire until you're sure to hit them!"

"On my way!"

Keeping his head low, Lazarov estimates the range of their attackers. "Vasilyev! Adjust range to four hundred! Cover the area wide, from ten to one o'clock! Steady!"

Now Ilchenko's machine gun opens up in the trenches, followed by the rapid fire of submachine guns. The howls get louder and closer.

"Three-fifty… steady!"

"Why don't you just fire, man?"

"Stay cool, Stalker… three-hundred."

"Adjusted!"

"Fry them."

Vasilyev pulls the release cord of the grenade launcher, grabs the holders and fires short bursts from the AGS, unleashing fast grenade fire into the mass of dark silhouettes running up the slopes. The dushmans' battle cry disintegrates into cries of pain amidst the detonations. Squirrel jumps back.

"*Damn!* I didn't take this shit for a machine gun!"

"Shut up and prepare the spare drum," Vasilyev shouts.

"They weren't prepared for that!" Lazarov tells them triumphantly. "Good job."

Looking down to the dushmans' broken wave and hearing Zlenko's and Skinner's voice directing their comrades' fire towards the retreating enemy, a stoic feeling of might empowers him. He watches the dushmans hastily retreat into the darkness, but what he views to the south makes him shudder. A gigantic shadow rises, darker than night itself, making the stars disappear. Lightning flashes on the horizon.

"Vasilyev, keep the settings. As soon as the second wave gets into range, open fire. Try to save ammo."

"Will do, sir."

"So far, so good," Squirrel says. "Time to relax."

He rises from the ground and lights up a cigarette. At the same moment as Vasilyev drags him back into cover, a muffled noise comes from the closest mountain. A bullet hits the spot where the Stalker's head had been less than a second before.

"Kravchuk," Lazarov shouts to the squad's marksman, "sniper to the east! Try to locate him!"

"I-I did this on purpose," the Stalker cries, "I wanted them to reveal their position!"

"Bloody good job," Lazarov replies.

The single bullet is followed by several more. A scream comes from the trenches. He hears Zlenko shouting. "Keep your damned heads down! Snipers!"

They know what they are doing. Not giving us a moment of respite until the next wave comes.

Kravchuk's Dragunov fires in response.

"Did you see them?"

"I think so!"

"Don't waste your damned ammunition on shadows!" Lazarov wishes Crow was here, although looking up at the massive mountain, he can't really blame his sniper. "Go back to your position and keep your eyes on the ridge. We only have a handful of Stalkers there!"

Lazarov doesn't waste his time with climbing down the ladder. He jumps down, throws himself into the trench and keeping his head low, hurries to the forward position. "Casualties?"

"A Stalker bought it," Lobov replies, ducking behind the sand bags as another bullet impacts close to them. "He was dead by the time I got to him."

"His name was Sashka the Hand," Skinner grumbles. "At least he won't be stealing first aid kits from fellow Stalkers anymore."

A clap of thunder rolls over the plains, echoing from the mountains. A second later an explosion rocks their perimeter.

"Mortars!"

"Hit the ground," Skinner shouts. "Take cover, Stalkers!"

Amidst more incoming mortar rounds the dushmans' battle cry bellows. Another flare flashes above them, casting its dire red light over the hill.

"Holy shit! I need a bigger gun," Ilchenko yells and points to the slope where hundreds of enemy fighters are advancing towards them. He opens fire without waiting for orders. The grenade launcher belches out a salvo but abruptly falls silent. After a moment, it sounds up again but firing in a different direction. Lazarov's face grows pale.

"They've got into our rear! Skinner!"

"Here!"

"Hold your position until you can, then fall back into the trenches around the bunker! Zlenko, Bondarchuk, on me!"

With the two soldiers in tow, he runs back to the bunker. Thanks to Vasilyev's quick reactions, the line of attackers falters, giving the handful of defenders a little momentum. Zlenko and the rifleman join the Stalkers in holding their thin line beyond the scattered cover of sand bags. Above his head, Kravchuk is firing his Dragunov.

"Last ammunition belt!" Squirrel shouts.

"Prepare the VOG-30s, Stalker!" Vasilyev bellows back.

The voices coming from the grenade launcher are desperate, just like Zlenko's.

"Kamensky is down!"

Lazarov cocks his rifle. "Vasilyev! Give them hell! Burn the ridge!"

Fiery explosions pierce into the enemy's line, throwing up rocks, sand and body parts in balls of fire. But before the grenades can stop them, the launcher stops firing. The first dushman appears over the wall of sandbags, aiming his rifle at Zlenko while he is reloading his rifle. A burst from Lazarov's rifle hits the dushman, but as soon as he falls three others appear.

"Get this, cocksuckers!"

Squirrel shouts a battle cry from above and the grenade launcher resumes firing. Lazarov quickly climbs up to the bunker. Vasilyev's body lies in a pool of blood. Kravchuk is still kneeling behind the sand bags, firing his Dragunov relentlessly.

Heavy rain begins to fall. The flashes of lightning fork so close together that the thunder merges into a ceaseless din that almost drowns out the frantic rifle fire that now spews from all directions.

Oblivious to the danger, Lazarov looks over to the perimeter to assess their remaining defenses. It looks bad. The Stalkers are already retreating towards the bunker, with Ilchenko in the rear covering their route. Beyond them, Zlenko is desperately trying to hold the line with the few remaining Stalkers.

"No more grenades!"

"Grab your rifle and help the sergeant, Squirrel!"

"Incoming!" Kravchuk screams.

A huge explosion rocks the bunker, throwing Lazarov and the Stalker to the ground.

"RPGs! The bastards come up now with RPGs!"

"Let's get off the bunker! Kravchuk, on me!"

Skinner and his Stalkers are already there when Lazarov reaches the sand bags overlooking the ridge. The wind has grown into a storm. Dust whipped up by the wind quickly mixes with the driving rain and covers the men with filth.

"The cocksuckers know what they are doing, Major," Skinner says, rivulets of rain running down his face as he glances in Lazarov's direction. "They pushed us back and now come against us from the rear! But you know... there was a moment when I almost thought we could actually make it." Skinner holds his rifle over the sand bags and fires a long burst. The dushmans' blood curdling cries are so close and their bodies so tightly packed together that he doesn't need to aim. "Take this, bastards!"

Lazarov looks around, squinting into the storm. Ilchenko is still there, firing his PKM with a scream that distorts his whole face. Kravchuk has dropped his sniper rifle in favor of an AK taken from a fallen Stalker. Squirrel drags a fallen comrade into cover; a man Lazarov recognizes as the other Stalker they met in the forest.

He realizes it's just a question of minutes before they are overrun and annihilated. Hearing their triumphant cries, he knows that the enemy is aware of this too.

"Zlenko!" Lazarov screams with all the air left in his lungs. "On me!"

The sergeant scrambles up to him. "Major?"

"Now is the time," Lazarov says, panting. "You know what comes next if we stay in the trench. Give me that flare gun and wait for my command."

A wide smile appears on the sergeant's blood-smeared face. What Lazarov sees in those shining eyes is the one thing he would have least expected: happiness.

"Nobody but us!" Zlenko bellows and raises his hand. "Fix bayonets!"

At this moment, Lazarov wishes he was a believer, not so he could pray for deliverance but so he could give his thanks. All ways to die are bad, save for that which a man chooses of his own will. Hearing the steely click as his combat knife attaches to the AKM's barrel, he feels that his wish has been granted. He fires the flare gun.

"Are you ready?" he shouts.

"Ready," the scattered defenders reply one by one.

Lazarov hears the attackers drawing closer through the pouring rain and darkness, appearing in the flashes of lightning like ghosts.

"Hold!" he shouts. "Keep steady… steady!"

In the moment when the flare bursts out into a bright cupola of blinding red light, he thrusts his fist towards the enemy.

"Charge!"

"Forward!" Zlenko shouts. "Vperyod! Rota k boyu!"

Soldiers and Stalkers jump out of their cover and charge down the hill. No one can keep up with Lazarov, his limbs quickened by the Emerald relic. He doesn't need his bayonet. Wielding his AKM like a club, he smashes skulls and shatters bones adding the weight of his down-hill charge into every punch. He sees the orange tracers from Ilchenko's machine gun form a deadly arc in front of him, the gunner's mouth opened wide by his terrible battle cry. Skinner runs down the enemy, then falls, still firing his rifle as he hits the ground and rolls over to jump up again. The tiny group seems to break up with every man fighting for himself.

"Keep the line," Lazarov roars over the battle noise. "Keep the line!"

He sees a Stalker firing his AKSU-74 with one hand and a handgun from the other. A Stalker falls, either dead or wounded, and another grabs his shotgun. A soldier screams in agony. Another throws his body between his wounded comrade and the attacker, his rifle spitting a full burst as he screams like a desperate animal. He recognizes Lobov.

"They are on the run! Press on, press on!" Lazarov hears a Stalker shouting.

Where is Zlenko?

Lazarov at last sees him appearing way down the hillside and dashes after him, hitting an enemy and kicking the dushman's head as he falls to his knees, jumping over him, tearing the pistol from his hand and shooting another enemy in the chest just as the dushman was about to smash the sergeant's head in with his rifle. Other enemies immediately close in.

But otherwise the dushmans are routing as the storm closes in, firing as they cover their retreat.

The thunder in the sky sounds as if it is right over the battle, the sand swirling above the shaking earth, turning into mud under their heavy boots.

Someone hits his left arm. As he turns towards to his attacker, he sees no one.

Shit, I'm hit! He empties his pistol magazine blindly into the darkness. The sergeant is gone. The full fury of the storm is now only seconds away.

"Men!" Lazarov cries desperately. "Fall back! Fall back into position!"

They run uphill, jumping and trampling over dead and dying enemies. Lazarov hears someone repeating his order, *fall back, fall back!* It's not Zlenko's voice.

"Ilchenko," he shouts, "cover our rear! Give us covering fire!"

But the machine gun's rattle is nowhere to be heard.

Panting heavily, he jumps over the sandbags and looks back to see the last man getting back to the hilltop. He grabs a wounded Stalker's shoulder and drags him into the bunker, not so much entering it as falling inside. The door slams. A Stalker makes sure it is closed tight.

His men are lying on the ground and over each other's limbs, totally exhausted. He sees Bondarchuk and Kravchuk. But where is Zlenko? Where is Ilchenko?

"Where are the sergeant and the machine gunner?"

"I didn't see them coming back," the medic replies. His voice is trembling.

Lazarov closes his eyes in pain. "You're in charge while I'm gone," he whispers.

"What? You can't—"

The storm almost knocks Lazarov to the ground as he opens the bunker door. He can barely see, his Geiger counter doesn't just click anymore; it bursts into a high-pitched *tikitikitik*. Photons dance in the radiating dust storm that is painted in an eerie green by his night vision goggles, mingling with the stars he is already seeing due to the pain behind his eyes.

A flash of lightning illuminates a bulky figure on the ground. Bending against the wind, Lazarov kneels down and realizes there are actually two bodies, one of them still crawling up to the hilltop. He grasps both men and, with an effort requiring a level of energy that would be impossible without the Emerald's power, drags them to the bunker. He tears the door open and pushes the bodies inside. His knees are trembling, forcing him to lean against the wall.

"K.I. tablets!" he snarls. "Pump them full of potassium iodide!"

"I only have one leaf and that's for myself," he hears a voice say. It's the former Intruder in the *Flecktarn* jacket. The major aims his pistol at him and pulls the trigger.

Clack. The magazine was empty, but half a dozen hands now open the armored suits on the two soldiers and push syringes into their arms.

"It's all right, Major," Skinner says, taking the pistol from Lazarov's hand. "It's all right now."

Lazarov is too weak to resist. Every molecule of adrenalin has been spent. He sinks to the ground.

We did it, flashes into his mind before his sight fades away.

Bagram, 23 September 2014, 18:23:32 AFT

"Sammy! Where are you when I need you?"

This sounds familiar. But from where?

"Leave me be, I'm feelin' so high right now!"

I hear words but don't understand them.

"Are you having sex with a gun barrel again?"

That sounds like the Zone.

"I wish I could me dear, but there're no tubes of heavy artillery around!"

"Then try a blowgun! That's the only thing willing to give you a blowjob!"

A blowjob... must have been ages. There is no blowjob in Hell. Would that put me in Heaven? There's someone close. Maybe it's an angel. Damn, I need a blowjob.

"GROUCH AND SAMMY - CUT IT! I REMIND BOTH OF YOU THAT UNSOLICITED USE OF THE INTERCOM WILL BE PUNISHED!"

Damn. I am alive. And in Bagram of all places.

Lazarov tries to sit up but as soon as he moves his head seems about to explode with pain.

"Oh, our local celebrity has woken up!"

He turns his head towards the figure standing next to his bed in the makeshift first-aid room.

"Crow? What the..."

"Rest, Condor," the sniper replies with a reassuring smile. "With all the radiation you collected up there you should qualify for a new call sign. Perhaps Liquidator, like those chaps who cleaned up Chernobyl?"

"What about my men?"

"Those who made it through think you're some kind of a demigod. Maybe I should tell them how I picked you up with a jackal at your throat."

Lazarov tries to laugh but breaks out in a horrible cough.

"Just rest now. To be honest, I'm bloody happy to see you alive. First I was thinking you'd become a zombie, but when you started murmuring *blowjob* and *Zone* I thought you would actually make it."

"How come you are here?"

"I was late to join your show," Crow sighs. "God knows that I wanted to give you a helping hand. Anyway, I better tell your men that you regained consciousness. They pretty much admire you now. But don't count on any blowjobs."

Lazarov grins. Now he feels he has bandages all over his face. "Hey, Sergeant," he hears Crow's voice calling, "Sleeping Beauty is awake!"

After a minute, the sergeant storms into the room. He is in bad shape with anti-radiation cream smeared all over his face and a bandage covering his forehead, but this doesn't prevent him from cracking an ear-to-ear smile.

"Major Lazarov!" he cries out. "I am happy to…"

"What about Ilchenko?"

"He's fine and should be here in a minute."

"And the rest?"

"Two dead, three heavily wounded. The Stalkers lost six men altogether."

"Squirrel?"

"The lucky bastard made it through without a scratch."

"How did we get back here?"

"Bone's truck came when the storm was over. But… well, Major, I think I better let you rest now."

Lazarov doesn't mind the sergeant leaving with his wounds torturing him. "It's good that you're such a thin little kid… I would have needed a crane to lift two Ilchenkos. Now stop baby-sitting me and see to the troopers."

Zlenko laughs as he leaves the infirmary. Closing his sore eyes, Lazarov doesn't see Crow pulling his silenced Glock from its holster.

Seconds later, a loud *bang* pierces into his aching head. Then he feels more pain all over his body.

Encrypted digital VOP transmission. New Zone, 23 September 2014, 18:50:33 AFT

#Did you get the shipment?#

#Positive. Good job. But he is still alive.#

#Forget him. Jerk off on those damned exos or do whatever you want. What the fuck do you expect me to do anyway? Shoot him myself?#

#Positive. You are running out of options. He is becoming troublesome.#

#Actually, you bastards have a point...[sharp, unidentified noise] Hey, wait... #

#Come again?#

#[sharp, unidentified noise continues]#

#Someone has sounded the alarm. Breaking contact.#

#I have difficulties in hearing you. Repeat...#

#[unidentified human voice]We have a man down! Man down in the base!#

#I have no copy on you. Check your transmission.#

#[another unidentified human voice] Everyone, to the infirmary! Now!#

#[static noise]#

#[static noise]#

25 September 2014, 16:45:27 AFT

"It was a flesh wound, but try not to exert your left arm too much... As your doctor, I forbid you from firing any pump-action shotgun for at least two weeks. Otherwise, you're in surprisingly good condition."

Placebo motions for Lazarov to stand. He does so, stretching his arms and back.

"Two days in bed with a flesh wound and a little radiation... not good," he says. "Am I feeling my age?"

"That's the best thing one can feel because it means one is still alive. You've had a close shave. Now, take care and stay healthy..."

The medic shuffles to the next bed where another wounded Stalker lies and the major freshens himself up from the bucket of water standing in the corner of the infirmary, enjoying the sensation of splashing cold water to his sweaty face. He can barely wait to get out of the metal container.

The sun hurts Lazarov's eyes as he steps out of the infirmary. A paratrooper guards the entrance. Seeing Lazarov appear, he stands to attention and salutes. It is one of the wounded they left behind to recover, which he obviously did well enough despite the bandage on his arm.

"As you were, Stepashin," Lazarov says after a brief glance at the soldier's name tag. "What's all this security about?"

The paratrooper gives him a baffled look. "Sir, you were probably unconscious. A Stalker tried to kill you. One of Bone's guards interrupted him. The Stalker shot him and disappeared in the fray."

"A Stalker?"

"Yes, sir. That bastard who was sitting at your bed. Probably he was waiting for the right moment."

That's odd. Why would Crow want to kill me?

"Where are the others? I'll need to talk to the sergeant."

153

"Three are still in the infirmary. Sergeant Zlenko was here earlier. He and the others have set up camp in that shack, just behind you."

"All right... I suppose you were guarding me?"

"Yes, sir. On Sergeant Zlenko's orders."

"Your watch is over."

"As ordered, sir," the paratrooper replies, shouldering his rifle with a relieved grin.

Still weak and light-headed from two days of lying around, Lazarov is on his way toward the paratrooper camp when Grouch's voice sounds from the loudspeaker.

"Sammy! Drag your sorry ass over here."

"Sorry me dear, I can't! I'm trying to find out why me new hash pipe ain't working!"

"Maybe before lighting it up you should remove your gas mask first?"

"You don't get it, do you? Me gas mask *is* me new pipe!"

"SAMMY! LET ME REMIND YOU THAT ANY MODIFICATION OF EQUIPMENT TO FACILITATE DRUG CONSUMPTION WILL BE PUNISHED!" Captain Bone's voice booms.

"I hear you, Captain, I hear you! What's wrong about me finding a new meaning for *'integrated breathing system'*?"

Bone's voice returns on the intercom, but this time it is not directed at the eccentric trader.

"Major! I am delighted to hear you're on your feet again. Come over here. Let's have a chat."

What the hell could Bone want from me?

Lazarov feels uneasy as he enters the Captain's fortified compound. Judged by the tower overshadowing the half-ruined building, it might have been the control center of the air base once upon a time. The guards salute and let him in, and he is about to open the door when one of them bars his way.

"You can't go there."

"I'm here to see Bone."

"The Captain's room is in the tower. Take the stairs."

Lazarov shrugs him off and climbs up the stairs to the former air traffic control room, from where the whole base can be seen. Encircled by the wall of containers, Bone's headquarters are at the center of the perimeter. Not far from here, a dilapidated transport airplane is collecting dust and rust. Wires run from its tail to the central building where the generators should be. Makeshift shacks and tents litter the cracked concrete, sitting among all kinds of war debris, from gutted military vehicles to helicopter wrecks. Stalkers with an affection for personal hygiene have set up a field shower by attaching a plastic water tank to the trunks of a metal structure that might have been a radio relay tower once upon a time. All looks peaceful except for the armed Stalkers keeping watch in the fortified positions, the look-out posts along the container wall and a watchtower where a sniper scans the horizon through his binoculars.

The commander is standing in front of a huge, detailed map of the area. He is wearing his armored suit with the helmet on.

Does he ever wash himself? comes to the major's mind. The sight of the field shower made him realize how much he desires a long, refreshing bath himself.

"You are feeling better, Major? Congratulations on a battle well fought. Now that you have proven yourself, I'll let you stay for a few days. A deal is a deal. But that's enough idle talk. I want you to do something for me."

Lazarov stares at him curiously, hoping that his anxiety is not too visible.

"Here," Bone says, pointing at a position on the map that lies to the north-west of Bagram, "is the location of a mercenary base. They constantly harass the Stalkers moving between Bagram and the small Stalker base at Ghorband, here. I want you to find and eliminate the mercs."

"I'll need to check on my men first."

"No need for that. I want you to do it alone, because your men are needed here."

"They are still under my command, Captain, not yours."

"Those cocksucker mercenaries have become very active recently. I need your men to help us defending the base, should we be attacked. You do this mission for me and leave your men here, or I'll have you all kicked out of Bagram. Period."

Lazarov has to admit that no matter how arrogantly presented, Bone's idea is not entirely unreasonable. "I suppose that only leaves me with two choices... to do it or to do it, right?"

"Exactly, Major," Bone nods. "At least your wounded men can recuperate while you are gone."

"That's very thoughtful of you. By the way... now that we defended the Outpost we can have our exoskeletons back, I suppose?"

"Well... I'm afraid, that's not the case." The helmet might hide Bone's face but his gestures reveal embarrassment. "Your suits were stolen from our armory."

Hearing this, all his suppressed anger is released into Lazarov's face. "Stolen? What the hell are you talking about?"

"Yes, it's... shameful. I have already initiated an investigation but... In any case, if Sammy is involved in this, I'll shoot him myself. That's a promise."

"Why on earth would he steal them?"

"Do you know how much such a suit costs, Major?"

"No but—"

"It's about eighty years of your salary. Yes! People turned into scoundrels for a fraction of that... Anyway, go talk to that no-good anarchist. And we are clear about those mercs, aren't we?"

"Yes," Lazarov reluctantly replies. "I'll see what I can do."

Leaving Bone's compound, Lazarov runs into Ilchenko and the sergeant. The machine gunner's nose is bandaged and his face blue from multiple bruises, but that does not prevent him from giving Lazarov a bearish hug. Zlenko acts more reserved, though equally glad to see his officer on his feet again, and it's Lazarov's turn to hug the young sergeant.

"What happened to your nose, Ilchenko?"

"That damned Stalker who wanted to kill you knocked me out."

"How come? One would need a sledgehammer to knock you out."

"Shame on me, Major. That piece of shit was a damned quick little son of a bitch," Ilchenko replies, embarrassed. "But if I ever see him again I'll break his neck. I swear it!"

"If you get close enough to him, that is."

"What do you mean?"

"Never mind. What about the squad, Sergeant Zlenko?"

"Privates Nakhimov and Obukov are still in the infirmary. Bondarchuk too. He got a nasty stab in the stomach during our charge. We had two KIAs."

"*Damn!*" A curse escapes Lazarov's lips. "I hope no one was left behind."

"No, sir. They're both here, Kamensky and Vasilyev."

Zlenko points toward two crosses close to the container wall, each made up of a rifle stuck into the sandy ground with a helmet on top. The boots of the fallen soldiers stand at attention beside them.

Lazarov bows his head. "Did Skinner make it?"

"Yes, but he didn't stay. He went on to a place called... what was it, Ilch?"

"Ghorband, Sarge. Actually, as soon as he got off the truck he wanted to kill the Captain but the guards kicked him out."

"Pity he didn't succeed," Lazarov grumbles, looking at the graves. "Two men. What a goddamned waste. And I suppose there's no priest among the Stalkers."

"We said a prayer and let off a rifle salvo for an amen."

"Proper funeral for our paratroopers." Lazarov sighs. "Well, then... let's have a toast on their memory. How's that famous Stalker bar?"

"We haven't checked it out yet."

"How so?" Lazarov is surprised.

"We held off on the toast until you were on your feet again."

"Well, I am... and your patience is appreciated, Viktor. It must have been a sacrifice second only to dying."

"Honestly? It was hard."

"Let's go. Where's Stepashin?"

"Last time I saw him he was taking a shower. I'll go and get him."

"Wait. On second thoughts I'm dying for a shower myself."

A few minutes later, refreshed and cleaned up, the soldiers make their way to the wrecked Antonov. Ripped off its landing gear long ago, two rusty tank hulls balance out the fuselage. It is covered with graffiti but the ghost of a single red star is still visible on the tail. The ramp below the tail gunner's compartment is lowered. Warm orange light permeates from inside, making the interior look cozy and inviting in the approaching dusk.

"I hope that Sammy character wasn't lying about the chilled vodka," Ilchenko mutters.

"There's only one way to find out. Inside, everyone!"

The order is eagerly obeyed: walking up the ramp, the narrow confines of the airplane reveal a den covered by carpets, cushions and pallets used for tables, some on the metal floor, others placed on wooden crates still bearing the word USAID on their age-worn sides. Under the humming ventilators, the jingle of vodka glasses blends in with a

Stalker's attempt at an old song on his guitar, the tune not quite matching the muted beats of reggae from the music player, but not jarring too bad either. Stalkers sit or lie around, some of them smoking on hookah pipes. Thick clouds of smoke float in the dim light of candles and petroleum lamps, and Lazarov detects the heady smell of marijuana too. The rusty metal of the fuselage has graffiti painted all over it.

За матер зону, за отца мутантов и за бутылку водки -
ЗОНА
Dzsíesszí monnyonle.
Jeg kneppede en mutant og jeg var vild med det.
J'ai pas le gout de parler avec cette arme pointer sur moi.
Hei suomilauta tälle seinälle! Ainoa tyyppi Venäjällä joka
käyttää kuvalautaa.
I ♥ Paravin.
Implikoi olevansa ainoa suomalainen.

At the other end of the fuselage, behind a bar made from crude battens, the barkeeper waves his hand holding a thick, hand-rolled cigarette.

"Welcome to the Antonov! She's gonna take you real high!" He protracts the word *real,* suggesting means for uplifting spirits the major has never been fond of.

"Sammy," he says, "don't even think about offering *bhango* to my men. But if you have a chilled *pollitra[1]* – spill it!"

"Yo, dude!" Sammy shouts cheerfully. "If no soft smoke, then a hard drink! Here you go. At me place, every hour is happy hour!"

Lazarov raises his dewy vodka glass. "To our fallen comrades!"

His soldiers repeat the toast and clink their glasses.

---

[1] A normal vodka shot is referred to as *sto gram* (literally: 100 grams). A *pollitra* – half liter - means more serious business.

"Oups…," Sammy retorts in embarrassment and lowers his tone. "Okay, maybe this one is not a happy hour… sorry, brothers! This round is on the house."

To the major, always fond of good vodka, the spirit tastes as if it had been watered down but the soldiers don't seem to care. Lazarov is about to announce another toast when his palmtop signals a new message.

Condor, I had to leave the base in a hurry. Sorry for your trooper's broken nose. There's a Stalker den at Ghorband. Get some sniper gear and visit me there ASAP. And watch your back in Bagram! Crow.

Lazarov frowns.

I wish that elusive son of a bitch had told me what this is about. Could this be a trap? I still don't get why Crow would be after me.

He listens to his soldiers' chatter, at first heavy-hearted as they remember their fallen squad mates but soon growing cheerful with the drink washing away their somber mood. Ilchenko is already regaling them with anecdotes about a prostitute and the 'special treatment' he'd ended up receiving from Lobov, but Lazarov is too lost in his own thoughts to follow the story.

"Hey Sammy," he says bending over the bar and continuing in a whisper. "Do you have any exoskeletons for sale? Or anyone else in Bagram?"

The barkeep recoils and almost lets the joint fall from his lips.

"What? Exos? Hell, no!"

"Why so jumpy? You look as if I asked you to kiss a upyr."

"Bro, ask me for a crow bar, a 10 millimeter pulse rifle, a golden Kalashnikov, a Gatling laser — any weapon made or not and I'll get it for you. But exoskeletons… I don't deal in that stuff here, nor does anyone else."

Lazarov carefully studies his face. "All right, never mind… It's actually something long and silent I need."

"Oh yeah, now we talk business!" Sammy says with huge relief, unlocking a huge metal cabinet. Inside, a dozen assault rifles and pistols are arranged in a weapon rack.

"Is that all you've got?" Lazarov asks looking down the rather motley stash of weapons.

"Come on, man, I have the whole Kalashnikov family here. Look at this AK47 in pristine condition. Want something more up to date? Here's an AKM. Okay, I see you already have one, but what about this AMD-65? Very practical with low recoil! I also have a Khyber Pass-copy Lee-Enfield. Not interested?"

"I need something like an AS Val with a PSO scope. A Vintorez would also do."

"It's so good to have at last one customer who knows what he wants! The only better thing than that is a seller who actually has that stuff... imagine, last week a Stalker comes to me shop and says, 'I want a Desert Eagle.' I show him me collection and he says—"

"I haven't got all day, you know?"

"You're late for a date? Come on, me dear, she'll have to wait. It's men talking guns now! But the problem is, I don't have any Vals. You know, last time you could get such weapons here was back in the Eighties, and even then only from the hands of a dead Spetsnaz. No offense, okay? Now it's from the hands of a dead Stalker expert... which means that even if I had such a weapon, let's say a Vintorez, it would be very, very expensive!"

Lazarov smiles. He already knows where the trader's story is going. "Do I smell a dead Stalker expert in your den?"

"He had that 'been there, done that' look all over his scarred face," Sammy replies with an ear to ear grin. "Then he went to a place he'd never been before and did something stupid: got too close to a Geyser at Hellgate. You know, the trap that can boil you. Must have been painful."

"I guess so, and I also guess that he had a Vintorez on him that miraculously found its way into your stock."

"Something like that. But first things first: do you have enough money? I accept dollars, euros, British pounds, rubles and of course relics. Why, what did you expect, me dear? Paying in bullets or bottle caps? I have no use for that, you see?"

"I do have money. Rubles and dollars."

"Excellent!" Sammy takes a long bundle from under the bar. "Ain't this a beautiful little baby? You pay the ridiculously low price of 75000 rubles or 2500 dollars for a 2-to-10 pancreatic scope with a 52 millimeters objective —"

"What?!"

" — with a nice Vintorez attached to it. And if you buy it in package with an AMD-65, I'll give you a set of scope cleaning tissues for free!"

"Are you kidding?"

"Of course! You think I'd give you the scope cleaning tissues for free, huh? But the tungsten-cored SP-6 ammo that I have on sale is no joke and one full magazine is already included in the price! Make up your mind! This Vintorez is the first and last thing a Spetsnaz like you needs!"

"I'm not convinced," the major says, studying the weapon. It's in dreadful condition and even if he made the trader lower his price, it would still take the better part of the money given to him to buy information. "It looks as if a herd of mutant elephants has trampled on it."

"Chill out, brother! What do you think we have Grouch for? He will only need to replace the trigger and the loading mechanism and maybe straighten the barrel but you'll get yourself a discount, don't worry."

Seeing the rare, silenced automatic rifle that performs equally well as a mid-range sniper weapon and at close quarters, Lazarov tries to fight the temptation but fails.

"What about 45000 rubles for the Vintorez with three magazines and three more boxes of ammo?"

"You wanna ruin me? Even an airsoft version costs 700 dollars and we're talking about the real stuff here! Sixty thousand rubles."

"What if I don't make a big fuss about you watering down your vodka, and you give it to me for forty thousand? Come on, don't make such a face. I'll throw my AKM into the deal."

"You're really a pushy one, you know that? Now take it before me heart breaks!"

Lazarov puts the money and his assault rifle on the table and happily takes the Vintorez, hoping that he won't regret the deal.

"Where is Grouch's workshop?"

"In an old Chinook chopper close to Bone's quarters. You know, he always wants to compete but his place is much smaller and shorter than mine."

"I'll go and check him out. This rifle badly needs an overhaul."

"There's an itsy-witsy little problem," Sammy replies scratching his head. "Grouch is... how to say... out of mood nowadays. His pet is missing."

"His — *pet?*"

"A young Stalker named Mac, actually. He used to run errands for Grouch. Since he left, Grouch is more useless than ever."

"I'll ask him about that. Don't let my boys get too wasted, all right?"

"No problem, man! But maybe *you* want another drink?"

"Not now. And Sammy — you forgot to give me the ammo."

20:14:53 AFT

Sammy was right... Grouch's hovel looks barely more than an ordinary wreck.

163

Lazarov bangs on the wooden plate covering the wreck's hatch with his fist but no one answers. He walks around the chopper and knocks again. Still no reply. Eventually, he starts kicking the wreck with his boots. At last a drunk voice comes from inside.

"Go away."

"Hey Grouch! A customer is here!"

"I said, go away!"

"I just need you for a minute!"

"I don't care what you broke. Go away."

"I need to talk to you."

"Damned rookies. You can't leave an old man alone…"

The wooden plate covering the helicopter's hatch swings open and a graying head appears. The wrinkled eyes look tired.

"Oh, it's you… sorry. I thought it's just another lad wanting an upgrade for his shotgun… come inside."

Empty vodka bottles litter the chopper's interior where a single petroleum lamp provides the only light. All kinds of tools and weapon parts lie around the floor. A work bench occupies the place where the cockpit once was although, judging by the dust on it, the technician hasn't done any work at it for a long time.

"Nice place you have," Lazarov says looking around. "How's life, Grouch?"

"Don't even ask. How should it be in this fly-infested fake Wild-West pile of rusty junk? Now tell me what you want."

"I have a Vintorez to upgrade."

Grouch rolls his eyes in frustration. "I knew it! Sorry but I'm not doing any weapon upgrades right now."

"How come? I heard you're missing your apprentice but a Vintorez is not something you couldn't deal with on your own."

Grouch sits down on his mattress and picks up a vodka bottle from the metal floor. Seeing it empty, he angrily throws it down again. "It all started back in Black Defile. I always worked alone. Then, one day, a young Stalker comes. Says he wants to learn the trade. I tell him, business is slow and I have no money to pay him. No problem, he says, pay me by upgrading my FN-2000."

"That's a pretty hardcore weapon for a rookie."

"Yes, but I didn't ask him where he got it from. It's none of my business. But you know how it goes... I had a look at it and first changed the scope. Then I disassembled the trigger mechanism just to admire its precision. It was such a pleasure after all the busted Kalashnikovs that the Stalkers keep bringing to me. I installed a new trigger, a synthetic bolt seal and a stronger return spring to reduce recoil. Then I adjusted the spring trajectory and... anyway, one thing led to the other and in the morning I had an already great weapon turned into something awesome."

"Let me guess—then the Stalker got hold of your masterpiece and disappeared."

"Well, not exactly. We arrived here together. Mac was a good kid, helping me out with things like test firing the weapons... my eyes are not as good as they used to be, you know? All went fine until one morning he said he'd grown bored of Bagram and wanted adventure. Then he disappeared into the wilderness to hunt relics and didn't return."

"That's tragic and all, but what about this Vintorez?"

Grouch doesn't even look at the weapon. "It could use a roll back moderator with a stop drive to make it more precise over medium distances... you know those silenced rifles are useless over 400 meters or so. Too bad I'm done with weapons and all that shit. I even sold my own Dragunov to a Stalker. You know what? I have a little money saved up and will use it to go home."

"But—"

"No 'but' and no pneumatic compensator on your rifle's butt. Even if I was willing, it would cost you a fortune."

"You'd let your business be ruined just because your apprentice ran away?"

Grouch buries his face in his hands.

"You don't get it, do you? For a decade I repaired and upgraded weapons here and in the Old Zone. And as soon as all the rookies got improved rifles in their hands they thought themselves of being tough relic hunters, wanting to get rich and usually died trying. It was like selling drugs. This time, here was this kid and I told myself, 'I'll teach him the trade to keep him away from all that faction war, relic hunting, mutant-shooting nonsense'. I failed. Damn it, he was so young, he couldn't have purchased vodka at Sammy's if he got asked for his ID card!"

"Anyway, I need that upgrade and repairs on my soldiers' gear too," Lazarov says. "I still have a few men left despite burying two of them who died to protect this place, you know? Their graves could also use an upgrade."

"All right, all right... You help me out and I help you out. Get that foolish kid back to me and safety. In exchange, you'll get the upgrades and repairs. I might even give you Beretta I used to experiment with. Just find him."

"Upgrades and repairs for free, if I get him back alive."

"I can't believe I'm haggling over this."

"No need for belief when it comes to facts. Any idea where Mac went?"

"If he was chasing those relics he was after, try the old textile factory to the north-west. Let me see your palmtop... here. Squirrel can lead you there. He knows all the shortcuts through the Shamali Plains."

"We have a deal then."

Lazarov is about to climb out though the hatch when he remembers something else. He pulls out the mobile phone he had found in the ambushed patrol car and hands it to Grouch.

"While I'm gone, could you check if there's any data left in this?"

The mechanic frowns as he studies the device. "Where did you find this trash?"

"In a wreck to the north. I'm just curious about it."

"I'll see what I can do," Grouch replies with a shrug.

"Thanks. But by the way… what about adding the thermal imaging enhancement as advance payment?"

"Poidi proch, Stalker!"

"I'm leaving, I'm leaving… see you soon, Grouch!"

21:10:39 AFT

The sun sets slowly over the mountains. To get rid of the stiffness that two days of idleness has left in his limbs, Lazarov strolls down to the base and watches the Stalkers lighting up the campfires for the night. He spots Zlenko at one of the lookout posts on the container wall.

Climbing up the ladder, he joins the sergeant who is busily discussing something with two Stalkers. Seeing him approaching, Zlenko salutes.

"Sir!"

"As you were," Lazarov casually replies and sits down on the sandbags. "What are you doing here? Did Sammy run out of vodka?"

The sergeant shrugs. "I've heard the troopers' jokes more than once before. And all that marijuana smell… it's nauseating."

"You're not into that stuff? That's good."

"I've played in a rock band. Enough is enough," Zlenko says, smiling. "Anyway, the Stalkers were debating whether the M or the AK family are the better. I argued for the Kalashnikov. What's your opinion?"

"My opinion is that the brothers will be discussing this for a long while. Come along Viktor, I wanted to talk to you alone anyway."

Walking away from the lookout, Zlenko takes a pack of cigarettes from his vest and offers one to Lazarov who, looking over to the dark mountains and the glowing red anomaly in the far forest beyond the sandy plain where the wind swirls up small clouds of dust, and listening to a Stalker tuning his guitar, he feels in the mood to smoke.

"Thanks. Now tell me about this mess with the dead guard and that loner."

Zlenko exhales the smoke before starting. "That's a strange story—" he begins, then breaks off as the Stalker finishes tuning up and begins to sing.

"I happened to be walking around
And I hurt two people by chance,
They took me to militia grounds
Where I saw her and broke down at once."

"Oh no, please no," Zlenko moans, burying his face into his hands. "It's Ilchenko's favorite song."

"I knew not what on earth she was doing there,
She was probably getting a pass.
She was beautiful, lovely and fair...
I decided to search out the lass.

I just followed her, walking behind her,
She wouldn't talk to a bully, I thought.
Then I made up my mind to invite her
To the nearest restaurant. Why not?"

Lazarov grins at the sergeant. "Hey Viktor! If a Vysotsky song makes you cry, I'll get you demoted!"

"As we walked people smiled at my pretty one,
I was furious, my mind on the blink!
I just smote the face of a weird man
'Cause he dared to give her a wink.

She found the caviar delicious,
And I didn't grudge the expense,

I ordered smash hits to musicians,
And the last tune they played was 'The Cranes'.

I made promises, showing my feeling,
I repeated one thing the whole night:
'For five days I haven't been stealing,
Believe me, my love at first sight.'"

"It's not the song, Major, it's how badly the Stalker's playing it. Permission to shoot him?"

"Denied."

"I said that my life had been ruined,
Blew my nose and wiped tears from my eyes,
And she said: 'I believe you, yours truly,
You can take me at a reasonable price.'

I slapped her on the face in despair,
I was boiling like crazy inside.
Now I knew what she really was doing there,
At the militia, my love at first sight."

"*Klass,*" a Stalker shouts as the song finishes. "Hey soldier boys, want some vodka? We can trade you some! One bottle for a medal!" The Stalkers laugh.

"Do you mind if I teach them some manners?" Zlenko asks Lazarov. "I mean, with a guitar."

"Permission absolutely granted."

The sergeant joins the Stalkers at the campfire. "Hey, big mouth! Give me that sad excuse of a guitar," Zlenko demands, sitting down at the campfire. The Stalker hands the instrument over and Zlenko plucks the strings experimentally before starting to play. His fingers, chafed and dirty from gun grease, move on the strings with astonishing grace. Then he starts singing:

"She's got a smile that it seems to me
Reminds me of childhood memories
Where everything was as fresh as the bright blue sky…"

"Here, take this vodka, just shut up," the Stalker says. "You play it well but that song makes me sad."

"Yeah, me too," another adds. "It reminds me of a girl I used to bang in high school. How blonde she was, oh God! Like a fairy queen!"

"You lie, Tolik. How would a blonde get into high school?" the third one asks grinning.

"Forget the school," says the failed guitar player. "What the hell was she doing out of bed?" They burst into drunken laughter as the two soldiers walk away.

"I have to admit, that was the best song I heard in a long time," Lazarov says.

"Did you like it? I screwed a chord or two, but… damn, how I wish I could have a real guitar to play on for a change!"

"It was fine. But enough pleasure for today. There's something I need you to do for me."

"Whatever you ask, *komandir*."

"Don't be too eager because you will not like it, son. I want you to stay put here in Bagram while I recon something. It's pretty far away, so I might be away for a few days."

"Indeed I don't like it."

"Your objection is duly noted. The truth is, I don't trust this place. I don't want to take the few remaining men with me and leave the wounded at Bone's mercy. You will stay here, watch over the men and be my eyes and ears while I'm gone."

"Understood."

"I'll take Ilchenko along. He'll come in handy with the PKM."

"Where are you going?"

"There's something to be done for repaired weapons' sake. When I'm done with that, there's one more obstacle that'll need removing from our path to the scientists."

Frowning, Zlenko lights up another cigarette. "Needle might be in danger and we can't just sit around here."

"I get your point, Viktor, but our destination is in the middle of hostile territory. The mercs, commandos or whatever they are—they aren't even the worst. If only half of what I've heard about the Tribe is true, there's big trouble ahead."

"Yeah, I heard some weird rumors from the Stalkers." Zlenko bows his head. "It seems that even mentioning the Tribe scares the shit out of them."

"You see? How are we supposed to fight our way through with me, you and only two other soldiers left capable of fighting? I hope I can at least remove the lesser obstacle from our path."

"I guess we have no good options here. As ordered, then. I'll watch the backs of the troopers."

"That's the spirit. Talking about spirits, didn't that Stalker give you a bottle of vodka?"

Zlenko smiles. "He did. Here you go."

"Cheers—here's to a good raid!"

Encrypted VOP transmission between the Exclusion Zone and Central Afghanistan, 26 September 2014, 06:41:08 AFT

#Eagle Eye, this is Diver, do you copy?#
#This is Eagle Eye on Sierra Bravo. Report.#
I have acquired the transport coordinates. Need reinforcements to interdict the transport.#
#Positive. A detachment will be dispatched. You will get further instructions at the next transmission time.#
#Roger.#
#Diver, be advised that we picked up several messages between the central and eastern areas. Watch your back.#
#Affirmative. A friendly element might be involved in further developments. I suggest to contact Kilo and keep them on stand-by.#
#Are you sure about sharing this intel with Kilo, Diver?#
#Positive. It is us who adapt to the situation here, not the other way around.#
#Affirmative. Kilo One will be informed. Eagle Eye out.#
#Understood. Diver out.#

"I didn't hide! I swear it on my mother's life, may she rest in peace," Squirrel says trying to blow the dust from a battered harmonica. "When the soldier manning the grenade launcher was shot, I got really, really angry. Had the sergeant not ordered us to charge them, I would have run down the freaks on my own, I swear it!"

"I'm sure they were spared a dreadful fate, Squirrel." Ilchenko gives the guide a skeptical look while he finishes cleaning his machine gun. "Am I not right, Major?"

"Squirrel is a killer, he's just hiding it."

"Exactly my thought, sir," Ilchenko sarcastically replies and takes a bite of the canned meat he's having for breakfast. His face contorts in disgust. "Do you think I could use this as gun grease? It tastes like that anyway. Jesus, how can you Stalkers live on this?"

Squirrel blows the harmonica but a discordant shriek is the only sound the instrument makes. Grimacing, he puts it back to his pocket. "I wish I had an MP3-player so that I don't have to listen to your moaning all the time," he says. "You know what? Don't have any food for two days and then you will love it. You could lose a few kilograms anyway."

"Come on, Squirrel. I am from Russia. I have a big soul and a big soul has big appetite. Why do you have such a shitty call sign, anyway? Squirrel... why not Hamster or Guinea Pig or Jerbil?"

"Because my political views are Red, I'm lightning-quick at picking up relics and have a long, big tail if you know what I mean."

"Is it bushy too?"

"Why so interested? I didn't take you for a *gomik*."

Lazarov yawns. He is tired after their night's march through the forest. Now the first light of dawn casts beams through the high trees, making the woods appear less threatening. Sitting against the wall of the derelict farm where they halted for a short break, he enjoys the simple pleasure of feeling the cool morning breeze blowing between his toes as he cleans his boots with a damp tissue.

"Did you hear that, Major? This rodent just called me a *gomik!*"

"And what do you expect me to do about it, Private? Killing him?"

"Oh no, *komandir!* Just looking the other way when I shoot him myself!"

"Now listen up, guys... On my last mission in the Old Zone, I had a technician with a welding torch with me. I wish he were here now to weld your mouths shut!" Lazarov says shaking his head. "You two are worse than Grouch and Sammy. So, Squirrel, instead of fucking with someone who is three times your size, you better tell me about that place called Hellgate we're heading to."

"It's a shortcut to the plateau where the factory is," Squirrel explains. "There's a road leading directly up, but it goes through an abandoned village infested with mutants. Sometimes dushmans also show up to say hello. Compared to that, this shortcut is a stroll in the park. In three or four hours, we should reach a perfectly nice Stalker camp at Hellgate."

"If it's such a perfectly nice place, why is it called Hellgate?"

"Oh... nothing, really. Just a few Burners and Geysers here and there, you know."

"Hey, rodent," Ilchenko butts in. "Why didn't you leave that RPG at Bagram? It was good loot but my back's aching just from looking at it."

"Was I supposed to leave it on that dead dushman at the Outpost? He won't need it anymore. And what if we run into a tank?"

"A tank? Here?" Ilchenko laughs. "You can't be serious."

"A bear then, would that be better? I want to tell all my buddies how Squirrel the Brave saved the asses of two military guys with one single RPG shot."

"I'll look forward to seeing that."

"If you want to know, back in the Old Zone—when I was still with the Intruders—we did it the other way round. The process was the same, except it was not about saving."

"Go ahead and make my day, rodent."

"Peace, man! Don't point that shooter at me. What are you compensating for with that machine gun, anyway?"

Meanwhile, Lazarov has finished cleaning his boots. "If you're done with the banter, let's move on."

"Let's," Ilchenko says standing to his feet. "Damn, how I miss those choppers! I hate walking."

He kicks the half-empty can, still holding the remains of his breakfast, into a bush.

"Don't do that," Squirrel says, looking around nervously. "The woods have ears."

"And the fields have eyes," Ilchenko murmurs. "Heard that before."

"Stop! Squirrel is right. Get down!"

Maybe it is Lazarov's tired eyes playing tricks on him, but for a moment he was sure he'd spotted a pair of eyes watching them from the bushes. They'd disappeared, but the movement of the branches and a barely audible crackle on the ground tells him that someone, or something, was definitely watching them.

"What was that, *komandir*?"

Crouching, Ilchenko aims his PKM and slowly scans the ruins.

"Squirrel, are there any upyrs here?"

The guide pales. "Oh shit! Did you see one?"

"How could I? They can make themselves invisible!"

"We were not supposed to run into them before Hellgate!"

"Holy Mother of Jesus Christ," Ilchenko exclaims. "It's just a few traps there, you said!"

"Ilchenko, take point. Squirrel, stay on my side and keep an eye on our rear."

The woods become sparse as they slowly approach the steep descent to the plateau. They proceed cautiously, moving from cover to cover. After fifty meters, Lazarov signals a halt.

"Wait," he murmurs, scanning the area through his binoculars. "Wait... I see a huge pack of jackals."

"Are they moving in our direction?" Squirrel whispers.

"I don't think they've detected us yet." Lazarov zooms in the optics to have a closer look at the mutants. "Look at that... they're fighting over something."

"Let's move on quietly and avoid them."

Lazarov glances over the mutants one last time, but just as he's about to lower the binoculars he spots something sinister.

"What the hell?" he whispers, adjusting the zoom.

"What is it, boss?"

"I'm not sure."

Something long and thin reaches out from behind a group of dried-out, lifeless trees. Switching to the highest magnification, he realizes that what he took for a long, straight branch of a tree is actually the rotor blade of a helicopter. Behind it, a dozen jackals fight each other. The biggest mutant chases down a smaller one and delivers a vicious bite. The small jackal drops something and scurries away. Lazarov focuses on the pack leader as it grabs the small mutant's prize from the ground and scowls when he recognizes it as a human arm.

"I'll be damned... they're fighting over a body. But that's not all."

The major gives the binoculars to Squirrel and points to the rotor blades. Immediately, a greedy smile widens on the Stalker guide's face.

"Rotor blades! And where there are rotor blades, there's a chopper crash site, and where there's a crash site, there's loot!"

"Give me that RPG, Squirrel."

"Let me blast them, man! Please!"

"I said: give me that RPG, Squirrel."

"Please, please, please let me fire the RPG!"

"All right, all right, but you better remove that protective cap from the warhead before you shoot... Ilchenko, show him how to do that. And now, Rambo, you don't want to miss the mutants. Wait until they are bunched up. Get your machine gun ready. After the grenade hits them, open fire and try to hit as many of them as you can. If we screw it and they come running at us... that won't be nice. Are we set?" His companions nod. "Don't screw this up, Stalker. Wait for my command."

Lazarov now sees the jackals gather around a corpse, half dug out from a shallow grave.

"*Gospodi*," he mutters when he sees what's left of the body.

"What is it?"

"I saw a— but no. That cannot be. I refuse to believe it."

At the moment when the most jackals gather over the grave, Lazarov gives Squirrel a signal. The projectile leaves the launcher with an ear-piercing *whoosh*. The pack leader tosses its head but by the time it realizes the danger it is too late; the grenade hits the pack and explodes in a sheet of orange flame. In the same second, Ilchenko's machine gun starts barking as he fires a long salvo into the strewn mass of wounded and half-dead mutants.

The pack leader, still alive, emits a vengeful howl and starts running toward them at speed despite having had one of its legs torn off by the explosion and the huge wound gouged into its side. Even so, the distance is so great that Lazarov can take a steady aim with his Vintorez. He fires a short burst and the mutant falls, its momentum still carrying it a meter closer to the three men, as if its predatory instinct drove it on even after life had departed.

Wish I had this rifle on the Shalang Pass when I needed it most, Lazarov thinks with a bitter smile.

"Good job," he tells his companions. "Let's have a look at that wreck. Keep your eyes peeled."

Getting closer, Lazarov recognizes the wreck by its tail as a Mi-24. With Afghanistan full of war debris the sight does not surprise him, at least not at first. However, as they get close enough to see more of the wreck between the sparse bushes, the major gives a ghastly cry.

"Damn! This was one of ours!"

Ilchenko and Squirrel turn their heads to look. The Russian ensign is clearly visible on the bullet-riddled fuselage.

"Where's that rotten stench coming from?"

The enthusiasm has disappeared from Squirrel's face. Indeed, the smell is so foul, it forces him to put his gas mask on.

Lazarov follows suit before carefully studying the wreck. It looks to him as if the helicopter was intact when it landed and had been attacked on the ground. Lazarov and Ilchenko step to the hatch.

"Looks like the hatch was blown open, sir."

"And judging by the mess inside, someone tossed grenades into the compartment."

Hundreds of cartridge cases lie in blackened pools of dry blood and Lazarov finds a few bloody bandages and empty medikits, but there's no sign of any bodies. Stepping out, he finds the pilots' hatches open.

"Maybe the crew made it through?"

Ilchenko looks around as if expecting surviving troopers to appear from the bushes, but Squirrel shatters any optimism.

"Major... Ilch... you better come and have a look at what I found."

A few steps away from the chopper's wreck, close to where the mutants were fighting, the grenade has blasted a shallow crater into the ground and unearthed two bodies. By the missing parts and advanced state of decay, Lazarov recognizes the corpse dug up by the jackals. Of the other, only the back and legs are visible but the sight of the half-decomposed flesh is enough to make Squirrel retch. The bodies are clad in nothing but cotton leggings and the army-issue T-shirts with blue and white stripes.

"Where is their kit?" Lazarov inquires, combating his nausea. "And who buried them?"

"Maybe surviving comrades."

"Ilchenko, give me your shovel."

"Are you sure about this, sir?"

"I'm sure that you want to put your gas mask on, soldier."

Lazarov opens the foldable shovel and starts digging. Ilchenko and Squirrel watch in horror as he soon unearths more bodies, most of them stripped almost naked like the two on top. Only one is different, and he still wears his pilot's suit. The major has seen enough corpses to know: they must have been buried several weeks ago. When he finds the seventh corpse, Lazarov stops digging.

"No need to dig any deeper… looks like the whole squad and crew were buried here." He leans closer to the bodies. The stench of decay and rot is so strong that it even penetrates Lazarov's gas mask. A sweetish, sickening taste develops in his mouth as he studies the bodies from a closer range. He points at a skull, barely connected by rotting sinew to the rest of the corpse. "Look… this might have started as a firefight, but ended in an execution."

Speechless, they look at the open grave, then at each other.

Ilchenko scowls. "Who did this?"

Lazarov shakes his head. His first thought is of the sinister commandos from the Salang Range. *But they use different means to clean up their mess,* he thinks. The burial also means that the dushmans are no option either. He can't imagine any reason why they would bother with digging a mass grave for their enemies.

"I don't know, but probably not the dushmans, and definitely not the Stalkers."

"I agree," Squirrel says. "One needs more firepower than a few Stalkers' Kalashnikovs to storm a downed chopper with a whole squad of paratroopers inside. No brother would be foolish enough to do that."

"Squirrel, can you read tracks?"

"Wouldn't be much of a guide if I couldn't, man."

"Let's check the area. Ilchenko, here's your shovel. Fill that back in."

"Damn this shit... I just can't believe it."

Looking for any traces the attackers might have left behind, Lazarov and the guide comb the perimeter around the wreck.

"I'm not a big tactician, man, and the whole place looks as if God had created it for an ambush... but if I had to take that chopper on, that position would have been as good as any. Look!" He waves Lazarov over to a tree stump, where the Stalker kneels and takes a handful of cartridge casings from the ground.

"9x39 millimeters... Russian-made. Lots of them. Here... and look, two more firing positions over there."

Lazarov examines a casing. Even a quick glance proves that the guide was right. He frowns. "Squirrel... do you know anyone who has a Val or a Vintorez?"

"Yeah, man. You."

"I assure you I didn't do this. Now tell me: here in the New Zone, which other rifle uses this caliber?"

"The Groza."

"And who is armed with assault rifles of that type?"

Squirrel removes his gas mask. It is the first time that Lazarov sees horror in his eyes.

"Exactly," the major murmurs and bows his head.

For a long minute, they look at each other.

"Listen Squirrel... I already know that you were with the Intruders once. I suppose there's not much love lost between you and Captain Bone's Guardians."

"That's not the correct way to put it. I'd rather say: please, let me cut their bellies open, tear out their intestines, trample on them, and suffocate the suckers with their own guts!"

"If you want to see that day, you must keep your mouth shut for now. Do not talk about this to anyone. Especially not to Ilchenko."

"Why?"

"Because I said so. Or do you want my six remaining men to charge down Bone while there are a hundred Stalkers around who don't know who they hate more, us or the guards?"

"They don't hate soldiers anymore after you helped us out at the Outpost. At least not you and your guys."

"Be that as it may, we are not ready to take the Guardians—or whoever they really are—on yet. Is that clear?"

"Yes sir, Major, sir."

"Spare me your jokes, I'm not in the mood for fun. Let's go back to that chopper and give Ilchenko a hand."

Stalker camp at Hellgate, 20:25:47 AFT

Night has fallen by the time they climb up through a valley to Hellgate. Lazarov scans the area through his binoculars. Beyond an empty area encircled by jagged, rocky hills, dozens of small fires dance under a huge archway leading to a cave entrance. The place looks like a ruined cathedral built to worship some evil entity, but it was the tortured earth itself that produced this wicked rock formation. Now he also realizes that what had looked like one single anomaly from far, is actually many: sizzling and pulsating purple flames dance among columns of steam. A dilapidated log hut stands a safe distance from the anomalies, most of its timbers having been taken away to feed the campfire that burns in the middle of the stone circle, further away from the anomalies but still close enough for the flames to lit up three human figures huddled around the campfire. "I see Stalkers there."

"That must be Beefeater and his buddies," Squirrel says.

"Beefeater?" Ilchenko asks.

"He prefers gin to vodka, would you believe that?"

"How could anyone set up a camp there?" Lazarov asks. "There are anomalies around, and the whole place itself looks creepy."

"Because they aren't stupid."

"And what makes them smart?"

"Mutants don't go too close to anomalies, and smart Stalkers make camp where no mutants go."

"Sounds reasonable. Let's join them at their fire, then."

As the three of them walk up to the fire, the Stalkers jump up, pointing their weapons at the newcomers.

"Peace, brothers! It's me, Squirrel!"

"Hey Squirrel," a Stalker says, lowering his weapon. "What's wrong with you? We're just sitting here, telling jokes and all, and you sneak up on us like this? You scared the shit out of us!"

"We mean no harm," Lazarov says. He switches his rifle's safety to 'on' and shoulders the weapon. "Do you mind if we spend the night here?"

"Haha! The military is looking for protection from Stalkers," another says as he sits down by the fire and goes back to tuning a battered guitar. "Come, you'll be safe with us."

"That's very reassuring," Ilchenko says, looking around.

"What's up, Squirrel?" The third Stalker turns to the guide. He is cleaning an old L85 Enfield rifle. "Got lost as usual, my old mate?"

"I'm guiding my soldier guests through the local zoo, Beefy," the guide says, sitting down next to the campfire. "They've already met the bears and dushmans. All that must have prepared for them for the worst attraction. Major, Ilch, I have the displeasure to give you Mishka Slash. He pretends to play guitar but he can't. The jumpy one is Sashka Commando and the brother with a taste for antique weapons is Beefeater."

"Slash? Commando?" Ilchenko gives Lazarov a puzzled glance. "How did these guys chose their call signs? Plucking them out of a hat?"

Lazarov shrugs the question off. He has already noticed something far more interesting.

"I don't give a shit about crazy call signs if the name on that label is for real," he says, eyeing the bottle of vodka that the Stalkers are sharing among themselves. "Is that really what the label says?" He takes off his heavy rucksack with a satisfied sigh and joins the Stalkers sitting around the fire.

"Sure! It's Stolichnaya, what else?"

Mishka Slash offers him the bottle. Lazarov takes a long swig, then hands it over to Ilchenko who has taken the place next to him.

"What brought you here then, lads?" Beefeater asks.

"We're on our way to the Factory."

"That's where we wanted to go a few nights back. Forget about it."

"Come again?"

"The last storm moved the anomalies. Looks as if it's swept all the damned Geysers, Mines and Burners into the archway. You could waste a million bolts but still wouldn't find a way through."

"Shit," Lazarov swears. "Have you at least seen Mac? You know, Grouch's apprentice?"

The Stalkers exchange a baffled look.

"Nope. Sorry, mate," Beefeater says.

"How far is it if we go the other route, through that abandoned village you mentioned, Squirrel?"

"Two days."

Lazarov glances at Ilchenko who returns the concern in his look. The major removes his helmet and rubs his temples.

"Damn it… we haven't got that much time. We must find a way through tomorrow."

"Let's keep tomorrow's worries for tomorrow," Squirrel cheerfully replies, "and now tell me buddies, you got any new stories?"

"We were talking about women."

"What women, Sashka?"

"That's the point. There aren't any around."

"Why would there be? Prada produces no Stalker boots, Mango has no protective suits, Louis Vuitton offers no relic containers and jackal puppies aren't cute. That's why they don't come here."

"Which sucks," the Stalker called Commando sighs with resignation.

"How would you recognize one anyway?" Lazarov asks. "All Stalkers wear gas masks, helmets or at least balaclavas."

"By her voice?"

"Come on, Mishka. Speaking through a gas mask makes anyone sound like a robot."

"True enough, Squirrel. By her tits then."

"Under the body armor she could have tits like a cow's udders and nobody would notice them."

"Okay, not the tits. Maybe a pink rifle."

"Or an armored suit with a 'Hello, Kitty' sticker on it?"

"Or just by being a pain in the ass," Beefeater grumbles.

"By dumping you for a Stalker with a bigger rifle," Ilchenko smirks.

"You talking about your own experiences, Ilch? Anyway, one wouldn't have to guess," Squirrel says laughing. "Just find out which Stalker the upyrs are after on certain days!"

"Now that was way below the belt."

The Stalkers all laugh, except for Beefeater who seems more intent on maintaining his weapon. Lazarov likes this attitude, all the more because Beefeater handles the disassembled weapon with a routine that can only come from a military background. However, for once he finds the

Stalkers' conversation more interesting than speculating in which army Beefeater had acquired his skills.

"I wonder where the Tribe got their women from?" He says, taking another swig from the bottle.

Suddenly, silence falls upon the camp.

"Hey Major," a Stalker eventually says, "don't ruin the party by mentioning those animals!"

"Sorry, Slash. Didn't mean to scare you."

Sashka picks up the thread of conversation. "*Kruto*, fellows," he says, clearing his throat. "So, assuming that a female Stalker was here, what would you do?"

"I'm a polite guy," Squirrel says. "I'd open the door to any underground area and let her enter before me. Ladies first!"

"I would give her a flower."

"Just a flower? You're a cheapskate, Sashka."

"I mean, a Blood Flower relic."

"Before or after?"

"Whatever. Eh, this makes no sense... let's talk about women in the Big Land. Hey, newcomers, tell us a juicy story!"

"Hell yeah! Tell us something naughty. I guess you army officers get the most pussy out there."

"Only on paydays," Lazarov jokes. "Women are expensive, you know?"

"Who's talking about whores?"

"*All* women are expensive," Lazarov sighs.

"Or all women are whores."

"I wouldn't subscribe to that, Ilchenko."

"No argument about women being expensive," Beefeater says. "But back in Bagram I heard a little bird twittering that you've been the commander of the Perimeter. If that's true, and you didn't get rich from all the relic trade, then, Major, with all due respect, you missed the opportunity of a lifetime."

"Maybe I did," Lazarov dryly replies, staring into the fire.

Ilchenko takes a long swig from the vodka bottle. "Everyone, listen up! Yoshkar Ola is the place to go. It's an ugly little *bydlostan* in Russia, but there's a big university and out of every ten students, nine are girls."

"Then what the hell are we doing here?" Beefeater muses.

"Wasting ourselves, Beefy," a Stalker replies.

"I'm not talking about you, Mishka, you old wanker."

"You've studied there?" Lazarov asks Ilchenko.

"No, I studied in Odessa, but she was from Yoshkar Ola. I got to know her during a student exchange, which ended up in an intense exchange of body fluids..."

"A story at last! That's what we need!"

"Right you are, Sashka! Come on, Ilch, get right to the juicy details!"

"It's a sad story, Squirrel. So, I am from Odessa and she was from Yoshkar Ola." Ilchenko suppresses a hiccup and takes another swig. Lazarov can only admire his drinking abilities – the soldier seems to knock back the vodka like water. "During a summer break, we met again in St. Petersburg. She and some other girls had a party organized. It sucked – there were several Western guys there too, and they were looking at our girls as if they were nothing but pussy."

"Which is actually true," Mishka Slash cuts in.

Ilchenko gives him a disapproving look and drinks once more. "So, I speak a little German, you know, because I studied Goethe and Rilke and helped them translate. When the suckers told a girl: *was möchtest Du trinken*, I just said: 'he wants to know if you'll lay for a Schengen visa'."

"Now that's what I call party-pooping," Squirrel says.

"Whatever... The worst thing was that some girls—not all, but some, you know what I'm meaning—just said 'yes'. But that was not the only thing that ruined the party for me. Imagine, there was a fucking negro too. Can you believe that? He was on some fucking fellowship to study fucking sociology or whatever. Officially. Unofficially, he was selling drugs. The girls let him come to the party because he had some pretty good stuff, I'll give him that."

Mishka Slash chuckles. "I don't even dare think what else might have interested the girls."

"Shut your mouth, Stalker. Anyway, I bought a few grams of dope to cheer myself up. And while I was getting high, that *kurvenok* fucked my girl!"

"Shame on you, man. You should have stuck to Coke instead of coke."

"Haha, very funny! That bastard gave me stronger stuff than what I wanted, Squirrel. It totally knocked me out. Yeah, okay, I admit I had too much vodka too but you're missing my point. My point is that my girl was fucked by a fucking negro!"

"I always knew you were compensating with that machine gun," Squirrel jokes. Ilchenko gives him a scornful glance, and now appears to be genuinely angry. Lazarov watches him, ready to intervene should a fight break out, but his soldier seems to be too drunk already to stand.

"Anyway, next morning I find my girl in the next room and the negro all over her. I told her to get out of my sight and go back to Yoshkar-fucking-Ola. Then I had a... conversation... with the negro."

"About the dope?"

"About why I shouldn't throw him out off the balcony, Stalker. He wasn't very... Major, how do you call it when an argument doesn't work?"

"In your case, it's called being totally pissed. You better go, brush your teeth and prepare your bivouac, son."

"Is this an order?"

"Finish the story first, if you still can," Lazarov says, softened up by the drink himself, and also curious about the end of Ilchenko's story, even though the soldier's words begin to turn into drunken blabber.

"I go, *komandir*, I go, but let me tell you this... I found out something very interesting about negros. Their skin might be black but their brains are white. Don't give me that look! I saw it with my own eyes when he hit the pavement one, two, three, four... five floors below the balcony!"

Squirrel chokes on the loaf of bread he is eating.

"That was the most interesting thing I learned during my student years. There was no more studying for me anyway, because who the hell wants to study once he's got a drug dealer's stash in his hands? So one thing led to the other and a year after I even had my own *bummer*, a nice black X6. Guess how many teachers drive one. So, in the end I couldn't care less about my degree, and all went well until one day a sucker scratched my car. I was a little too rough on him... anyway, while waiting for my turn at the *militsia*, along came a recruiting officer and told me that I could either go to jail or join the army."

"With a past like that, one day you'll make it to general," Lazarov says.

"Major, I love you. You are a badass, but I love you! Please, Major, don't tell the others that I didn't finish university. You know, we're all supposed to be badasses but being a badass with a university degree makes me a special badass. Am I not right?"

Lazarov softly pushes Ilchenko's arm away as the soldier attempts to embrace him. "That's your only concern after you've killed a man?"

"Come on, it was in St. Petersburg! Someone would have killed him anyway..."

Finally wasted, Ilchenko stretches out on the ground and starts snoring immediately. The Stalkers are quiet.

"Why does someone drink too much vodka if he can't handle it?" Beefeater eventually says. "Let's go to sleep. Mishka, it's your turn to keep the first watch."

"That was a very touching story, but we still don't know where to find women," Mishka Slash says, stretching his back. "Oh God! Relics, guns, freedom, adventures... What good is there in all of this if there's no pussy around?"

Beefeater, the only one who has kept his mind sober, gives Lazarov a questioning look. "One doesn't just need to mention the Tribe to poop a party, I see."

"He's proved to be a capable and reliable soldier to me," the major replies with a shrug. "I don't care about what he did before."

"That's the kind of soldiers you have in your army? And I thought the Stalkers were a rough enough bunch."

Lazarov looks at the snoring machine gunner. "My job is to command them, not to judge them," he says. "And besides... if you are in battle, you need men like Ilchenko at your side."

"You have a point. As a matter of fact, sometimes I'm glad we have no women around."

"Agree."

Lazarov takes Ilchenko's sleeping bag from the soldier's rucksack and opens it. Before covering the snoring soldier, he looks him down for a minute. "It's probably better for the women too."

"Do you think it was true, or was he just bragging?"

"I don't care. But to be honest, I guess you're not from the former USSR and have no idea of what some women, like Ilchenko's girl, are willing to do to get away... to London, for example."

"What an irony," Beefeater says with a smirk. "Because you have no idea of what men like me are willing to do to get away from there, mate."

Beyond Hellgate Camp, 27 September 2014, 13:12:48 AFT

"Shit, we've been here already!"

The better part of the day has already passed when Squirrel smashes his palmtop to the ground. "I'm sorry, man. There seems to be no way up to that cursed plateau!"

"I can't believe this shit. You're supposed to be a guide, Stalker."

Ilchenko looks tired and angry. Lazarov can't blame him for his frustration: since they left the camp at dawn, they've spent all day wandering through the rugged crevasses with walls that tower several dozen meters above them. With their heavy gear, the walls themselves are too steep to climb, forcing them to seek an easier way.

"And you're supposed to be airborne, man," Squirrel retorts. "Why do you need me? Go, fly up there!"

Lazarov scans the area with his binoculars. No matter how many approaches they've tried, all have ended at an impassable section or another dead end. All he can see now is a labyrinth of sand-colored rocks and steep hills, no matter how far he looks.

"One week on *havchik*... maybe you're right, Squirrel. All I need is to fart and it'll propel me right up to the plateau."

"Gas masks on..."

"Cut the crap, *patsanni*," Lazarov says. "I think I saw something. Squirrel, have a look at that." The major hands his binoculars to the guide and points to the mouth of a cave. "Maybe there's an underground passage leading up in there. I don't know... do you think we should check it out?"

"It's your call, man," Squirrel replies, increasing the magnification for a better look.. "It could be a mutant lair."

"At least we'd get the chance to shoot something rather than just walk around completely lost. Let's go."

As they approach the cave, Squirrel points to a path leading up to its mouth. It is surprisingly well-trodden.

"Keep your weapons ready," he whispers. "Might be a dushman hideout."

"What the hell would dushmans do here?" Ilchenko snorts.

The guide sends a scowl towards Ilchenko. "Looking for relics, like everyone else... why, what did you think? Pilgrimage?"

"Squirrel, step back. I'll take point," Lazarov says, covering the last few meters to the cave entrance with utmost caution, ready to shoot. Before entering the cave that overlooks the plains below, he switches on the flashlight he has fastened to the Vintorez with duct tape. Keeping his index finger on the trigger, he enters the cave. Then he juts his head out, signaling his companions to move up.

"Ilchenko, be prepared to mow down everything that moves. Squirrel, watch our back. We're moving in."

Signs of human habitation appear in the light circle of the torchlight: a mattress and a fireplace.

"Steady, *rebyata*. Steady."

A shadow moves in the darkness. The major points his rifle toward the corner where he sensed movement, but what appears in the torchlight gives him a bigger scare than any mutant.

"Hold your fire!" Lazarov shouts.

It is an emaciated man with a wildly grown, dirty beard covering the lower part of his weathered face. His skin bears deep scars and wrinkles, giving him the look of a burnt out shell of a man, thin and old like a mummy. A dusty Talib turban covers his head, but the most unnerving thing is the ragged coat he is wearing. Lazarov has to force himself to believe his own eyes: it is the coat of a Soviet officer from many years ago. One of the shoulder patches has been torn off but the other, dirty and faded, still shows a captain's rank. He recoils into his cave and covers his eyes from the torchlight's blinding light. His toothless mouth utters senseless blabber. "*Wiy... nashi?...*"

"Lower your weapons," Lazarov tells his companions, and reaches out towards the ghost-like figure. "We mean no harm. Who are you?"

"*Nash...* our column."

"If we stumbled upon a Soviet guy from that war, I'll piss myself," Ilchenko murmurs.

"*Sovietskiy? Da! Da!*" The figure steps forward and grabs Ilchenko's arm. "*Nashi, ti nashoi sinok!*"

Before the soldier can do anything, the old man kisses the hand holding the machine gun. Then he touches the small, white-blue-red patch on Ilchenko's sleeve and his eyes open wide in bewilderment.

"We're Russians, not Soviets," Ilchenko observes. "We always were, actually."

Squirrel takes a bottle from his rucksack and offers it to the old man. "*Vipyi!* You look like you could use a little vodka."

"Me too," Lazarov says.

"Count me in," adds Ilchenko.

Holy Mother of God, Lazarov thinks, looking at the old man as if he were a creature from outer space. Then he realizes that he actually is: a living time capsule that has turned every abstract memory of the past into reality, even if it is a hardly conceivable one.

"All right... come, sit down. Are you hungry?" he asks, pointing to his mouth and making a chewing gesture. To his surprise, the man shakes his head. "Let's get out of this cave. Ilchenko, help him walk. Squirrel, get that bottle back from him. He's confused enough. Look around, maybe you find something useful that helps us know who he is... or was."

"I'll be damned," Ilchenko says offering his hand to the old man. "Come, Papa, grab my hand. Otherwise I'll think you're a ghost."

The old man might be worn out, but he is not helpless. He takes a heavy wooden staff and, laughing, pats Ilchenko on the back as he walks with them into the light outside.

"Ours... you are ours... you have arrived," he says. His words sound like those from someone who hasn't talked for a very long time.

Ilchenko watches Lazarov pensively. He seems to be at a loss over what to do and say. Lazarov doesn't feel much smarter than his soldier.

"I am Major Lazarov, Armed Forces of the Russian Federation. This is Private Ilchenko. And the other guy is... well, call him Squirrel. He is our guide."

"Russian forces? How?"

Ilchenko is about to launch into a long explanation when the major signals for him to hold his tongue and turns to the old man. "Who are you?"

"Who... I am. Now I am. Again. I am this." The man reaches into his duster and gives Lazarov a barely readable ID card, issued by the Soviet Army. The major holds it in his hands as if it were a relic that he had never believed existed.

"Captain Igor Vasilyevich Ivanov? 40th Army, 276th logistics division?"

"The column."

"What column, Captain?"

"My column. Ours."

"This gibberish makes no sense," Ilchenko says.

Lazarov tries to tackle the situation by sticking to their basic needs. "We must get through to the factory on the plateau. We can't get through. Do you know a way to the factory?"

"My column is lost."

"We are the new column. And we must get through. Captain Ivanov, you must lead us through."

"I hoped... that the war ended. Did it end?"

"Not exactly," Lazarov says with a sigh. "We are here to settle unfinished business with the dushmans. Getting to the factory is part of that. Do you know a way or not?"

"I do... I know. Old neck-grabber is hiding there. Me, I'm hiding here. I don't like leaving my hiding place. What news?"

"Captain... please give me a moment."

Lazarov waves to Ilchenko to follow him a few steps away.

"Things have taken a turn for the surreal, Private. What's your view on this?"

"Sir, with all due respect, it's 2014 now. Do you really believe that one man could have survived here for almost thirty years, all alone? Look at him. He's more a walking skeleton than human being!"

"His ID card seems genuine enough. Look." Lazarov gives the weathered card to Ilchenko. "Plus he claims to know a way to that damned factory. This means we need him, and need to play along. Let's assume that what he says is true and he was left behind somehow by the Soviet army. What do we tell him? That his country, the mighty USSR, was humiliated and ran like a whipped dog?"

"I don't know, sir... I don't know."

"And then that his country doesn't exist anymore? And all that has happened ever since? The CIS, the putsch, Yeltsin, Putin, all that shit? Damn, maybe this guy never heard about Chernobyl either! As far as he's concerned, his commander in chief is still Leonid Ilyich Brezhnev!"

"If we tell him, he will probably have a heart attack and we won't get to that bloody place. And telling him all that would take so long that we would be sitting here till doomsday. I can't see any option other than lying to him, Major."

"Well, Ilchenko, one thing is sure—we can't leave him here."

"It's your call, sir."

"Yo, Major! Look what I've found."

Squirrel emerges from the cave and gives Lazarov a note book.

"What the hell is this?" Lazarov says looking at the cover.

"Uhm... that's a Homer Simpson sticker, sir."

"I realize that, Ilchenko, it's not me who's been living in a cave for decades. But how did the old man obtain this? Anyway, let's not waste more time."

"So what shall we do with him, sir?"

"Put him out of his misery."

"What?"

Seeing Ilchenko's scowl, the major smiles. "Out of the time capsule, I mean. Let's hope it will not be too painful on him."

Lazarov steps back to the old man. He is sitting on the ground, staring into the distance, repeatedly murmuring only two words: *the column, the column.*

"Igor Vasilyevich, listen up." Lazarov squats in front of the old man and looks deep into his eyes, slowly, clearly repeating his name once more. "Igor Vasilyevich Ivanov. Listen to me: it is now the year 2014. The war ended twenty-five years ago. The USSR is no more."

"What? Brezhnev is dead?"

"He is."

"And no more USSR?"

"It's gone."

"Thank God Almighty! Oh, God has worked wonders, wonders!"

"You don't know half of it. Now we will bring you home. Home... to Russia."

"Russia?"

"Wherever your home is, it is time to return now."

"Did we win the war?"

"Well... some of us were victorious. You will be among them, if you carry out a last order — from me."

"But —" The old man touches Lazarov's arm patch. "You are not from my army."

"I am a major. Ranks did not change. You will follow my orders and guide us to the factory. We will finish our mission. Then we'll take you to a safe place. You will be transferred home from there."

"You speak differently... everything is different about you," the old man says, touching Lazarov's bulky body armor. "Your uniform is different also... so much better than ours. Oh no! You are not of my army. You are of no use to me."

"*Komandir!*" Ilchenko speaks in a forced whisper, but Lazarov feels that his soldier can barely suppress his anger. "Let's leave him to his fate or just drag him with us. This makes no sense!"

"But he has a point, Ilch," Squirrel says. "You guys are not from his army."

"That's fucking right, Stalker! How in the hell could we be Soviet soldiers?"

Suddenly, an idea comes to Lazarov's mind. "You are a genius, you know that Ilch?"

Lazarov reaches into his body armor's breast pocket and shows his father's photograph to the Captain.

"You see that? That is me! Kunduz, 1988! Look at it!"

The old man looks at the picture, then at Lazarov. His eyes open wide.

"Yes... that is you, Sergeant. So someone did survive! I knew it! The whole column couldn't all have been lost... it could not have been that everyone died..."

For a moment, Lazarov's mind almost blackens out. He closes his eyes, falling into a vortex of memories where time, dates and history have no meaning, turning his heartbeat into stormy waves of emotions that threaten to drag him down into dark depths where he would lose his mind, the desire for revenge being the only straw he can hold on to. When he opens his eyes, he finds himself back where he was, stranded in reality—a reality he needs to bend if he wants to keep his sanity.

"Captain, our shoulder flashes have been changed but you should still recognize a major's star," Lazarov says, pointing at the small patch on his sleeve indicating his rank. "I am a major now and outrank you, Captain Ivanov. We did not forget you and the others. Never. Do you understand?... I am here to bring you home." He swallows hard and releases his grip. "You must come with us. This is an order!"

A shadow of doubt visits the Captain's face. "Is Brezhnev really gone?"

"Really." Lazarov puts his visor on to hide his eyes.

"And he can't rest in peace from the noise of all the BMWs and whores in high heels walking on Red Square," Ilchenko says, gritting his teeth. "Major... for God's sake, bring him back to his wits!"

"Captain Ivanov, I gave you an order. Come, we go home."

"But I cannot go home."

"Whatever you mean by that can be settled. For now, you will guide us to the factory. I will not repeat my order."

"No… not everything can be settled. But I will bring… guide you there, yes. I will guide you and take orders from you, if you will do something for me."

"We have no time for more side missions, sir!" Ilchenko is almost shouting at Lazarov. "If he wants to send you to Kabul to fetch his lost Party membership card — I beg you to say no!"

"Not now, soldier, not now. After I have guided you to the factory. Please. Will you do something for me, Major?"

"What more could I do for you than getting you out of here?"

"It will not need much time."

"All right. I will, if it can be done quickly. We have a mission to complete, Captain, and I guess you want to get to a safe place as soon as possible too."

"Thank you! Good! *Davay uhodim!*[1]"

"Where?"

"You don't want to get to the factory?"

"Oh… of course. Are you sure that you can — "

"I am. I can." He takes his heavy staff and starts walking up the hill. "What are you waiting for, *komandir?*"

Wilderness, 17:11:38 AFT

After a few hours of walking, Lazarov looks at the old man through different eyes. Maybe it's the reduction of a human body to bones, sinew and muscles that keeps him moving quickly, or just the freedom of movement he has compared to the three companions who carry their heavy kit and weapons, but at times they have had a hard time keeping up with the pace of their new guide. He leads them through crevasses and over ridges on a path they would have never found by

---

[1] Let's go/move out/leave, quickly

themselves. Squirrel occasionally stops to record their progress in his palmtop.

"This new path will make me rich, man... I will be the only guide who knows a way to the factory!"

"I doubt that too many Stalkers would come here," Ilchenko says, breathing heavily from their recent ascent through a narrow ravine. He stops and wipes sweat from his face.

"You couldn't be more wrong about the factory, man. Rumor says there's more relics than used condoms in a brothel."

"Mention brothels one more time and I'll just shoot you. Mention cold beer, and I'll shoot you twice."

"I wouldn't care about you shooting me a hundred times if I had a Heartstone."

"What's a Heartstone?"

"A very rare relic. It's said it boosts one's health like nothing else... just telling you because they're supposed to be found around here. Sell one to Placebo back at Bagram and you'll be filthy rich. Sell it in the Big Land, and you'll get dirty filthy rich. Or keep it and it will make you live for a hundred years." Squirrel scratches his head. "Pity there's no relic that would make you dirty filthy rich *and* live for a hundred years."

"I'm not sure I want to live for a hundred years. Live fast, die pretty is my philosophy."

"You'll have a problem with dying pretty, Ilch."

"It's not far now," the Captain says, standing on the ridge while Lazarov and his companions are still climbing up a narrow crevasse in the hillside.

"What do you mean by 'not far'?" Lazarov asks him, nervously looking at his watch as he toils up the last few meters. "The day will soon be over."

"About three hundred meters, Major."

The Captain points forward as Lazarov at last reaches the ridge. Panting heavily, leaning with his hands against his knees to give his back a minute of rest, he looks in the direction that is shown. Just a few minutes march ahead of them stands a high wall made of concrete slabs. Beyond the wall, the auspicious buildings of a ruined industrial site loom. But what he sees between them and the factory fills him with frustration.

Breathing heavily, Ilchenko and Squirrel finally catch up with them.

"That's great," the Stalker says looking at the factory. "We could have just stayed at Hellgate. Shit!"

On the open rocky ground between them and the factory, deadly anomalies sizzle. They slowly move and burst out in fountains of fire when contracting, as if they were trying to deny any path leading through.

"And now?" Lazarov asks.

"And now we go to into the lair. *Vperyod*, to the factory!"

Carefully keeping a safe distance from the anomaly field, they follow the Captain to a low knoll covered with thorny bushes. At one point he stops, reaches into the bushes and moves the thorny branches aside. A large hole lies beyond, big enough for a man to climb inside.

"Here lives old neck-grabber."

"Only one upyr, then?

"And his family."

A nasty curse is all that comes to Lazarov's mind.

"We rest here for a few minutes. Ilchenko, Squirrel, weapon check."

"Yes, we better rest now," the Captain says. "I will show you the way."

Lazarov notices that the Captain's speech is improving. *Maybe if I talk to him more, he will fully regain his speech,* he thinks. *Maybe his memory too.*

"But you have no weapons, no armor, no light. Nothing at all, Captain."

"My staff never runs out of bullets. It also keeps the upyr away."

"How do you keep a upyr at bay with a wooden staff? By beating it, or what?"

"You will see."

"And what is this?" Lazarov asks taking the note book from his vest pocket. He ponders through the pages. It is full of neat handwriting and, to his surprise, even a few drawings appear among the notes.

"Oh, you took it… you can keep it. I don't understand. It's about a country called 'Zone'. I found it a few days ago at an abandoned campsite."

What Lazarov finds in the notebook pages surprises him. Several pages with notes and text about the old and the new Zones, mutants, probably of those its owner encountered here. Judged by the first entries, written in very bad Russian, the book's owner must be very young, a kid even.

"Damn! After playing airsoft so many times it amazes me how inaccurate an AK-47 is in reality. Anyway, at last it's time to get into the real stuff!"

Lazarov smiles. *Hello, Mac,* he thinks. *Nice to meet you.*

The notes he can decipher tell of missions, fights with mutants, expeditions with rookies, experienced Stalkers, and claims the owner has been everywhere in the Zone whilst under the protection of Grouch, whom he had joined on his trip to the south in search of a new bonanza of relics. Lazarov smiles when a few familiar names appear. On one of the first pages, he discovers a note mentioning his own base. It is written in rudimentary Russian, mixed with words in a language he doesn't understand but guesses to be Spanish.

"Day 3, 2014. R. warned me not to perform what the trader asked me. He said that Perimeter has new commander and it is not longer the… un completo desastre (¡Maldita sea! ¿Por qué esta maldita palmtop no viene con un diccionario incorporado?) and that no matter how much I was promised for it I should not attempt to steal ammo. I better skip this task."

Praising the young Stalker for his wise decision and cursing the traders' shady business deals at the same time,

Lazarov keeps on browsing through the pages. The language and vocabulary of the notes improves from page to page. Some early notes have been written entirely in the Stalker's native tongue, but in the end the notebook tells of a steep learning curve in using the Russian language. Later notes tell about the journey of the kid and Grouch to the New Zone, posing as tourists in Uzbekistan, buying their way into the new Zone and finally to Bagram. To his disappointment, the language of the last notes returns to Spanish, giving him no clue as to why the kid left Bagram or where he went. He turns to the Captain.

"I hope you did not find this on a corpse."

"No, no. I heard someone coming and hid. Next morning I found it."

"You're ready to enter a mutant lair armed only with a staff, but a Stalker scares you?"

"A — what?"

"Uhm... a human."

"I know beasts. But about men one can never know."

"You have a point about that," Lazarov replies and turns to his companions who are lying on the ground, exhausted. "Hey, you two! Ready to go?"

"Must we? I'm dog tired," Squirrel whines. "It's getting dark now. Let's make camp and continue tomorrow!"

"I guess it's pitch dark in that lair anyway. Let's move."

Ilchenko and the Stalker grumble with discontent as they get up, but follow him to the cave entrance. The Captain, however, grabs Lazarov's rucksack, halting him.

"We need fire first."

He takes a small pouch from the pocket of his duster. Carefully, as if handling a great treasure, the Captain unfolds the dirty linen and removes a pair of broken eyeglasses. He plucks a few branches from the nearest brush and starts collecting sunshine in the glass.

"Hey grandpa, if you don't mind...I have something better." Squirrel kneels down and, using a lighter, gets a small fire going in a second.

"Nice. Very nice!" The Captain says admiring the lighter.

"You can have it if you want to," Squirrel generously says.

The Captain waves it off. "I played with that when I was a little child. Now I have better fire."

He takes a small, black object from his knapsack and fixes it into a nook at the point of his staff. Looking closer, Lazarov's eyes open wide. It is a black stone, shaped into the form of a blade as if crafted by cavemen. The Captain holds the chopped stone into the fire. After a few seconds, it glows, illuminated from inside and emitting a small sphere of light.

"This is my torch," he says, giving Lazarov a proud smile from his toothless mouth.

"I have never seen a relic used like that before," Squirrel says in awe.

"You like it, young man? Good! I like it too. Upyr does not like it."

The Captain wraps the Talib turban's end over his mouth and steps inside the lair. Lazarov follows him. As soon as he is inside, an unbearable stench hits his nose: the stink of rotten meat, dry blood and animal feces.

"Gas masks on, *rebyata!*"

Upyr lair, 18:27:30 AFT

Lazarov finds his night vision equipment has been rendered useless by the unnaturally bright glow emitted by the Captain's relic. He reluctantly switches on his head lamp and gives a sign to Squirrel and Ilchenko to do the same.

I hate such tunnels, he thinks as they proceed in the narrow cave shaft. *No space for flanking or maneuvering, only backward and forward.*

"Ilchenko, keep your shooter's barrel out of my back," Squirrel whispers.

"Maybe you should move quicker, you lame duck?"

The Captain turns to them and puts his finger on his lips. "Quiet! Upyrs have bad eyes but sharp ears," he whispers.

"We do know that, Captain. But we should hear them coming – they try to scare the shit out of their prey with a howl before they attack."

The Captain frowns. "Then you haven't met a upyr here, Major."

"Squirrel! Why didn't you say anything about this? You're supposed to be our guide, after all!"

"Sorry, man, but I supposed you already knew everything!"

Damn it, Lazarov thinks, *of course, that's what Goryunov mentioned during the briefing.*

"Shit! Sneaky upyrs are the last thing we need. All right, one more reason for you two to stop teasing each other. Let's move on!"

Walking with steps as quiet as possible on the rocky and sandy ground, they proceed. The Captain's relic lights up just a small part of the cave, as if they were walking in a sphere of dim, red glow.

"Stay in the light."

Lazarov moves closer to the old man, wondering if staying close to the glowing relic is a good idea. It gives more light than their headlamps would alone, giving them a better chance to avoid stumbling in the hazardous ground, but it could also make it easier for a upyr – or anything else that might lurk in the dark caves – to detect them. However, his better judgment tells him to rely completely on the Captain who is leading them through a maze of tunnels with firm steps, never hesitating before taking turns into shafts to the left and right where no one but him would know which direction to take. Lazarov hopes that the old man's sense of direction doesn't fail him, since the only thing he can detect is that they seem to be gradually ascending.

After long minutes of sneaking and climbing, they reach a point where the tunnel widens. Lazarov grimaces under his gas mask when he sees a dead body on the ground, the torn Stalker suit bearing the marks of huge claws. Thousands of flies swarm around it.

"Squirrel, fall back into line!" Lazarov whispers angrily when the guide moves to inspect the pockets on the dead Stalker's body armor. "This is no time for scavenging."

"But…"

"Shh! Quiet!" the Captain whispers. "I heard something!"

Now Lazarov can hear it too. It's a muted roar coming from the depths of the tunnel lying ahead. Instinctively, he raises his weapon.

"If we hear it, we don't need to fear it," the Captain whispers. "It means that the upyr has not detected us. Howl is good, but silence is deadly."

"I hate upyrs," Squirrel whispers back. "Especially sneaky ones."

The long, tedious march takes its toll on Lazarov's energy. Walking is easy on the hard ground and the ascent is mostly gentle, but constantly keeping his eyes peeled and ears pricked becomes more and more exhausting as the time passes. As his mental energy depletes, a creepy sense of claustrophobia sets in.

Damn this spelunking… these narrow shafts sap on my energy with every step I take, no matter of the Emerald I carry.

He delights at the sight of the tunnel widening again into a long, oval-shaped space, and is already considering a short break when he sees the Captain freeze in his steps. Then he hears the noise of footsteps approaching them.

"Jesus Christ, here it comes!"

He doesn't need Squirrel's desperate scream to realize the danger. In the red glow of the Captain's relic, the shadow of a upyr appears on the rocky wall only a few meters to their right. Lazarov raises his rifle to shoot but the Captain's fragile figure is standing between him and the mutant.

"Upyr! Hold it! Don't approach!"

Lazarov is about to shout for the old man to get to the ground so that he has a clear shot, but realizes that it's not him or his comrades the Captain is talking to: he is directing his words to the mutant.

"Hold your fire," the major whispers to his companions.

The Captain raises the staff holding the glowing relic higher and steps forward. "Move away, old beast... move."

With eyes wide open from dread and surprise, Lazarov watches the mutant's shadow taking a step backwards, as if mesmerized by the relic's light. With a nod of his head, the Captain signals them to proceed.

Cautiously, they walk by the Captain who still keeps the relic high and close to the upyr's snout where Lazarov can now see his eyes reflecting the light. When Ilchenko, the last man in their row, has reached the far end of the cavern, the Captain slowly takes a step back. Still facing the mutant he seems to hold under his command, he retreats towards them with slow, cautious steps.

"Now go away," the Captain says in an almost fatherly tone of voice. "Go away until your sight returns."

"I'll be damned," Lazarov exclaims. "Did you actually blind that beast?"

But before the Captain could answer, Ilchenko steps forward. "A blinded mutant is good but a dead mutant is better."

Before Lazarov can bark to him a quick order to hold his fire, the machine gunner pulls the trigger on the PKM.

After the long silence the machine gun's fire is deafening, made even more thunderous by the echo in the cave. Guided more by instinct than reason, Lazarov also opens fire, aiming his rifle from the hip at the center of the mutant's shadow. Emitting a cry of pain, the Captain falls to the ground. Now Squirrel's AK joins the fire. The shadow approaches them as their bullets hit the still invisible body. Blood splashes from ever more visible wounds and now the mutant emits a dreadful, long howl. Then it falls, swirling up clouds of dust as it hits the ground. A few seconds later, the natural color of its body appears as the mutant's brain, which made it appear invisible by whatever mysterious ability it possessed, finally dies.

"No, no, no," the Captain moans. "Why?"

Lazarov quickly helps him to his feet and notes with relief that the old man is unscathed. His relief quickly evaporates as he hears several howls echoing through the cave – coming from the shaft ahead, the tunnel they have left behind them, and from unseen caverns above and below.

"You see what you did?" The Captain casts an angry look at Ilchenko.

"Yes! I killed a mutant!"

"Useless, stupid private! You killed one mutant and called up a dozen!" The Captain turns to Lazarov. "Since my times, discipline has become even worse!"

"I'll reprimand the soldier later," Lazarov shouts back. "We must get to that damned factory, quickly!"

"The howls are getting closer!" Squirrel screams.

"Run!" The Captain shouts. "Run!"

They run, slowed down by Ilchenko who keeps turning back to fire short bursts from his weapon. If their march had been careful up to now, it has turned into a heedless rout as they follow the Captain who is sprinting ahead. He almost gets thrown to the ground when he suddenly stops and collides with Lazarov, who has no chance to maneuver around him in the narrow tunnel.

"There's one ahead of us!"

The major empties his magazine into the mutant blocking their way ahead, cursing himself for not having loaded a full magazine after they'd finished the blinded mutant.

"Squirrel! Reloading, cover me!"

The heavy rattle of the PKM joins with the assault rifle's clatter, the noise of both weapons almost obliterated by the upyr's howl. When Lazarov's fires his now reloaded rifle, the howl turns into a pain-filled growl, but he keeps firing nonetheless until the mutant falls. They jump over the lifeless body and run forward.

"*Vperyod, vperyod!*"

"Squirrel, watch your back!"

"*Damn it!* We have been here before!"

"You must be kidding me, Stalker!"

"No, Major! Forward!" The Captain, now also tired and breathing heavily, points forward. "We're almost there!"

"Any more side turns ahead, Captain?"

"No! This leads straight to the factory!"

Lazarov peers back into the tunnel as the machine gunner and the guide arrive. Upyr howls are still echoing in the darkness, but none seem to be close enough to indicate an imminent threat.

Howls are good, silence is deadly, he recalls what the Captain said.

"Ilchenko, Squirrel! Haul your asses behind me! Cover me, I'm preparing a booby trap!"

Lazarov removes his last two hand grenades from his ammunition vest and carefully removes the fuses. At a position where any of the heavy-limbed upyrs would move it, he places one grenade on the ground and cautiously puts a stone on the release grip. Then he does the same with the other one, not giving any chance to a mutant who was lucky enough to avoid the first grenade.

"Done. Let's move on, and be quiet! Especially you, Private!"

The Captain's guidance proves to be correct. After covering a short distance, the natural walls of rock and earth end in a wall made of bricks.

"We have reached the cellars," the Captain says. "But this tunnel has always been open before. Strange!" He steps back, scratching at his beard.

Lazarov examines the wall. The rows of bricks are loosely laid and the balance of the whole structure seems to be borne by a single, if massive piece of timber in the middle. Overall, it looks like a makeshift barrier hastily erected to block the passage.

"This was not built by a upyr," Squirrel whispers. "That's for sure."

"Ilchenko, come over here," Lazarov says. "Consider yourself our combat engineer. This wall must go."

"Consider it done, Major."

The burly soldier steps to the stone wall and gives it a kick with all his force. After a few more kicks, the timber yields. One more kick, and the wall collapses with a huge rumble, leaving a hole big enough for a man to climb through.

"Forward," Lazarov orders. "Let's hope we haven't called up even more mutants by this racket!"

One by one, they enter the room on the other side. It is definitely man-made, looking like a cellar with rusty pipes and wires running along the concrete walls.

Suddenly, they hear a yelp.

"Jackals!" Squirrel shouts.

But only one mutant appears in the light of his headlamp. It seems to be frightened and hides under a pipe.

"It's a pup," Lazarov confirms without lowering his weapon. "I wonder where the rest of the pack is?"

"They seem to be one big loving family," Ilchenko says, pointing his torchlight at some textile rags arranged in a nest-like structure and a metal plate on the ground. A bulky rucksack lies next to the pet's place. "And quite sophisticated for jackals, too."

"I hate jackals. Especially sophisticated ones." Squirrel raises his submachine gun to shoot the helpless yelping mutant. But before he could even aim, a voice comes from the darkness. It is accompanied by the auspicious noise of a rifle being cocked.

"If you even think about hurting my dog — I'll fry you!"

"That's not a dog," Squirrel shouts back, "that's a bloody jackal!"

"It's a dog and his name is Billy. Lower your goddamned weapons!"

A beam of strong light flashes from the headlights of a human figure standing in a corner, maintaining a perfect firing position over all four of them.

"It's okay," Lazarov says. "We won't hurt your... pet. Everybody, relax!"

Slowly, with his hands up, he cautiously steps closer to their opponent. The jackal pup darts out from its cover and hides behind its master. By now Lazarov sees that he is wearing an exoskeleton and keeps his FN2000 automatic rifle squarely at aim. The Stalker's face is hidden behind the helmet's dark, protective visor and integrated gas mask.

The major frowns. It is not looking into the barrel of one of the best weapons of the world that gives him an odd feeling about this encounter, nor the relatively small size of their opponent, but how perfectly the exoskeleton fits its wearer. It suits him perfectly, as if tailor-made.

Strange. Grouch works wonders with rifles but armor has never been his strong side.

"Mac the Apprentice?"

"That's correct. Who are you?"

"My name is Lazarov. Ilchenko and I are from the military..."

"Friends call me Ilch," Ilchenko adds with a grin.

"... and that Stalker is our guide. Name's Squirrel."

"And who's that? Did one of you bring his grandfather on this joyride?"

"The grandfather holding that red light is... well... he's with the good guys too, he only stepped into a time vortex. Call him Captain. Can we all relax now?"

Mac laughs. "The Captain looks like a lich king from some stupid RPG!"

"You have something against RPGs? Best loot I ever had!"

Squirrel asks, stepping forward.

Lazarov grins and waves him to halt. "That's not the kind of RPG the kid means. Mac, you are right about the Captain, but he is a chaotic good lich. We're all with the good guys, believe me."

"Behave and I won't shoot you. But if you ever look at Billy the wrong way—"

"I love that puppy," Squirrel quickly. "Hey puppy, you want some rations?"

In reply, the jackal pup snarls at him and emits an angry yelp that was probably intended to be a frightening bark.

The tension eases as Mac cradles his rifle. Ilchenko and Squirrel do the same.

"So, let's get down to business," Lazarov says. "Grouch has sent us to get you back."

"How is he doing?"

"He'll be doing better once you get back to him."

"Forget it. Tell him I'm off to the Panjir Valley."

"What?"

The Captain's frightened cry surprises them all. "Operation Magistral is still going on? We went there five times… always beaten back! That place is hell! The column! The column was heading there—"

"What's wrong with this dude?" Mac asks. "The valley is like heaven for Free Stalkers. There are fewer mutants, and no arrogant Guardians poking their dirty noses into Stalker business."

"Never mind the Captain," Lazarov replies. "He's not really up to date."

Suddenly, the jackal named Billy starts to growl even without Squirrel bothering him.

"Uh-oh," Mac says readying his rifle. "Here come the upyrs!"

"How do you know?" Lazarov asks in surprise. Then he looks at the jackal pup called Billy. "Don't tell me that…"

The pup's low growl is suddenly subdued by an aggressive howl coming from the tunnels.

"You must have pissed them off, Stalker... you see, all animals seem to hate you."

"It's mutants, man, not animals! And actually, it was this trigger-happy *boyevoychik* who woke them up, not me!"

"We should leave," the Captain anxiously says.

"Yes, man! Let's go or we become upyr food!"

"Let's," Mac shouts, grabbing his pet and putting him into a bag hanging over his chest. He opens a metal door leading to a corridor to their left. "Get in there. Move!"

"You first, kid," Lazarov says, readying his rifle.

"Billy, cover your ears!"

Mac steps to the opening in the wall and fires a projectile from his rifle's built-in grenade launcher. The low *thump* is followed by a huge explosion inside the tunnel, strengthened into a thunder by the narrow space, followed after a second by two more detonations. Rocks and earth fall in and block the tunnel, while Mac gets his rucksack and even finds time to comfortingly caress his jackal.

"Did you booby-trap the tunnel? All the better, at least I could save some grenades!"

"Why did you bother building that stone wall?" Lazarov asks when they step into the corridor and Mac closes the metal door tight. "You could have blocked it with a few grenades from your rifle's launcher!"

"I have only a few grenades left, but there's more than enough bricks lying around here. Pity to leave it, though... it was a good place to hide. Hey, fat boy, let me through!"

Ilchenko lets Mac pass him by and take point in the corridor. "I am not fat, you little dwarf," he grumbles.

"Nobody calls me a dwarf," Mac says, looking back at the machine gunner towering behind him.

"I suggest you two settle this later," Lazarov snaps. "Mac, where to now?"

"You've probably guessed that this is the cellar of the textile factory. Normally, the way up should be clear. If not, Billy will warn us."

"How so?"

"He has a good nose even for a dog. Smells out any mutant, no matter how far away. Anomalies as well."

"Maybe that's because it's a jackal!" Squirrel says.

"*Gospodin* Lazarov, where did you find such an imbecile guide who can't tell a dog from a jackal?"

"First, you will address me as Major or *komandir*. Second, Squirrel is cool. He eats bears for breakfast."

"Yeah, I guessed that. His breath smells like that."

"And you—"

Lazarov cuts into Squirrel's words. "Zip it! Let's move!"

The corridor is narrow and dark, but at least man-made which a relief in itself after the maze of caverns they have left behind. At regular intervals, Lazarov sees metal doors with little hatches at eye height; most unusual for a cellar of a factory, making him wonder what this place might have really been. One door stands ajar. He peeks inside, and what he observes looks like a prison cell.

"This place is just damn creepy," he says.

"You want to see something really creepy?" the kid replies.

"I've had my share of creepy things for today, thanks."

"Too bad. Nothing is as creepy as an underground torture chamber."

"A factory with prison cells and a torture chamber? What the hell was this place?"

"Guess what? The factory levels are above. Below it was KGB, CIA, whatever." Mac halts at a winding, metal stair case. "You sure you want to miss the torture room?"

"Sir! If I may ask you," Ilchenko says behind them, "I'd like to see it."

"Why am I not surprised? Forget sightseeing, Ilchenko. Dammit, am I the only one who wants to get out of this dungeon as soon as possible?"

"No, man! I'm with you, as always!"

"We shouldn't tarry here too long, Major."

"Up we go then," Lazarov says.

The rusty staircase creaks and heaves under their steps, as if it could collapse at any moment. Two more corridors appear, which Lazarov is glad to leave unexplored as they continue their ascent.

When they reach the top of the staircase, Mac signals them to halt and looks around with his rifle poised to shoot before waving them to follow him.

"What made you hide in the deepest and darkest place?" Lazarov asks as he joins the kid above, and finds himself in a large, rectangular room with no windows. Empty plastic bottles, sheets of paper and other garbage litter the floor among turned over tables, chairs and collapsed shelves. The room has only one proper door, situated at the far end.

"Sense of safety, what else? Only a creepy guy like Ilchenko would hide in a prison cell, or a crazy one like Squirrel in the factory level..." He crosses the room and cautiously opens the door. "Appears to be clear. Let's go..."

"Mac, wait a minute. Close the door." Lazarov looks at his watch. It is a few minutes past midnight. "What's behind that door?"

"The factory hall."

"Is it over ground?"

"Of course. Why?"

"It's pitch dark now... we should stay put until daybreak. This room looks like a safe place to rest."

Ilchenko and Squirrel release huge sighs of relief. Even the Captain grumbles something like *it's about time to rest.*

Mac shrugs his shoulders. "Chickening out?"

"You better watch your tongue, kid. We left Hellgate this morning, stumbled upon the Captain and crawled through the caves in just one long leg. The last time we had *havchik* was early this afternoon. We need to rest."

"Besides, you, being a sneaky little bastard, could run away in the darkness, making this whole trip count for nothing," Ilchenko says, taking off his rucksack and placing his machine gun on a table that still stands upright.

"Indeed! You do have a tendency to run away, Mac. Ilchenko, take that table and block the door. Just in case."

"Spare your efforts, guys," Mac says, waving his hand in resignation. "That wouldn't block the door. It opens the other way, to the outside."

"Never mind the door, man," Squirrel says, already holding a dried sausage in his hand. "After all this mess today, there's probably nothing coming through that we couldn't handle."

"Yes, especially with you around."

"Come on, Ilch, didn't I help you kill that upyr?"

"Don't even mention it!" the Captain exclaims. "Major, isn't this soldier to be reprimanded for opening fire without being ordered to?"

"Ilchenko, consider yourself reprimanded," Lazarov casually says. Ignoring the Captain's frown, he takes a can of 'tourist breakfast' from his rucksack and opens it.

"How can you Stalkers eat all this shit? If I had to feed on nothing but this crap, my farts would have a bigger blast radius than a hand grenade."

"Why, Ilchenko, are army rations any better?"

"No, sir, but at least in the army we get a leave once in a while, and with that a chance to eat better food." No matter how much he bitches about the processed meat, Ilchenko still takes a big portion and continues munching, talking between mouthfuls. "For me, sir, surviving in the army means surviving to the next leave... I wish I could be a camel, stocking up enough *galipots, blunts, piroshky* until the next time I get something decent to eat."

"Camels stock up on liquids, you moron."

"Come on, kid. I didn't mention beer and vodka because that's self-explanatory for a real man. Which you obviously aren't."

Lazarov expects a snappy reply from the sharp-tongued Stalker, so Mac's silence surprises him.

"What's up, Mac? It's your turn. Did Billy bite off your tongue?"

"I didn't even hear what your pit bull was saying... Captain, does that strange light of yours never go out?"

Obviously happy that someone is talking to him, the old man jumps at the opportunity to talk.

"Never. Only when I remove it from my staff. There is another stone inside the staff and when this one is on fire and they get into... when they... meet?"

"You mean, contact?"

"Yes, young man! When I let them contact, it burns on and on and on."

"When we get out of here, you need to explain all these things to me," Squirrel eagerly says. "I have a great interest in relics myself!"

"If there is enough time, young man... Remember, the Major has no time, and he promised to do something for me."

"Vodka, anyone?"

Lazarov waves Ilchenko's offer away. "Please, Captain, let's forget that for now. First we have to get out of here. And you might want to keep that bottle for later, Ilchenko. We're not back at Bagram yet!"

"Sorry, sir."

"Offer it to the Captain, but here and now I don't want to see you drinking. Clear?"

"Certainly, sir."

"Hey Mac, how did you find your pet jackal anyway?" Squirrel says, before the tension in the air can thicken any more.

"A snake got to *my dog's* mother, Squirrel. Billy is the best companion. He doesn't tell boring jokes, doesn't beg me for a first aid kit and always warns me of dangers ahead."

"That's cool, man. You know, I always wondered why Stalkers didn't use dogs in the Zone to smell out mutants and anomalies."

"Probably because no one has ever made a protection suit with armor plates and gas masks suitable for dogs," Lazarov says. "Besides, not even dogs could smell anything while wearing a gas mask."

"Hmm... that's true. But anyway, it's still a jackal."

"All right. You won. He was a jackal. You happy now?"

"Happy, man. But he still is."

"No. He's a domesticated canine now. And that makes him a dog."

"Whatever. It won't be my balls he'll bite off when he grows up."

"He will not bite my balls either, you can be sure of that."

"Yes, he will."

"No, he won't!"

"You better be careful with mutants, kid. They grow quickly." The major stretches his arms and releases a tired sigh. "All right... Mac, first watch is on you. Squirrel, you're up next. We move out at five sharp."

"You men can sleep," the Captain cuts in. "I need no rest."

"Come on, Captain. You need to rest. And who has ever heard of an officer taking the first watch? It's grunt privilege."

"But I really need no sleep. I had some food, now I don't need to rest. Later, I will rest for a very, very long time."

"That's actually true," Lazarov replies with a shrug. "Because once you get home, your only worry will be journalists and all... you'll be a celebrity. A hero, even."

"I don't think so, Major."

"You don't have to. For now, take my rifle if you insist on keeping watch. I trust you still know how to handle it."

The Captain knows. Lazarov takes his helmet off, rubs his weary eyes and lies down on the ground, crossing his fingers behind his head. His eyelids feel like lead. But before he falls into an uneasy sleep, he turns to the Captain one more time.

"And Captain... if you want me to do that favor you'll have in mind, do not let the kid sneak away... if he has to crap, pee, do his prayers or jerk off, whatever, he will do it in front of you. That's an order."

"But—" the young Stalker tries to cut in.

"Shut up, Mac. Have some rest. Kids like you need at least eight hours of sleep, but four and a half is all you're going to get."

Factory grounds, 28 September 2014, 04:55:00 AFT

The long years spent in the army have made Lazarov's mind develop a strange sense of time. No matter how tired he'd been, when he wakes up and looks at his watch, it shows five minutes to five – just in time. Anxiously, he looks around but relaxes when he sees the seemingly tireless Captain standing at the door, the unnatural light of his relic still glowing and Lazarov's rifle in his hands. Seeing that he is awake, the old man smiles at him.

This man really deserves a medal, Lazarov thinks as he gets up and gives the snoring machine gunner's boots a soft kick. *Or who knows… maybe he'd be better off staying at Bagram. There's so much he could teach the Stalkers.*

"Moving out already?" Ilchenko grumbles, still half asleep.

"Get your gear and check your weapon."

Yawning, Ilchenko gets to his feet and steps over to Mac. Ignoring the jackal pup's growl, he kicks the still sleeping Stalker's leg.

"Hey, dwarf. Get up."

"Jesus, Ilchenko… I've had a nightmare about a upyr chasing me, but waking up in the same space as you makes it appear like the sweetest dream I've ever had."

"Damn it, man. I hate getting up early," Squirrel yawns, awakened by the noise.

"*Dobro utro,* Captain," Lazarov greets the old man. "Any events?"

"Nothing to report, Major," the Captain replies, still smiling. He removes the glowing relic from his staff and puts it into his shoulder bag.

"Mac, give me light over here... You want a little water, Captain Ivanov? Here you go... Why so happy?"

"Today you will do something for me," the old man says, giving back the field flask. "I have been waiting for it for a long time."

Lazarov pours water from his canteen into his hands and rubs it onto his face, then puts on his helmet. He switches on his headlight, but hopes that they will see daylight soon.

"Everyone ready?"

"Last time I take soldiers on a trip," Squirrel grumbles. "No breakfast, no relaxing, no guitar playing, no jokes, only *get ready* and *let's move* and *hurry up*. Like joining the Guardians. It sucks, man."

"You're lucky we don't have time for a little healthy morning exercise. Now fall in line, Squirrel. Ilchenko, you—"

"I'll watch our six. I know, sir."

"— and you, Mac, take point. Captain, you stick with me."

Mac opens the door and cautiously looks around with his rifle ready to shoot. "Clear."

Stepping out of the dark and dilapidated room after many hours in almost complete darkness and confinement, Lazarov feels relief when he finds himself in a spacious hall. Through holes in the roof that looms high above them, he can see the overcast sky. Wherever he looks in the hall, rows of heavy machines stand, although most of them look like little more than heaps of rusty scrap metal. On some of the concrete columns supporting the roof, metal ladders lead to a gangway that runs around the factory hall, apparently to grant access to the pipes and wires above. Here and there, they hang loose, torn or fallen from the fittings that had held them once upon a time.

The relatively open space might be a relief for his senses dulled by the narrow caves, but the intensifying noise of the Geiger counter is anything but relaxing.

No wonder... everything here is metal. This place is one huge radiation trap.

"I detect high radiation readings. Masks on, switch to breathing systems," the major orders.

Seeing that the Captain has only his age-old gas mask to protect himself makes Lazarov wonder how he had survived after the nukes went off, even if the radiation in this area is not as high as it must be in the areas south of the Outpost, closer to the epicenter of the detonations.

How did he manage that?

Although there are no signs of mutants or any other hostile elements nearby, they keep their weapons at the ready as they follow Mac to a huge gate that stands wide open to a courtyard containing several wrecked trucks and other disabled vehicles. Beyond the wrecks and a wall of concrete slabs, earthy brown hills come into view with the towering peaks of the Salang Range beyond them on the far horizon.

Only a dozen meters separate them from the gate when Lazarov hears the noise of metal falling on metal. For a few seconds, he wonders if one more of the decaying fittings has yielded to the weight of pipes and wires above, letting a loose screw fall and hit one of the machines below.

Then he hears a burst from an assault rifle. He ducks, barely avoiding the bullets that hit one of the machines instead. A ricochet hits the back of his body armor.

"Dushmans!" Mac screams. "Dushmans at two o'clock!"

"Take cover! There's one firing from that ramp above us!"

Ilchenko's PKM sprays the ramp with bullets and a dushman fighter falls headlong from above, his cry of agony ended when his body smashes into one of the machines.

"Where did they come from?" Squirrel shouts, peering out from under the cover of a machine. A bullet barely misses his head. The Stalker ducks and fires a burst, holding the weapon out over his cover position.

"Everywhere!"

Seeing that they are trapped between two rows of machines, offering an easy target to the enemy fighters shooting at them from above, Lazarov realizes that the only way is forward, into the courtyard, shooting their way through any enemies who might be waiting outside. But he knows that if he were leading the attacking party, he would have laid an ambush outside instead of attacking them in the hall where the machines and concrete columns offer more than enough cover. Presuming that the commander of the opposing fighters is no fool, he is sure that the dushmans themselves had not been prepared to find them here, and their lack of tactical preparation could mean the advantage lies with him and his men.

"Ilchenko, take out those dushmans on the ramp!"

"Yes, *komandir!*"

"There's one! At eleven!"

Crouching, Ilchenko swings the machine gun in the direction instructed by the major and fires. "That's one less!"

"Squirrel! Move forward! Cover the Captain!"

Squirrel does as commanded, reloading his rifle as he proceeds with the Captain in tow. He has almost reached the last machine in the row, from where the gate is only a few meters away, when a huge dushman fighter appears behind them and turns toward them to fire his AK. With Ilchenko and the Captain directly in his line of sight, Lazarov has no clear shot on him.

"Behind you!" he screams. "Get down!"

The dushman fires, but he has barely pulled the trigger when the Captain's staff smashes into his head. Squirrel's rifle completes the kill.

"Wow, man! Never seen anyone fight like that!"

"Ramp is clear!" Ilchenko shouts. "No more fire from above!"

"Wrong!" comes a voice from the ramp.

Aided by the built-in scope of his assault rifle, Mac lays down lethal and accurate fire on the attackers. Now the roles have been reversed: it is the dushmans hiding while Lazarov and his companions dash towards the gate, while Mac makes full use of the high vantage point.

Lazarov, Squirrel and the Captain quickly find cover behind two mangled trucks covering their flanks. In a few seconds, Ilchenko joins them. Lazarov is about to call the young Stalker out of the hall when more enemies appear and Ilchenko immediately opens fire.

"How many more dushmans are in this goddamned place?" he roars over the rattle of his machine gun.

"Captain! Get under that truck, quickly! Mac, can you hear me?" Lazarov shouts into his intercom, hoping that the kid has switched on his own.

"Loud and clear, big brother!"

"More visitors from the south! From your position, that's nine o'clock. Make it here quickly and let's catch them in a crossfire!"

"On my way!"

Aiming and firing his weapon as he lays concealed under the truck, covering the Captain with his own body, Lazarov sees Mac climb down a ladder and move towards the truck from the corner of his eye. He has almost reached it when a dushman, whom he already believed dead, raises his weapon.

"Mac! Hostile at your left, on the ground! Watch out!"

His warning comes too late for Mac. The dushman lifts his weapon and fires at Mac from point-blank range. Hit in the side, the Stalker cries out in pain and collapses.

"Ilchenko! Mac is down! Cover me!"

The machine gunner fires a long burst into the direction of the attackers. Using the momentarily lapse of hostile fire, Lazarov fires a burst into the still moving dushman who had shot the kid, then dashes to the Stalker's body to drag it into safety. Suddenly, the PKM's fire cuts out.

"Weapon's jammed!"

"Squirrel! Keep on firing!"

"Just loaded my last clip!"

Immediately, the hostiles open fire again. Lazarov drags Mac's body away from the gate and inside, hoping that no dushman remains alive in there to give him a nasty surprise. Ilchenko's PKM fires up again outside.

"They are withdrawing!"

"Keep on firing! Squirrel, watch out to the right!"

"Come, dushmans, come! Papa Ilchenko is waiting for you!"

Relieved that the battle's balance is shifting in their favor, Lazarov places Mac into cover between a cabin that must once have been a guard post watching over the entrance and the machine hall's wall, and begins to check the Stalker's condition. Billy emerges completely unscathed, but an inch away from the carrying bag holding the yelping mutant, two bullets have penetrated the body armor's weaker side panels.

Thank God for making the third bullet fired in a Kalashnikov's burst almost always miss the target.

First, he lifts the visor of the helmet and tears the gas mask off the Stalker's face to facilitate his breathing, leaving only the sand-colored balaclava as a cover. Then, pushing the snarling mutant away, Lazarov opens the zipper and buckles on Mac's exoskeleton, preparing himself for the sight of blood and gore under the armor plates.

What he sees makes him forget about Billy who bites into his thick weapon gloves, trying to pull Lazarov's hand off of his master's body.

Tits. Nice ones.

A smile comes to his face as he remembers Mac's words about the jackal pup not biting off 'his' balls. *She was wrong,* he thinks while opening a first aid kit. *She does have balls. Much more than some men do.*

To his relief, the bullets hadn't penetrated the armor. He quickly applies an adhesive bandage from his first aid kit to the bruised body parts and closes the armor.

Outside, among the ceasing gunfire, Squirrel gives a triumphant cry. "Yeah! This will teach them not to come to places they aren't invited to!"

"Are you okay, Major?"

"I'm fine, Ilchenko. The kid will make it too."

"Damn. One can't have it all... You need assistance?"

"No! It's not time to relax yet. Wait a little longer!"

Lazarov takes a deep breath and pulls up the balaclava still covering Mac's face. The young Stalker opens her eyes, which twinkle in the harsh light falling through the gate, now untamed by the helmet's dark visor.

Normally, Lazarov would have taken the face for that of a handsome young man. Now that he knows Mac's secret, he is not misguided by the short hair and grimy face. He recognizes the soft features characteristic of a female face, even if Mac had obviously done everything she could to hide her beauty – because even with her face dusty and grimy, she does look beautiful. Not breathtakingly gorgeous or irresistibly desirable, but in the way of natural beauty that only young women have, in the way of natural sex appeal assigned to the trappings of youth.

"What are you staring at?" Mac tries to get up to her feet, but immediately emits a moan of pain, reaching for her bruised side. "Shit... hurts like hell... am I hit?"

"Just a bruise, thanks to your exo," Lazarov replies and, to cover up his knowledge of Mac's secret, he adds, "you're a lucky son of a bitch, you little bastard. We had to finish the dushmans while you were groaning and moaning. Next time try not to get shot so easily, is that clear?"

"Clear. Ouch—hey, what's that?" She asks patting the armor above the place where Lazarov has adjusted the bandage.

"First time you get patched up by someone else?" Lazarov turns his face away to hide an ear to ear grin. "Stupid little kid! You should have stayed home and played video games until you became man enough to enter the Zones of Alienation."

"*Andate a la mierda, forro...!*"

By the sound of the curse that Mac whispers, Lazarov can tell that she understood his message and is not very happy about what he has found out.

"Ilchenko," he shouts over to the machine gunner. "All clear?"

"All clear!"

"They ran like dogs!" the guide shouts. "Hope they'll tell the other freaks that Squirrel was here!"

The major supports Mac as she gets to her feet. To his relief, it appears that everyone outside is unharmed.

"Wouldn't be the New Zone if getting back to daylight was easy," Lazarov tells Mac. "But hey… at least the view is not so bad."

Through a torn-down section of the factory wall, a view opens to the plains below. Followed by his companions, Lazarov walks to the edge of the plateau.

Strong winds throw up dust from the ground and drive dark clouds across the sky, covering the sun. Long rays of sunlight pierce through the clouds, as if combing the hills and forest stretching out below their feet. Not far from their position, Hellgate is looming where the orange flames of the anomalies burst up into the sky and cast a purple haze over the stone arch. From up here, it looked like the claws of a giant predator reaching out from the earth, and to Lazarov, they seemed to be the claws of the New Zone itself, threatening the sky with all its menacing power. The dark clouds finally chase away the last ray of light, making the Shamali Plains appear in pale shades of gray and blue.

"Getting down should be easier," Squirrel says. "With just a little caution, we can simply climb down."

"Yes. No need to go back the same way we came. You don't need me any longer."

All faces turn to the Captain.

His shoulder bag lies on the ground. Exhaustion is written throughout his fragile figure, but it's not from the rigors of the past twenty-four hours. Leaning on his staff, his worn out duster and long beard blown by the wind, he looks just like what he is: an emaciated, weary old man with a million wrinkles on his bearded face.

"Major Lazarov... I see that you have found what you were looking for," he says, jerking his head at Mac. "And now, will you carry out a task for me?"

The major frowns, knowing that it is high time for him to continue with his mission.

"Don't worry," the Captain says, seeing Lazarov's hesitation. "It will not take much of your precious time. What is your answer?"

"First, tell me what you need."

"No. First, you need to hear me out."

The Captain takes a few steps toward the precipice and turns towards the vast plains, standing still with the wind slowly playing with his ragged coat. He stretches out his arms, as if he wanted to bless, or at least embrace, the hopeless wilderness. Then he turns back and looks into Lazarov's eyes.

"It's about the column... The column that was lost."

And I was hoping he'd have got his wits together by now, the major thinks.

"The column left Kunduz in early January 1988. Twenty Ural trucks, three T-62 tanks, five BMP troop carriers, three fuel tankers full of petrol and gasoline. It had to get through."

"Yes, I guess it had to," Lazarov replies impatiently.

"The column was going to Khost. It never arrived. It was betrayed."

"I heard you couldn't trust the Afghans about anything."

"The Afghans... first, they killed the armor driving up front. With RPGs like that." The Captain points at Squirrel and gestures firing a rocket propelled grenade with his hands. "Kaboom! Kaboom! Then those in the rear. Bang! Kaboom! No vehicle could move. It was snowing heavily, and no helicopters came to help. When the trucks were burning, they stormed down on us. They slit the throats of those who were not shot. They captured our *komandir* and beheaded him, praising their god. Some were left to die in the snow, to freeze to death or be eaten by jackals and wolves."

Mac suddenly stops stroking the mutant pup. Lazarov is surprised about his own lack of emotions over this story – instead of sadness or anger, all he feels is exhaustion.

"What was left of our load, weapons, ammunition, fuel, went into the dushmans' hands. It never reached the *desantniki* fighting in the Panjir Valley. It is safe to suppose that they also died. All this happened because of a traitor."

"How did you get away, Captain?"

"It was not the Afghans who betrayed us."

Lazarov frowns. He already suspects where the story will go, but he wants to hear out what the old man still has to say. "Carry on, Captain."

"I see you have already guessed it, Major. I was the traitor. I sold out the column to the dushmans in exchange for passage to Pakistan and then to America. They let me down. I deserved it."

Lazarov looks at his comrades. Ilchenko is staring at his boots. Squirrel is toying with his anomaly detector, watching Lazarov's reaction from the corner of his eyes. Mac is standing with her face mask open, her hand resting on Billy's head. A cloud of sadness hangs over all three of them. He clears his throat and turns back to the Captain.

"You certainly deserved twenty-eight years in prison for that, and I cannot imagine a worse prison than this place."

"You really think so?"

"What do you want from us now?" he asks back, shunning the Captain's eyes.

"I want you, Major, to court-martial me and execute me for treason."

"What?"

"You heard me."

"Captain... what you did was horrendous, but you have paid the price. The country that should have court-martialed you doesn't exist any longer. Let's forget what you've just said. Come with us."

"I can't. How could I look into the faces of people? I could meet the mother of one of the men who died because of me. Or a son who had grown up without a father. How would that be: the dear one dead, the traitor alive?"

Lazarov bows his head. "That's just an imagined situation."

"Even if I was wrong, a Soviet... a Russian officer's lost honor is not just imagination."

Mac gives him a startled look, but Lazarov ignores her.

"For a long time, I longed for this," the Captain continues. "I prayed day and night to survive here and to be spared being shot by dushmans or torn apart by mutants when I grew too old to defend myself. I prayed to live until the day came when I could die a proper death. A traitor's well-deserved death, but at least delivered in an officer's manner. This is what I ask of you in exchange for guiding you, Major Lazarov."

Lazarov draws his pistol. Seeing this, Squirrel and Mac start shouting at him.

"Hey man, you can't be serious about listening to this lunatic?"

"Put that gun away! We must take him to safety!"

Only Ilchenko stands silently. He buttons up his body armor and stiffens his stance. Lazarov turns towards the two Stalkers.

"You two, step back. Now. And you, Captain, excuse me for a moment."

With the others out of hearing range, Lazarov turns to the machine gunner. "What do you think of this?"

"I am just a grunt, not supposed to judge officers."

"Cut the crap. You grunts do nothing else behind our back."

Ilchenko gives a scornful glance towards the Captain. "Honestly, sir? To a dog—a dog's death!"

"But we don't have capital punishment anymore."

"*We?* He is not one of us. I mean, he is, but he belongs to the Soviet army, and in the USSR, such treason was punished with death."

"But the USSR doesn't exist anymore, neither does her law, and capital punishment is no longer applied in Russia either."

"Sir... permission to speak freely? It is not a legal argument that's expected of us now."

"True."

"I'm sure you'll do what's right, sir."

Now I know what it means to stand in front of a man whose betrayal killed my father, Lazarov thinks. *But I also know what he has been through. He survived twenty-five years in Afghanistan and three years in a new Zone. As much time as I have spent in the old Zone. Fate was the only thing that kept me alive. It is not up to me to judge him. I can't judge fate.*

"Taking him home would be of no help to him, and you are right. Maybe he wouldn't deserve it at all. All we can do is to restore his honor and dignity."

"Deserters have no honor and dignity, and traitors even less so."

"Honor is not born with us. Neither is dignity. I don't believe in all that bullshit about human rights. One has to earn honor and dignity the hard way and can lose it the easy way. At least that's what life has taught me."

"Sir, if I may ask, were you brought up on the streets?"

"No. I had a very happy childhood, apart from the absence of my father who died when I was very young. He was as a

BMP driver with the other soldiers of the very same column that the Captain has betrayed."

Ilchenko takes a step back in surprise. "*Gospodi...* I was a bit confused when you showed him that photograph, but now I understand. May he and the others rest in peace... I was just asking because I did grow up on the streets and I agree with you two hundred percent!"

"If so, then you probably also agree if I say that this man has by now regained his honor and dignity?"

"And if he did, does this change the past?"

"Not at all. But only those with honor and dignity can pass a fair judgment upon themselves."

Turning away from the puzzled soldier, Lazarov clears his throat and addresses the Captain.
"Captain Igor Vasilyevich Ivanov, stand to attention! You have committed the most despicable crimes an officer can commit: treason, resulting in the deaths of your comrades, and cowardice in the face of the enemy. Your infamy is all the worse for your base reasons. Such crimes are punishable by death."

The Captain stands stiffly to attention and eagerly listens to Lazarov's words, but now he also has to say something. He points to the shoulder bag that lies on the ground. "You forgot to add the forfeiture of all assets."

"And the forfeiture of all assets, yes." Lazarov takes a deep breath before continuing. "Nonetheless – your ability to survive for so many years in the direst of environments and your readiness to assist your fellow soldiers to complete a dangerous mission in times of war, has proven that you are once more worthy to be called an officer of... any army, living up to and even surpassing the highest standards set for honor and dignity. Therefore I... uhm, this court-martial concludes that your honor and dignity as an officer is restored."

With a bow of his head, Lazarov hands his pistol to the Captain.

A smile appears on the old soldier's face. He takes the pistol and salutes. Lazarov and Ilchenko return the salute.

"Thank you, Major, and God bless you. All of you."

The Captain looks up to the gray sky. Then he closes his eyes, puts the weapon to his head, and pulls the trigger.

The shot is still echoing among the hills when Captain Ivanov's body falls backwards from plateau and disappears below, his fingers still clutching at the weapon, the evil land itself having finally claimed his tormented soul.

Squirrel and Mac step up. For a minute, the four companions stand there as if turned to stone. Then Ilchenko speaks up.

"Major... that was awesome."

"I need a new sidearm," Lazarov replies with a shrug, and turns away from his companions.

Stalker camp at Hellgate, 22:38:04 AFT

The fire slowly burns itself out. Mac rakes the fire with the Captain's staff while Billy sleeps in her lap, digesting a huge portion of 'tourist breakfast'.

"So, that was the story of our raid," Squirrel says, watching as the last sparks fly high from the fire into the starry sky. He takes a long draw at his joint and slowly exhales the smoke. "I can't complain. I didn't find a Heartstone, but the Captain's glowing relic is a nice one. Probably I won't sell it. Nah, I'll keep it for sure."

"What is it called?" Mishka Slash asks.

"No idea. That's what I love about this place. New Zone – new relics and all."

"Then you should give it a name."

"What about... I don't know. Hey, Ilch, give me that bottle!"

"Lich would be a good choice," Mac says gazing into the fire. Her helmet is placed at her side, and through the balaclava's holes that leaves her eyes and mouth visible, the trace of a sad smile appears.

"Cool, man. Lich it will be then. But what's a lich, anyway?"

"All kids know that. A lich is a magician who stays alive through many centuries. Usually, they are evil. Do you agree, Major?"

Lazarov, who lies there resting his aching feet and watching the stars, just shrugs the question off.

"I don't know... maybe not all of them."

"Anyway, maybe one day I'll come back to find a Heartstone," Squirrel dreamily says. "I could sell that for a million dollars, rubles, euros, whatever. Or maybe if the Stalker legend is true, I'll just hold on to that relic and it will keep me healthy for the rest of my life."

"Then I beg you not to find it."

"Oh come on, Sashka! Don't spoil a poor man's dreams, man!"

"A million dollars, you said?" Lazarov asks.

"Yup. Okay, maybe just a half million, but still... Why?"

"Just asking." Lazarov hides his smile and puts his hand over the relic container on his armored suit, where he has put the relic he found in the Captain's bag.

Forfeiture of assets... If he hadn't mentioned that, I would have completely forgotten about his bag.

"That was a very nice story, fellows, but we still don't have the answer to Question Number One," Mishka Slash says and finishes the sentence in a chorus with Sashka Commando: *"Where are the women?"*

Lazarov sits up and looks at Mac from the corner of his eye, trying to suppress a smile. She sits quietly, not looking at any of the Stalkers.

"And what about you, kid?" he asks. "Where do you want to go now?"

"Panjir. Anywhere but Bagram."

"Grouch will be disappointed."

"That's not my problem."

A shout comes from the darkness. "Stalkers coming through! Try not to shoot us, will you?"

Beefeater and Ilchenko appear from the darkness.

"All clear, sir. Everything is quiet around the perimeter."

"That's a camp, not a perimeter," Mishka Slash says, feigning embarrassment. "Relax, soldier! You're among Stalkers now!"

"Welcome back, *patsanni*," Squirrel greets them. "I was just in the middle of telling a joke to these bores here. So: what does a whore give her best client for Christmas? AIDS."

"Not bad, but I know a better one, " Ilchenko says. "How do you make a little girl cry twice? Wipe your bloody dick on her teddy bear!"

"Cool!" Sashka Commando hands Ilchenko a vodka bottle. "I'll need to remember that, haha!"

The Stalkers laugh, only Mac scowls. "Screw that. I heard it a thousand times."

"What's wrong with you?" Ilchenko asks, still laughing at his own joke.

"You better ask what's wrong with your jokes. They are disgusting. And even worse, they're boring too."

"Apologies, Prince Myshkin," Ilchenko says, faking a polite bow. "I didn't mean to offend your sensitivity!"

"If there's an idiot amongst the two of us, Ilch, it's certainly not me."

"I guess you have met your match," Lazarov says smirking at the machine gunner.

"You're all pricks. I can't wait to leave with Beefeater for the Panjir Valley in the morning."

"Two tree-huggers teaming up... a match made in heaven!"

"Slash, stop teasing the kid or I'll kick your teeth in," Beefeater grumbles while taking notes on a writing block.

"At last something that could distract you from your scribbling."

"I need to remind myself that I still can write, Sashka, not just push buttons on a palmtop. I'm writing a book — *'Zone and the Art of Weapon Maintenance'*."

"Sounds strangely familiar, somehow," Ilchenko says rubbing his chin.

"God damn it," Mishka Slash shouts. "I need a woman, now!" He gets to his feet, takes his rifle and imitates copulation.

"Keep the bees in your fucking pants, you daft bugger!" Beefeater says, waving the Stalker's rifle away from him.

"Mac," Lazarov quietly says, "let's take a hike. We need to talk."

Lazarov offers his hand to help Mac up but the Stalker jerks it away.

"Don't even think about talking me into going back to Bagram."

"How's that bandage doing? You might need me to apply a new one. "

"No... no... okay, maybe having a little walk is a good idea."

"Indeed. Eases the heart, refreshes the soul. Right?"

Lazarov waves for her to follow him to the ruined hut where they will be out of hearing range, then takes a deep breath before questioning her.

"So... I guess you owe me an explanation, Mac."

"I don't owe you anything."

"Yes, you do," Lazarov says, taking Mac's diary from his side bag. "I guess every honest finder deserves a reward. All I ask you in exchange for your notebook is to tell me the truth about yourself."

Mac grabs the notebook from Lazarov's hands. She eagerly looks inside, and hides it safely in the map compartment of her armored suit.

"Where did you find this?"

"The Captain found it after you'd left a campsite, obviously in a hurry."

"It was when a dushman patrol came too close during the night... Thank you very much. There's no more to say."

"Listen, *devushka*, I am not in the mood to play along any further."

"I didn't take you for such a pushy dickhead."

"Agreed, sometimes I can be a pain in the ass. It's part of my job as an officer. And now listen up. I must take you back to Grouch."

"Why?"

"I didn't exactly do this mission to gain favor upstairs. Grouch will only fix my squads' kit and weapons if I bring you back. Besides, his heart is broken. Ignore that if you can."

"Emotional blackmailing is pathetic," she replies, biting her lip.

"But I see it works. Let's start from the beginning. Where are you from?"

"Argentina."

"A woman from Argentina..." Lazarov makes a low whistle. "This place never ceases to surprise."

"So what? Are you still under the effect of what you've seen under my armor?" Mac asks with a coquettish smile.

"No reason to deny that. Actually, I do find you beautiful... even by Argentinean standards."

Mac laughs. "You should see my niece... but come on, have you ever met a woman from Argentina?"

"Uhm... no."

"See? Don't try to be a flirt, it doesn't work for you. Just be who you are. You're a cool enough guy."

"Those Stalkers have a point about women... Here in the New Zone, and back in the old one, we can be who we are. And you too have a point saying that one is cool when he is what he is. But outside... I feel like a fish out of water. No woman out there would ever understand what the Zone of Alienation is about and what she means to me. That's why it's bad that we have no female Stalkers."

"I can't grant wishes, but hope that sooner or later you'll run into a woman who appreciates your radioactive charm. I guess her heart will beat faster than a Geiger counter. Anyway, I know you didn't just want to sob on my shoulders about how lonely you are."

"Well said. And I have no intention of blowing your cover, missy, whatever you have to tell me."

"Is that a promise?"

"Depends. But by now you should know that I keep my promises... just think about what I promised to the Captain."

"Look... Grouch didn't tell you everything. Where should I begin?... It appears to be on another planet now, but anyway, back home I was just tired of everyone, stupid married friends always showing off about their so called wonderful lives, stupid society putting the pressure on me to be a wonder woman..."

"You are."

"I don't need your stupid compliments. I mean it in another way... I hated the expectations of being a woman based only on appearance and pretension... Damn it, many of my friends would have sooner died than let themselves be seen without make-up and stuff. Do you have any idea how tiring it is to live up to all those stereotypes? But one has to, because if one just says 'no' to all that beauty-industry bullshit she gets treated like a weirdo. So, when I heard about the Zone I took a flight to Russia and sneaked in, disguised as a Stalker guy, and I realized that, in there, I needed no more makeup, no short skirts, no eyelashes, nothing that is required from me before others accept me. In my disguise, I could be who I wanted— no expectations, no clichés, no pressure to do something just because fucking social rules pressure me into it... I could just be who I really was. Posing as a male I didn't even have to bother about guys offering their 'help' and 'assistance' at every step. I didn't want to be taken as someone who needs 'help' because I happen to be born with no dick. It's not even flattering, because what the fuck did I do to be treated with all this circumstantiality? Nothing! For once, I wanted to be judged by what I do and not my looks. No flirting, no more stupid games. It's not as if I'm a man-hater or a lesbian, mind you… I do love men. Occasionally, I met some nice Stalker guy and when I was sure he would keep his mouth shut, I gave him the fuck of his young life. There's more things one can do during the night than sitting around a campfire and telling dumb jokes, you know? And if I met a tough guy who bitched at me because he took me for just another Stalker, I bitched back at him. *Vsyo zaebalo, pizdyets, na huy, blyad, idi na huy, huyesos!* How's that?"

"Not bad. Start smoking and soon you can pronounce the most important word like we Russians do. *Khui.* From your throat. By the way, how do you say it in Spanish?"

"*Pija*, and something inside me says you're a *pijudo*. Anyway, I eventually made my way to the center where I prayed for the Zone to unsex me…"

"Good God."

"…and what did it do to me? I saw a bright flash and after a second my G36 and Stalker suit were gone and I was standing there in this exoskeleton with an FN2000 on my shoulder, and later I realized that all my hair was gone!"

"It's growing back."

"I'm not talking about a bad hair day, you moron. Imagine, I couldn't take off that damned exo! I was imprisoned into it! I made my way back to Grouch because he was the closest mechanic. It took him eight hours to get the suit off me without totally destroying it, because it's a pretty good suit after all. Then I stayed with him because grew to like him… Eventually he got me out of that suit and of course saw what I couldn't hide, but he was cool enough to keep it to himself. Now don't give me such a jealous look. Grouch could be my father! He actually tried to act like one… kind of."

"He's quite fond of you indeed. So, when Grouch moved his business to this new Zone you went with him, but left him nonetheless when you got bored. Right?"

"That's correct. I'm sorry, but that's just the way I am. I can't stay put in the same place for too long. It's got me into a lot of trouble. Grouch is cool, but listening to his monologues about optical image enhancements and titanium rod replacements and soft trigger mechanisms all day long... it's hardly exciting after a while."

"I'd disagree. But why did you pick such an English-sounding name if you're from Argentina?"

"If you'd ever read something apart from weapon manuals, you'd get it by yourself. My real name is Elisabeth. Well, almost. I always wanted to go through a sort of Lady Macbeth transformation — getting rid of my weakness, or better: of my quality to be interpreted by others as weak and soft, something to be patronized, just because... Anyway, Beth — Mac — Macbeth. *Ti ponish?*"

"Yes, I understand. Let's hope Ilchenko doesn't find out about this."

"How would he?" Mac shrugs. "He's an idiot."

"He studied literature before he... never mind, my point is that he's smarter than he seems."

"If that's what Ilchenko is like when he's awake, I'd hate to be in his dreams."

"That's just the way he is. I don't want you to walk hand in hand and pluck flowers on the way back to Bagram... there aren't too many flowers here anyway."

"Forget it. I want to go to the Panjir Valley and check out that Stalker paradise."

"Why do you make my life so difficult?" Lazarov sighs. "I asked you nicely. Let's do it the hard way then... I think I'll just ask everyone to put out the campfire by peeing on it."

Aghast, Mac steps away from Lazarov.

"You wouldn't dare!"

"That would be the moment of truth for you, wouldn't it?"

"You really are a jerk, you know that?"

"Hey, what happened to 'cool enough guy'?" Amused by the fear and anger dancing in Mac's eyes, Lazarov gives her a grin.

"Shit!"

"We're all deep in it. So, will you come and see Grouch or not?"

For a minute, Mac bites her lower lip. Then she slowly sighs before responding. "The deal with Grouch was just to take me back to Bagram, not about making me stay there. Is that correct?"

Lazarov nods. Mac sighs again, this time in submission. "Okay, you win. I'll pay Grouch a visit but only if you promise me to never, never ever tell anyone about my secret."

"We have a deal."

Mac mumbles something in Spanish that sounds like a very obscene curse.

"You are free to bitch at me if you want," Lazarov says with a shrug, "but I appreciate that you don't make my life any harder, Beth."

For a minute, she examines her dirty fingernails, then fixes Lazarov with a piercing stare. "I lied to you... actually, I liked your compliments. It's been a while since anyone called me beautiful... Anyway, I guess you did read my diary."

"Parts of it."

"Can't blame you. I'd do the same. That's why I kept writing about a few things in my language. Not much... but important things. I had a lover back in the old Zone. His name was Raider."

Now it's Lazarov who almost recoils with surprise.

"Raider? The idol of all Stalkers?"

"Yeah", Mac continues, "It was love.... tough love. He loved me through hurting me. On the outside, he was guiding me. Educating even. But he lost his wits to the Zone. He took pleasure in my pain, and I took the same pleasure in being hurt by him because, for me, he was the Zone himself."

"*Himself?* Strange... see, I'm a man and always think of the Zone as a *she*."

"Define ultimate attraction. But those big mouths over there," Mac says pointing at the campfire, "they know nothing. Anyway, have you ever met Raider?"

"Never," Lazarov says, avoiding her sad gaze.

"Then you do not understand what it means to find another human being who resembles everything about what the Zone means. A new reason for staying alive. For me, it was love. Finding such a love and losing it is worse than your heart being ripped out by a mutant's claws. I do hope, Major, that one day you will find such love, so that you understand what I was talking about... maybe a woman who is as much an avatar of the female Zone as Raider embodied the masculine Zone to me."

"I do understand what you mean," Lazarov replies although Mac's words strike home more in his heart than his mind. "Now we better take a few logs from this hut to feed the fire."

She ushers a long, tired sigh. "No, you don't understand... one needs to hack your alpha ego down to size but I'm not up to that. All right... let's get back to testosterone wrapped up in niceties. If I'm a woman and you're a man, that means *you* carry the wood, right?"

"With pleasure," Lazarov says and smiles.

06:17:58 AFT

At sunrise, Lazarov watches the two Stalkers and Ilchenko walking ahead towards Bagram. Mac has the Captain's staff over her shoulder, occasionally swinging off towards Billy who tries to grab it with its teeth. Beefeater and Ilchenko walk at her side, their weapons cradled. All three seem to be in a good mood and Lazarov cannot shake off a niggling feeling of jealousy.

"From the Perimeter to the center, from the Old Zone to the New, from Bagram to that place that's supposed to be a Stalker's paradise... Will some people never stop chasing dreams?" he asks Squirrel, pensively.

"See... to me, that's what being a Stalker is all about. Why, you don't have any dreams left to dream?"

"My dream is to find a place which I would never want to leave again."

"Now look at that! Who would have thought that you have a free Stalker's heart beating under that dirty armored suit... Will we also go to the Panjir Valley, then?"

Squirrel's question hauls the major back to reality. He shakes his head. "Maybe another time... Let's get back to Bagram for supplies. Then we go to Ghorband."

"Cool, man," Squirrel says. "You gonna make me rich. This trip already cost you a fortune, you know that?"

Encrypted digital VOP transmission. Central Afghanistan, 29 September 2014, 08:44:13 AFT

#We did not get the shipment. The transport was ambushed.#

#What the hell are you talking about?#

#Your little games are annoying. You were supposed to maintain order in your area.#

#I'm so sorry about this. I could almost cry. Boo-hoo! And now listen to me you bastards. It's not my fucking problem if your incompetent monkeys got whacked. I delivered your stuff. The rest was up to you.#

#Negative... #

#Negative, positive, negative...could you speak like a human being instead of a robot for once?#

#Negative. We learned that you failed to get rid of the outsider. We are through with you. You have been warned.#

#Don't think you can scare me, you slit-eyed little monkey.#

#[static noise]#

Wilderness, 1 October 2014, 18:10:14 AFT

The New Zone does have her beauty, the major thinks as he scans the landscape through the state of the art scope on his newly-upgraded sniper rifle.

Evening is approaching and Lazarov is standing on the top of a hill overlooking the road in the meandering valley. Not far from him, Squirrel is trying to lure a decent chord from his harmonica, without much success.

Since leaving Bagram an hour before daylight, they had been advancing cautiously, sneaking from point to point, scanning the towering mountains for enemies and keeping an eye over the gloomy forest in the valley beneath the snowy peaks.

Abandoned villages and war debris offered more than enough cover, and they have passed many Soviet wrecks: tanks with their turrets blown off, BTRs with ripped open hulls… A defaced, bullet-riddled memorial that might once have marked the location of a successful break-through or the death of a high-ranking officer had served as a rest stop while they had eaten their ration-pack lunch.

In the afternoon, he had observed a pack of jackals as they were finishing off a deer. Saving the defenseless mutant had been a good opportunity for Lazarov to test the abilities of his upgraded weapon, and he'd managed to shoot the pack leader from a safe distance without the mutant even realizing what had hit it. It had been hard not to laugh as the death of their alpha sent the rest of the pack into a leaderless sprawl and Lazarov had been more than satisfied with the smooth handling and accuracy of his silenced rifle, though he hoped that he would never get into a situation requiring the use of his other reward: a shiny black Beretta M-9 pistol with enhanced automatic fire mode and extended magazine to compensate for the somewhat underpowered 9mm bullets. He'd had enough of underground tunnels and close quarter fighting, at least for a while.

Caves, appearing as dark dots among the rocks, had tempted them to seek refuge and rest, but they had toiled up the road to this hill, and now the valley stretched out beneath his feet. The sun, slowly sinking behind the peaks, paints the white ridges a fiery red and sends the valley into gloomy oblivion for the night.

Turning westwards, a tiny orange point appears in the scope. A drop of rain blurs his view and Lazarov wipes it off. As he walks down the hill and waves to Squirrel to follow him, the rain begins to cascade down, covering up the magnificent sunset with a curtain of grey clouds.

Deep in the gorge to the west, a campfire shimmers.

Ghorband, Stalker base, 19:51:08 AFT

"Lower your weapons!"

Signaling his peaceful intentions, Lazarov halts his steps. He shoulders his rifle and waves to the heavily armed Stalker guarding a road block. Beyond the low wall of sand bags, a fire blazes in what was once a tank's engine compartment. The flames cast a flickering light onto the massive, strike-marked mud walls nearby. Raindrops sizzle as they meet the flames. Another Stalker is watching them from the hatch of the wreck, his long-barreled shotgun ready to fire.

"We seek no trouble," the major says.

"What's your business here?"

"Whatever it is, it's not about standing here in the rain with two would-be Rambos pointing their shooters at us," Squirrel impatiently says. "Come on, man, I've tamed this soldier boy. We're passing through and seek shelter for the night."

"Squirrel! I didn't recognize you. Get into the compound, brothers!"

Passing the wrecked, trackless tank, they arrive at the gate of a building surrounded by a high wall. More Stalkers guard the entrance.

"Come in! Don't stand there," one of them says, gesturing to him. A sign on the gate says 'NO WEAPONS BEYOND THIS POINT' in English, apparently ignored by everyone.

There is a campfire inside, lit up in a fuel drum riddled with bullet-holes, that casts a dim light into the compound. Another wrecked vehicle that Lazarov recognizes as a US-made personnel carrier sits close by. A few Stalkers are sitting under what had been a veranda once upon a time, trying to find cover from the rain pouring through the holes like bullets from a machine gun. From the wilderness outside, jackals' howls pierce the drumming sound of rain and Lazarov thinks that nothing in the world would tempt him to swap position with the sentries walking along the walls. He notices that apart from the Stalkers hiding under the veranda who look like rookies, most men wear better armor and heavier weapons than those in Bagram.

"Get me out of this hellhole," a rookie Stalker groans. "I swear to God, I am done with relics and stashes and loot. I only want to get out of here!"

"Hey bro," another one says, reaching out to Squirrel. "I'll give you my shotgun if you guide me back to Bagram!"

"Pull yourself together, man," the guide snarls back, shaking the Stalker's hand off.

"I can't... not since I saw them taking Danylo away. I told him not to wear that damned dushman armor but he said it's still better than a leather jacket... since then they must have ripped him to pieces!"

"What are you talking about?" Lazarov asks.

"The Tribe... they are close. I heard the bell and ran. I want to get out of here... If only someone could help me!"

"You heard the—*what?*"

"The bell of the Tribe! Those cannibals must have been out on a man hunt!"

Inside the building a few petroleum lights fight the shadows. Someone has improvised a table from a simple wooden board laid on two fuel drums. The Stalker standing at it, nursing a half-empty bottle of vodka, looks familiar.

"Skinner?" Lazarov asks, stepping closer. "Is that you?"

"Yep," the renegade Guardian reluctantly replies.

"I'm glad you made it through here. How are you doing?"

"Spare me the bullshit, Major. A buddy of mine, Vaska, was supposed to return yesterday from a raid. Still no trace of him. 'Nuff said… if you need company, talk to the Shrink. I'm not into gum-beating right now."

Lazarov shrugs and turns towards the stout Stalker manning the bar. Seeing the major approaching, the barkeeper stops wiping the shot glasses and looks at him with smart, curious eyes.

"At last one who doesn't smell like he's shit his pants," he says by way of greeting to the major. "Welcome to the Asylum, soldier. I'm Borys the Shrink."

"Why do they call you a shrink?"

"Because I can heal your brains with vodka or your rifle with ammo. Seeing that you still have your wits, it's obviously ammo that you need."

"Ammo is not exactly my problem."

"So you want to talk? Vodka, then. Here you go."

The local vodka tastes purer and cooler than in Bagram, and Lazarov licks his lips as the spirit flows down his throat, creating pleasant warmth inside his body.

"That's good stuff you have here. What is this place?"

"It used to be a fortress and then a prison, until some Western do-gooders turned it into an asylum. That was back before the nukes went off. Now it's a fitting place for those who were crazy enough to go farther out and lucky enough to make it back."

"Gone farther? I heard there's a place called Shahr-i-Gholghola to the west."

"That's correct. About two or three days' march from here."

"Have you been there?"

"No." The Shrink leans over the bar and lowers his voice. "That's where Skinner's buddy went... People say it was freaky enough before the Bush war began, after the Taliban blasted those big Buddhas away, but recently..." The barkeeper cuts his sentence short. "This is no kindergarten here like Bagram. Frankly, sometimes I'm glad we have the Tribe between us and that place."

"The Tribe? That's why everyone's so scared around here?"

"They aren't scared, they just haven't had enough to drink... anyhow, to answer your question: the Tribe is a bad enough neighbor but things got really weird recently. A few days ago, a Stalker appeared. He was gone for many days and we all presumed him dead, saying toasts to his memory and all, and then he came back. He was not happy to see us again, though... he opened fire on us. His own friends had to shoot him."

Lazarov is too absorbed in the vodka's calming effect to say anything compassionate. "Give me and my guide another shot."

"Cheers! Wouldn't be much of an event if killing him had been easy, but he kept standing up again and again like a freaking zombie. I had to apply the strongest remedy I know."

"And that would be?"

"Emptying a full magazine of Parabellum bullets into his brain."

"I see. Anyway, have you seen a Stalker called Crow around? He uses an SVD and wears a camouflage coat. Black balaclava, cold eyes, slightly necromantic... I mean, he likes putting half-smoked cigarettes into the mouths of people he has just killed and stuff like that. Well trained, probably ex-military. Know anyone like that?"

"Let me think... Maybe you mean that Loner who was waiting for some soldier boy who is fond of vodka, has a cynical, bossy attitude, and keeps trying to squeeze others for information? Sounds like you and must be you," the barkeeper says with a smirk. "He arrived in a hurry from Bagram two days ago, then went to raid a patrol of mercs. At least that's what he said. He was waiting for you afterwards but disappeared again. There's a pen drive he left here for you... Here it is."

Lazarov plugs the device into his palmtop and a new message appears on the screen.

Hey, Condor. I wanted to make sure this didn't get to your palmtop before you reached Ghorband. It wouldn't have been nice if the wrong person had found it after killing you. Proceed two klicks to the west, where you'll find a memorial and the wreck of an APC. Check the engine compartment. There's a stash waiting for you. Shrink is cool but don't forget to delete this message just in case. I have to hurry back to the Shamali Plains. I have a feeling the place will turn hot soon. C.

"Do you know where to find Crow?"

"No. He's a strange character, coming and going without telling anyone where he goes and what he is up to."

Lazarov shrugs. "Anyway... at least Crow, or whatever his real name might be, seems to be on our side. But tell me, Squirrel, do you know of a way around the Tribe's territory?"

"No way, man. I agreed to guide you here, not beyond. Sorry."

"And you, Shrink?"

"There are barely passable mountain ranges to the south and north. Between them there's a long canyon called the Red Idol Gorge, leading from here to the ruins across the Shibar Pass. Unfortunately for you, everything between the Pass and the City of Screams is the Tribe's turf. The only safe way to avoid them is to go back to Bagram and forget about Red Idol Gorge."

"Then I do have a serious problem," Lazarov sighs.

"I'm listening."

"Never mind, Shrink. Is there a place where we can spend the night?"

"Suit yourself and help yourself. We have enough empty cells... but the rubber room will cost you extra. That's the only one with its roof intact!"

Wilderness, 2 October 2014, 11:40:52 AFT

"I don't mind missing the view, seeing as this fog keeps us hidden from any enemies... but I wouldn't mind a little break either, man."

Lazarov agrees with Squirrel. The road is shrouded in a fog so dense that a pack of jackals could be just a few meters away and they would never see them. The ghosts of occasional bushes and stunted trees emerge from the surrounding gloom wherever they had grown close to the road, but apart from that there's nothing to see.

"Should be coming into a built-up area soon, according to the palmtop," the Stalker reports.

Lazarov nods, not relying on his eyes so much as his ears to detect problems. But the world is almost silent thanks to the deadening effects of the fog bank.

Soon the gray walls of a lonely building appear along the road. It might have been a traffic check-point long ago.

"This place is as good as any," the guide says, sitting down under a bullet-riddled metal sign that says *'DANGER! MINES! KEEP TO MARKED ROAD'*. "I wish we could make a campfire."

"Later. Let's move during daylight as much as we can."

"We better find them soon, man... I have a serious case of itching in my index finger and it can only be relieved by pulling the trigger. Do you have a plan for how we do this?"

"It depends, Squirrel. We have to recon that stronghold first."

"I only ask because I have a plan already."

"Please, do share it then."

"We move in, kill everyone, loot the place and get out of there. That's step one. Then we sell all the loot in Bagram and become dirty filthy rich. That's step two. Then I fuck all the whores of Russia and die a happy man from physical exhaustion. That would be step three. What do you think, man?"

"That's a very good plan," Lazarov smirks, "like those taught at the military academy. You ever considered becoming an army officer?"

"With all due respect, man, I might be crazy but I'm not an idiot... Do you have some bread? If I had gear like yours, I'd carry a full kitchen with me!"

"You'd be better off if you didn't carry that RPG launcher with two warheads."

"Come on, man. They make me look cool!"

"Why don't you at least disassemble them?" Lazarov asks, shaking his head over the guide's inexperience with heavy weaponry. "It would be safer for you to carry that shit with the warheads dismounted."

"What? You can remove the warheads?"

Lazarov sighs. "Of course... I'll show you later. Now, it's *havchik* time."

He offers a loaf of bread to Squirrel. They have enough resources now.

He'd set out to find Crow's stash at dawn, following the road west until the APC's wreck emerged from the fog like a sleeping monster. The huge stone slab serving as a memorial was smashed, an only faintly readable English inscription still bearing a clue to the battle — itself just one of many — that had ravaged the place a few years ago.

When Lazarov had cautiously peered inside the wreck, he'd expected to find the usual stash: ammunition, food or first aid kits, perhaps some common relic. He was therefore surprised to find a huge crate with a hand-written note on top of it: *This suit rocks! Now I only need to find out who's killing your soldiers to get these exoskeletons and who's paying him. He won't see my bullet coming. Or if he does, I don't care. I hope you don't mind that I took one of the two suits I found with the mercs. I'll consider it your thank-you to me for saving your ass at Salang. We're quits — for now! C.*

When he donned the brand new exoskeleton and the armor's built-in instruments — radiation meter, relic detector, kinetic motors, life-support system — quietly started to hum in the silence of the mountain dawn, with his heavy kit becoming almost weightless once fitted to the titanium-alloy body frame, Lazarov felt as if he had boarded a gunship after many days on a perilous foot patrol: safe at last. With the exoskeleton's silicon carbide ceramic armor protecting him, he felt as if he has become a walking juggernaut.

Once back at Ghorband he tried to talk Squirrel into joining forces with him. Since he had nothing else to offer but a fight, the major had eventually had to offer his own, serviceable body armor, rendered a dead weight now that he had the exoskeleton. Albeit feigning reluctance, the Stalker had accepted it gladly in exchange for joining him on the raid.

However, his period of confidence had made way for concern soon enough when it came to his mind that this wonderful suit had actually been *taken* from him and his men. There was nothing in Crow's messages that would give him a hint to the players in the shady dealings going on behind his back. As he walked behind Squirrel to the north, he tried to put together the pieces of the puzzle he already knew: Bone's men ambushing the squad sent in before them, the mercenaries hunting him, Crow's hints at danger in Bagram…

Crow might be his ally in this game, but the sniper certainly knew how to keep his findings to himself; that is, if he actually knew any more than Lazarov.

"Hey, man, don't look so down," Squirrel says, interrupting the major's thoughts. "Let me cheer you up with my harmonica. Do you have a favorite song?"

"Let me think... I love *Steppe, endless steppe* for example."

"Nah, sorry man. I don't know how to play that."

"What about *The Ships* then? You know, that Vysotsky song?"

"Actually, the only tune I can play is the Soviet anthem."

"Then why did you offer me to play my favorite song? That's certainly not one of them."

"I just asked about it. I didn't say a word about playing it."

"You are totally crazy, Squirrel. You know that?"

"Of course. After all, I slept at an abandoned asylum last night."

"Squirrel... where do you come from, anyway?"

"Germany. Berlin, actually. You know I was a guerilla there, fighting against the oppression of the poor."

"Sounds like a tough battle."

"Hell, yes! Each night, me and my buddies used to set a few big fat BMWs and Porsches on fire. Just to show the rich bastards that the resistance was alive and kicking!"

"Setting cars on fire doesn't really sound fair. They don't fight back."

"But it's fun! You should try it, man. Anyway, then one of our night raids went wrong. I picked the wrong car. It belonged to one of the lawyers defending our comrades from injustice. Things got a little messy and I decided to join our comrades in arms in Russia. So I volunteered to deliver another shipment of... let's call it humanitarian aid to the villages around the Zone of Alienation, and two days later I was drinking vodka with all the Intruder guys."

"Anarchists," Lazarov grumbles under his breath.

"Don't worry, man. Those days are gone. I changed a lot."

"How come?"

"You see... once you find a relic to sell, you think differently about the distribution of riches. Then I heard that in the New Zone there's even more to find. Less hunters, more game, you see? And here I am now. Are you sure you don't want to hear the Soviet anthem?"

"Play it, if that makes you happy..."

Listening to the jarring tune from Squirrel's harmonica, it occurs to Lazarov that this would be a good time to check out the text messages that Grouch had found on the old mobile phone and uploaded to his palmtop. The date and time is not recorded, but it's obvious enough that the messages are from the times of the Bush war.

Hey Frank! Here's why I'm pissed off. They want to conduct a disciplinary procedure against the sergeant but why? All he did was getting some aftermarket replacement parts for his G3 rifle to bring it at least to semi-modern condition. What was he supposed to do? The new rifles we're supposed to use are crap. For God's sake, we can't switch off the safety on the new G3 DMR while aiming because our thumbs are too short to reach the switch. Did they design those rifles for pianists? Besides, we can't use them because we don't have proper sniper ammo. We were told to use MG3 machine gun cartridges but that's only accurate up to 500 meters. You get it, Frank? They give us sniper rifles which we can only use at less than 500 meters! That's a true stroke of genius! On one hand, they order thousands of new rifles but on the other, they don't provide us with the proper ammo to save money. And as if that were not enough the night vision goggles will not work together with the telescopic sight. Until I find the eyepiece of the scope when wearing the goggles, the war is over. My army should be performing in a circus, not Afghanistan!

The second message is shorter:

After what happened at Kunduz we are not allowed to ask for air support. Not as if the Brits nearby would have any choppers available, anyway. We asked the French to beef us up with a squad for this mission but they are low on ammo. The Hungarians wanted to give a helping hand but their Mercedes jeeps are broken down as usual. We must not ask the Americans for assistance because we're supposed to maintain security in our sector on our own. Now we move out with a company of Afghan troops which is an invitation for trouble. SNAFU like always, my friend! Anyway, I'll hook up with you later, we're moving out now. Wish me good luck. In two weeks, my tour of duty will be over.

The major switches off his palmtop and looks into the thick fog, sadly, wishing he was a believer so he could say a prayer for the soul of the dead soldier.

Mercenary base, 3 October 2014, 12:39:28 AFT

Lying prone on the top of an ice-cold, rocky hill, Lazarov studies the narrow ridge connecting their position with the mercenary stronghold through his binoculars. Their target encampment lies atop another hill, not quite as high as their narrow vantage point, and overlooks the wide landscape, easily commanding the valley below. Far in the distance, the major can see the flat, sandy plain between the mountains and the Amu-Darya.

The conical shape of the concrete structure looks similar to the many Soviet-built pillboxes and bunkers he has seen before.

"Must have been a *zastava* or observation base during the Soviet war," he mutters to Squirrel.

No mercenaries can be seen on the ridge.

It could still be mined or booby-trapped. We'll still need to exercise some caution.

A jeep track leads up to the stronghold, passing by another bunker with a radar dish and a forest of other antennae on top. Lazarov gives a sigh, wishing he could use the radio facilities, but it is bound to be heavily defended. At least the terrain ahead looks advantageous enough to him with its many rocks and boulders. It should make their approach a little easier.

"Mount your silencer, Squirrel."

"That PBS won't help me much. The shots will echo like hell among these mountains."

"At least you won't be deafened when I tell you to cease fire."

"Fair enough. So what's the plan?"

"We stick to your plan."

"You must be kidding, man. I was."

"Take these binocs. Keep your eyes open while I'm aiming. Warn me if a hostile pops up where I can't see him. Watch our six. Clear?

"Like the sky."

"All right. Let's get this over with."

Lucky for them, the sky is actually overcast, regardless of what Squirrel said. Relieved that he doesn't have to worry about his shadow betraying his movement, Lazarov moves quickly forward and crouches behind a rock. Scanning the sandbag walls through his rifle scope, a mercenary soon appears in the reticule. Lazarov follows his movement. Seemingly bored, the guard moves in a predictable back-and-forth pattern along the wall, making no contact with anyone else. Another hostile stands on top of the wall with his back towards them.

I can only see these two. There must be more around. If they fall, the whole place will be stirred up.

"You asleep?" Squirrel whispers. Ignoring the guide's impatience, Lazarov weighs his options.

I must get closer.

254

He signals the Stalker to follow him. Watching their steps in case of booby traps, they move forward until they reach more cover. The major takes another look at the bunker.

"Squirrel, I see one on the wall and one on the top. Do you see any others?"

"None."

"Take the binocs. Keep your eyes on the bunker and the road while I'm focusing."

"Okay, man."

Lazarov adjusts the scope.

After the quiet, when only the wind whistles, the sharp, piercing sound of the silenced shot seems to be deafeningly loud. In the middle of the reticule's dark circle, the first guard's helmet flies off. His blood has not yet made contact with the wall behind when Lazarov already moves the rifle towards the guard on top. Another shot pierces through the howling wind. The second guard falls forward, as if an invisible fist had punched him in the back.

"See any more?"

"No."

"Keep watching! I'm moving in."

In a few seconds, Lazarov arrives at the sandbags. Sensing no movement from the other side, he signals Squirrel to follow him. Taking a deep breath, he quickly climbs over the sandbags, keeping his rifle ready to fire. The dead guard stretches out in front of him, his head in a pool of blood. Now Squirrel arrives and immediately aims his weapon into the opposite direction, covering Lazarov's back.

"Let's move."

The sound of footsteps comes from around the corner. The guard has no time to be surprised. Lazarov's shot hits him while he is still opening his mouth to shout.

The major peers around the corner before cautiously moving forward. Behind the building he finds a platform that he could not have seen from his vantage point. Three mercenaries stand there, grouped around a huge weapon even though they must have been startled by the noise: the first is already climbing up the stairs to raise the alarm..

"Squirrel!" Lazarov shouts as he pulls the trigger. The Stalker is prepared and fires two short bursts from his AKM. The two guards on the platform fall to the ground in the same moment as the third rolls down the stairs, hit in his chest by a single round from Lazarov's Vintorez.

"Clear," Squirrel reports.

In any other situation Lazarov would stay cautious, but now he stands in front of the weapon on the concrete platform, trying to believe what he is seeing, his brain bewildered and oblivious to any danger that might be still around.

"What the fuck is this?" Squirrel sounds just as confused as he is.

"This is… not supposed to exist."

The weapon looks like a giant version of one of Russia's most secret weapons: a long barrel running through several small spheres, all held together by a metal frame and lots of electric wire.

So, this is the device that shot my chopper down!

There are no ammo crates lying around, nor can Lazarov see any batteries. The gun in fact seems to be powered via a thick cable that disappears through a hole in the platform.

Lazarov shakes his head in disbelief.

This piece of artillery should be able to take down virtually anything… But who are these guys? How did they snatch this monster?

He crosses over to one of the corpses and removes the balaclava and dark eye protectors from its face. Then, still not believing what he is witnessing and rejecting the reality he is beginning to realize, he exposes the faces of the others too, as well as checking the bodies for anything that could clarify his suspicions. His search yields a plastic ID card. A low moan escapes his lips.

"*Oh Gospodi.*"

"God is not here, man. Only mercs with a bullet in their brains."

"No... they are not mercenaries at all. They're Chinese. Spec-ops or whatever, but it's the People's Liberation Army!"

"What? What the hell are the Chinese doing here?"

Lazarov rubs his temples and looks around. For the moment, they seem to be alone in the compound.

"We tried to protect the Zone of Alienation from outsiders but all the world, the Chinese, the Americans, the Western Europeans, tried to sneak in and grab their share of relics. We... frustrated them, so to say. It would be no surprise therefore to find Chinese expeditions lurking in the New Zone, where they can do as they please. But what amazes me is this weapon... It's enough for you to know that... okay, anyway, I saw similar weapons before but they were classified Above Top Secret. Thinking of the Chinese laying their hands on them gives me the creeps."

"So, what now?"

Lazarov peers over to the radio station that lies about two hundred meters from their position along the jeep track, thinking: *I must inform the FSB about this.*

"First we need to clear this bunker and disable this weapon. Then we'll see if we can get into that radio station."

"We've only killed five of them. That leaves us with... let me think... more or less three billion more hostiles! Will we have enough ammo?"

"Stop kidding, Squirrel. Check the bodies for grenades."

Using his combat knife, Lazarov cuts the wires running along the gun barrel.

Damn, how I wish Goryunov could see this. At least he knows how these things work.

By the time he is finished, Squirrel has returned with three frag grenades.

"It's not much, but if we add ours too it will make for a nice firework display. I also found some food rations on them... I love dim-sum."

"Let's go inside and find the power source."

Cautiously opening the metal hatch, they enter a room with bare walls and a row of mattresses. The smell of old socks and unwashed bodies assaults Lazarov's nostrils, and empty food cans and water bottles litter the ground. Next to the wall, in a thick, green sleeping bag, a guard seems to be asleep.

"With this snoring, no wonder they didn't hear us coming," Squirrel grins.

"Be quiet, unless you want him to wake up."

With silent steps, Lazarov moves over to the sleeping guard. For a moment, he considers interrogating him.

We haven't got much time... besides, I'm not even sure I'd understand whatever he said.

He reaches for the spot where the guard's head lies under the sleeping bag's hood and pulls it backwards, pushing his knee into the guard's back.

This is for Sparrow One, bastards.

The snoring turns into a rattle as his combat knife cuts through the guard's throat. After a time that seems to be endless, the rattle becomes a gurgle as blood enters the respiratory tract, adding drowning in his own blood to the suffering of the dying enemy. It only takes a few seconds for the ghastly noise to cease. When the body doesn't move anymore, Lazarov lets go of it and wipes the blood off of his knife onto the sleeping bag.

"Once I had a girlfriend who hated my snoring," Squirrel whispers, "I'm glad she didn't take the sort of measure you just did, man!"

Lazarov smiles, but immediately freezes. "Ssh! Listen!"

They hear the muted sounds of conversation from the hatch leading to the level below, and the Chinese words cast away Lazarov's last doubts about the origin of their opponents. They can't understand what is being said, but the voices sound alarmed.

"They must have realized something's not right outside by now. Squirrel, duck behind that crate!"

Lazarov hears someone climbing up the iron ladder. Quickly, he moves behind the hatch. Two hands appear, then a head with short black hair. Using his left hand, the major grasps the man by his neck in a chokehold, lifts him up and cuts his throat with the knife held in his other hand. Slowly, he lowers the body to the ground, its hands and legs still shaking in the spasm of death. Lazarov holds the dying man down until he stops moving.

"Let's move," he whispers to Squirrel as he wipes the blade clean.

"You're a fucking butcher, man," the Stalker silently remarks, shaking his head in disgust.

Peering down, the major can't see anyone below. They quickly descend the ladder. As he arrives below, Lazarov hears a startled shout. A Chinese in civilian clothing jumps up from his computer, drawing a pistol and frantically firing in their direction. Two shots from Squirrel's rifle send him to the ground. Lazarov quickly checks the body. His search yields a key in the technician's pocket with a label attached.

"You don't speak Chinese, do you?" Lazarov asks Squirrel showing him the label.

"It says, 'generator room key'".

"Don't tell me you *do* speak Chinese."

"Just guessing. But there's only one door here and it has 'generator room' written on it in Russian and the same cramped characters as the key label."

"Clever," Lazarov observes as the key glides softly into the lock.

A huge device stands in the room, emitting a low, humming noise. One thick cable goes up from it and disappears into a narrow shaft leading upwards.

"Whatever that thing is, it's certainly not running on diesel," Squirrel says.

"I wish I had a timed fuse," sighs Lazarov. "Give me those grenades." He carefully places the grenades in a spot that seems vulnerable. "Move back to the entrance."

"What about you?"

"I'll have about three seconds to get out of this room. Move!"

Left alone, Lazarov looks around for something worth taking before blowing the generator up, but only sees some tools left on the ground.

All right... here I go.

He takes a grenade and pulls out the safety pin's ring, puts it with the others and dashes to the exit with two long leaps, where he throws himself down behind the wall. He has barely hit the ground when the deafening thunder of several detonations shakes the structure, unleashing a rain of concrete fragments and steel splinters through the door, followed by a cloud of dust and smoke. The air becomes thick with the stench of burning electronics. With the lights gone out, Lazarov switches on his headlight and quickly climbs up the ladder. Squirrel is waiting in a firing position at the entrance hatch, aiming his rifle at the outside.

"Whole of damned China woke up! I see the bad guys approaching!"

Looking out, Lazarov sees them too. A dozen commandos are running towards them, with more appearing from the radio bunker below, hastily putting on their armored vests and helmets.

Damn it, he thinks. *There goes the opportunity to contact Goryunov... Too many of them for us to take on.*

"Let's get the hell out of here," he yells. "Back, same way we came!"

Jumping over the sandbags, they run. The first bullets fizz by. The enemy must have reached the bunker with the gun by now.

"Squirrel, run!" Lazarov turns back, firing his rifle from the hip for suppressing fire, but the commandos have him outgunned.

"I'm hit, I'm hit!" Squirrel shouts. Lazarov runs up to him, yanks him to his feet and flings the wounded guide over his shoulders. He can barely feel the weight in the exoskeleton, but the suit also prevents him from running as fast as he would like.

Leaping from cover to cover, he soon reaches the relative safety of the ridge and places Squirrel down behind some boulders, reloads his Vintorez and aims to pick off any hostiles that have been stupid enough to follow them into the open. None have. They seem content to remain behind their cover. Lazarov fires a few rounds into the top line of sandbags all the same. Squirrel's AKM joins the fire.

"You all right?" Lazarov shouts.

"I got hit in the leg but can still shoot!"

"Lean on me! Let's move, move!"

Hostile fire tapers off as the Stalkers move out of rifle range. Occasionally, just to keep the Chinese at bay, Lazarov fires a few shots. By the time he reaches the ridge, his own panting and Squirrel's groaning is all he can hear. Casting a final glance back before descending the safe side of the mountain, he notices smoke rising over the bunker and grins triumphantly. The grin disappears from his face as he hears a loud, roaring drone. In a few seconds, a black helicopter emerges from the valley below.

"Can you still fire that RPG?" he yells. "We must take that chopper down!"

"Help me kneel up," the Stalker shouts back. "Load this shit!"

Lazarov quickly removes the aluminum cap from the grenade and, with the piezo-electronic release bolt now open, places the grenade into the launcher tube.

"Ready!"

Pain is all over Squirrel's face as he aims the rocket launcher and fires. The projectile misses. Lazarov quickly takes the other grenade from his back. The chopper looms closer and opens fire with its onboard machine guns, showering them with stone splinters and dust as the bullets hit the ground close to them.

"Bring it down," Lazarov desperately shouts. "Bring it down or we're finished!"

Peering out of their cover, the Stalker aims for seconds that seem to be endless before he fires the launcher at last, this time scoring a hit. The grenade detonates towards the chopper's rear, sending the helicopter spinning around for a few seconds before it crashes into the mountainside, hitting the rocks with a loud, shrieking noise. Lazarov grabs Squirrel's shoulder and drags him over the ridge at last.

Eye for an eye, chopper for a chopper, the major thinks, grimly, and rushes down into the valley, carrying the Stalker on his shoulders to safety.

Wilderness, 16:27:00 AFT

"You'll be limping for a day or two, but you'll survive," Lazarov says reassuringly while fixing a bandage on Squirrel's wounded leg. "No need to look so gloomy. Here you go!"

After doing whatever he could to ease his companion's pain, the major goes to the entrance of the shallow cave he has chosen as their shelter and looks out, watching for any signs of pursuit. There are none. Nor is there any sign of mutants.

"All this shit for a couple of food cans," Squirrel bemoans. "This was the worst raid of my life!"

"Apart from you getting wounded, we've been successful. We have lots of intel now, and the slit-eyes will be licking their wounds instead of harassing the Stalkers around Ghorband... at least that's what Bone had been hoping for."

"Yeah, man, that really gives a new meaning to my life. Making Bone happy and getting shot in my fucking leg in exchange."

Despite Lazarov's best efforts, Squirrel's wound had gone from bad to worse. Before long, he would be unable to walk. Lazarov had already taken to carrying some of the guide's gear but quite soon, the major knows, he will be carrying Squirrel *and* his gear.

Lazarov contemplates for a moment, and then opens his relic container. "Look... I don't know what this thing does, but it feels good to have it active, somehow. Here, take it, it's yours," he says, giving the Heartstone to the Stalker. "Maybe it will speed up your healing, I don't know."

Squirrel's eyes almost pop out of their sockets when he sees the relic. "Look at this—a blue, opaque shell with a red core, like a big chunk of glass... This is a Heartstone, man! That's incredible! Where did you find it?"

"Uhm... close to that log hut at Hellgate, while collecting firewood with Mac. I didn't know it was a Heartstone."

"And you'll still let me keep this?"

"Sure."

"Oh, man, if it wasn't for my busted leg, I'd dance right now! And for you, this trip is for free! Wherever you want to go, the Panjir Valley, Kabul, Tokyo, Hawaii—I will guide you everywhere for free! Especially Hawaii!"

"Sounds like a deal, but now let's eat something."

He opens a can of processed meat and offers it to the Stalker, who is still happily admiring his new relic with a broad smile.

I hope it will have a good effect on his wound. Otherwise we'll be really screwed.

After his hunger is satisfied, Lazarov opens his palmtop and tunes it to Bone's frequency.

"Bone. This is Lazarov. Mission accomplished."

"That's excellent news."

"Your intel was wrong. It wasn't really a base... it was an AA battery. We took care of it."

"*Doesn't matter. This hit should give our boys some respite. Good job.*"

"One more thing: the place was manned by Chinese. Special forces, commandos or whatever."

Bone falls silent for a minute. "*Keep that to yourself for now.*"

"Returning to base. Out." Lazarov turns to Squirrel. "Bone has asked us to keep the Chinese presence a secret. Can you keep your mouth shut?"

"I guess so... it's no wonder if Bone is scared, man. The last thing we need is a confrontation with them, if it's really the Chinese army out there."

Lazarov removes his helmet and rubs his eyes. Wild thoughts are buzzing in his head and he cannot share even half of his concerns with the Stalker.

"I don't know, Squirrel... I don't know. This whole thing stinks like a mutant's lair. In any case, let's get our asses back to Bagram. If we're lucky we can make it to Ghorband before nightfall."

"This food is rotten," the Stalker says spitting out a piece of greasy meat. "I wish I was back at Shrink's den, having a shot of vodka... *Damn!* I never believed I'd ever want to see that wretched place again... Oh man, I can hardly wait to see his face when I show him my Heartstone!"

Wilderness, 19:40:05 AFT

These jackals were either very dumb or very hungry, Lazarov thinks while reloading his Vintorez.

The small pack of mutants had been far below the path that descends steeply from the hillside into a barren canyon, but knowing how sharp their ears are, he didn't want to take the chance. Sneaking is no option anymore with Squirrel barely able to drag himself, and they're making further noise when they occasionally tread upon loose stones, causing the rocks to roll down the path.

Approaching the carcasses, he sees what they were fighting over: the remains of what had once been two dushman fighters. The stench of putrid flesh assails his nostrils as he steps closer, but it's the sight of what has been done to them that causes a shiver to run down his spine.

The genitals have been stuffed into the mouths of the decaying faces, which still bear expressions of horrible pain as they gaze down from wooden poles to their own corpses. Their weapons lie in the dirt, disabled, together with the few other belongings the dead Taliban once carried. Judging by the state of decay, whatever happened here had occurred only two or three days ago.

"Obviously it wasn't mutants that killed them," the major says, motioning his thumb toward the corpses. "They aren't advanced in evolution enough to be capable of such a thing."

Squirrel's face hardens. "No, man... This is how the Tribe deals with its enemies."

"Aren't they supposed to be cannibals? I see three rifles on the ground, but only two dead dushmans."

"I'm not too keen to find out for sure. Let's get the hell out of here, man... Let's move!"

Before they leave the grim scene, Lazarov draws his pistol and shoots the corpses.

"Just to make sure you don't turn into zombies."

"Could you make a little more noise, please?" Fear lingers in Squirrel's voice as they move along a dried-up creek. He draws some water from the camelback fastened to his armored suit and looks at his palmtop. "No way to make it to Ghorband today... we better hide somewhere for the night."

Twilight has already fallen and they are still some distance from decent shelter. The going had been slow, largely due to the guide's wound. The relic has indeed improved the guide's condition, but enough pain still remained to hinder Squirrel's pace. A rest of one or two days would help even more, but they had both used up most of their ammunition during their raid on the Chinese outpost and, with being low on medical supplies as well, Lazarov knows that it wouldn't be advisable to linger too long in this unwelcome area.

Suddenly, Squirrel stops.

"What is it?"

"I don't know," the guide replies with a whisper. "Look at that."

Lazarov switches the night vision on and peers forward into the valley. There's something big and man-made ahead of them, partly obscured by bushes as if someone had wanted to hide it.

"What's that?"

"Still no idea, man... let's stay put."

A pebble falls from the rocks on the hillside. Squirrel immediately raises his weapon. Lazarov too turns his rifle in the direction of the noise, but sees only rocks. Nothing moves in the night vision's flickering green display.

"Can't see nothing."

"Dammit," Squirrel whispers. "I hope it's a shelter... an abandoned bunker or whatever. I don't know how much longer I'll be able to drag myself along."

After a few minutes, their curiosity prevails. Slowly, careful not to step on anything that would make a noise, they move closer. Lazarov gives a sign. Squirrel, limping, moves behind a boulder and aims his rifle forward to provide covering fire if needed. Lazarov, crouching from cover to cover, approaches the high bushes hiding the strange object.

His eyes suddenly explode with pain. He tears the night vision goggles from his face but the blinding brightness remains. Helpless, he covers his eyes with his hand. Squirrel's rifle is silent, meaning he must also be blinded — or dead.

"*Freeze!*" a voice yells in English, as loud and sharp on the ears as the light is blinding to the eyes. Slowly, Lazarov slumps down to his knees.

"We mean no harm," he shouts back, in English. "Don't shoot!"

"You are sitting ducks, scavengers. Drop your weapons, or you will be dead ducks."

He does as commanded and raises his hands in surrender. No way could he fight an invisible enemy. He hears the noise of several heavy boots approaching but cannot see his captors. Someone roughly takes off his helmet and handcuffs him from behind. A kick in his back sends him to the ground. A body lands in the dust at his side. He recognizes Squirrel's heavy breathing. Someone barks short commands.

"Secure the prisoners!"

"Sir!"

"And switch off those fucking high-beams on the Humvee."

Strong arms grab them and manhandle them into the vehicle. Metal doors slam. Lazarov detects the sickening odor of sweat, engine oil and cordite inside.

"The Tribe," Squirrel groans, "Mother of God, it's the Tribe."

Wilderness, 4 October 2014, 07:20:23 AFT

It was not the Stalker's words that made Lazarov's blood freeze, nor even the horror and pain in his voice; it was the sight of children armed to the teeth, kids who now chat among themselves in a strange, but not unpleasant-sounding language with the occasional English word thrown into the mix. The third one remains quiet, and Lazarov doesn't need to look up to know that he is holding his rifle ready.

"*Khosh haal hastam az inke in gasht tamaam shod. Mesle sag khasteh hastam,*[1]" the driver says.

---

[1] "I'm glad this patrol is over. I feel dog tired."

"Are, man ham hamintor," the other boy laughs. *"Chandin rooz ast ke inja sabr kardim ta in suckers saro kaleyeshan peida shaved![1]"*

"Fekr nemikoni bayad be Lance Corporal Bockman begim ke biaad va be motor negahi bendaazad?" The driver's voice sounds concerned. *"Zaaheran dandeh moshkel darad. [2]"*

"Dar har haal," the boy in the passenger seat replies with an air of authority. *"Man patrol leader hastam, to raanandegiat ra bekon![3]"*

"Aslaheye khodkaare jadide Benelli shotgun ra didehyee? Boxkicker yek mahmooleh.[4]"

Lazarov hears the senior boy yawn.
"Dar haale haazer hich selaahi barayam mohem nist. Bogzaar bekhaabam![5]"

He can only guess what they are talking about. It could be about women, but about the most effective way to torture their prisoners too. But even though the boys now talk in their own language, they had used English as their command language when capturing them and judging from the way they talked and the vehicle they are riding in, Lazarov is sure that they have some connection to American forces. Recalling the gruesomely treated Talibs and what he had heard about the Tribe so far, the prospect of being their prisoner does not look good to him at all. Moreover, in his present condition, squeezed in between the seats of a Humvee with his hands shackled and being driven to an unknown destination, the prospects for escaping and getting back to Bagram are definitely limited; and if he thinks too long about Squirrel's

---

[1] "Yes, me too. We've been waiting for days until these two suckers showed up."

[2] "Don't you think we should ask Lance Corporal Bockman to check the engine? Something's wrong with the gear shift, too."

[3] "Whatever. I'm the commander, you just do the driving."

[4] "Have you seen the new Benelli shotguns? Boxkicker got a shipment."

[5] "I couldn't care less about weapons now. I'm dog tired."

fretful words and the scared Stalkers at Ghorband, they look downright frightening.

Tribe perimeter, 09:48:29 AFT

He blinks into the pale morning light as the Humvee finally stops and their captors drag them outside. Rude kicks to their limbs remind them to stay on their knees.

"Scouts reporting back, sir." The adolescent boy speaks like a well-trained soldier, but his English has a strange, hard accent. "We secured two scavengers."

"Let me see them, devil pups."

The deep, hoarse voice does not promise anything good, even though it clearly came from someone who speaks American English as their first language.

Looking up, Lazarov sees the tallest soldier he has ever seen standing before him. An exoskeleton, similar to his own but looking even heavier, hides the soldier's massive body. The man's face remains hidden behind the dark eye protectors and gas mask. Without apparent effort, he holds a M249 machine gun in one hand. In faded red letters, the words SEMPER FI are painted on his helmet. A long ammunition belt hangs around his neck.

This soldier looks like a killing machine made flesh, Lazarov thinks, struck with awe and fear.

"Yes sir, First Lieutenant Driscoll, sir!" the young scout replies.

The major is hauled to his feet. Although he is a tall man himself, the exoskeleton-clad warrior still towers over him as he frisks Lazarov carefully. Finding his wallet, he opens it and takes the old photograph along with his army ID card.

"What the hell?" he says, slowly. "The Russian army is here?"

"I am on a search and rescue mission," Lazarov protests in English. "There is no reason for you to —"

"The prisoners speak when they are ordered to," the warrior addressed by the scouts as First Lieutenant Driscoll barks, and delivers Lazarov a lightning-quick punch to the pit of his stomach with his free hand.

Gasping for breath and with his sight darkening at the edges, the major falls to the ground.

"Devil pup, take this to the Khan riki-tik. Tell him we have an English-speaking Russian here. Probably spec-ops."

The apparent senior boy performs a perfect salute and hurries off with Lazarov's wallet.

"Is he a spy, sir?" the other boy asks. Bloodlust lingers in his voice.

"Not even the Russians are stupid enough to send a spy with ID on him. And look at the other one. He is wearing a military suit but has the face of a scavenger. They were together?"

"Yes, sir."

"I no soldier! No spy!" Squirrel desperately screams in broken English, still on his knees. "Just suit! Please!…"

"He speaks the truth," Lazarov interjects, still panting from the blow he received. "He is just a Stalker!"

"The officer might be a good catch, but we have no use for a scavenger," the First Lieutenant continues. "Plus, his leg is rotten."

"Please, no! I love America!" Squirrel whines, almost with tears in his eyes. "Johnny Cash! Star Wars! Semper Fi!"

Lifting Squirrel with his left hand, who already shakes with fear and pain, the warrior now raises his machine gun to the Stalker's head.

"What did you just say, scavenger?"

When he sees the warrior is raising his weapon to shoot him despite his desperate pleas, Squirrel spits on the Lieutenant's armor.

"Fuck you!"

Eyes wide with dread, Lazarov watches the warrior shoot Squirrel in the head with one single shot and lets his lifeless body fall to the ground. Driven by the collapsing Stalker's last heartbeats, blood fountains from the wound into the sand.

Without giving Squirrel's body even the slightest attention, the Lieutenant wipes the spit from his armor.

"No worthless scavenging scumbag is worthy to utter *Semper Fi*," he grumbles.

"I could have slit his throat while he was still on the ground to save your bullet, sir," the driver boy says.

The warrior takes a handful of sand from the ground and rubs his glove clean, unhurried. "Now listen to me. No man dies on his knees with his throat cut from behind. Not even scavengers. Only rag-heads. Rag-heads you are free to kill any way you can," he tells the boy in a lecturing tone. "And rag-heads you *must* kill any way you can. Is that clear, pup?"

"Oorah, sir," the boy replies, his voice revealing a tone of shame.

"Take this Russkie piece of shit to the Gunny. Tell him that he is to be taken to the Brig until the big man decides his fate. Now get out of my sight!"

Lazarov's stomach is still aching when the two young warriors lead him away. Now that daylight had arrived, he can better see the vehicle that brought him here: it is a sand-colored Humvee with a row of high-beam lights across its top. To his horror, a human skull adorns the vehicle's bull guard with chunks of rotting flesh still clinging to it. In hand-painted red letters, HAJI HUNTER stands on the hood.

Looking around, he sees that they are in a fortified perimeter at the narrow entrance of a valley. Ahead, on the top of the almost vertical, jagged mountainside that towers over the valley, an ancient citadel nestles. Bastions and battlements guard the path leading up to it and are reinforced with concrete at intervals where the pale red walls of mud brick have started to collapse. They pass pillboxes that have been camouflaged so well that Lazarov only notices them at the last minute, giving the impression that no effort or time was spared when the ruins were turned into a massive, impregnable stronghold once more. Short poles stand along the path with small, round objects attached to them and Lazarov first believes them to be lamps. Only when he approaches does he realize that the round objects are human heads – some mere skulls, some with the rotting face still visible, and all of them still wearing Taliban headdress. The sight relaxes him, because what he sees are his own enemies too, but his relief lasts only for a minute: among the dushman heads, he discovers that of a Stalker with a gas mask still covering the face.

They halt outside an arched gateway that is protected by two more pillboxes. FIRE BASE ALAMO stands emblazoned on one of the walls. High atop the walls, a flag flies in the morning wind. Based on the rumors he had heard about the Tribe, Lazarov had expected to see the flag of the United States appear here sooner or later. But this flag, though being American, is different: he recognizes the symbol of the Marine Corps in the middle, but it stands on a red field crossed by two blue stripes with white stars.

The Confederate battle flag, he thinks. *Who the hell are these people? Rebels? Renegades? They are certainly too well-equipped, and too well organized to be a bunch of deserters.*

Several warriors are standing around, weapons held casually. They are wearing lighter body armor than the First Lieutenant and their faces are open under the Kevlar helmets, but the sand-colored camouflage pattern is the same. Their rifles look well-maintained and their outfits are spotlessly clean.

Whoever these warriors are, and whatever they have in mind for me, I give them that they do have discipline.

One of the warriors, his face evidently blackened by dust, approaches. It is only as the warrior gets closer that Lazarov realizes it's not just dust darkening the soldier's face: it actually is a black man, the first one he has seen in real life.

I wonder how Ilchenko would feel now if he were in my shoes.

"Reporting back from patrol, Gunnery Sergeant Anderson," one of the boys reports. "First Lieutenant Driscoll ordered the prisoner to be taken to the Brig until the Khan decides his fate, sir!"

To Lazarov, the black non-com seems to be a more easy-going superior than First Lieutenant Driscoll because he greets the scouts with a friendly smile.

"Welcome home, devil pups! That was a squared away patrol. Keep it up, and you will not be devil pups for much longer."

"Is that so, Gunny?" The two boys sound happy like normal children upon receiving a special reward.

"It's the big man who decides, but you are making good progress. Soon you should be real warriors. Now, take off this man's handcuffs. Dress him down to skivvies and put all his gear into his ditty bag."

With any resistance being foolish, Lazarov lets the young fighters take all his belongings. They make him remove his exoskeleton, boots and all, until he stands in front of them barefoot, wearing only his shirt and light cotton leggings. No matter how humiliating the process is, what hurts the major most is that even his watch is taken by one of the boys, who then straps it onto his own wrist with a happy smile.

"Wow," he exclaims, "a tough watch!"

"And this pistol's cool, too," the other scout replies studying Lazarov's Beretta. "Boxkicker will pay me well for this."

The gunnery sergeant, who in the meantime had been giving Lazarov's kit a thorough search, now commands a stern and disapproving glance towards the boys.

"Give me that watch, devil pup! And you, that pistol. You are not supposed to behave like scavengers!"

"Sir!"

The boys bow their heads in shame as they hand over the loot to their superior, who puts them into the exoskeleton's rucksack with the rest of Lazarov's gear.

"Where in the hell did he lay his hands on this?" He says examining the major's exoskeleton. "A Russkie spy in one of our armors. Anyway, we'll find out soon enough."

"I am not a spy," Lazarov angrily protests, "and I demand to—"

"Shut up, Russkie!"

One of the boys hits Lazarov in the chest with his rifle butt. Moaning with pain, he staggers but manages to remain standing. Spitting saliva that tastes like blood, he looks defiantly at his captors. This time, the gunny remains indifferent to the boy's action, neither does he care about Lazarov's angry look.

"Put his handcuffs back on," he orders the scouts. "The brothers will take care of the rest. Now go, stir up some trouble."

He waves two soldiers over to him. "Sergeant Polak, Sergeant Hillbilly! Blindfold the prisoner and take him to the Brig!"

The sergeants are young but adult men, one with red hair and full beard and the other with a pale, Slavic face and blue eyes. Their faces are the last thing he sees before he is blindfolded and, guided in the right direction by the blows of rifle butts on his back, led through the massive gate to the inner stronghold.

The gate closes behind him, and Lazarov hears something he would have never expected in this frightful place: female chatter and laughter. Even though they are speaking a language he can't understand, he feels the mockery directed at him. He can't see the women due to the blindfold, but the voices are young and cheerful.

His guards stop again and he hears a heavy door opening. One of his guards takes off his blindfold and handcuffs, and shoves him into a dark, tight cavern before Lazarov has a chance to look around.

"You'll have a rag-head for company," the bearded guard says as he chains Lazarov by the neck to a ring in the wall.

"Driscoll was in a merciful mood and didn't cut off his tongue," the other one adds. "If he talks too much, feel free complaining to Amnesty International about psychological torture. I forgot where I've kept their telephone number... ask me later, will you?"

The door slams closed.

The Brig, 12:10:41 AFT

It is completely dark save for two beams of light falling through holes above. The chain leaves him barely enough room to move. Lazarov leans his back against the stone wall, emitting a long, defeated sigh.

I'm screwed. No way to escape from here.

His eyes slowly adapt to the darkness. Shapes begin to emerge in the dim light: first, the walls, made from rudely hewn stones, then a shape near the base of one of them. He makes out a pair of legs, then a man dressed in something now little more than dirty rags.

He remembers the first time he wanted to kill dushmans, way back in his childhood when he was big enough for his mother to tell him how his father had died. The fight for the Outpost had been personal enough. But now he is locked up together with the first dushman he has met outside of battle, by an ironic twist of fate bound together as they wait for death. Shuffling over, the major kicks the man's legs.

"Hey! You still alive?"

The other prisoner looks up at him. Lazarov has seen the faces of his enemies many times distorted by pain, effort, hate, even a sort of bitter resignation – very much like how he must have looked while killing them. Now, in this man's eyes, he is surprised to see nothing of that enmity. Even in the gloom, Lazarov can see that the dushman has been brutally beaten, but still the eyes in the round face appear calm, devoid of fear.

"I am talking to you. Do you speak English?"

The prisoner slowly shakes his head.

"Damned dushman..." Lazarov murmurs to himself.

"I am no dushman," the prisoner replies in almost impeccable Russian.

"You speak Russian?" Lazarov asks, startled. "Where are you from?"

"Dagestan."

"That still makes you a dushman."

"I am no dushman."

"Then what the hell are you, apart from being a mindless, brain-scorched, child-murdering son of a bitch?"

"I am a student of God."

"And where is your God now?"

The prisoner lifts his hands in a gesture that could equally mean 'here' and 'I don't know'.

"Son of a bitch... anyway... who are these people?"

"Devils."

"And what are they going to do? Kill us?"

"No."

"Then what?"

"Only you will be killed. I will be martyred."

"Good riddance, you bastard. Are we at least going to die a soldier's death? If I can call you a soldier at all..."

The Talib stares into the beam of light.

"Come on, tell me how. A bullet in the head?"

"No."

"Hanged?"

"No."

"Then?"

"The women will come."

"And then what?"

In response, the Talib takes pebbles from the ground and tosses them one by one into the dark corner of the dungeon.

"Curse on you, *dagi*," Lazarov snarls. "Whatever death you die, you'll deserve it for killing all those children in Beslan!"

"Beslan was wrong, but if I deserve to die for that, you deserve to die for what happened in Grozny. That was wrong, too."

"I had nothing to do with what happened there!"

"Beslan was nothing to do with me, either, since I was not there and would never have been. In any case, it is not up to you or me to judge. No judgment is fair but God's. If we die, it will be because we deserve to die. I can trust his judgment. And you? Is there anything left you can trust in?"

"Now listen up, you... "

Lazarov's words end in empty curses. The Talib has hit a nerve in his mind. Desperately, he refers to the only supernatural power he had experienced.

"I have bested a place worse than hell. It eats the laws of your god for breakfast. Whatever created it is far more powerful than your pathetic god!"

"Really? Will this power come and save you?"

For a moment, Lazarov falls quiet. "It's you who's praying to get out of here. Not me."

"I pray for strength to accept my fate, not for a chance of escape. But you are angry. You are not brave enough to face your fate. I feel pity for you, weak man, and pray to God to have mercy on you. Why are you laughing?"

"Because fate is so absurd. If I believed in God, I would have prayed each day to give me revenge. It was people like you who killed my father. People like you turned this land into a wilderness with stolen warheads..."

"Those were to be used elsewhere," the dushman protests. "The Americans came on my brothers and left them no choice but to martyr themselves. Curse on their SEALs! It's all the American's fault!"

"You bastards!"

Lazarov tries to move closer to the Talib but the chains cut into his neck. He coughs heavily before he can continue. "You deserve to die a thousand deaths. And I would gladly give them to you but I can't reach you, and instead of smashing your head against the wall all I can do is just sit here listening to your bullshit!"

But no matter how much he shouts and shakes his fists, Lazarov knows that he is losing this war of words, as if fate wanted to prove to him how empty he is inside.

"You are a cruel man," the Talib murmurs, "and even if you could kill me now, I wouldn't accept mercy from you. Mercy from an infidel would disgrace me. But you should have mercy on yourself. These devils will not have mercy on any of us. I am prepared to die happily. And I pray to God that he gives you—"

Lazarov spits all his anger into the Talib's face in four words.

"Shut the fuck up!"

Exhaustion and despair overcome his senses.

I will die anyway... but even if that wasn't so, I can't keep myself awake any longer.

16:39:00 AFT

The sound of opening doors awakes Lazarov from his uneasy sleep. Startled, the Talib moves back into the darkness but it is Lazarov the guards are after. Seeing the anger that still presses hard on the major's face after the argument, the blue-eyed guard gives him a grin.

"So, Russkie, do you want to make that call to Amnesty International?" he says, removing the shackle from Lazarov's neck. "I found their number, but now I've misplaced my mobile phone."

"You are very absent-minded today, Brother Polak," the bearded guard says, shaking his head. He grabs the major by his arm and hauls him to his feet. "Get up, Russkie. The big man himself wants to see you."

Whether because Lazarov's fate is sealed or for a reason only known to them, this time the guards don't bother blindfolding him. The sun is already low and the clean, cobble-stone streets are empty save for a few fighters sitting here and there on carpets laid around small campfires, smoking hookah pipes and curiously looking at Lazarov as he passes them by.

The guards lead him through a maze of mud houses to a massive tower. Climbing up several stairs, they arrive at a wooden door guarded by two warriors, as big and frightening as the First Lieutenant who killed Squirrel. They too wear heavy exoskeletons and are armed with machine guns.

Good God. There's more of them.

Without saying a word, they open the door and signal for him to enter.

Lazarov finds himself in a small room with only one window, its walls covered with carpets and large maps. A paraffin lamp casts a weak light onto a chair and a simple field table, where Lazarov sees a switched-off laptop, a radio, an ashtray full of cigarette butts and several books: Napoleon's memoirs, Sun Tzu's *Strategy*, a novel by Joseph Conrad and a collection of Rudyard Kipling's short stories. Thinking for a moment that he is alone, Lazarov reaches for the books.

"Do you like literature, Major Lazarov?"

The tired, yet deep and dominating voice comes from a dark corner of the room. The words are spoken slowly, in the way of a Texan. Straining his eyes, Lazarov makes out a man in the shadows. A small flame flares as he lights up a cigarette, but the light is strong enough for the major to see something of the man's face: graying hair cut short though his age could only be roughly estimated, with eyes that are sunken deep in their sockets. The leader of the Tribe—if that is who he is facing—has the appearance of a hard, and hardened, military man.

"Bring the light here," the man says, and Lazarov is about to reach for the lamp when another shadow emerges from the darkness. A young woman with a scarf draped over her head appears and places the lamp closer. For a moment, the light falls on her face and Lazarov notices a tribal tattoo on her forehead. But as she turns and the lamp casts light on the right half of her face, he sees a horrible scar—the skin looking almost molten. The sight makes him shudder, the impact of the old wound made worse by the realization that, without it, she would have possess an exceptional beauty.

"Yes, I like literature," he finally replies with a dry throat.

With a grunt of satisfied laughter, the Khan steps forward. Lazarov takes a step back, stunned by the size of the man. He is a giant, maybe even surpassing the superhuman size of his exoskeleton-wearing warriors, though he wears only a loincloth. He wears the emblem of the Marine Corps tattooed on his chest, but a long, deeply cut wound runs across over it, ending right above his heart.

"So what the report said is correct. You do speak English."

"Yes."

"Do you like English literature?"

"I like all kinds of literature... in general."

"That's good, Major. Literature begins where strategy ends."

The Khan sits down on the chair standing next to the table. His consort starts tending to the wound above his heart. Something cold runs down Lazarov's spine as he sees her sewing it up. Judging by the many stitches in the bronze-colored skin, she is not doing it for the first time.

"*A scrimmage in a border station, a canter down some dark defile, two thousand pounds of education drops to a ten-rupee jezail.* That is my favorite quote. It sums up everything about us and them."

Not knowing where the quote comes from, Lazarov does not reply.

"Kipling, Major. A much underrated author nowadays."

Lazarov feels the Colonel's eyes studying him. The urge to stand to attention comes over him, but he somehow manages to resist.

"Let's get down to business, Major. Judging by your ID card and the obvious similarities, this must be your father here. Am I right, Mikhail Yuryevich?" the Colonel asks, holding the photograph of Lazarov's father.

"That's correct," he replies.

"Your father and his comrades were brave men," the Khan continues. "Is it true that they were given inferior equipment because the suppliers had sold the best pieces to the enemy?"

"I heard that such things happened. But that was long ago."

"Yet here you are. First the father, now the son, fighting the same war in the same country. Proof of what a fateful place this is. And obviously, it is now our suppliers who send our best equipment to our enemies."

"I am not your enemy, and the armor —"

"That's not why I want to talk to you. You were brought before me because you are a Russian officer," the Colonel says, deeply inhaling the smoke from his cigarette.

"That doesn't make me your enemy."

"The story I want to tell begins when you were enemies to us, and our friends were shooting at your Hind gunships with their *jezails*. I was still a young cadet back in the mid-Eighties, but like everyone else I pulled for the mujahedin and rejoiced in the end when I saw on TV how your army ran like a whipped dog."

Lazarov's eyes fall on the cigarette. The Colonel catches his eyes but doesn't offer him a smoke, making the major wonder if this, together with the derogatory remarks about the Soviet army, is part of a subtle way to torture him. He shifts on his feet as the Colonel pauses for a moment, wondering what the warrior might be building up to.

"Yes, I was young... and utterly ignorant, just like our government who helped the mujahedin beat your father's army."

Hearing this, Lazarov becomes very curious about what the Colonel is going to tell him. For a minute, the battle-hardened warrior stares into the grey cloud of smoke that slowly snakes upward in the light of the lamp.

"I remember," the Colonel continues, "while I was still commanding a recon battalion of the United States Marine Corps, we went into a village on a hearts and minds operation. It was just a few months after Nine-Eleven. We felt we were liberators. The locals welcomed us. There were lots of handshakes and rations shared. We left, but next morning we had to drive through the same village to another destination. We had barely left it when an IED went up, blasting one of trucks and killing five of my Marines. The same kids who we gave candy to the day before were cheering when they saw what had happened. Usually soldiers are rewarded for killing... Have you ever been rewarded for killing, Major?"

"I was only rewarded for bravery."

"Bravery. That's nothing, Major. Nothing. It must be the nature of a soldier, not a virtue. And we should have been rewarded for *not* killing anyone that day. It was that day, when I had to tell my Marines sad excuses for what had happened—the villagers bribed into looking the other way when the insurgents planted the IED, or being coerced into doing it themselves, whatever—that I realized our war was lost. Not because our enemy cannot be beaten, but because history proves that we have to fight them on their terms. That means: if they can't be won as true friends, then we must treat them as true enemies. No excuses, no mercy. We lost the war because we were fighting it the on wrong terms... on the terms of those back in the States who sent us into war, but didn't let us fight it the way a war should be fought. My spoilt and naive country has long forgotten the true rules of warfare. Our rules were made by those crying out for the respect of the human rights of an inhuman enemy, by those who let a nineteen year old sailor load a two-thousand-pound bomb onto an airplane but punished him for writing 'HIGH JACK THIS FAGS' on it because a bunch of faggots and dikes ten thousand miles away found it offensive, by those who let the Afghan peasants produce heroin to save their children from starvation which then poisons our own children and turns them into drug addicts... It dawned on me that the real obstacle on our way to victory was not the insurgents, but those who wanted us to fight this war with one hand tied behind our backs. A hundred years ago, a fearsome enemy called the Marines *devil dogs* out of respect. But what good is there in being devil dogs if you're kept on a tight chain by a corrupted government? That chain had to go, and I had to take matters into my own hands."

The big man crushes his cigarette in the ashtray lying on the table and lights up another one before continuing.

"One day we were ordered to secure another village. There was a nursing school for adolescent girls from the Hazara tribe. The insurgents burnt it down a few days before. Only one girl was brave enough to stand in their way. She stabbed one of them, right in the heart. They sprayed acid into her face as punishment, but not without a dozen of them raping her first. She was cast out by the elders for bringing 'dishonor' on her village and walked ten miles to our nearest position to alert us with half her face burning and blood running down her legs."

The Colonel looks down at the girl bandaging his wound. "As soon as we arrived at the village, they hit us with RPGs, AKs, machine guns, everything. This time, I let my Marines fight like true warriors. It was... marvelous. After that, no shots were fired from the village anymore. It was the greatest satisfaction a soldier can feel: at last fighting a war as it should be fought. In war, there is no such thing as excessive firepower. That concept is a peacetime invention. It is pure irony that the rules of war are made in peace. But irony turns into tragedy when the rules of peacetime are forced upon soldiers fighting a war. That's why my superiors didn't approve. They didn't understand what I'd come to know. Neither did my own son. I tried to explain but he didn't get my message, or it was distorted... After what happened, he wrote me this."

The Colonel opens the Joseph Conrad book and takes a tattered sheet of paper from its pages, then hands it to Lazarov. It is a print-out of an email, with two of its faded lines encircled with thick red ink over and over again by a shaky, maddened hand, opened and folded again a thousand times. The major reads it and, without a word, gives the note back.

"The battle was recorded by a TV team. All those people on the streets back home called us baby-killers, a shame on our country and worse. Nobody listened to our side of the story. I understood: there would be no way for me to go home. My Corps, my country, even my own son's soul was taken from me by those who didn't know what war means, yet dared to judge me and my men!"

The Khan wipes beads of sweat from his head as if he wanted to crack his own skull open in despair. Until now he has spoken slowly, without emotion, making sure that Lazarov understands and remembers every word. But now his voice trembles with suppressed rage and the major narrows his eyes. He wants to ask something, but by the time the correct English words come to his tongue, the Colonel has continued in his tired voice.

"Later on, I was thankful to them for burning the bridges behind me. It made it easier to do what I had to do. We were sent to mop up a place called Shahr-i-Gholghola. It could have been easily blasted by bombs but it's a world heritage site, so a dozen of my Marines had to die to keep its mud bricks intact. And after we fought our way into its depths, I found myself standing in a place that Genghis Khan had been the last to see before me. And then I saw his glory and his power and understood the mightiest of warriors!"

The big man's eyes now burn with obsession. His face is like that of a prophet who once experienced otherworldly bliss and tries to convey just a fraction of it to a lesser mortal.

"I bathed in his grandeur with my men and let it wash away the bonds shackling me to the past. He opened my eyes and made me invincible. Cast away that doubt from your eyes, Major! It was the fear in his enemies' hearts that made him invincible. To be invincible, you must be feared! Kill one man, terrorize a thousand! The rules of war haven't changed from the times of Sun Tzu and Genghis Khan. But in our war, whenever my country killed one man she apologized to ten thousand! Could such methods ever lead to victory, Major?"

"Sun Tzu also said that none can see the strategy from which comes victory."

"Because Sun Tzu was no Marine!" the big man proudly exclaims. "But we understood that even if our country was not to be feared anymore since her backbone was broken, we could still be — *I* could still be feared. By the time I emerged on the surface I was filled with power and strength. The men who were with me in those catacombs were no longer simple Marines. The... *Spirit* had turned them into true warriors and they became my Lieutenants. The Spirit imparted our bodies the strength to follow the call and crush anyone in our path. The Spirit... it is powerful beyond your wildest imagination, Major. Had our willpower not been tempered and honed like fine steel by the discipline of my beloved Corps, it would have crushed us and turned us into wild animals. We closed the tunnels after we left to prevent anyone from finding it again. I know about your scientists, Major Lazarov, and also about the people wanting to hijack their mission. They will all die, if they are not dead already."

"Will it be the Tribe that kills them?" Lazarov cloaks all his vulnerability behind a simple question.

The man who would be Khan looks at him like a father whose son has asked something of a futile nature. "If I am talking to you, Major, you'd better not interrupt. But to answer your question: no. They will not be so lucky. The Spirit knows how to defend itself."

He falls silent for a moment, smoking his cigarette. Lazarov doesn't dare speak.

"After we emerged from the catacombs, there were a few grunts who still didn't understand. My warriors were only too eager to finish them off, and a day after the battle I was finally relieved of my duties. They charged me with mutiny, with operating without any decent restraint and beyond acceptable human conduct. But the generals no longer had any power over me. They sent people after me to terminate my command, but they either joined us or died."

The Khan discharges his cigarette and falls quiet.

Lazarov hesitates before asking the Colonel how the Marines, supposedly the most loyal unit in America's armed forces, could cope with apparent treason. But, emboldened by the thought of being executed anyway, he risks asking one tricky question without caring much about the big man's possible reaction to it.

"What happened to 'semper fidelis'? No matter what reasons you might have, what you did was, after all, plain mutiny!"

"What makes you think you can judge me?" the Khan questions him, grimly. "We had to choose between heeding the call of the Spirit or keeping true to a morally corrupt country that has no appreciation for our way of life anymore. Do not dare to judge me and my Marines."

"And to keep up with your losses, you took in Afghan children to let them fight for you?"

The Khan waves a hand towards the table. "Have you studied Napoleon's works, Major?"

"Yes, we had to study his battles."

"That's only the surface of his genius. Back at Quantico, we too had to read Napoleon. In his memoirs, he wrote that his soldiers could have stayed in Egypt forever, had they used the local women to supply the army with new soldiers. Back when I read that, it sounded like madness, or at least like a broken old man's desire for the young women he must have enjoyed in his youth in a foreign land. When we found ourselves here on our own, I wasn't laughing about him anymore. Strong and desperate men come to join us now and then from all over the world, but they are not like my Lieutenants. And while invincible, my warriors are not immortal. Yes, we need natural born warriors, who have the spirit in their heart as soon as they are born, who are like the flesh growing from the rocks of this land. The Hazara are not just any tribe, Major. They are the direct descendants of Genghis Khan's warriors. Once I took up his heritage, it was my duty to protect his lost tribe. With my guidance, they have recovered their roots."

Lazarov feels odd. At the beginning, what the big man told him sounded like the ranting of a lunatic, but the longer he listens to the big man, the more it seems to him that his words start shaping into a steadfast theory; a cruel and savage, but nonetheless logical theory. It is the logic in this man's words that he finds the most frightening.

He looks at the girl. Using a short pause between the Colonel's words, he dares to speak again. "It seems that in the end you did win over some hearts and minds."

"In these valleys, Major, the Pashtu were fighting the Tajiks and the Taliban both, and all three were murdering the Hazara. We offered the Hazara widows protection and their orphans education. Proper education. You call us mutineers, but where are the billions of dollars my country spent to 'help' these people? What did all the NGOs, the civil rights activists and other idealists accomplish here? It is only us, the warriors you dare call mutineers, who remained and accomplished the mission we were sent here to do. Don't you think so, Major Lazarov?"

"But you didn't do it to give them freedom and peace."

"Both freedom and peace have a different meaning here than in our countries, Major. This is what our politicians could never understand. Here, freedom means to be free to live according to a code of honor. Peace means that this code is upheld. Our code of war and their code of life created the Tribe. The only real treasure this land can offer is its women. They will never betray you. They will never want to rip off your manhood by claiming to be equal to you. They *want* you to be stronger than them, to protect and care for them. All they ask in exchange is loyalty... and fair justice. They use the same word for justice and revenge: *badal*. For the mistreated, be it orphans or widows, nothing makes a better leader than one who offers *badal*. And we were all thirsting for — for someone who would at last appreciate our code of honor, our strength and our loyalty."

While the big man spoke, the girl sewing up his wound has finished the last stitch. The big man sends her away with a pass of his hand. He reclines and sighs, apparently relieved of torturing pain.

As the girl passes by Lazarov with a jingle of bangles that adorn her ankles, she gives him a look of curiosity. Their eyes meet for a moment and Lazarov shudders once more, but this time at the regret that his life will soon be over and he will have no more chances to meet and love beautiful women like her who, as it seems to him now, has eyes yielding some unique quality that makes him forget about her gruesome scar.

"What happened later only proved me right," the Khan continues, "so right. Thanks to the Hazaras, we found shelter. We were well equipped and survived the nukes. Thrived, even. Soon, when enough men have joined us and the sons of our women grow up, there will be enough of us to conquer more of this land. And after that—but there's no point in telling you more. I wanted to share this long story with you so that I don't have to shoulder its burden alone. It is not often that I meet a fellow officer, and only men like you could possibly understand. And now, Major Mikhail Yuryevich Lazarov, tell me—what do you think of my methods?"

The thought that his reply might save his life if it was to the big man's liking paralyzes Lazarov's mind. He hesitates which path to take: telling him something that he would find flattering, or the truth.

"You don't have to worry about how to reply," the Khan replies upon observing his hesitation. "You will die anyway, and if I had not wanted a chance to talk, you would be dead already. Repay me the extra time you've been given with your honesty, Major."

Lazarov clears his throat.

"I don't know if you defeated this land or this land defeated you."

The big man smiles, but it is a somber smile. "Only the end of war will tell who is defeated. And who has seen the end of the war?"

Lazarov knows this quote. "Only the dead have."

The Khan nods. "Tomorrow, you will see it too. And to reward honesty with honesty: I envy you for that. Now go and see the last sunset of your life. You will see the death of this day and the next day will see yours. Corpse by corpse, we carved out a piece of the world that belongs only to us now, where we can preserve our honor. This is our Promised Land, and this Stronghold our Alamo. You are nothing but a trespasser here. That's why you have to die."

Lazarov stands motionless, waiting for a sign that will allow him to ask all the questions still flooding into his mind. The Khan closes his eyes.

"You are dismissed."

Lazarov pulls himself together and speaks out. "My fate is what it is. But give my guide a proper burial... please. His dignity deserves that much."

"My First Lieutenant has already done that," the Colonel softly replies without opening his eyes. "May that scavenger find in death the peace he was looking for in his restless life."

At a slight motion of the Khan's hand, a Lieutenant appears from the shadows and leads Lazarov out of the room.

Alamo, 18:17:00 AFT

"Take him up," the Lieutenant commands the two prison guards who were waiting outside.

"Good news, Russkie. No more climbing stairs for you," one guard says leading Lazarov to a narrow staircase.

"Just a few more steps up," adds the other. "From there, your only way is down."

After a minute, they reach the roof of the tower through a trapdoor. The guard with the beard signals Lazarov to step forward.

"This is our valley. You are to enjoy the view before you die," he says.

"Not bad for a last sight," the blue-eyed guard adds. "Ain't it beautiful?"

Seen from their high vantage point atop the tower, the Tribe's hidden valley stretches out in the canyon below. The sunset makes the jagged hills appear as if they are glowing with even deeper shades of pink and red than at the break of dawn, while the green fields in the canyon are already darkened by the shadow of twilight. Now, with lights appearing in the windows and campfires being lit, the maze of narrow alleys reminds Lazarov even more profoundly of a medieval town come to life. He also realizes that the town built into the hillside is but a small part of the Tribe's stronghold: more fortifications loom above, the stalwart, concrete-enforced bastions giving way to smaller pillboxes as the hill steepens. Partly covered by the highest rampart running along the top of the hill, the tips of antennae and satellite dishes are visible. Beyond this forest of steel, in the deep blue sky a full moon rises, glowing with orange. Compared to this stronghold, the Stalkers' base at Bagram appears like a gipsy camp.

"It is beautiful," Lazarov agrees.

"Say your prayers if you want," the blue-eyed guard says. "We don't speak your language, so feel free to curse us and ask your god to destroy us in the cruelest way possible."

"Yeah, Brother Polak. That's what prisoners usually pray for."

"And their god usually doesn't listen to them. Or did he ever listen, Brother Hillbilly?"

"Nope. And even if he does, he better not do it during *our* watch."

Lazarov has given himself up to enjoy the scenery and have a last peaceful moment under the open sky, but the two guards begin to casually chatter amongst themselves, seemingly oblivious of his presence.

"I love this part of the job, Brother Hillbilly. Makes me feel being on top of the command chain."

"It literally does, Brother Polak. Talking about chain of command, how's your woman doing?"

"Pretty well, well and pretty. She's learning English really fast but still has an issue with articles. Last night, I tell her 'could you please, please say *the* bed?' and she puts her sweet little tongue to her upper lip and says, '*dzeh* bed'. So, I just tell her, 'never mind, never mind...'"

"Yeah. I heard that they all have a problem with that."

"I don't mind, Brother Hillbilly. I love everything about her except her name—Forozenda. Geez, it's so long and complicated."

"Why don't you just call her by another name? Being her man has its prerogatives, after all."

"My thought exactly. I'll call her Lechsinska. Easier for me to pronounce."

"Cool. I call mine Peggy."

"Sounds sweet."

"Yeah, women are one's only comfort."

"You don't sound too enthusiastic today, Brother Hillbilly."

"Yeah. Day after tomorrow I'm scheduled for a patrol with Driscoll. Oorah."

"I feel for you. He's a badass, even for a First Lieutenant."

"Not as much a badass as the Top, though."

"Hell, yes! The Top rocks!" The guards high-five each other. "Where's the patrol area, anyway?"

"To the south. Rag-heads keep creeping up the passes."

"Like moths to a flame."

"I guess we're marked on their map as Martyrdom Central."

"Anyway, did you hear that one of the newcomers was cast out last week? He said the L-word in the presence of the big man."

"You mean, *Liberal?*"

"No, *liquor.*"

"Guess he couldn't wait until his first covert recon to Bagram."

"Yes, that's the only way to get a… you know what I mean, Brother Hillbilly. I won't say it twice."

"Too bad for the Lieutenants. No way for them to disguise themselves as scavengers."

"Being suspiciously oversized comes at a price."

"By the way, have you tried one of the new M27-s, Brother Polak? Lieutenant Ramirez says that beast can take a bear down with only one STANAG clip."

"Come on, that's overkill. What do we have the Benelli for?"

"Good point. But Ramirez likes hurting mutants. He hates them."

"Lieutenants like to hurt everything, especially if it bleeds... which everything that can be hurt does. But who loves mutants, anyway?"

"The witch maybe. She only uses her blade to kill them. Or so I heard."

"Come, on, Brother Hillbilly. I don't buy that."

"I swear I heard it myself from a guy in Lieutenant Bauer's platoon, who saw it for himself! A few weeks ago, they escorted the healer on one of her forays to the west, looking for swags and whatever. They enter a cave, and what's in there? A snake? Negative, sir! *Two* snakes."

"No kidding?"

"The fighters stand there shitting bricks, but what does she do? *Zap* — she draws her blade, jumps to one of them monsters, and *whoosh* — off goes the snake's head. Then she turns around, jumps, *whizz* — and that's that! After that, Bauer's platoon was living off snake steak for a week."

"I could imagine Bauer and his men eating nothing but snake meat even for a month, but not that Lara Croft bullshit. Sorry!"

"True or not, it would be one badass way of killing monsters. Way more awesome than, let's say, burning their lair with a flamethrower."

"Or pumping them full with double-0 rounds."

"Or mowing them down with an SAW."

"Or blasting their heads off with a grenade."

"Although driving through a pack of jackals with a Humvee also has its thrill, wouldn't you agree? Anyway, that woman is old school."

"Yeah, very. Poor little witch. Must have been quite a babe before that shit happened to her."

"She's still got her nice side, if you ask me."

"If you look at her the right way."

"Yup. Because if you look at her the wrong way, the big man himself will cut off your balls."

"You ever see such a thing happen, Brother Hillbilly?"

"Never mind... So, about those M27-s... I wish I could test-fire one soon. Oh, Russkie, by the way," Hillbilly says, as if suddenly becoming aware of Lazarov's presence again. "Talking about a wish. We're authorized to grant you a last wish."

"Everything can be granted, except three things: booze, women and letting you go."

"That's why most prisoners don't even bother asking."

Lazarov sighs. Instead of enjoying this moment of contemplation, he feels as if his ears are already buzzing from all the chatter.

"I do have a last wish," he says turning to them. "I want to enjoy my last sunset but your bullshit drives me mad! Could you shut up, at least?"

"Uhm... We're supposed to say 'yes we can' but that means we're still talking, doesn't it?" Polak replies. "You better ask for something else."

"Do you have a cigarette?"

"At last! I thought you'd never ask." Hillbilly takes a pack of cigarettes from his pocket and offers it to Lazarov. "I had a gut feeling that you were a smoker. You seemed so nervous without a smoke."

Polak readily gives him a light from a Zippo.

"I was nervous because of your chatter," Lazarov says. "But thank you for the cigarette, anyway."

"Don't mention it. We're glad that we could do something for you. Ain't we, Brother Hillbilly?"

"Second best part of our job, Brother Polak."

Lazarov gives the guards a skeptical glance, but they seem serious. "Why so compassionate, Marine?"

"You're Spetsnaz?" Hillbilly inquires, curiously.

Lazarov nods, smoking the cigarette.

"You're cool guys, you Spetsnaz," Hillbilly says. "I used to watch all the Spetsnaz videos on YouTube when I was a kid. Actually, they inspired me so much that I joined the Marines."

"Uh-hum," Lazarov mutters, unsure whether this was meant to be mocking or whether it was a bizarre way to express respect.

"Shame that a Spetsnaz officer has to die in the Pit," Polak tells him, almost comfortingly. "Such a waste. Wouldn't you agree, Brother Hillbilly?"

"Such is life in the Tribe, Brother Polak."

Suddenly, Lazarov is not enjoying his last cigarette anymore. "I have one more last wish," he says, tossing the cigarette away and giving a long sigh of resignation. "Take me back to the Brig or whatever you call the prison. I want to have a good night's sleep before I die."

"That's awesome for a last wish. First time I heard it, though."

"Spetsnaz," Hillbilly says with an appreciative nod. "You see, Brother Polak? They're awesome to the bitter end. Fighting *them* would be so much more fun than just martyring the rag-heads, day after day..."

The Brig, 5 October 2014, 10:57:00 AFT

Uncertain of how much he slept, if he really slept at all with the big man's words still haunting his mind, Lazarov awakes to the sound of softly muttered prayer. The beams of light are again falling into the dungeon, allowing the major to see the Talib's face. He looks like a man who has left all earthly worries behind, and deep in his heart, Lazarov feels envy.

"Too bad you can't bang your head into the ground, chained to the wall by your neck as you are," he snaps. "Looks like your God will not come to save you."

"So you're awake," the Talib says, still going through his praying routine. "Today, I will be in Paradise, if God wills."

"Suit yourself."

Before the Talib could reply, the door opens and the two talkative fighters enter the dungeon.

"Upsy-daisy, rag-head! Your seventy-two women are waiting for you," Polak says, grabbing the Talib.

"Too bad they ain't virgins no more," Hillbilly adds with a grin while removing the chain holding the prisoner.

Now that death is no abstract thought anymore, primordial horror appears on the Talib's face. Kicking and screaming, he tries to free himself from the fighters' grasp. The reek of urine bites into Lazarov's nose. Mercilessly and without saying any more words, the guards haul the Talib out.

The door slams shut, but the doomed man's desperate screams are still audible. Somewhere outside, a crowd has gathered. Lazarov, now alone in the darkness, wishes he could move as far away from the door as possible and hide in a dark corner.

I don't want to hear what's coming up next.

Even so, his ears strain to catch an audible detail of the Talib's fate. Trying to distract himself, Lazarov begins to hum songs learned at school. He wanders through the hits of his youth, songs that were the soundtrack to a few successful and many failed love affairs. He tries to recall something from his training to prepare himself for a dreadful death. Nothing works. Not even the heavy doors can suppress the noise of screams, soon to be suppressed by the roar of a cheering crowd. In despair, he wishes the Zone was a god he could pray to so it would unleash a horde of its worst mutants upon his captors. Then the words of the two 'brothers' come to his mind.

That's pathetic... The Zone will not help me. The Zone calls all men, but when men call the Zone they get nothing. The Zone is the Zone and I am nothing without it. But what is good about the Zone if it has no power beyond its boundaries?

He knows that the Zone will send no mutants to tear the Tribe's warriors apart, or turn the stronghold into a meat-grinding anomaly. His Zone has let him down.

No one could have prepared me for something like this.

Lazarov realizes that he, a survivor of seemingly hopeless battles against mutants, mercenaries, vengeful Stalkers, anomalous fields and worse, is now in the grasp of mortal fear.

I will be listed as missing in action... and in twenty years when nobody remembers me anymore, the army will close my file as KIA. A merciful lie. And I only have my mother to think of when I die. Just like when I was born. Full circle, game over.

The door opens and the 'brothers' appear.

"Get ready, Spetsnaz. It's nothing personal. Orders are orders."

Polak says nothing, but as he carefully removes the chain from Lazarov's neck he gives him an encouraging pat on the shoulder.

Lazarov lets them grab him, knowing he has no chance if he tries to resist. All he can do is to meet his fate with dignity, and that means not being dragged along the floor as the dushman allowed himself to be.

Struggling to his feet, he tries to walk for himself as the guards haul him towards the heavy wooden gate of an enclosed compound. All kinds of people have thronged here: children in tribal dress, boys in miniature uniforms and holding real weapons, fighters laughing and mocking at him. But only men. He tries not to think about the reasons why the women are not present, but for a moment, Lazarov catches a glimpse of the girl from the Khan's room. She is the only woman he can see in the crowd, and her scarred face is the only one looking down at him with the least hint of compassion. She stands next to the Khan, who looks down at the pit devoid of any emotion, surrounded by several of his Lieutenants.

Lazarov has no time to return her gaze. He is dragged through the gate into an area of narrow, sandy ground surrounded by huge blocks of wood, like an old Roman arena. A pole stands at the far end. The guards drag him to a chest-deep hole dug into the ground close to the pole, and the major spots the remains of a human being not far away. The head and torso have been smashed to a bloody pulp, presumably by the stones that are lying around the corpse.

Thus far, Lazarov has faced his fate bravely, but upon seeing the hole and the corpse, he pulls together all his strength to resist.

"Not like this!" he yells, "I did nothing bad to you!"

"Save your breath for later," Hillbilly says. "As an officer, you will be spared of the hole. It's the big man's orders." He binds Lazarov tightly to the pole. "Die bravely, Spetsnaz."

The Pit, 11:52:37 AFT

The rope cuts into Lazarov's flesh as he desperately tries to free his wrists. The guards have done their work well: no matter how he struggles, his efforts are all in vain. All he can do is stare at the wooden gate in front of him. He knows that whoever comes through it will bring his death.

"Brothers and sisters of the Tribe!" The voice sounding over the crowd is cruel and cold. "We have here a soldier from an army that once brought death to your people. They laid the way for the destruction that came down upon you at the hands of those who call themselves the students of God. Now they are back to spy on us. Tell me, what is the just punishment for such trespassers?"

"Death," the crowd roars.

"Brave women of the Tribe, you who have suffered so much! The time of *badal* has come. Cherish the sweetness of justice!"

Angry female voices hiss from behind the gate.

Maybe they are discussing who will throw the first stone. I must free myself before they come. I won't make it but at least I'll die putting up a fight.

The shackles still hold, remaining intact as he helplessly watches the gate open. Led by an elderly crone, dozens of women enter the Pit with faces as hard as the stones in their hands. A cold breeze stirs up the black scarf of the leader as she stands motionless in front of him, her hand clutching the stone she intends to throw at his head.

She looks like a dark angel avenging a sin I have never committed. So be it. Let this be done.

Lazarov raises his head and looks into the woman's dark eyes, preparing to die with her scornful face as the last thing he sees. The woman's breast rises as she draws breath before unleashing a scream. But it is just two words that leave her lips.

"*Zendeh bogzaaridash!*[1]"

The crowd suddenly falls silent.

Lazarov has already prepared his mind for the pain of the first strike when the woman drops her stone to the ground. An astonished murmur spreads throughout the crowd like a

---

[1] "Spare his life!"

wave. The women behind her look at each other. She looks up to the Khan and shouts out again.

"Man behesh tarahhom kardam![1]*"*

Her wrinkled face radiates confidence and pride as she waits for a response. From the corner of his eye, Lazarov sees the big man rising from his seat. If the Pit appears like an arena, the Khan now acts like an emperor who is about to decide over life and death of a gladiator to who quarter was given.

The eyes of the Khan and the woman lock as if wrestling in a contest of willpower; then, after a long minute, the big man nods. In reply, the woman bows her head in a sign of respect, covers her face with her scarf and turns around. She leaves the Pit with slow and dignified steps, ignoring the crowd that now erupts with disappointment.

The two guards hurry to the pole and untie him before dragging him out of the Pit.

"Don't be too happy," Polak tells him, "I would sooner die than face what the Beghum has in mind for you."

Realizing he might yet live, Lazarov's stomach lurches seconds after the wave of relief hit him and, unable to control his mind and body, he retches as the wooden gate slams closed behind them.

After giving him some time to recover, the 'brothers' pour water on his face to clean him up before taking him to a mud house nestled on the hillside. It is bigger than the others and clay pots stand along the walls with colorful herbs planted inside.

Stepping through the wooden door decorated with a jackal's skull bearing strange, painted symbols, Lazarov feels a refreshing herbal scent, an odor so pure and sweet that it brings tears to his eyes. The two guards remain outside.

---

[1] "I have mercy on him!"

"Good luck, Spetsnaz!" Hillbilly whispers, while Polak remains silent and crosses himself.

With his mind full of doubts about what is in store for him, Lazarov enters the house.

With the Beghum, 12:37:29 AFT

Rubbing his chafed wrists, he wanders further inside and finds himself in a cool, tidy room smelling of herbs, spice and other exotic, but not unpleasant aromas that linger in the air. The earthen floor is covered by tribal carpets. Smaller rugs adorn the white walls among shelves holding a disorderly host of pots, jars and jugs. On another shelf, strange-looking containers are arranged with a few tools among them, their purpose remaining a mystery to the major, except for a copper mortar and pestle.

Facing him is the woman who saved him from the Pit. She sits on a bench beside the hearth, with a girl sitting at her feet. Lazarov recognizes her as the girl who tended to the Khan's wound.

He wipes the tears and dust from his eyes so he can see her better. From under the scarf covering her hair and the tattoo resembling a gently undulating line on her forehead, a pair of dark green eyes study him curiously. Lazarov guesses that she could be around twenty years old. He can't help himself shudder again, like he had the first time he saw her scarred face, though now it was for a different reason.

Her eyes...stunning, but old beyond her years.

She is wearing a long, blue gown and a leather belt which holds a long, curved knife. Its scabbard and grip are adorned with precious stones. As she sits there with her legs crossed, her gown permits view of her bare feet and ankles that are encircled by delicate golden bangles.

Lazarov looks at the bare skin as if mesmerized, and finds it hard to turn his eyes elsewhere. The girl feels his stare. After a long minute, making a face that has embarrassment and nonchalance equally written upon it, she covers her feet with the gown.

"*Dokhtram tarjomeh mikond*", the elderly women says, "*chun man englisi sohbt nemikonam*[1]."

"Beghum not speak English. I will translate," the girl tells him in slightly broken English, but her voice, surprisingly deep and sultry, causes Lazarov to ignore her mistakes.

"My English is not perfect either," he rasps, his throat dry and sore from inhaled dust and retching.

"Your knees are trembling. Sit down," the girl says. Lazarov gladly complies. "Warriors brought you here because we have tradition. If one woman says not to kill the man in Pit, he stays alive."

"I am… very grateful."

"First you drink our water." The older woman passes an earthenware jug to Lazarov, and he greedily gulps down the cool, pure water inside. "Now you are guest of Beghum Madar. She wants speaking to you."

The woman looks at Lazarov and starts talking in a language he cannot fathom. Now, without rage distorting her features, it appears to him that she isn't an elderly crone at all. Indeed, she can only just be beyond the years when her face would still have retained some of the attractiveness of her youth, and Lazarov becomes aware of a slight similarity between the two women. While she speaks, the younger woman keeps her eyes on the major. Her gaze discomforts him. There is a quality to it that he can't stand for too long.

"*Daastaani toolani va ghamgin ra bayad be to begooyam…*[2]"

"It is long and sad story," the girl translates. "Beghum Madar is from village where everything began. She survived and knows what happened. She wants to save our leader's soul."

---

[1] "My daughter will translate because I don't speak English."
[2] "I have to tell you a long and sad story…

302

Beghum Madar continues. Slowly, her voice becomes more forceful, as if gripped by powerful emotions, while at other times she falls silent, giving the impression that she is telling a story that is hard for her to bear. After a few minutes, the girl speaks up again in an almost humble voice, as if she reinstates words of immense importance.

"Colonel not permitting to talk about our village. But she knows what killed our people. It is still there. Beghum Madar wants you to find it. Colonel is not letting warriors to go there, but you can. She will tell you where it is. You will find it and bring it to him. This is price of your life."

"If so, that warrior should have left my friend alive. He was innocent, and could have helped me find that thing!"

"Scavengers are not innocent," she replies without bothering to translate his words to the Beghum. "They are not warriors."

"The hell they aren't –" Lazarov begins.

"Quiet!" the girl commands. "You speak bad words. Your friend was a weak man." Her angry eyes pierce into Lazarov's but he withstands her look.

"Squirrel was as good as any of your... warriors!"

"Our warriors fight for honor, not money and loot like scavengers." The girl's voice softens as she turns her eyes away. Lazarov doesn't answer back. Inside his heart, he admits to himself that the girl has a point.

"You also not fight for such things, soldier. You fight for something else. When Beghum Madar was looking to your face, she saw shadow of death in your eyes."

Lazarov frowns. "Please... what is your name?"

"You need not know my name."

"Whoever you are, I beg you: tell Beghum Madar that I am just a soldier from a land far away, trying to find some lost people."

She translates his words. While answering, the Bhegum looks at Lazarov with eyes that seem able to penetrate into his soul.

"You were an ordinary soldier once perhaps," the girl translates, "but what you have seen has changed you. Not here. Long before you came to our land you met death. Beghum Madar sees that you cannot breathe the air of peace. You came from a place that signed... no, *marked* you with love of danger. This is why you can find our leader's... medicine." Uncertain if she has used the right word, the girl exchanges a few quick sentences with Beghum Madar. "It is something he has to see. It will give him peace."

"What exactly do I need to find?"

"You will find it close to Shibar Pass. Turn south from road and look for village in the valley. Beghum Madar says, you will find a big car with white color on a hill."

"Your men took everything from me. How am I supposed to do this?"

"I told you: you are now guest of Beghum Madar. Before you leave, everything will be given back to you. But until then you must stay in this house and not go outside. Now rest. Beghum Madar is tired, too. She wants you to leave."

"But how can I leave when I must stay here?"

She translates his words.

"Marde shayesteyee baraye to khahad bood." Beghum Madar replies directly to her, not Lazarov who looks from one woman to the other without a clue. Her voice is hard and commanding. *"Be harhaal hich marde dighari to ra nemikhahad![1]"*

The young woman blushes and covers her scar in shame.

"Be entekhab man etemad kon, dokhtra.[2]"

Beghum Madar's last words must have been comforting, because when the young woman looks at Lazarov again, the coldness vanishes from her green eyes. She looks him up and down with a mixture of anticipation and hesitation.

---

[1] "He will be the right man for you. With the scars on your body, no other man wants you anyway."
[2] "Trust my choice, my daughter."

"Beghum Madar… my mother says you have blood of true warrior," she murmurs, "and you will stay in my room… because tonight you will make me mother of a warrior."

This is not happening to me.

She girl leads him into a small room furnished only by a thick, woolen mat. Rays of sunlight lance inside through splits in the crude shutters that cover the arched window and reflect off of dust motes as they perform their slow, swirling dance. An opening in the wall, covered by a colorful curtain, leads to a small, water-filled cistern.

"Rest here for now," she says. "You will need your strength." She gives him a cotton towel and a piece of soap. To Lazarov, in his grimy condition, they smell pure like heaven. "Clean yourself. Beghum Madar will bring you food. I come later."

She shuts the door, and the major hears a heavy lock being engaged. Lazarov feels as if he is a prisoner once more.

5 October 2014, 23:42:58 AFT

Dark rain pours down. It would be filthy weather to be out in, but Lazarov is resting his head on the desk in the command room, feeing such an exhaustion that he had never experienced before. He wonders why the view outside doesn't resemble the Perimeter. The lush vegetation has disappeared and the barren hills are full of crevasses from which herds of small mutants stream like ants.

I am back in the Zone of Alienation. My Zone.

The thought brings him some relief, though he shudders; it is cold in the command room. Through the rain, drab apartment blocks loom beyond the hills.

I am home.

But the watch rosters and maps are gone from the wall, a ragged carpet hangs there instead. Memories from the New Zone flash into his mind.

I want to be back there. The Zone of Alienation has let me down. It is not my Zone anymore and I don't belong there. I want the New Zone. I want its rage, its darkness, its mysteries.

The light goes out and the window's frame blurs, slowly narrowing and assuming an arched shape. He hears a female voice from above.

I am here.

Lazarov gives a start. Looking around, he realizes he is in the Beghum's house, in the Tribe's stronghold, somewhere in the New Zone that had been once Afghanistan. He relaxes with odd, unexpected relief.

"I am here," the female voice insists. "Wake up!"

Now he sees the girl, a lamp and a jug in her hands, and his heart starts beating fast.

"What is your name?" he asks.

"I not tell… yet. Stand up."

Her words are authoritative but she speaks with a softness in her voice that Lazarov wouldn't have expected. Getting up, he sees that she barely reaches up to his chest. As she removes the tattered camouflage shirt from his shoulders, her fingers touch his skin, stirring excitement throughout his body. She stands close enough to let him detect the sweet aroma of female sweat, mixed with a strange scent that reminds him of pomegranates with a hint of wood smoke. She takes a small sponge from the jug and pours a balm-like liquid over his shoulders and chest. The salve emanates a spicy scent, pungent and pleasant in equal measure.

"What is this?" he whispers.

"An ointment," she replies, moistening his skin with gentle strokes. "I prepared it myself from herbal oil and powder of glowing stone."

"Glowing stone? You mean, a relic? A swag?"

"No… it is from stones of Samal."

"Samal?"

"Guardian of lost valley."

"Tell me more…"

"No."

As his coarse skin absorbs the salve, Lazarov is aware of a relaxed sensation in his muscles, as if they are thawing from inner warmth. It is pleasing but strangely unnatural. He feels her touch becoming more and more sensual with every stroke of her hand.

"Have you done this to men... before?" he asks, swallowing hard.

"No." It seems to him as if her voice carries a barely concealed note of shame. "Men are scared of my scar. English is funny language. Men are scared because I am scarred. Is that right word?"

Now it's his time to reply with a *no*. "No. I think beautiful would be a better word."

"You lie," she replies, with the nuance of a smile on her lips.

"Are you with me because your mother ordered you to... do this with me?"

"Why?"

"Uhm... actually, because I wish you were doing this because you wanted to."

Now a smile runs across her face, like the smooth oil streaming down on Lazarov's body. "Before Colonel and his Marines took us in, girls could not refuse if parents chose a man. But now I could have... and did not. I was watching you when I was healing him. You had respect of him."

"Honestly? He was frightening."

"He is. But you remained proud. You didn't beg him for mercy like many men did before you. You are a brave man, soldier. Besides..." She moves her index finger along Lazarov's eyebrows. "...you have beautiful eyes. And besides..." Her hand slides down over his neck and shoulders to his chest. "...you are strong. I like you. Do you have a woman, soldier?"

"No... and does all this mean that I will be your man?"

"Maybe," she replies with an enigmatic smile.

"And after we do this, and I find whatever I have to find, what then? Will I be free to leave?"

"You will be free..." She kneels down at his feet, applying the soothing balm everywhere except his loins. She looks up to his face. Their eyes meet. Her hands, softened and warmed up by the balm, now touch his body where no woman has touched him for a long time. "...but you will not want to leave."

What is that thing you're pouring over me, Lazarov wants to ask, in fear of being bewitched by some supernatural act of sorcery, but all he can do is to emit a soft moan. Looking at the girl's face on which the last evidence of shame has vanished, making way for a barely withheld, wild desire that yet has something pure and honest about it, he moves to caress her. She gently pushes his hand away.

"Lay down now," she tells him.

Looking up from the mat, Lazarov watches the girl remove her scarf. A rain of dark brown hair falls over her shoulders, streaming down to her delicate hips. She loosens the buttons on her apparel, letting it slide to the ground, then takes the jug and pours the balm slowly all over herself, standing motionless with her eyes closed, letting the viscous liquid flow down on her sinewy body.

Now he sees that her scar doesn't only cover half her face. It runs down through her neck to her breast, making the untouched, inch-width space between her nipple and the scar look like divine intervention or at least mere luck.

His glance glides below, to where a woman is supposed to be touched in the most gentle way and where her skin, from where even the thinnest of hair had been plucked, reveals scars left by long claws or knifes.

The orange light from the lamp glimmers on her small breasts and hardened nipples. Her lips move in an inaudible whisper, as if praying. The warm oil flows down her body. Mesmerized, Lazarov's eye follows a drop of oil run down from her aroused breast to her scarred belly, then to her inner limbs and drop down, as if it were the moisture of her flesh.

Then she looks down at him. The reflection of the flame dances in her eyes.

""Will you give yourself to me?", she says solemnly, as if concluding a mating ritual.

"Even if I had a choice, I could only say yes."

"Then you are my man now," she whispers, lying down at his side. She closes her eyes and stretches out her arms, offering herself to him. "And I am your woman. Take me."

Her voice is barely more than warm breath in his ear. Feeling her lips touch his skin, he closes his eyes, succumbing to the waves of heat engulfing his body.

6 October 2014, 06:08:51 AFT

Lazarov awakes to a loud knock on the door. From under half-opened eyelids, still heavy from sleep, he sees light falling in through the window. It must be morning.

Damn it, let me sleep. If this is a dream, I don't want to wake up.

The knocking gets impertinent. Lazarov stretches his arms and, feeling that the girl is not lying beside him, buries his face into the mattress to detect the smells of sex, oil and sweat again.

"You don't have to look for me like that. I am here."

Lazarov opens his eyes and sees the girl standing at the door. What he took for knocking was actually her nailing his father's photograph to the wooden door.

"It is my surprise to you," she says. "Because this is your home now."

"Hey," he exclaims, jumping up from the mat, "where did you get that photograph from?"

"Driscoll was here. He brought your things."

She points to the corner where Lazarov's Vintorez stands propped against the wall, a neatly rolled bundle sitting beside

it. His watch lies on top. The exoskeleton stands there too –
cleaned, and to his surprise, now bearing the desert pattern
camouflage of the Tribe warriors. Moreover, in a much
smaller bundle he recognizes a few things that had once
belonged to his guide. Even the Heartstone is there. The sight
of it, and that of Squirrel's battered little harmonica, saddens
him, but this soon makes way for appreciation. In hindsight,
he now fully understands the girl's words about the difference
between Stalkers and the Tribe.

*Men like Driscoll or the Khan might be brutally cruel, but they
seem to have more respect towards certain things than the Stalkers...
and Stalkers can be nice, but they're not called scavengers without
reason.*

"Hey... that's great!" Lazarov joyfully exclaims as he
straps on his watch. "But out of all this, you are my best
surprise."

The girl giggles. "You don't have to call me 'best surprise'.
My name is Nooria."

"Nooria," Lazarov slowly repeats. "You have a beautiful
name."

"It means: *light*. And your name is Mikhail. What does it
mean?"

"Archangel, leader of Heaven's armies, things like that,"
Lazarov replies with a shrug. "My mother was very religious
at that time. But how do you know?"

"I have been looking through your things."

He gets up and steps to the door. For a moment he feels
like taking the photograph down, but as he looks at the girl
called Nooria and her—or by now rather *their*—mattress,
which is still in a mess from the intense night before, he leaves
it in its new place.

"Thank you, Nooria," he says. "Thank you for everything."

"For what?" Nooria replies with a smile. "Say thanks to my
mother."

Lazarov doesn't know how to reply. Clearly, it was the
Beghum who saved his life and who eventually put him up

with her daughter, but it was Nooria who had accepted him and, although it feels difficult for him to admit, made him happy. Now, as he looks into her pure, green eyes and sees the happy smile on her scarred face, his suspicions about being used as a buck or being bewitched seem utterly ridiculous.

"You don't have to thank me," she says, repeating her meaning. "Today you will go away, but you will return to me."

Her words sound neither like a request nor an order but a statement about something that needs not to be asked, because there is no way for it to happen otherwise.

"Yes, I will," Lazarov softly replies, and looks at the photograph fixed to the door with four rusty nails. "You got me nailed, Nooria... nailed for good."

"*Tora dost daram,*" Nooria replies.

"What does that mean?"

"You should know," she says and turns her gaze away from Lazarov's eyes.

Road to Shibar Pass, 10:15:47 AFT

"You are one lucky son of a bitch, you know that?" the Tribe warrior shouts to Lazarov as he drives the Humvee along the bumpy, curving road at reckless speed. When they'd set out on their way to the pass in the vehicle bearing the name MULLAH MOWER, the driver had introduced himself as Lance Corporal Bockman. His face is red from the strong sun. "I've only seen this once – it was a rag-head with long blond hair. He came all the way from Germany to join the Taliban. The women admired his looks for a while, but then tore him to pieces anyway. But you... not only did she save your ass, defying the big man's will, but she even picked you for Nooria!"

"The Beghum must be a very important woman."

311

"You can say that about the big man's ex, yes!"

"What?"

"What what? I thought you got that already, partner. She was the big man's woman. Still is, to some extent. The Bhegum's the only one among us who can take him on. Okay, the Top too, but in different matters..."

"But this makes me —"

"Yes, you can consider yourself the chosen man of the big man's stepdaughter, whatever degree of kinship that is!" The warrior shakes his head as if he were talking about something that's hard to believe.

"Now I understand her attitude," Lazarov shouts back, grinning. *Yes, she is used to having things done her way,* he thinks. *All my bones are aching.* "But I can't complain. She can be cute if she wants to."

"That's none of my business, partner... and that's not what makes her special anyway."

"She does like doing strange things... But what do you mean?"

"Well, it's been a while ago... One day we went on a rag-head hunt with Lieutenant Ramirez. Now, Lieutenants are cocky sorts and Ramirez wandered off to check out a cave on his own. Turned out it was crawling with jackals. The beasts tore his armor off in seconds. By the time we dragged him out, he had more poisonous bites on his body than hair on his ass. But the healer fixed him up in less than a day... Tellin' ya, that girl ain't natural."

"Then how come she couldn't heal her own face?"

"Once you have acid sprayed on your skin there's no skin left to restore, is there?"

"I guess not. Anyway, it was strange too that she only told me her name this morning."

"That's good for you. Because if she hadn't told you her name, it would have meant that you failed to impress her. You'd have ended up back in the Pit by midday, and no woman would have saved your ass then!"

"Do you have many such weird customs?"

"More than you could ever imagine."

For several minutes, Lazarov watches the barren mountains, remembering the previous night and that same dawn, when Nooria had explored every inch of his body in the candlelight. *"How did you get this big scar on your chest?" "That was an upyr." "What is an upyr?" "Something very bad and smelly that bites people's necks." "You have very ugly scars, you know? We make a nice couple, soldier."* He remembers her giggles when she called him as ugly as herself. He tried to convince her about how wrong she was about herself by kissing her scar, only to be pushed back to the mattress for another round of pleasuring her.

Oh dear. Will I ever see her again? I better think of something else.

"Can I ask you something? The two prison guards, Hillbilly and Polak... why do they refer to each other as 'brother'?"

"They go *way* back, ages. The 'brothers' were among the first retainers of the big man, way before the nukes went off. Originally they'd been military police. Guess who they were after... Anyway, for one reason or another, they'd hated each other's guts in the beginning. Then, during a patrol, they got themselves into a really bad clusterfuck. Those who made it out alive started to call each other 'brother', and the two of them have been best buddies ever since... especially nowadays, when they are the last ones still alive from that band of brothers."

"I see... And what about you? You are not one of the Lieutenants, nor a Hazara boy," Lazarov casually remarks to the Lance Corporal. "You must also be a newcomer, or how to say. What brought you here?"

"California ain't what it used to be no more," Bockman replies. The grin leaves his face. "Life is safer here... Anyhow, when I heard about the Tribe, I heeded the call."

Lazarov is taken by surprise. Not even Goryunov and the FSB, and even more so, not even the Stalkers in the New Zone, had heard much about the Tribe.

"Heard about the Tribe? How? Where?"

"Now listen up, partner... just because the Beghum asked me to take you to the Pass, you shouldn't think we're friends. Clear enough?"

"Enough."

"We're cool then. Yippee!"

"Hey, what are you doing? You are driving straight into a trap!"

"Oh yeah!" Electrical emissions crackle outwards and explode under the Humvee with a row of sharp, crashing thunder, but to Lazarov's astonishment nothing happens to the vehicle.

Lance Corporal Bockman gives him a triumphant smile. "State of the badass art!"

Shibar Pass, 11:10:39 AFT

Lazarov watches the dust cloud disappearing behind a hill as the Humvee returns to the Tribe's stronghold, far away beyond the canyons and mountains to the west, and opens his palmtop.

The map shows a valley to the south of his position where the ruins of Bhegum Madar's village supposedly lie hidden amongst the overgrown vegetation. The valley appears mostly green, just like on the display, but the digital map fails to reveal the red and blue, pulsating areas that look to Lazarov like dense anomaly fields. The path marked on the palmtop tells him to find the village first, and from there guides him to a trail leading up to a plateau overlooking the valley.

He unslings the Vintorez from his shoulder. When he was reunited with his gear that morning, he'd found that someone had cleaned and applied a strange, antistatic substance to the gun metal that repelled even the finest particles of dust. Now, switching the safety catch off, Lazarov starts walking towards the valley, his eyes ceaselessly scanning the surroundings.

Jackals yelp from a short distance. Hiding behind a rock, he observes them fighting over something that looks like a body. Indeed, it had to be some kind of food: the mutants were so intent upon it that they remained unaware of his presence. The major cautiously raises the rifle. Two jackals become startled as he hits the first, and even the last one runs away after the second victim falls too. He fires again. The yelp abruptly ends.

A bumpy, broken tarmac road leads into the forest. On the roadside, a blue sign stands with white Pashtu and Latin letters. The latter have all but disappeared, blasted away by many bullet holes, but the number 2 is still visible.

I hope that is the correct distance to the village.

Keeping close to the low mud walls lining the road, he cautiously moves on. The trees have grown so high that their foliage intertwines above the road, forming a kind of tunnel. Rays of light seep through and illuminate the dense vegetation.

Lazarov sees a vibrant spot ahead, as if the cracks in the tarmac emanate steam. Approaching within a couple of feet, he notices that it's not the only occurrence: the whole road looks like a landscape of miniature volcanoes.

Small but lethal, Lazarov thinks as he tosses an empty pistol shell into the closest anomaly and watches it evaporate with a fizzing sparkle. He switches on his detector and bright lights appear on the green display, indicating many anomalies. It also indicates one green dot deep inside the anomaly field.

Too far. Damn it, I could use another relic.

He sees a single whole mud brick lying on the ground near to a wall and, guided by sudden inspiration, kicks more bricks from the dilapidated wall before throwing them in the direction of the indicated relic to form a path. Cautiously stepping on it, he makes his way through the anomaly field and finally reaches the spot where a small spherical object gleams in one of the cracks. The Geiger counter's ticking gets faster as he crouches down to pick the relic up, the indicator reaching almost into the yellow area.

I'll need to ask Nooria if she knows more about this one.

The Geiger counter's indicator drops back to a safer level when Lazarov puts the relic into the container on his belt and, after a few leaps, he is out of the anomaly field and free to move on.

The undergrowth becomes more dense as he proceeds until the road narrows into a path. Lazarov ducks as something moves not far from him and he raises his weapon, waiting. The bushes rattle again, as if something large and heavy has moved behind them. A little distance away, a mutant appears, and for a moment Lazarov and the hind look into each other's eyes. Spooked, the creature gracefully leaps back into the forest, leaving Lazarov to sigh with relief before pushing on once more.

After a protracted period of more watchful sneaking, an ochre ruin appears. Once it must have stood directly on the road, but now high bushes hide most of it from view. Looking around, Lazarov sees the ruins.

The village at last.

Haunted Village, 13:46:02 AFT

Lazarov is creeping deeper into the ruined village when he hears a noise so strange that at first he doesn't believe his ears. All the same, he stands still, listening, but hears only the beat of his heart and the Geiger counter's slow ticking. But then the sound comes again.

No way. It cannot be.

But when the sound arrives a third time, there seems to be no doubt: it is the faint noise of someone crying.

Damn, this place is creepy.

A glance at his radiation meter assures him that the area would be too dangerous for anyone to enter without a protective suit and helmet. But the crying is there, somewhere deep among the overgrown ruins.

I better check it out instead of turning my back on it. This place reeks of danger.

Following the cry, he reaches an opening in the forest that must have once been the central square of the village. The wreck of an American truck stands in the middle of the area, its tires having rotted away long ago, the bullet-riddled windows opaque with dust and age. The absence of Tribe-like decoration tells Lazarov that it must have been destroyed during the Bush wars.

I can probably skip checking this one out.

His compass tells him that the trail to the plateau should be close. Turning to face that direction, Lazarov hears the crying getting stronger. A human figure suddenly appears in a dark hole that was once a window, passing by so quickly that he wishes he could rub his eyes under the helmet's visor. The crying is louder, clearer, and Lazarov realizes it is a child sobbing. Unable to bear the sound of the disconsolate voice, he takes one step closer… and sees a man standing by the next ruin. He is about to call out, but then notices details other than the long white gown that the silent stranger is wearing and his grey beard. The major falls back a step as he realizes that the man's eyes are missing, together with the top of his skull. The beard grows red from the blood that now pours out from his wounds. Gasping, Lazarov ducks and raises his gun, as if he could hit an apparition with a translucent body.

There are no ghosts. But this is one. But there are no ghosts.

Undeterred by the fear crawling under his skin, he steps closer. Now he sees the crying child, sitting on the ground, sobbing, tugging on the dress of a dead woman with a still fresh wound on her chest. The child looks up at him and Lazarov sees a hole in its head. The apparition raises its hand as if showing a way and, as the major involuntarily looks in the direction shown, a group of people appear, shuffling ever closer, with the row of ruins faintly visible when their bullet-riddled and mutilated bodies should be blocking them from view.

Instinctively, he grabs a grenade from his armor and throws it towards the group. It falls through them and detonates without having any effect on them. The crying becomes so loud that Lazarov feels as if he could touch its source. Turning his head to locate where the sound is coming from, he switches on his headlight and steps to the door of the house where the child first appeared. The fresh body of a woman lies in front of it. There is no visible wound on her body, but blood streams from between her legs.

Pulling all his courage together, Lazarov kicks the door in.

The blood-curdling howl is almost a relief after the sobbing. A human-like mutant stands in the headlight's beam, its unnaturally long arms scything towards him as if throwing something, but it is no weapon or projectile that hits him, only more images of dead people, their wounds heavier and their bodies more horrifically mutilated with each step he takes.

Lazarov aims his weapon and fires. He has barely emptied half the magazine when the mutant falls, its limbs writhing in agony before becoming still. The crying continues, so the major takes out his pistol and fires more shots into the creature's head. Now, the crying weakens, and finally disappears, leaving only the buzzing sound of flies in the filthy room.

He grins.

That was a nice try, but don't threaten a whore with a dick or a Spetsnaz with corpses.

But as he exits the house, his knees tremble so strongly that he has to sit down. Only now does he realize that the most horrifying thing about this experience was not the sight of wounds and corpses, but the natural way they appeared. They had been nothing but apparitions, yet all of them had been in realistic poses: the dead woman's hand reaching out for a wooden beam as if to help herself up; the child grabbing her dress as if it was a tangible thing; one of the dead men stepping over some bricks lying on the ground… It was as if he had just seen the eerie reenactment of something that had actually happened here.

The Khan's words come back to Lazarov's mind: *"It was… marvelous. After that, no shots were fired from the village anymore."* Now, confronted with what the renegade officer's idea of warfare could mean in reality, Lazarov now views him in a different light, and the respect he had for his brutal philosophy vanishes.

It is odd, though… he only hinted at a firefight. He said nothing about slaughtering civilians and rape. What the hell is it that the Bhegum wants me to find here?

He moves on. The trail leading upwards is steep, but he can soon see over the dark green foliage as he climbs higher and higher up the path.

Reaching the hilltop, he sees a cluster of trees with a large vehicle among them. Looking through the binoculars, he zooms in to identify the wreckage of a white van with a broken satellite dish on the top. With his weapon held ready, Lazarov approaches the wreck.

It was an unusual car, obviously civilian but heavily armored. Behind the tarnished windshield he sees a white sign with the word *PRESS* on it, written in huge letters. The bullet-riddled doors are locked and show the signs of several attempts to pry them open from the outside.

That car was like a tank… but somehow whoever was after these guys must have gotten inside, because there are no survivors here for sure.

He looks around. Close to the wreck, the heavy branch of a tree almost reaches the ground. Carefully balancing his weight, Lazarov climbs up it. After a few steps, he can comfortably leap over onto the top of the van.

They cut a hole in the weakest part... too small for a man to climb through, but big enough for a grenade. Now how can I get inside?

A closed hatch lies next to the satellite dish. Taking his pistol, he reaches through the hole and fires, aiming towards the hatch as best as he can. After a lucky shot the hatch moves, as if its lock has been suddenly released. After that, it is easy to force it open. Leaving his bulky backpack outside, Lazarov lets himself slide down into the compartment.

Three grimy skeletons appear in the dim circle of his headlight, their clothes long rotted away, along with their flesh. Without knowing what he is looking for, he rummages amid the debris. A camera lies on the ground alongside a broken laptop and he picks them up. The computer is nothing more than garbage now so Lazarov lets it fall back to the ground, where it breaks into small pieces. Something shiny falls out, a CD or DVD, and when he leans down to pick it up, his headlight falls on a tiny orange object amongst the bones of one of the skeleton's hands. Upon closer examination, the major realizes it is a pen drive.

Climbing out through the shaft, he seeks a safe spot where he can have a closer look at his loot. Behind a boulder, hidden from any hostile sight, he plugs the device into his palmtop.

Now let's pray it's not encrypted... Ah! It seems to be my lucky day indeed.

A folder system appears on the screen. Some are labeled in a script he recognizes as Arabic, but most of the folders have English names. There is one titled DIARY, but only one message is readable.

July 2, 2006. Kabul. Hooked up with Gardi and Hetherington at the Mustafa Hotel over a few cans of contraband Heineken. Those boy scouts still dream about being embedded with a USMC unit. Had to listen to their endless lectures over ethics again. Gardi was quite happy with his photographs of Medecins sans Frontiers turning an old prison into an asylum. I couldn't care less about such BS. They just can't understand that the real story is on the other side.

He opens ARCHIVE. It's empty. Switching to a folder titled *MISSION REPORTS 07/2006* brings more success: a few readable files appear on the screen.

08.13. AM, July 6, 2006. ISAF's new rules of engagement make it difficult to provide the coverage that our peak-time audience is seeking. Phyllis hopes to find local sources to get behind the scenes. She better do it, otherwise we'll all lose our jobs.

09.24. PM. July 14. Phyllis came up with a new source today. The idea is pretty risky but if it works out we'll have a really big story. We leave tomorrow morning. I hope Mahmud and Phyllis know what they are doing.

11.30. PM, July 15. If I hadn't got my fucking divorce to deal with I'd not go along with this, but I need my damned salary to pay that bitch. Fucking English legal system, robbing bastards... Anyway, this is our chance to land the scoop of our lives. The source has prepared everything. We only need to wait till morning and then keep the camera rolling.

01.57. PM, July 16. That was one hell of a show. The Yanks took the bait and were busted as soon as they arrived in the village. And we got the whole thing on tape! We wanted to move in quickly after they left but the source didn't let us. For our own security, he said. But when we eventually saw it... shit! Chuck-Up Central. Anyway, the only thing that counts is that the suckers have now their second My Lai coming.

02.43 PM, July 16. Something is not OK. While Phyllis was arguing with the source about money I saw the mujahedin dragging their fallen from the ruins. I also saw a shepherdess approaching the village. I grabbed my camera to take a photograph of her face when she saw what had happened – it would have been my WPP winning shot - but then the mujahedin wanted me to photograph a dead civilian. As I went there he moved and they just shot him in the head. Could it be that... it's too late now, we have already transmitted the footage. Should be on air tonight. The shepherdess ran away though, and with her went my chance to take the photograph of a lifetime. I'd better check on Phyllis now, it looks like their argument is getting out of hand.

03.55 PM, July 16. Shit shit shit! I can't believe I am part of this. They fucking drove the villagers away before the battle! They fucking shot them after the Yanks left, then arranged their fucking corpses. They even raped a woman, at least that's how it looks...That's why we had to wait and that's why they demanded extra payment. We want to drive away like hell but those bastards have blocked the road. We are now hauled up in the van. Phyllis is desperately calling the bosses to sort this mess out.

13.25 PM, July 16. We're fucking screwed. They're not letting us go. We wanted to ask ISAF for help but our comms are down because those bastards climbed up and smashed our antenna. I just hope the hatch will hold...

Lazarov removes the pen drive and carefully puts it away, thinking deep, dark thoughts

This explains a thing or two... Bhegum Madar was right. I must take this intel to the Khan.

He is about to close his palmtop when a LED indicates that somebody is calling him. He switches to the helmet's intercom.

"Lazarov here."

"*At last! I have been calling your for two days. Where have you been?*" Captain Bone's voice sounds anxious, even terrified.

"It's a long story. What's up?"

"*We came under attack yesterday. It was the damned Chinese during the day and the dushmans by night, but now they've joined forces! Major, you need to collect all Stalkers from the Ghorband area and relieve us!*"

"That's bad news..." The events of the last couple of days have kept him so preoccupied that Lazarov had almost forgotten about Bagram and the Stalkers. Then his soldiers come to his mind. "What about my men? They should be assisting you, Bone."

"They are but we lost two of them already. Many Stalkers too."

"What? Who is dead from my squad?"

"I don't know their fucking names and I don't care to, either. The only thing that counts is that you get all the men you can assemble in the west and help us! Now!"

Lazarov hesitates. If Bone is panicking, the situation must be dire. But he also has to deliver the pen drive. "How long can you hold out?"

"One and a half days, two perhaps. We are already running low on ammo but they just keep coming!"

"There aren't many Stalkers in Ghorband. What am I supposed to do with a dozen men?"

"Every Stalker and bullet counts. Bring everyone you can gather or we are done for... including your precious soldiers."

"I'll do what I can."

Lazarov receives no reply and he looks toward the north where the road, invisible in the vibrating heat, forks to the west and east. To the west, there is an opportunity to restore the honor of renegade Marines, because what he found has made it clear that they had been lured into a set-up and hadn't committed the crimes they had been charged with. To the east lay the strong chance that he would die in a futile attempt to protect Bagram, or even before getting to it, taking the white van's secret with him to the grave. Go east, and he might be able to help the Stalkers and his soldiers as they fight for their lives. Go west, and they would surely die horrible deaths.

Nooria is to the west. My men to the east. Where do I go now?

Then an idea comes to his mind, so daring that he himself doubts it could ever succeed.

"You disappoint me, Major. After all that I have told you, you still fail to understand."

The notes from the pen drive are still flickering on the laptop's screen, but though he has finished reading it, Lazarov can't see any change of expression in the Khan's face.

"But this proves that you were framed! You did not commit those crimes!"

"Can't you understand that we were not running from justice? We are not renegades and outlaws. We are the Tribe now!"

Lazarov sighs. *I don't even know what I was hoping for.*

"No," the big man, staring out of the window into the wilderness. "We will never return. This is our home now. Tell this to the Beghum. I know it was her who sent you to find this. She could never comprehend…"

After a long minute he turns back to Lazarov and takes something out from a wooden box. "Anyhow, you have my gratitude for your efforts. This is for you. I will also let you re-supply from our armory. Take whatever you like. I'm sure you'll find something useful."

"Thank you," Lazarov quietly replies.

"You have also proven yourself worthy to be called a warrior. For many, we are the worst enemy but for you, we will be the best friends."

Removing the oilcloth wrapper from the Khan's gift, Lazarov sees a beautifully forged combat knife. A delicate pattern runs down the blade, and its razor-sharp edge glows with a pale red hue. The weapon is not only beautiful as an object in its own right, but has obviously been alloyed with fire-emitting relic too.

"This is our special Ka-Bar, as used by our warriors. Take it and bear it with honor."

"You didn't even ask me if I wanted to join your Tribe," Lazarov boldly says. "I do have my own duty, that of my own country."

The Khan looks at him as if Lazarov has uttered the lowest profanity. "Don't mistake a gift for recruitment. Even if you begged, I wouldn't take you in. You are a friend, no more and no less... for now."

"Fair enough." Realizing how much he has overestimated his standing with the Tribe, Lazarov hesitates for a moment before continuing. "But there is something I need to ask you. As a friend, with all due respect."

"And what would that be?" the Khan asks, his voice promising nothing good.

"The Stalkers at Bagram are under attack by the dushmans and their allies. If the Tribe doesn't help them, they will be annihilated."

"So what?"

"If you helped them, you would have an ally to watch your back. They have traders too who could supply you with everything."

The big man mockingly laughs. "We don't need anyone to watch our back. Nor do we need Sammy's rubbish."

"You seem to have excellent spies, but they didn't report everything to you. There is a technician there too. Name of Grouch. He can work wonders with weapons."

"You test my patience, Major. Didn't you see that blade? If we go to such lengths to improve the most basic of weapons, what do you think we do to our rifles? We need no tinker man. But why do you care so much about them? You are with the military after all."

"You think they are without honor, and you are right: many of them are scavengers, trespassers, adventurers, killers and robbers. They are, because in the end Stalkers can rely on no one but themselves. Right now you can teach them what honor means and make them your friends, and that would be a good thing for the Tribe. Because what good is there in being everyone's worst enemy, without being anyone's best friend?"

The big man keeps looking at him with the same measured state. Lazarov is at the end of his wits. *There is no way to influence this man. Whatever I say keeps rebounding off him.*

Leaning against the wall with his hands, the former Marine now turns back to the window, drumming his fingers. Lazarov stands patiently awaiting a reply for so long that he begins to get the feeling that the Khan has forgotten about his presence. It therefore startles him when the Khan suddenly addresses him again.

"Would you be ready to die for your men, Major?"

"I am a soldier, trained to kill and to stay alive," the major replies without hesitation. "But if dying would make a difference… I would take it on as a sacrifice with meaning."

"Well spoken. Too bad there are bigger sacrifices than dying!"

Lazarov gives the Khan a baffled gaze but the big man turns his back on him to look out into the dusk again. "Go and see to your woman now. I will have my decision in time."

The major knows the Khan has nothing more to say. He also knows that, while the Lieutenants are standing at the door like statues, they are watching every move he makes. With nothing left to say and no action to be taken, Lazarov salutes and takes his leave. The Lieutenants let him pass and, stepping out of the Khan's tower, the major becomes silently preoccupied with his own concerns.

So… probably it will be me alone, maybe with a few Stalkers from the Asylum at best. I'll leave at dawn.

The Alamo, 18:41:56 AFT

It is the first time he finds himself unguarded and free to roam the Tribe's stronghold, and it comes as a surprise to him how peaceful, even romantic the encampment appears. Small fires light up the narrow street leading down to the gate, each one with fighters sitting around, relaxing. Warm light emanates from the small windows of the mud houses overlooking the valley that is now cast into darkness by the approaching night. Some homes have been built into the rocks with rope bridges leading up to and connecting them. The jagged mountains gleam crimson for a few minutes before the sun sets, leaving only shades of deep blue and purple on the horizon. But with the eyes of a well-trained soldier, Lazarov can also see that every stone in the stronghold has been placed with only one goal in mind: defense. The serene lights from the fighters' homes come from a direction where the valley could easily be kept under fire. The way to the gate is winding, with pillboxes perfectly aligned at positions to intercept intruders with machine gun fire. The fighters themselves may be chatting and smoking on hookah pipes, but all keep their rifles within reach, and here and there sandbags lie uniformly stacked up, ready to bolster the defenses. On the ramparts and bastions, rifle lights shine as guards keep their watch, and he also recognizes the small but well-trodden path that leads to the Pit. The thought of a home here with Nooria waiting for him almost makes him regret his words about not joining the Tribe.

"Are you lost?"

Lazarov jumps even as he recognizes the voice of the black gunnery sergeant.

"As a matter of fact, I am."

"Don't worry. It's easy to get lost in this warren. If it's the healer's house you're looking for, keep walking up the alley, always uphill."

"That's not exactly how I meant it..." The fighter seems friendly enough, so Lazarov decides to ask him the questions that are on his mind. "Do you have a little time?"

"Sorry, I don't."

"Just a few questions."

"My watch is coming up. If I'm late, the sergeant major's gonna get my ass."

"Then at least tell me where the armory is."

"Boxkicker's den? Up that alley to the right and across the bridge. He should be around with a few fighters doing PMCS." Seeing the confusion on Lazarov's face, he adds: "Preventative maintenance checks and services."

The fighter hurries off. Following his directions, The major passes by a few campfires where the warriors stop chatting and watch him with curious, distrustful eyes before turning back to their chat and the fruity-smelling smoke of their hookah pipes.

Lazarov has a strange feeling about them. Then he realizes that one thing is missing, something he had thought no soldier could live without: alcohol. He can't see any bottles being shared, any glasses filled with spirits. Only teapots steam over the charcoal fires.

No way could I ever join them. No booze.

Passing by a home hewn into the rock he hears a woman chastising a misbehaving child.

"Hush! Go to bed or Osama will get you!"

"But Mom, the Khan killed Osama long ago!"

"Go to bed, big mouth, or you'll not be going to the shooting range tomorrow!"

Walking over a rope bridge, Lazarov sees a bunker ahead. A sign on its metal door says *PROPERTY SHED* in neatly painted letters.

Before entering, Lazarov examines his equipment. He has only two magazines left for the Vintorez. It will barely be enough for the trip to the Asylum, never mind Bagram.

I'll need an arsenal for fighting my way to Bagram. Let's see what they have.

Stepping inside, he finds a few warriors tending to their rifles under shelves that are beginning to sag under the weight of the weapons on them. A man is standing at a work bench, welding something that looks like heavy armor plates for a machine gunner's position in a Humvee.

"Look at that! You got yourself a new customer, Boxkicker," a fighter says.

The technician switches off the welding torch and removes his mask. Heavy sweat runs down his red, snooty face.

"Spare the introduction," he says wiping the sweat away, "I know you're in for a free ride."

"Where did you get all this gear from?" Lazarov asks, scanning the shelves. The amount and variety of first-class weaponry leaves him in awe: what he can see from a mere glance blows Sammy's stock, or even many military armories, out of the water. From pistols to Gatling guns and submachine guns to heavy assault rifles, every lethal weapon ever made in the Western hemisphere lies here in perfect order and condition.

"*Where* is none of your business," Boxkicker says. "Suffice to say, we still have... sympathizers. Rest assured, it's not Human Rights Watch or the ACLU."

The warriors burst out laughing but Lazarov doesn't get the joke.

"What's the ACLU?"

The armourer grins. "No clue, eh? You Russians don't know how lucky you are." The warriors laugh again. Lazarov looks back at the weapons, feeling like a child in a toy shop.

"We got the word you're in for some cumshaw. Make your choice, but we have no Kalashnikovs or other slavshit here," Boxkicker says, eyeing Lazarov's rifle covetously. "I dig your Vintorez, though."

The technician's American slang puzzles Lazarov. *Dig a weapon?* he thinks. *Never heard that before.* "What do you mean? Why would you... use my rifle for digging?"

Seeing his confusion, the technician gives him a wide grin. "Never mind, Russkie. If you can't choose between a forty-mike-mike and a gimpy, just ask."

"I'd go for the nightwatch," a warrior adds. The others eagerly join in the mocking.

"Forget that. No man is man enough without a bushmaster."

"Check out the Ma Deuce, Russkie."

"You ever fired a Pig?"

"I love firing my boomstick in the morning. Sounds like victory."

"Once I dumped a girl because she made me chose between her and my blooper."

"So, Russkie," Boxkicker says, turning to Lazarov, still laughing and wiping more sweat from his face. "Tell me what you need."

Lazarov looks around. The abundance of Western-made arms is overwhelming. "Boxkicker… what about that SOP-modified M4A3, including the ACOG? You could throw in a few 30-round magazines as well."

"Hear ye, hear ye… we have an educated Russian here."

"And the Heckler & Koch M27 with a C-Mag on that shelf to your right. Can I see it?"

"Come on, that's too good for you. I can offer a PIP M249 with a cloth pouch holding two hundred rounds."

"Only if it comes with enough duct tape to prevent it from falling apart."

"You have a point about its wear, I give you that. All right… Ammo for this one? Suppose you want to take some full metal jacket M855's."

"I don't need it for pea shooting. Are those Match bullets over there?"

"Bingo. Two boxes is all you get."

"I could use that Benelli M4 too with a few boxes of slugs."

"You are a rat-fuck, you know that? Take this shotgun."

"What about that one?" Lazarov points at an ochre-painted, heavy rifle.

"Uh-oh… you want to make my life really difficult, eh?"

"Is that so?"

"I don't know what's screwing me up more, giving you that Gepard M6 or ignoring the big man's orders... how would an anti-material rifle help you, anyway?"

"By making a material difference between life and death, I suppose."

"That's a real ass for sure. But it only works with Russian 12,7 millimeter rounds and we don't have many of them around here."

"I ask you very nicely: may I take the Gepard, please?"

"No way. You better keep your dickbeater off that."

"Stop being so shit-hot, Boxkicker," a warrior says quietly. "He's Nooria's mate. Unless you want her pissing into your wounds next time you need first aid, you better give him what he wants."

"Oh, yes, Nooria." The armourer smacks his lips. "I guess before eating her out, you've had to let her soak in hot water for an hour, scrubbed and disinfected her, and then put a bucket over her head to cover her face?"

Lazarov's face reddens with anger.

"You don't want any trouble for yourself," another warrior tells Boxkicker. "Give him what he wants, big mouth."

"I won't give the Gepard to this rat-fuck. He can kiss my ass. But only if he washes his mouth after kissing that pus-faced little witch who –"

The armourer doesn't get to finish the sentence. Quick as lightning, Lazarov's fist darts out and slams into Boxkicker's cardia and arm, followed by one more punch to the throat that sends him sprawling among the neatly arranged weapons. Knocked out, he stays on the ground with rifles, tools, grenades and ammunition magazines raining down onto his head from the ruined shelves.

"Fuck," Boxkicker eventually groans, spitting out blood and teeth.

"I'll take that as a 'yes, have anything you need'," Lazarov says firmly, and piles the weapons and ammunition into his exoskeleton's rucksack.

"Respect, Russkie," a fighter laughs, "that's what I call a ninja punch!"

"Wrong, *pindos*," Lazarov grumbles back as he leaves the armory. "It's called *Systema*."

Nooria's home, 7 October 2014, 21:57:13 AFT

"I'm back."

Upon entering Nooria's home and putting his new weapons down on the floor, the irony of his situation makes him smile.

It feels like returning to a perfectly normal home after a day's shopping.

"Welcome, my warrior!" Nooria beams happily from the hearth, where she is boiling something spicy in a blackened pot. She looks different now, wearing a white gown with beautiful embroidery with her loose, freshly washed hair shining with the fire's reflection. "You look happy. What did he say?"

"He is still thinking about it," Lazarov shrugs while taking off his armored suit. "I couldn't impress him enough."

"I told you when you arrived from village. His heart is hard like..." Nooria knocks on the iron pot.

"I will have to leave you again tomorrow."

Lazarov is concerned about her reaction. Nooria is a woman from the Tribe and he couldn't blame her if she couldn't understand why he wanted to go off helping the Stalkers, who her people considered to be nothing but worthless scavengers. Looking at the white dress that barely hides her dark-skinned, delicate figure, he almost regrets his words.

"Of course you will," she casually replies taking the pot from the hearth and putting it on the table. As she moves close to him and waves her hair from her face, Lazarov smells her scent. He knows enough about women to know that her hair did not need to be fussed about. "And now eat. You look hungry."

"What is this?"

"Stew. Devil pups hunted down a deer."

After all the things he's heard about Nooria, Lazarov is a little suspicious of the thick, spicy broth, but it tastes like a normal soup, even if it is spicier that what he is used to. He savors the first few spoonfuls. The last decent, warm meal he had was at his mother's apartment, but Russia, the Old Zone and Moscow now seem to be on another planet.

"You don't like it?" Nooria asks with concern, studying his face. She sits down on the rug, watching Lazarov eating. "I have some powders to make it more tasteful."

"Oh no, thanks, it's delicious," Lazarov quickly replies. "But listen… could you please sit with me here, at the table?"

"No. Women always wait until men finish their meal."

Lazarov puts down the spoon. "But I can't eat like this."

"Please do. I have something to do until you finish." Lazarov opens his lips to swallow down another spoonful but his mouth stays open in surprise as Nooria grasps his rifle and, before he can say a word, starts disassembling it.

"What are you doing, Nooria?"

"Cleaning your weapon."

Lazarov rolls his eyes. "Leave that rifle alone, woman. It's loaded."

"Of course it is. But I didn't treat this yet. Wait."

She disappears in the back room. When she returns, she brings a small pouch and a piece of cloth. Nooria skillfully disassembles the rifle and applies a greasy, gray substance on it that the gun's metal immediately absorbs.

"I made it from your new swag," she explains seeing Lazarov's puzzled look. "It will keep your gun clean."

"*What?* You made gun grease from my relic?"

"But of course. Some are better used like this than carried around. From some I make refreshing ointment. From others, I make oil for wounds. I make powder, mix it with herbs, glowing stones... Things like that." She shrugs and gives Lazarov an innocent giggle.

"Where did you learn all this?"

Nooria's giggle turns into a mysterious smile. "Ask me something else."

"All right... Why do you call those kid soldiers devil pups?"

"The Khan's former tribe called themselves devil dogs. He loves tradition. That is why the children are called pups. They will become warriors one day, if they prove themselves."

"Uh-hum... Did you give him and his Lieutenants some of these special powders of yours? Because all of them are so huge..."

"No... that was..." The smile vanishes from Nooria's face. "They were with Colonel when they went into..."

"Where?"

"Depths of Shahr-i-Gholghola."

Lazarov slowly begins to understand. *Whatever they found under the City of Screams turned them into human, living juggernauts. But how could this happen?* He wishes he could ask Nooria more questions about the village and the battle that had happened there, but she doesn't look too eager to be pressed.

"I saw something weird in the village..." he says carefully. "It was a mutant, but instead of attacking me it made ghosts appear. Strange ghosts... they looked very real."

"Was it difficult to kill?"

"No."

"I know its kind... we call it djinn. It is very weak and hides in caves and ruins. It tries to scare its enemies away. If jackals come, it makes them see snake. If snake comes, it shows him bear. And to men, it shows dreadful things. You are brave."

"Curious would be a better word... and now I feel miserable for killing a weak mutant that only wanted to scare me away."

334

"You have good heart."

"Now this is something no one has told me for a long, long time." A feeling of compassion comes over Lazarov as he looks down at the fragile girl, who returns his look with a smile on her scarred face. "About those ghosts... were they for real?"

"My village has seen many sad things," Nooria replies, getting up from the ground and taking the empty plate from the table. "Let us not talk about such things tonight. We have something more important to do."

All Lazarov wants to do is to relax after the hearty soup. *I wish I could have a beer now.*

"Nooria, you are good with all kinds of powders and potions... do you know how to brew beer?"

"A bear? You did not like deer stew?" She asks, disappointedly, going back to cleaning the rifle. "Because a bear tastes very bad."

"Never mind..." Suddenly, Lazarov's eye falls on a large pot and a pile of stale, dark bread next to the hearth. "Is that made of rye?"

"Yes. But it is old bread."

"All the better. Do you have... you know, that thing used for making bread..."

"Yeast? I think so."

"Raisins and sugar?"

"Yes, but why?"

"All right... now it's my turn to teach you a secret recipe. Cut and dry the bread. Boil water in that big pot. When boiling, take it from the fire and stir. Cover the pot and let it rest in a dark, cool place. After half a day, filter the liquid. Mix yeast with warm water and a pinch of sugar. Wait until the yeast gets foamy. Stir it into the filtered liquid with a little sugar... can you still follow?"

Nooria nods while removing the magazine from the carbine. She wraps the cloth around her finger and starts cleaning the breech. Her finger moves slowly and gently inside the rifle, as if caressing it. Lazarov stares at her eyes, still fixed on him, and suddenly finds it hard to concentrate on the recipe.

"Okay… anyway… after a day, filter it into a pitcher and add the raisins. Wait for a couple of days, then serve it cold. The warriors will love it."

Nooria gives him a suspicious look. "Hm… is that *sarab*?"

"What? Oh no, it's not alcoholic. My mother prepared it for me when I was a child… it's a very good drink… but why don't you drink alcohol, anyway?"

"Long time ago, Colonel found two drunk fighters during their watch. He got very angry. Since then, no *sarab* for fighters."

"*Gospodi*… Don't worry, nobody will be shot for having my kind of drink."

"I can give it a try…"

"Please do, but don't add any stone powders, swags or relics to it, all right?"

"All right. But I will not prepare it now. Now I have something else in mind."

"And, uhm, what do you have in mind?"

Nooria now moves the cleaning cloth up and down the rifle barrel, softly, gently and very slowly. She gives him a broad smile, flashing her white teeth.

"What do you think I have in mind?"

Nooria's home, 8 October 2014, 05:48:59 AFT

Knowing that it could be the last time he sees her, Lazarov leaves no inch of Nooria's body untouched. While kissing and caressing her scars as if tenderness could heal them, Mac's — or better, Elisabeth's — words come his mind: *to find another human being who has everything about him what the Zone means: a new reason for staying alive.*

Her body stretches out like a landscape, undulating female curves that smell of sweat and the scent from the body oil, prepared from a relic that seems to have the powers of an aphrodisiac; not as if he would need any such help tonight.

Staying alive... I wouldn't mind if I died right now, with her as my last sight.

He fondles her breasts and lets his hand glide up to her scarred neck and face, fondling her loose hair, and rests his head on her belly with her taste still on his tongue. Lazarov wants to fall asleep there, feeling the warmth emanating from Nooria's body against his face.

He closes his ears to the commotion outside, not willing to get up even when Nooria gets to her feet and, quickly covering her nakedness with her long gown, leaves their sleeping place.

From somewhere in the distance, the noise of heavy engines being started sounds through the night.

Doors open and Lazarov hears an agitated male voice outside, but ignores it still.

"Wake up!"

Nooria sounds anxious.

"What's happened?" Lazarov mumbles, half asleep. "Why are you so upset?"

Through his half-open eyelids, heavy with tiredness, Lazarov sees his rifle in Nooria's hands. Its impeccably clean gun metal shines in the candlelight.

"Take it and use it with honor," Nooria says with a hint of sadness in her voice, "because you must leave me now. Bockman is here for you."

"But... why?" Lazarov asks. A frightening thought agitates him. *I hope it's not the Khan ordering me away from her after I pissed him off last night.* "What is this about?"

Nooria gives him the weapon. "Our Tribe is going into battle. Be brave and strong, warrior... and return to me with victory."

Ghorband, 11:34:26 AFT

Hidden behind a BTR wreck, Lazarov studies the Stalkers guarding the roadblock at Ghorband through his binoculars. They seem nervous, keeping their rifles ready to shoot and barely moving out from the cover of the sand bags.

"Don't shoot! Friendly coming through!" Concerned that he might be shot on sight, the major slowly steps out of cover and starts walking towards the Stalkers with his hands held high. "Don't shoot, brothers!"

"Lower your weapons," he hears Shrink shouting, "it's the *boyevoychik!* Hey, come quickly! I hope you're here to help us!"

"Indeed! We're going to Bagram to kick ass!"

Shrink looks at him with utter disbelief. "No way. We'll be lucky if we stay alive here. We heard vehicles approaching… it means we are really screwed. Bagram is under siege and soon the Tribe will be at our throats too… This will be our last stand. Come, have some vodka while you still can!"

"No vodka today, thanks, nor will there be a last stand. I brought men with me… a few good men."

"This is no time for jokes. Where are they?"

"Behind me. You better holster your weapons." Lazarov presses the button on his intercom. "Bockman, the road is clear. Proceed. Have a truck take a few hitchhikers aboard."

The Stalkers become startled as they hear the noise of heavy engines approaching.

"This can't be real," Shrink murmurs. "But if it isn't real, it does *sound* real… and then it's me who needs professional help because I'm hallucinating."

"No, you aren't. Look!"

From beyond the next bend in the road, a Humvee appears. Then a dozen more follow and after them a long column of a hundred heavily armored vehicles, decorated with decomposing Taliban and mutant skulls, the Tribe's red banner proudly blazing on the antennae.

Bagram area, 13:07:51 AFT

The Humvee, driven by the Lance Corporal and carrying the Khan and Lazarov, turns up a trail leading to a high hill overlooking Bagram. The main convoy halts, still covered by the forest between the road and the sandy, open plain to the east. Two trucks leave the convoy and follow the Khan to the hilltop where they stop, covering the flanks of their leader's vehicle.

"You won't need your gear," the big man says upon observing that Lazarov is about to take his new M4 carbine with him. "Take the scope from the Gepard only. It's longer than your toy binocs."

A dozen Lieutenants jump down from the trucks and assume a protective position around their leader. They are led by a warrior wearing an exoskeleton that is entirely different to the others, since it has been painted entirely black – even his helmet, held under his arm, on which the red SEMPER FI inscription blazes out even brighter. Out of all the warriors around, except the Khan, he is the only one without his helmet on. Blue eyes stare out from a sun-baked, wrinkled face topped by gray hair cut to stubble, radiating the composure of a senior fighter who has already seen many battles like the one unfolding in front of them. Although taller and leaner, there is something confidence-inspiring in his presence that reminds Lazarov of *praporshchik* Zotkin.

More trucks and Humvees arrive on the hill, carrying mortars and heavy machine guns. Their crews quickly start preparing them, but obviously not quickly enough for the senior warrior.

"Don't be scared of breaking your fingernails, ladies! You are not just a fire support team, you are *my* fire support team!

Anderson, do you want the big man to think that *my* fire support team is made up of pussies? Do you want to let me fucking down, gunny?"

"No, sir, Sergeant Major Hartman, sir!"

"Then speed up! That also includes you, Corporal Hendricks! You're not in the Belgian army anymore! Haul those ammo boxes!"

"Oorah, sir!"

"That's the spirit! Move, move, move, warriors! Maybe the gunny told you that we're here for a lazy pussies convention. That's damn wrong! What are we here for today?"

"For the kill!" the warriors' chorus replies.

"And what am I here for?"

"For the thrill!"

"I want that kill! I want that thrill! Move, you lame pussies!"

Standing in front of his command vehicle and studying the besieged base through his binoculars, the Khan orders a command into his radio.

"Assault team, proceed towards Phase Line Akron."

"*Affirmative. Assault team is Oscar Mike*," comes the reply.

"Keep it steady, Ramirez."

"Fire support team is prepared, sir," the sergeant major reports to the Khan, who glances at his watch.

"It took them three seconds longer than I expect, Top."

"Apologies, sir. I'll talk to Anderson about it once the show is over."

At that moment, a volley of RPG projectiles hit the gates of the Stalker base, blasting a machine gun post and sending half a dozen defenders to their deaths.

"Looks pretty hairy down there," the big man calmly remarks.

"Nothing we couldn't handle, sir."

"Top, have the fire team stand by." The Khan speaks into his radio set. "Driscoll, proceed with the security team to grid Zulu Bravo Seven Niner."

Through his binoculars, Lazarov watches a few lighter armored vehicles leaving the main column, and cannot shake off a steady flow of bad memories when he hears the cruel First Lieutenant's voice reply through the radio.

"Affirmative. Security team moving out."

The vehicles speed up, driving around the hill the Khan has chosen for his command post so as to stay out of the sight of the enemy, and quickly move towards the road leading to the south.

"Driscoll is closing the kill zone," the sergeant major tells Lazarov with a grin. "No rag-head will get out of here alive, not even if they're disguised as Minnie the Mouse!"

Two small, light trucks arrive on the hill.

What are they doing here? Lazarov asks himself. *No armor, no nothing...unless that thing under the cover is some piece of artillery.*

"Looks bad for the scavengers," the sergeant major observes pointing towards the besieged Stalker base. "They're in deep shit. A real clusterfuck."

Lazarov raises his binoculars. The container wall around the Antonov is shattered, while here and there tracer bullets still fizz towards the waves of enemies who swarm around the Stalker base like a sea of ants.

"Major," he hears the Khan calling, "you will not take part in this battle. You will only have the pleasure of watching it. But before it begins, I give you a mission."

Lazarov turns to him with a bad feeling festering in his guts.

"You were right, Major, we have no friends here. But I don't think that Stalkers and the Tribe will ever be friends. I ordered my men into this battle because I want you to be in my debt."

This doesn't sound good, the major thinks.

"I want you to be in my debt because I will task you to do something that is almost impossible," the Khan says. "I give you the task of staying alive until you have done what you came here for. Afterwards, I want you to find my son and give him what you have found in that village. Tell him what you have seen here – everything. Are you willing to do this for me, in exchange for the miserable lives of a few scavengers?"

"What if I die, no matter how hard I try to stay alive?"

Another huge explosion rocks the Stalkers' defenses.

"Would you dare to disappoint me?" A grim smile appears on the Khan's face. "You better make up your mind now, because your friends seem to have only minutes left to live."

"Yes, I will do that for you. *If* I can stay alive."

"Consider that a direct order from *me*. Take this damned pen drive and guard it with your life. I have saved everything on it that you'll need to know to find my son. When you find him, you will understand what I said about heroin, and why we littered the poppy fields with corpses. And now... now you will see me unleashing the greatest warriors the earth has ever seen."

"*Assault team has reached Phase Line Akron. Sierra Bravo,*" Lazarov hears a voice crackling in the radio.

"*Security team is in position,*" comes another report.

The Khan looks up to the endless grey sky and takes a deep breath. His trembling nostrils tell of excitement barely withheld. "I love battles at dawn... let the sky crumble. Top! Send the assault team in!"

"Assault team, proceed through Phase Line Boston to Phase Line Charleston," the sergeant major commands through his radio. "When you reach Charleston, wait for the big man's command before you strike."

"*Assault team. Affirmative.*"

Lazarov raises his binoculars to his eyes. The column starts moving, turning eastwards on a narrow road through the forest.

The vehicles keep precisely the same distance from each other, as if they were railway carriages pulled by the same locomotive, even upon reaching the plain where they accelerate and swirl up a huge plume of dust and sand.

"*Assault team crossing Phase Line Boston.*"

So far, all the call signs, orders and destination codes sounded to Lazarov like a normal military operation, but now the big man barks an unexpected command.

"Sound the bell."

"Oorah, sir!" The sergeant major waves his hand to the light trucks. Their crews remove the canvas from the tops but, to Lazarov's surprise, it is not a weapon that they are carrying but a massive set of loudspeakers.

Suddenly, Lazarov hears the toll of a huge bell, its sound so deep and menacing as if it heralds the Apocalypse itself, and so loud that it feels as if it is crushing his eardrums. The dreadful toll rolls through the plains and echoes back from the hills far away.

"Our way of letting them know that doom is coming," the sergeant major shouts over with a wide smile, putting his helmet on.

"*Assault team has reached Phase Line Charleston,*" comes through the radio.

"Assume assault formation, Ramirez," the Khan commands. "Fire support team, the kill zone is yours."

"Fire for effect! Give'm hell!"

On the sergeant major's orders, the mortars fire a salvo and the heavy machine guns on the Humvees start barking.

The column has reached the plain and deploys into a semi-circle, outflanking the enemy like a gigantic snake raising its head to strike its prey. The Humvees slow down for a minute and turn towards the enemy who are already being hammered by the Tribe's mortars and heavy machine guns.

"*Assault team in position.*"

"Assault team – go!" the Khan commands. "Fire support, shift your fire!"

The sound of guitars now screams from the loudspeakers at skull-crushing volume, playing a symphony of pure rage. A desire for destruction overwhelms him and Lazarov feels the urge to run down from the hill with all guns blazing, unleashing a scream to join the singer's brutal cry. He feels like a puppet moved by the toll of the bell, blending with the merciless rhythm coming from the loudspeakers.

A glance from the Khan stops him dead. In the gray glow of dawn, the massive roar of battle blends with the music rolling over the plain below.

Lazarov believed that the Tribe had earned its notoriety by pure cruelty. But what he sees now unfolding is the most impressive deployment of mobile firepower he has ever witnessed.

The line of vehicles accelerates, the mounted machine guns and grenade launchers spitting bullets and explosives into the enemy ranks. They don't slow down as they smash into the dushmans, throwing bodies and shattered limbs into the sky. Now the warriors jump off and charge forward while the machine guns on the vehicles cover the area ahead of them with a deadly rain of fire. Lazarov sees a warrior blasting the heads of two enemies with his machine gun while devil pups charge forward, their fixed bayonets red from the glowing alloy and blood.

A Humvee gets separated from the line and is soon surrounded by the enemy, only to unleash a massive streak of fire from a mounted flamethrower and clear a circle filled with burning corpses around it. He sees a devil pup dying, then another one who had tried to protect his fallen comrade. For a moment the line falters, but a few senior warriors fill their loosened ranks and mow the enemy down with rifle fire. The Tribe's iron gauntlet closes around the enemy, mercilessly and irresistibly pushing them forward to the container wall, where the defenders' bullets rain down into their massed ranks.

Lazarov swings the binoculars towards the Stalkers who are fighting a pitched battle against the dushmans, several of whom are climbing up the wall. A Stalker in a heavy suit kicks one in the head, only to be shot in the back by a dark-clad figure crawling up the wall. Two rounds from a defender's shotgun blow the dushman's head off. Lazarov sees the enemy starting to falter, but at the gate, blasted and half ruined by RPG hits and hand grenades, a group of heavily armored Chinese commandos hold their ground among the terrified, routing dushmans and pushes on towards the gate.

"They do have guts," he hears the sergeant major commenting. "Not bad - keeping their cohesion under fire like that. The scavengers throw everything at them but the kitchen sink."

Something must happen or it was all for nothing, Lazarov reflects, barely able to keep himself from charging into battle. He switches to his sniper rifle's scope to have a closer look and sees a group of Stalkers pouring out of the gate led by two figures in military armor, one of them raking the enemy ranks with his machine gun and the other relentlessly firing an assault rifle. To his incredible relief, he recognizes Ilchenko and Zlenko.

Thank God they're still alive. But where are the others?

He watches the Stalkers surge forward, screaming, killing and dying until they run into the steel wall of Tribe warriors with only dead and dying enemies left between them. For a moment, Stalkers and warriors face each other.

"Assault team, regroup. Commence pursuit," the Khan commands, unmoved.

The Tribe's warriors turn and jump on the Humvees, some of which now carry fewer men than before the battle. Lazarov spots a few daring defenders join the warriors, with the Shrink and his die-hard Stalkers from the Asylum among them. The vehicles speedily pursue the routed enemy, crushing those who get under their massive wheels, the warriors firing their weapons at those too far away to be squashed as they drive the few surviving enemies towards First Lieutenant Driscoll's position, where they will be trapped in a final crossfire.

"All right, Top," the big man says. "Order them to cease fire before we go blue on blue. We're done for today."

"Cease fire, cease fire," the sergeant major orders into his radio. "Show's over!"

"Let Bauer and Ramirez mop up the area. I want the rest of our warriors to gather at the gate of that pathetic shithole. Let the corpsmen move in, and have a Humvee take our friend to his men."

At once, the vehicles turn around and, with the warriors finishing off the few enemies still alive, return to the shattered Stalker fortress, where they line up like a cavalry unit – dusty, smoky, flecked with blood, their riders jumping off and joining the Stalkers in celebrating victory. At the sign of the sergeant major, the music fades to a less ear-splitting volume, then tapers off.

"Security team. A few rag-heads have surrendered. Awaiting instructions. Over."

The Khan calmly lights up a cigarette. "I'm not in the mood to take prisoners today, Driscoll," he replies through his radio.

"Affirmative."

After a few seconds, the chilly wind brings the noise of short machine gun bursts from the First Lieutenant's position.

The old warrior takes off his helmet and slings his carbine over his shoulder. "Damn this shit," he tells Lazarov as he shows him to the nearest Humvee. "For men like us, watching such a battle and only smelling the cordite from far away – it's like torture, ain't it?"

"I could hardly agree more, Sergeant Major," Lazarov replies, climbing inside. "But it was hell of a battle either way."

"Of course it was. It was *my* Tribe fighting, the best men in the world. Semper Fi!"

"What was that music? Once I heard something like that in a movie, with choppers and all, but didn't believe that you Americans really played music when going into battle."

Sergeant Major Hartman gives him a smile. "Wagner is for pussies. We prefer Metallica."

"Grouch! You have a minute?"

"What? I can't hear you Sammy. My ear drums are blown."

"That's nothing, me dear! I have bullets in me ass."

"Actually, I got stabbed in my neck too."

"C'mon, man, that's nothing compared to me amputated toe!"

"Sorry, I can't admire it. I'm wearing a patch on my better eye."

"So you have no seen me boots? I can't find them since Placebo patched up me feet!"

"You removed your boots? Now I understand why they ran away!"

"YOU TWO! THE INTERCOM WAS NOT REPAIRED TO FACILITATE YOUR SMALL TALK! AND YOU, MAJOR... COME OVER. WE NEED TO TALK."

Fuck you, Bone, Lazarov thinks as he gets out of the Humvee and looks around.

The siege has taken a heavy toll on the Stalkers' base. Incoming RPGs have pounded the walls of Bone's command center. The old Antonov is in even worse shape than she was before, with one of the wings broken away from the fuselage, probably due to mortar fire, and now lying on the ground riddled with bullets indicating how the Stalkers had converted it into a makeshift firing position to compensate for the steel container that had been blasted away at the gate. Close to a relatively intact part of the container wall, Lazarov sees a dozen freshly dug graves. The watchtower still stands, with one Stalker on top of it behind the sandbags that have been darkened by the smoke of explosions. The only comforting sight is that of his two battle-worn soldiers hurrying up to greet him.

"Major Lazarov!" the sergeant greats him cheerily. "It's good to have you back!"

"Wish I could have come earlier."

"What happened to you? You look… different."

"It's a… long and sad story."

"In one sentence, Major," Ilchenko says, "please. You left with Squirrel and returned with a whole army!"

"In one sentence? All right… we destroyed the AA battery that shot down our choppers and ran into the Tribe who killed Squirrel and wanted to stone me to death, but a woman preferred that I get her witch daughter with child and sent me to a mutant-infested village to find some old intel and then I agreed to do their leader a favor in exchange for saving your asses. Well, more or less."

"Wait a minute… did you just say, you got laid?" Ilchenko asks with envy. "Come on, give me the juicy details! Please!"

Zlenko just shakes his head. "Damn… stone you to death? "What on earth are those people? Savages?"

"Far from it."

"The only thing that counts is that you are finally back with us!"

Lazarov doesn't know how to counter Zlenko's enthusiasm.

If I wanted to be honest with him, I would admit that I no longer know where 'back' and 'away' is and who 'us' might be. This land has got me good.

"Be happy it didn't happen to Ilchenko. If it were him telling this story, we'd still be listening to him till Christmas!"

"Don't worry, Sarge, I'm looking forward to make nice story out of this once I get home!"

"Zlenko, what's the status of the squad?"

"Permission to speak freely, sir?"

"Go ahead."

"With all due respect—I've missed that bossy tone of yours."

Lazarov smiles. "I must admit that I met my match."

"He must have been a very tough guy."

"You couldn't be more wrong. It's a *she*. So, what's our body count?"

"Only the two of us are left from Sparrow Two. Ignatov died during the first night. Obukov and Stepashin fell the next day. Bondarchuk was killed by a sniper. We received heavy mortar fire during the first night and the bastards hit the infirmary with Saitov and Lobov inside."

"They got our medic? Damned *baystrukhi!*"

"Then Kravchuk and Nakhimov fell during a raid to take the mortars out."

"Who was leading the raid?"

"It was the initiative of a Stalker called Crow…"

"Best sniper I ever saw, Major," Ilchenko cuts in. Lazarov gives him a disapproving look but the soldier refuses to allow being interrupted. "He showed up with a band of real badass Stalkers just before the siege began."

Zlenko clears his throat. "In fact, it was me executing the operation. All went well until we took out the mortars – we could sneak up to their positions without being detected. But we ran out of luck making our retreat. I ordered Kravchuk to take a mortar with him to bolster our defenses and Nakhimov grabbed two boxes of mortar shells." The sergeant's face darkens when he continues. "Those bastards fired RPGs at us. One landed close to Nakhimov as he was carrying the ammo. Both of them died immediately, together with a Stalker who was covering our rear."

Lazarov is sad to hear how the remains of his squad have disintegrated but cannot blame the sergeant. It might have happened the same way had he been in charge, and there was nothing to prevent bad luck from happening.

"Things like that happen. Good job. What about resources?"

"We are very low on ammo. I have three magazines left, Ilchenko only one. We shared everything we had with the Stalkers. Honestly, sir, now I'm glad that Captain Bone took half our ammo when we first arrived. Had we wasted more at the Outpost, we would have run out of bullets after two days here."

"Yes, Bone and his actions," Lazarov grumbles, keeping his doubts to himself. "Always more reasonable than one would expect."

"I need to replace the barrel on the PKM as well. It could crack now any moment and the breech jams all the time. It would be more lethal to throw the bullets."

"What about Grouch? The base technician?"

"He only works for money and we don't have that much."

"Damn! Ilchenko, you and I went through hell to make him work for us for free!"

"I mean, he doesn't ask *us* for money. He only wants to finish the paying jobs first."

"Bloody anarchists… oh well, I should have known. Mac and Beefeater?"

"Mac is still around somewhere but the Stalker bought it." Seeing that Lazarov wants to hear more, Ilchenko adds, "His rifle jammed at the worst moment."

"Sad to hear that… Anyway, at least we don't have to worry about faulty weapons. I brought some new stuff."

"Really? From the Tribe?"

"Yes. A shotgun for you, sergeant, and a heavy *avtomat* for Ilchenko. They're stashed on one of the trucks. I'll get more ammo once we get to their stronghold." Seeing that Ilchenko doesn't look too happy, Lazarov adds, "Don't give me such a sour face. I know you'd like to stick to our weapons, but at least theirs are in mint condition… or even better than that."

"We could have used those during the siege," Zlenko observes. "It was a close shave, even though the Stalkers fought like hell. But no matter what, we were thinking it was game over for us until we heard that riff—"

"What?"

"I mean, those guitars playing from the loudspeakers on the hill. The dushmans totally panicked when that bell sounded and even more so when the guitars started up. And when the mortars and machine guns started hammering them... *Gospodi*, what a sweet sight it was! The dushmans were cannon fodder, but the mercs gave us a pretty hard time until I saw the moment right to turn the tables around. So, I took the bravest Stalkers and Ilch, and..."

Zlenko stops in the middle of his sentence and looks to the base gate, as if seeing the devil himself. "Holy Mother of God, who are they?"

Lazarov looks to the gate. "My in-laws," he casually replies and leaves the two soldiers staring at the Khan, the sergeant major and two Lieutenants in admiration. So do the few Stalkers at the gate, even if they also keep a respectful distance from them as they enter the compound.

"Many good warriors have sealed our pact with their blood, Major," the Khan says by way of greeting. "I hope you will not forget about your end of the bargain."

"You have my word as an officer," Lazarov replies.

"That shall suffice." The Khan looks around. His face resembles that of someone who hates dogs but has business in a kennel. "Such a miserable excuse of a base... but I have to admit that I am impressed, to some extent. Your Stalkers seem to have guts after all."

"The Stalkers are not mine. *These* are my men." Lazarov waves towards Zlenko and Ilchenko who approach with a mixture of awe and distrust sketched upon their faces. "*Desantniki*, this is the... uhm, the Khan, the leader of the Tribe. *Smirno!*"

For a long moment, the Khan studies the two soldiers, who stand in attention and appear as if there is nothing in the world that could make them look into his eyes.

"Good men are all that an officer needs," he says, turning back to Lazarov, "and good men are made by good officers. Maybe one day I will give you a chance to join us."

"First I have to come up with my end of the bargain," Lazarov cautiously replies.

"Fair enough. And now?"

"I ask your permission to cross Tribe territory. We have a mission to accomplish there. I had hoped you would let me pass with a few dozen Stalkers."

"Let me give you some advice: forget the City of Screams."

"I am needed there," Lazarov replies. "We have a rescue mission to finish."

"It's you who will need rescuing in the end, and no help will come."

"Honestly, I would prefer another place to go, one I don't even need to tell you. But my orders still stand."

His hands crossed behind his back, the big man looks down to the ground, contemplating.

"Those who gave your orders do not know what lies there. Under normal circumstances, I would not let you approach the place. When you hear the call, you will understand..." The big man seems to fight against his own better judgment. "On the other hand, you being involved with Nooria now places you in a unique position. There are more things connecting her and the City of Screams than you would ever imagine."

The sergeant major clears his throat. "Sir, may I add something?"

"Speak your mind, Top."

"Maybe he can finish the job, sir. Remember, I told you right at the beginning that those diggers might pose a threat. Let him clean up the mess. Once he's there, he'll know what to do."

The old warrior's words seem to aid the Khan in making up his mind.

"You may pass, Major. I'll provide you with a few trucks to carry your men. Not because I want to help you get there, but because it's you whom I want to deliver to your woman as soon as possible. She will have something to tell you and you better listen to her. Understood?"

"I could hardly ask for more."

The big man nods. "Till we meet again, Major Lazarov. Remember my order." He turns to Hartman and the

Lieutenants without saluting or offering his hand to Lazarov. "Let's shove off, warriors."

Lazarov watches him and his men leaving the base in a Humvee amidst a cloud of dust. It seems to him as if the Khan had taken his good mood with him to far away, to a mud house overlooking the Tribe's hidden valley. He knew that one day he would have to conclude his mission, but now that it is only a matter of days or perhaps hours, he wishes there was more time left. As he turns back, slightly downcast, he realizes that the two soldiers are still standing there at attention.

"As you were," he says, wondering if his own face had looked as awestruck as those of his soldiers when he met the Khan for the first time. "Come, we could all use a shot of vodka now."

But as they walk towards the bar and pass by the watchtower, Lazarov hears someone calling down from above.

"Hey Condor! Come up here and enjoy the view!"

He looks up and recognizes Crow, standing atop the lookout.

"Crow? I thought I'd never hear from you again!"

"Why? Did a grenade blow your eardrum like Grouch's?"

"I need to talk to this man. We'll meet in the Antonov," he tells his soldiers, leaving them to walk away while he clambers up to Crow's position.

"You were the last one I expected to run into here. But where's your exoskeleton?" Lazarov asks after climbing up the ladder, looking up and down the battered Stalker suit Crow is wearing.

"In my stash, safely hidden far away. I didn't feel like answering to some nasty people's nasty questions about where I got it from."

"I see. How did you end up back here?"

"Kind of a long story... Bone accused me of killing one of his bodyguards, but offered me amnesty when he called in all

Stalkers to protect the base. Hell of a joke, eh? The man was so scared I could smell the shit in his pants even through all the armor... so I got together some of my buddies and we had lots of hot fun around here. Especially me when your machine gunner recognized me. At first, he was very keen to kill me but... but hey, what are you carrying there?" Crow points at the heavy sniper rifle on Lazarov's shoulder. "*Bozhe moi!* That's a Gepard, and a Mark-6 above all! I have been looking for one of those for ages. Where did you get it?"

"First things first, brother. Who the hell are you, really?"

Lazarov can only see Crow's eyes in his balaclava, and now they narrow in a squint.

"Listen to me, Condor. All you need to know is that I am on your side. Let's not make life more complicated than it already is."

Lazarov looks into Crow's cold eyes, admitting to himself that the sniper has a point— he'd saved his life twice already. What difference would a name make?

"All right. But what was that mess with Bone's guard?"

"He came to kill you. You've become a nuisance for Bone."

"I could have guessed..." Lazarov sighs. "I'd had a feeling that he'd do anything to get rid of me, one way or another. That bastard son of a bitch...Maybe I better go and just finish him!"

"I wouldn't do that, brother. First, you and your two remaining men are no match for his guards. Second, without him, this place would fall into chaos and it would be only a matter of time until the Stalkers started killing each other over relics. He might be a bastard, but he keeps order here, one has to give him that."

"There's another thing, Crow. A few days ago I found one of our choppers. All the soldiers inside were dead. Executed. And I can't think of anyone else doing that except for Bone and his guards. They probably did it to get to the equipment."

Crow scowls. "I told you that Bagram is a messy place... But we're Stalkers, not assassins. And even if we were

354

assassins, we have no proof that it was him. Let's see what happens... probably now that the Tribe has taken you under its wing, he will be less eager to fuck with you."

"Yes, the Tribe. They trust me now, but this trust was earned in blood... especially Squirrel's blood."

"That's the local currency here," Crow shrugs. "So, what about that rifle?"

"It was a wedding gift. Kind of, so to say."

Crow laughs. "I didn't take you for such a funny one. Anyway, would you be interested in trading it for a relic? Come on, you are not really the sniper type, but I could make good use of it."

"I don't know... why do you want it so much?"

"That's the best anti-material rifle in the world – at least of those I have tried. With that, I could take down an elephant wearing an exoskeleton. Or a chopper. Even a chopper carrying elephants in exoskeletons."

"Even so... Did you outgrow your Dragunov?"

"This would be for different purposes... a waste on mutants and dushmans, but those are Dragunov-prey anyway."

"You told me we were quits after you took that exo. If I agree now, you'll owe me another favor."

"Sounds like a deal. And to sweeten it up, I'll throw in a Jumpy. With that relic equipped you'll be able to walk through any acid anomaly as if it was sweet green grass... just keep it away from fires and impacts. It's explosive."

"I am not really convinced... a bullet could hit and trig it. I tend to get shot at from time to time, you know?"

"Don't break my heart, *bratan*. I've been carrying a pack of 12.7 millimeter rounds for ages, hoping to find a rifle that fits them."

"All right, I'd hate to make you cry. I probably won't be needing sniper gear in the catacombs anyway."

"Thanks! I really do owe you one more!"

Lazarov can't suppress a smile when seeing the almost childish happiness in the sniper's eyes. Crow cradles the heavy rifle in the same fashion a little girl would with her doll.

"So my gut feeling was right," he says, adoring his new weapon. "You still want to finish your mission?"

"Yes," Lazarov replies as he carefully puts the relic into one of his containers, "and I could use a fighter like you to command the Stalkers outside, while I deal with whatever lies beneath."

"Thanks, but no thanks. Don't worry, I'll be there with my buddies... just don't ask me to join a bunch of trigger-happy Stalkers. That's just not my style."

"I got it... but don't let us down. I'm a little tired of you always popping up when I least expect you, and missing you when I need you most."

"Sorry, but predictability is a sniper's worst enemy. Have a good one 'til we meet again!" Crow aims the rifle towards the mountains. "Damn... why are there never any mutants around when I need them for target practice?"

The Antonov bar, 18:17:46 AFT

"Hey bro! It's mighty good to see you again," Sammy shouts when he sees Lazarov entering the airplane. "Come in, don't stand there!"

The barkeeper wears a brown Pashtu cap and listens to the tunes of his music player, humming a slightly altered version of a reggae song that even Lazarov recognizes.

"Said I remember when we used to sit
In the good old Antonov bar
Oba, ob-serving the Guardian freaks
As they would mingle with the good people we meet
Good friends we have had, oh good friends we've lost along the way

In this bright New Zone you can't forget the Old
So dry your tears I say –
No dushman, no cry

Said, said, said I remember when we used to sit
In dusty Bagram
And then dushmans would open fire all right
Tracers flashin' through the night
Then we would cook jackal dick porridge
Of which I'll share with you –
No dushman no cry."

"Don't cry, dushmans? Are you kidding?" Zlenko asks, who has already made himself comfortable in one of the airplane seats together with Ilchenko. "Even Bob Marley would shoot you for that!"

"Nah, I mean that in a different way. If there's no dushman, there's no reason to cry!"

"Very funny. What happened here?" Lazarov asks looking up to the hull, where an explosion had burrowed a huge hole into the rusty metal. Someone has placed a fuel drum under the opening and a few Stalkers are warming themselves around the fire inside it.

"A mortar round," explains Ilchenko. "Blasted a hole big enough into it for us to see all the stars of the southern Zone!"

"As you say, bro, right as you say! The good old Antonov is no longer five but... eh, I forgot how many stars!" Sammy says.

"Too bad the fire makes so much smoke that one can't see any stars," Zlenko says as he opens a can and dips a slice of dry bread into the meat inside. "But at least it's cozier here."

"Did you go dushman, Sammy?" Lazarov asks, pointing at the barkeep's new headwear.

"It's cool, bro, ain't it? I found it after the battle. The previous owner's head was still inside but I had it disinfected, don't worry! And now, tell me... when I saw them tribals coming I didn't believe me own eyes! How did you manage that?"

"Ilchenko will tell you, and many things too that are not even remotely true. But for now, I could use a drink."

"For you, I always have one. Actually, I can't wait to get rich from selling all me vodka reserve to them thirsty tribals."

"Forget your high hopes. They don't drink."

"Can't comply, bro. Me hopes are always high."

"Neither do they use drugs."

"I knew they weren't human! All the better, I'm low on vodka anyway."

"How come?"

"I've been serving nothing but Molotov cocktails the past few days, if you follow me meaning. Our visitors couldn't get enough of them!"

"At least business seems to be back to normal. But what is that guy doing over here?" Lazarov jerks his thumb towards a Stalker drawing on the metal plates of the fuselage.

"Oh, I decided that this was a good time to make the Antonov even nicer, and asked Zenmaster to paint the walls."

"I see, but what is he painting?"

"Portraits," the Stalker called Zenmaster shouts back, obviously possessed of very sharp hearing. "That of the first Stalkers: Arkady, Boris and Andrei. They were awesome, dude!"

"Never heard about them," Lazarov shrugs.

"It's your loss, dude... your loss. It all started with them going for a roadside picnic into the Zone..."

"A picnic? In the Zone?"

"Yep. If you don't know their story you don't know what you're missing, man!"

A Stalker interrupts their conversation. "Hey Sammy, turn off that Jamaican shit. Could I borrow your guitar?"

"Sure, Vitka. Here you go. Watch gonna play?"

"Something that suits the mood better," the Stalker replies. Sitting close to the fire, he starts to strum a melancholic melody.

"It seems sometimes that soldiers
who didn't return from the bloody fields of war,
weren't buried under the ground,
But turned into white cranes.
That always happened since the dawn of time,
They always fly and call us,
Maybe that's why we so often sadly
and silently, look up into the sky.

They fly and fly up in the sky,
They fly from dawn until night falls,
Keeping an empty place in their high line,
And I think that will be mine.
My day to fly will come for me,
To join these cranes in the same blue sky,
I'll be one of them, and calling
the names of loved ones I have left behind."

A Stalker bows his head. "Good one."

"You better sing about those black ravens circling in the sky," another one adds. His head is wrapped in a bloody bandage. "They will feed on the bodies of many good Stalkers tonight."

"I came here for relics," the Stalker with the guitar says, "but it turned into a really bad raid."

"Hey Sammy," another one shouts, "give us another *pollitra*... to Kolya Pimp, brothers. He was a good Stalker. Let's drink to him once more!"

"How many Stalkers died?" Lazarov asks Zlenko.

"I don't know exactly, but what the guy with the bandage said is true... too many."

"You're cool with the guitar, Sarge," Ilchenko says. "Maybe you should try to cheer them up?"

"Good idea," Lazarov agrees.

Zlenko pats the Stalker on the shoulder and takes the guitar. "Give that to me… and let's put mourning behind us."

"Hello Mama, here I'm writing you again,
Hello, Mama, all is well just like before
The sun is shining, everything is fine
But there's still fog in the hills.

Mother doesn't know how hard it is for us
Mother doesn't know how we walk in the mountains
How our youth is passing here
In Afghanistan, where there's war."

Lazarov is familiar with the old song. He'd heard it sung before about Dagestan, the Caucasus and other blood-soaked places. Now Zlenko is eloquently adapting the lyrics to Afghanistan. His swift play and strong voice, filled with the zest of a young man who just survived a horrible fight, give it intoxicating energy.

"You kick ass, dude," Zenmaster says, clasping. "Back in Canada I used to have my own band. Did you ever think of playing in a band?"

"Here! I switch on the loudspeakers! The radio too!" Sammy says. "All Stalkers must hear this!"

The Stalkers in the bar follow the rhythm with their heads nodding, and by the time he gets to sing the refrain, more and more join in the chorus:

"Among exploding grenades our unit walks
There is shooting in the mountains far
Among grenades exploding and tracers flying by
We march forward, with the trembling earth beneath,
The helicopter's taking off and we go forward

And some of us will not make it back.

We were so young on the day when we arrived
To Afghanistan, where there's war
I'll not forget those warm days in May
And the face of friends who died..."

Slightly under the influence of vodka and carried away by the song, Lazarov imagines Placebo tending to the wounded and looking up, wiping blood and sweat from his face; the Stalkers in the compound fixing the blasted URAL truck while Captain Bone's bodyguards halt their steps around his command post; the men in the Outpost's bunker gathering around their radio; Grouch listening in while fixing a hopelessly jammed machine gun; the Stalkers on the container ramparts watching the herds of jackals feeding on the corpses outside; and even Crow, the hard-boiled sniper, smiling as he cleans his new Gepard rifle, looking down at the Tribe's desert Marines who don't understand the words and just shake their heads while removing dismembered Talib's hands and fragmented skulls from the chassis of their gruesome trucks.

Zlenko's voice flies over Bagram like the sound of victory, relieved and joyful but without trying to hide the grief. As soon as he finishes the song, the responses start pouring in through Sammy's radio.

"This is the Outpost. Play it again or we join the dushmans."

"Guards here. Stop that. We can't concentrate on the gate if you play such songs."

"Switch that shit off. It made me fix a PKM barrel to a Kalashnikov... wait a minute, it works perfectly! Play it again, Sammy!"

"This is Placebo. The wounded want to hear that again. It's good for their recovery."

And finally, Bone's voice comes. *"Major... once this fucking Woodstock is over, come and see me."*

361

Lazarov is under the assumption that it was either their training or superior equipment that kept most of Captain Bone's guards alive, because they are in far better shape than the Stalkers. The Captain himself, who is wearing his usual full armored suit and helmet, is unscathed, making Lazarov wonder if he and his men took part in the battle at all.

"While you were promenading around, we found some intel on one of the attackers," Bone says. "We know where the rest of the mercs are hiding. They're in the ruins of the City of Screams."

"We expected that."

"Well, now it's confirmed. Why, would you have preferred to have tracked them down in dushman country? No? I thought not. Anyway, our goals are the same now. We're going to smoke that place out. But first I'll take my guards and see to it that the Outpost is reinforced. Those zombified freaks might strike again."

"I presume they won't be back anytime soon, knowing that they are also messing with the Tribe now."

"You can afford to presume things, but I have the responsibility to keep this place safe. Take a few capable Stalkers and move to the west. I will meet you there in two days at the City of Screams."

"You will not return to Bagram first?"

"Why, for fuck's sake, would I do that? To drink that junkie's watered-down vodka in the Antonov? We have no time for that now."

"You better make it there in time. We will need the firepower of your guards."

"We will be there, don't worry about that. Do you think those savages could give us a helping hand?"

"First, Captain Bone, they are anything but savages. Second, they won't help us, but at least they will let us pass us through."

"All the better. Maybe now we can show them that Stalkers can also fight."

Lazarov finds Bone's words strange. He can't shake off a feeling that the foul-mouthed commander is actually relieved about the Tribe staying out of the operation, even if their help would shift the odds tremendously in their favor. He wishes he could look into Bone's eyes.

"We're set," he finally confirms.

"Then why are you still standing here? Move!"

Ramparts, 22:45:14 AFT

This mission makes quit smoking real hard, Lazarov thinks as he enjoys a drag on a cigarette he was offered by a Stalker.

Observing the base from the container wall, he sits down to enjoy a brief moment of satisfaction. The road to their destination is clear and the Stalker base safe, at least for the time being.

Warm light falls through the round windows and many cracks on the Antonov's hull where Stalkers are still celebrating. Others have gathered around the dozen or so campfires inside the compound. Moonlight paints the battlefield outside in shades of grey and blue, with the odd jackal howling — probably to invite the rest of its pack to feast on the corpses that appear like dark rocks in the night.

Lazarov has almost finished his smoke when he hears a soft voice calling him.

"Glad to see you again, Major."

"Call me Mikhail, Mac."

She sits beside him and offers Lazarov a bottle. Expecting vodka, he coughs when it turns out to be gin.

"Sad to hear about Beefeater," he says handing the bottle back.

"Today you, tomorrow me," Mac observes and draws on the bottle. "Ilch has taken over the bar, talking all kinds of bullshit."

"Another racist rant?"

"He's bragging to everyone about you owning all the Tribe's women, but they'll have an even better time once he gets to their stronghold."

"He'll need serious amounts of ammunition if he wants to get even remotely close to them."

"Is it true about Squirrel?"

Lazarov nods, sadly.

"Poor sod," she says.

For a minute none of them speaks. Then Lazarov gives a sigh. "It's partly true what Ilch says. I met a woman there. She reminded me of what you said at Hellgate, because she is... how to say... she is... somehow... eh, never mind. Give me that bottle."

"Oh you." Lazarov doesn't need to see her face in the darkness to know she is smiling sarcastically. "Men can be really pathetic when it comes to words."

"Maybe we all are when it comes to what the Zones are about," Lazarov replies.

The flames of the nearest campfire rise higher as the men around it feed it with more wood. In the light cast over Mac's face Lazarov sees her sarcastic smile vanish and change into an expression of *I told you so*.

Road to the Tribe stronghold—Red Idol Gorge, 9 October 2014, 14:37:51 AFT

"I liked that song, Viktor," Lazarov shouts, trying to make himself heard on the back of the truck taking them westwards, "and it was probably a good idea to omit the last part."

"About being demobilized and going home?" the sergeant shouts back.

"Exactly."

"Do Stalkers ever get demobilized?"

"That's my point!"

"What?"

He shakes his head and waves to Zlenko, meaning: *we'll talk later.* The truck is roaring along the bumpy road and the dust dredged up by the other truck in front of them covers them from toes to teeth. Not the best time to talk.

Passing by the intersection leading to the abandoned village, Lazarov wishes he could tell Zlenko more about the unit of framed US Marines who had turned into a tribe of proud and free men against all odds, but it will have to wait. For now, he can only watch the scenery pass by, but the sight of the wrecked Soviet tanks and trucks that still litter the roadside makes him sad.

Does this land never have enough of death? The sand absorbs blood like a dry sponge absorbs water.

The more he thinks about the Khan's philosophy of strength, the more he finds himself able to understand him.

Maybe, of all the conquerors that have passed along the very same road that we now drive upon, he was the first who truly understood this land. But where is all this evil coming from? Is the only way to be victorious over evil to become evil ourselves, no matter how respectable evil can be?

A quote comes to his mind: *For what can war, but endless war still breed?* though no matter how hard Lazarov tries to remember, the name of the writer who wrote it escapes him. Even so, the quote seems to fit perfectly with this barren and inhospitable land, where the rules of life had been those of war since time beyond memory, and where the appearance of the New Zone undermined even the laws of nature in an evil and deadly way.

For Lazarov, Nooria's home was now the only place where he found true shelter for his life and comfort for his soul.

Thinking about her, he realizes how fond he had grown of the girl: his feelings, which had been initially a mixture of gratitude, desire and maybe even a little pity, had turned into a deep affection that he, who had always been rough and skeptical towards his own feelings, did not dare to define yet.

The truck slows down, awakening him from his daydreams. They are approaching the entrance of a narrow canyon. Tribe warriors appear from out of nowhere. A Lieutenant raises his hand, signaling them to stop.

"We have the Khan's permission to pass through," Lazarov shouts.

"So we heard," the warrior replies. "Speed up! A supercell is rising to the south. We expected a storm hit before nightfall."

Lazarov returns his salute as they drive on. "We're entering Tribe territory now," he shouts to Zlenko. "We'll stop before we arrive at their stronghold. I need to tell the Stalkers a few things, lest they get themselves in trouble."

"It's weird," Zlenko shouts back. "The tribals saved our skin all right, but I have an uneasy feeling about spending the night in their lair!"

The Alamo, 16:53:06 AFT

The horizon has already sunk into a moody, purple haze when Lazarov walks up the path to the Bhegum's house. On their way here, he had hoped to see Nooria waiting for him, looking down to the road leading into the hidden valley. He'd imagined her scarf blowing in the wind as her fragile shape appeared among the rocks and mud walls, but she was nowhere to be seen. Thoughts of jealousy interfered with his growing anxiety. No matter how tantalizingly close he was to Nooria, first he had to give a crash-course to the Stalkers on the customs of the Tribe.

Forget about vodka and grass. Do not stare at their women. And never ever try to impress them by saying things like 'Semper Fi' or calling yourself a 'warrior' – in their eyes, you are not worthy of that.

He had actually been relieved when the Stalkers had been excluded from the inside of the stronghold, being put up in a huge cavern that served as a shelter for the Tribe's vehicles instead. It offered shelter from the impending storm for the Stalkers, whilst simultaneously providing an easy way for the Tribe to keep a wary eye on their guests. The cavern also gave Lazarov a clue as to where and how the Marines and their Hazara followers could survive the nuclear blasts back in 2011.

He'd had to tell Zlenko the whole story too, though the sergeant, being a young man in his prime, had been more interested in Nooria's looks than in his officer's adventures, and Lazarov's possessive heart secretly rejoiced when the warriors hadn't let Zlenko enter the stronghold either, despite Lazarov's half-hearted attempts to convince them otherwise.

Here and there, warriors are still sitting around their hookah pipes, but they seem more relaxed than usual. Passing by a bonfire, the major overhears a conversation.

"...so I come home after the hunt, and... the big man knows my soul, I would never break the Code, but I was dying for something better than water and *chai*. And then my woman says, *'try this'*. And man, I tell you, it was... awesome."

"Yeah, me too. I wish the witch could have discovered that recipe a little earlier."

"I don't care what she'd put into it. Maybe it was powdered rag-head dick, I don't give a damn."

"You disgusting pig. I'm drinking it right now!"

"You don't get my point. No matter how she prepared this stuff, it makes life so much better."

All jealous thoughts vanish as he opens the door and sees Nooria sitting on the ground with pestle and mortar between her legs, grinding herbs. The hearth is lit, its fire casting a spell of coziness over the room. A thousand words come to his mind but his lips can only utter two.

"I'm back."

She looks up with an impish smile that hides joy in the corner of her eyes. "That's good."

"Where's the Bhegum?"

"She is with Colonel. Sometimes they talk. She will not be back soon." Nooria fixes her eyes on him, still smiling. The pestle crushing the herbs in the mortar moves faster.

"Maybe we also talk?" Lazarov asks. He puts his heavy gear down on the table.

Whoever designed this damned exoskeleton didn't have a way of quickly getting out of it in mind.

"No. Why?" The pestle moves even faster and deeper into the mortar. She licks her lips.

"Well… where I came from, I mean, normally, when a man comes home to his woman…"

"But now you are not where you come from," Nooria whispers and licks the pestle, as if tasting the balm she is preparing. "You are where you arrive to."

Lazarov sits down in front of her, watching her hands moving the pestle in the mortar, slowing down to gentle movements, then speeding up and crushing the herbs inside with a heady rhythm. The scent rising from the mortar between her legs cleans his mind, shifting the concerns from his soul, making way for the basic instincts erupting from his heart.

He grasps her hands and, putting the mortar aside, takes its place between her legs, eventually entering the safest refuge a man could find from the clasps of thunder and the raging storm outside.

10 October 2014, 03:14:39 AFT

"We need to talk."

Nooria's whisper awakes him from his half-sleep. One single candle is flickering in the darkness. The storm is still roaring outside.

"Not now," he moans.

Nooria stands up and, covering her naked, sweaty body with her scarf, takes a little box from a shelf where all kinds of old and enigmatic things lie.

"Wake up and listen. I have something to tell you."

Her words remind Lazarov of what the Khan told him. Suddenly he is fully awake. Looking at Nooria's face in the candlelight, the emotion he least expected grasps his heart: fear. She sits there, looking into the candle, with a face that seems to battle the most terrible demons in the darkness beyond the dim light. Her face appears ageless and, with the shadows hiding her scar, inhumanly beautiful.

"All was lost after they destroyed Samal and all was unleashed after he fell. It took over Colonel's soul but he crushed darkness with its own weapons. But he was not victorious. He is now part of darkness. As we are all who live under his protection. Power of darkness shed its light on him. His strength reflected it like ancient stone shining on Samal's head, but he was not Samal. Darkness stained him. You will go into darkness to find its power. But Samal is no longer there to protect you. And you have not strength of our leader."

What the hell are you talking about, Lazarov wants to ask, but a look into Nooria's eyes stops his tongue. She looks into the candle with her eyes wide open, but he can only see their whites. Nooria seems to be lost in a space where he could never follow her.

"I hold a bridge between old time when Samal was our sentinel and today. What I hold is here." She closes her eyes. When she opens them, he can see her pupils again. Nooria looks down at a small, red stone in her right hand. "Sit up."

Obeying her words, Lazarov raises from the mat. A knife flashes in Nooria's left hand, cutting deep into the flesh above his heart. The cut fills him with burning pain as she pushes the stone deep into the wound and holds her palm over it. The pain eases a little but blood is still pouring from the wound, flowing through her fingers and down her arm.

"Why did you hurt me?" he groans.

"I would never hurt you."

Even through his pain, he can only think about her lightning-quick cut as he realizes that this fragile woman, who now takes her hand off his chest and licks the blood from her fingers, must be as good at killing as she is at healing.

"Now you are bearing last stone that once adorned Samal's crown. And I bear your blood and your life inside me. That is what I took in exchange for protecting you."

"For protecting me?"

"One part protects you. Two parts bond the darkness."

Lazarov opens his mouth to say something but Nooria puts her finger on his lips.

"Do you want to see me again and live with me?"

"I do, Nooria."

"Forever?"

"Is there such a thing?"

Nooria caresses his head. It is domination, not tenderness – but powerless domination, because while her hands are soothing his pain, her eyes seem to be begging with him.

"Remember your own words when you find shadow of darkness. You will shed blood and last drop will be yours. If you want me to live, you will have to make a sacrifice."

"I am still in pain and not understanding anything."

"You will. Lie down."

Nooria kneels over him, her left hand on Lazarov's wound, the right on his forehead. He feels the pain finally fading away from his chest, just like the fear from his mind. Closing his eyes, he hears Nooria whispering words that melt into a long incantation. His heart is beating under her warm hand, as if it were pumping his blood into her veins.

"It is done. Samal will be with you from now on," she says. "You will carry him to his last battle. Now I must cause you pain. Just a little."

Lazarov struggles for breath when he feels the sharp sting of the needle, but Nooria's soothing touch seems to suck all pain out of his body. Her swift fingers quickly finish sewing up his wound. She bites off the yarn protruding from the wound.

"Your mind can rest now," she whispers, letting herself glide down to his groin. "But I will keep your body awake. I must quench thirst of my flesh now, because it will parch until you return."

"Will there be such a day?"

"I know what past has brought, but not what future will bring." Nooria caresses his face. Lazarov feels his eyes closing. The words she whispers into his ear sound like an ancient melody.

"When your star is unseen, and all is dark, your despair itself becomes a star... Sleep now, my strong warrior. Sleep..."

Encrypted voice transmission between the New Zone and Moscow, 10 September 2014, 08:41:07 AFT

#Kilo One, this is Diver calling. Do you copy?#
#Kilo One to Diver. Copy you loud and clear.#
#Eagle Eye authorized me to tell you to confirm – your suspicion was correct. The squad has been located. All KIA.#
#Affirmative. Carry on.#
#It was a friendly element that discovered them. If he is who I suspect he is, so far your plan is working. #
That's classified, Diver. Proceed with your mission and provide us the proof.#
#I think there will be an opportunity for that… Is this man of yours doing all this to escape a court-martial or something?#
#Kilo One to Diver. Transmission wasn't clear, repeat. #
#I asked you because he will surely make our objective show his hand, but no man deserves to be punished like that. I guess not even you know what is waiting for him. You must hate him if you send him there. #
#[static noise]#
#Kilo One to Diver. That's classified.#
Diver to Kilo One. Eagle Eye is bad enough but you are even worse. All right, team is relocating. Will contact you and Eagle Eye when proof is obtained.#
#Kilo One. Roger on the voice transfer.#
God damn you Kilo One, he was a fine man. Over and out.#
#[static noise]#

Red Idol Gorge — eastern approach to the City of Screams, 10 October 2014, 06:20:41 AFT

"I had hoped to find more here than a pile of rubble."

Lazarov hands the binoculars to Zlenko, who is lying on his belly next to him as they take cover from behind a bush on a hill overlooking the wide valley below. The ancient site rises up on a barren hill, surrounded by dense forest and a spider's web of roads leading to it that are littered with all kinds of wrecked Soviet tanks, civilian cars and trucks. Far beyond the forest, where the valley meets the steep wall of the hills, the rocks are riddled with caves, all dwarfed by a huge, high cavern. The night still keeps its hold over the western horizon, but to their left, in the east, the first touches of light are already feeling their way through the darkness, painting the hills a soft pink. Soon, the valley will be filled with shades of red and orange, casting a deceitful beauty over the ruin that crawls with enemy fighters.

"How I wish that our gunship could be here now… it turns out it would have been a good plan after all," the sergeant replies. The electric zoom of the binoculars whizz as Zlenko adjusts the distance. "Only the logistics went wrong, right from the beginning."

Oh boy, you have no idea how bad everything went, Lazarov thinks, but says, "A frontal attack is out of question. Do you have any ideas how to deal with this mess, Viktor?"

"It's all screwed up, *komandir…* I can't even see an entrance to the underground where we could concentrate our attack."

"Probably on the southern side… you see that road to the south-west? The map on my palmtop shows a track branching off and up to the hill, towards the ruins. The entrance must be somewhere there. Can't see it clearly on this low-resolution image, though... I wish we could properly recon the place before moving in."

"If the entrance is to the south, it means we'd have landed at the wrong end of our target anyway."

"As far as the infiltration team is concerned, you're right... so, Viktor, if there's a well-defended enemy position between you and your objective, and you have no artillery or air support, how would you proceed?"

"The plain around the hill is covered with a dense forest and probably full of mines and anomalies... but there are trails leaving the main road right beneath our position. If there's any logic left in this place, they'll skirt the hill and join the other road coming from the south-west. A small unit should be able to get through there without stirring up too much trouble. That is, if the defenders have something else to do than watch their back: like bracing for an attack from the north or something."

"What do you think? Could it work?"

Zlenko studies the area carefully. "Good luck is all we need."

"Let's move back to the Stalkers."

Positioned behind the hill from where they reconnoitered the site, a bunch of tough-looking Stalkers wait for Lazarov's orders. He had gathered far fewer Stalkers than he had hoped for, but at least the men now huddling around him are the elite of their sort: veterans, well armed and disciplined. He feels reassured when looking at their faces, a few of them are already familiar: Skinner and Mac are among them.

But where in the hell are Bone and his Guardians? And where is Crow?

"Listen up," he tells them in a low voice, "we can no longer wait for the Guardians. We'll lose the advantage of the low sun in half an hour. If we approach them now from the east, they will have the sun in their eyes. We have to move in and have to move in quickly. We expect to find an entrance to the caverns to the south. The distance is about two kilometers. I'll move in with a small infiltration team. The rest of you will unleash hell to divert attention from us moving in. Borys, come over here… check the intercom. You, Stalker with that PKM, give me that flare gun. You don't want to shoot dushmans with that, do you? All right… you are Stalkers, so you will stalk down to that stream between our position and the ruins. You will assume firing positions there but hold your fire. Once we get close enough to the entrance, I'll fire a flare and you start the party. Meanwhile, we move in. Remember: all you'll you have to do is to keep the enemy occupied and attract as much attention as possible to your diversionary attack. Should they move up, there's a large free space between the stream and the forest. They will be sitting ducks there. Use the terrain to your advantage."

"And once you're out?" the Shrink asks.

"Don't worry about that."

Zlenko looks at Lazarov in a concerned manner. "*Komandir*… I'm with the Stalker on this. What about exfiltration?"

Sorry, son, Lazarov thinks. *All we have to plan for is reaching the lower levels. Getting out would be like planning for a miracle to happen.*

But he also knows that his two faithful soldiers, and any Stalkers brave enough to join them, deserve some sort of proper explanation.

"Once we're inside, we have to locate whatever's left of Needle… the expedition. Expect heavy resistance. Let's hope we kill enough of them on our way in to make our way out a little easier. Shrink will be in command of the Stalkers waiting for us outside. Once we're out, we haul ass back to Bagram. Any questions?"

"What if there's no entrance on the southern side after all?" Zlenko asks.

"There must be one."

"Why?"

"Because that's our only chance."

The Stalkers remain silent. Lazarov quickly orders them to take positions which fits their equipment best: machine guns to the flanks, riflemen to the center, the few Stalkers with Dragunovs and scoped assault rifles to the rear.

"Paratroopers, weapon check. Ilchenko, I hope you got acquainted with that M27."

"Took her virginity last night. Tends to bear a little to the right and above, but should be all right, sir. I have eight magazines, and I'm locked and loaded."

"Zlenko?"

"Ready for close quarters," the sergeant replies, pumping the first round into the breech of his Benelli shotgun.

"Check coms and night vision."

While the soldiers do as ordered, Lazarov picks two Stalkers. His first choice is Skinner, now armed with a Remington shotgun, who proved himself a capable fighter at the Outpost. Then he picks a Stalker wearing an old exoskeleton and a heavy shotgun with a drum magazine.

"Hey, you with the Striker shotgun! You come with us too. What have you got loaded?"

"Slugs. Still have plenty."

"What's your name?"

"Zef."

"Where do you come from with such a name?"

"South Africa."

The Stalker's exoskeleton is patched and has repair marks all over, bearing witness to many gunfights and mutants' claws. He opens the helmet of his armor and bows his head to Lazarov with respect.

"What the hell?" Ilchenko gasps. "We have a fucking negro here!"

"Shut up," Lazarov says angrily, almost at the same time as Zlenko and Skinner.

"And you, Skinner?"

"Nagorny Karabagh."

"You're Sammy's countryman, then?"

376

"No way. He's from Yerevan," Skinner replies in a disdainful tone. "People there take a cucumber, paint it yellow and sell it as a banana. But we from Karabagh—we are fighters!"

Lazarov shrugs. "Are your men set to go or do they also discuss home-made differences?" he asks Shrink.

The old Stalker responds with a grim smile. "My patients are cool. They've just been promoted to research assistants! If the enemy comes, we'll have a closer look at what's going on in their heads…"

"Hey, tough guy!" Mac sounds almost insulted. "I want to go with you too!"

For a moment Lazarov feels temptation to take her with them. Something inside tells him that this strange young woman will still play an important role in future events, be they five minutes or five years out, and he wishes to keep her safe until her time comes; maybe it is the very male attitude to keep a female out of harm's way, or perhaps the feelings stirred by the sight of female youth in a man's heart that has aged too fast. Eventually, in a very Stalker-like way, it is the sight of her weapon that gives Lazarov an excuse to leave her out of the journey ahead.

"You're the only one with a grenade launcher, Mac. You stay with Shrink."

"But I—"

Lazarov gives her the could shoulder. "We're set fair then, Shrink. Keep your position and give them hell when the time comes. Infiltration squad! All ready?"

"Ready," the soldiers and Stalkers reply.

"Follow me!"

12 October 2014, 08:23:58 AFT

Using the low walls along the dirt road to their advantage, they sneak into the forest. Lazarov wishes he could properly ·

scout the area but gambles everything on the one chance they have: surprise. They cautiously walk down the path weaving through the forest. It is still dark under the dense foliage, with the ubiquitous tank wrecks giving them the chance to gather in cover when the distance between their ranks becomes too large.

Zlenko suddenly stops, raising his fist. "I see hostiles at twelve o'clock."

Lazarov moves to his pointman and looks in the direction shown. Ahead of them, a half dozen hostiles sit around a campfire, one of them assigned to keep lookout on top of a wreck that once was a civilian all-terrain vehicle.

"The bad guys also seem to have made a brotherhood," Zlenko whispers. Four enemies wear the tight body armor of the Chinese commandos, the rest are Taliban, their gas masks comfortably hanging from their shoulders with their long black headscarves.

Lazarov pulls the safety off on his M4 and switches to single shot mode. On the narrow road between the mud walls, there's no way of finding a good firing position or flanking the enemy.

"Sergeant, you and Ilchenko take the guys to the left. Skinner, you and Zef go for the others to the right. I'll drop a grenade. When it goes up, hit them hard and don't miss. If one of them gets to use their radio, we're in trouble! Clear?"

His men nod. Lazarov takes a grenade from his webbing and removes the safety pin. He lets the fuse burn for two seconds and tosses the grenade into the group of the unsuspecting enemy. When the grenade explodes, his companions jump from their cover and spray the enemies with a hail of bullets and shotgun shells. In just a few seconds the one-sided firefight is over.

"So far, so good," Lazarov affirms, pleased at seeing the fallen hostiles. "Let's hope we didn't make too much noise. Ilchenko, now you take point. Move on, men."

They have covered almost half the way when Shrink's agitated voice crackles in Lazarov's intercom. *"Major! Can you hear me?"*

"What's up, Shrink?"

"They are mounting their trucks and are driving away to the south!"

"Do you see civilians among them? Any equipment?"

"It's hard to tell from this distance. All I can see is that since a few minutes ago the whole place is stirred up like an ant's nest. Wait... what the hell is that? Many are trying to get into the truck, but they're just driving away. Looks like they are fleeing!"

"You say they are abandoning the ruins?"

"Not exactly... they just want to... I see them climbing on the trucks as they leave, and the others already inside just kick them off the trucks... the freaks are panicking!"

"All the better. Wait for the flare." Lazarov turns to his comrades. "Something is going on up there. The Chinese are fleeing the place... and I don't like this."

"But it makes everything easier for us," Zlenko says.

"Depends on why they are spooked. Let's move, quickly!"

If there had been other sentry posts on the road they must have been abandoned in a hurry, because Lazarov's team does not encounter any other hostiles along their way. The path soon turns to the west. Now Lazarov can see it for himself: a dozen trucks making a hasty departure from the ruins, all loaded until their axles groan. Mercenaries are running after them in the dust whipped up by the heavy vehicles.

No one wants to be left behind... I wonder what's going on in that damned place.

They wait until the last truck has passed then, on Lazarov's signal, the small squad moves on and at last reaches the main road.

"Hostiles!" Ilchenko whispers. "One hundred fifty meters, one o'clock!"

Lazarov waves at his men to halt and hold their fire. He sees mercenaries coming in their direction. They don't seem to be prepared to fight and look as if they are thinking only of getting away from the ruins as quickly as possible.

The major fires the flare gun. The projectile climbs into the sky and in a few seconds bursts out into a fireball over the hill. Immediately, heavy gunfire breaks loose as the Stalkers get into action beyond the hill.

"Open fire! Open fire!"

He realizes that he has given Ilchenko a bad weapon, seeing as the machine gunner empties the first magazine within seconds. "We don't need a hail of bullets," he shouts. "Concentrate your fire, Ilchenko! Don't waste your damned ammo!"

Picking off the unprepared enemies, they move forward, covering the last two hundred meters to the dust road that leads up to the hill. He sees Skinner running forward.

"Don't scatter! Keep together," Lazarov shouts, but his warning comes too late. A heavy machine gun opens fire and the Stalker falls. Zef grabs his body and pulls it into the safety of a low stone wall. Dust and stone particles fly around them as the machine gunner keeps firing.

Before crouching down beside the wounded Stalker, Lazarov sees where the bullets are coming from: a massive bunker guards the road intersection, its crew either too slow or too stubborn to escape with the rest.

"Show me the wound, brother," Zef says, taking a first aid kit from his backpack. His voice is surprisingly calm despite the machine gun bullets darting above their heads. "You'll survive. I'll patch you up."

A look at the Stalker's wound assures Lazarov that Skinner can probably continue provided the wound on his hip is properly bandaged, and Zef's skillful first-aid looks reassuring enough to him. Then his thoughts return to more immediate dangers. He takes a stone and tosses it over the wall. Immediately, a long burst of machine gun fire rips into the stone wall.

"Shit," Ilchenko swears angrily. "They don't seem to be low on ammo yet!..."

"Anyone got a smoke grenade?"

"I do, *komandir*."

"Give it to me. Stay put. I'll try to cover our approach. Then we make a dash for it and finish that bunker with frags."

Lazarov knows it's a bad and desperate plan. Even if the smoke pops, there will still be about fifty meters between their position and the pillbox where they could be mown down. But with only four men, there's not much room for textbook-style suppressing and flanking maneuvers.

He crawls to the end of the wall and throws the grenade as fast as he can towards the pillbox. In a few seconds thick smoke covers the path. Dashing forward, he has covered only a few meters when the machine gun opens up again and hits him in the chest. The bullets don't penetrate his armor, but their impact is strong enough to knock him off his feet. He quickly crawls to a huge rock and takes cover behind it.

No way out of here. That bastard doesn't need to aim to hit me with that damned machine gun.

Suddenly he hears a rifle firing a dozen rounds in a slow sequence. Concrete splinters as heavy bullets blast the pillbox. The machine gun falls silent. Peeking out from his cover, Lazarov doesn't need to think twice before running up to the pillbox to toss a fragmentation grenade through the loophole.

The concrete shakes from the explosion inside and, his ears still ringing, he can barely hear the familiar voice in his intercom.

"You wasted your grenade, Condor. The bastards needed stronger walls to stop the bullets from my Gepard!"

Lazarov sighs with relief. *At last that elusive bastard is here.*

"We are not quits yet, Crow! I could have handled this on my own!"

"Like always, eh? No time to relax! Hostiles at your ten!"

By now his men have run up to the rock. Lazarov rises from behind the cover to aim his weapon, but Crow is quicker and the effects of his rifle leaves Lazarov amazed for a second. Where a mercenary had appeared in his reticule a moment ago, he now sees a human torso that has been torn apart by the impact of a heavy bullet. Ilchenko is already firing, not bothering to wait for orders, while Zlenko and the two Stalkers who wait for the enemy to get into range of their close-quarter shotguns.

Cautiously peering out from his cover, Lazarov looks over to the hill on the other side of the road, the only position where he would hide if he were a sniper, and frowns. For a second, it seems to him as if there are several fighters in black armor at the top of the hill. However, he has no time to think over what Crow would be doing with Bone's men — if his eyes didn't fail him, that was — and Bone's squad was supposed to back them up, not hide. Turning back to the road and sensing that the momentum has shifted, he orders his men to charge.

"Zlenko, Ilchenko, you're fire team one. Lay down suppressive fire. Skinner, Zef – fire team two. Run like hell up to that gate and take position there. Once you get there, Zlenko's fire team will move up. Clear? *Vperyod!*"

His plan seems to have paid off. With the gunfight on the other side of the hill and the still-unexplained retreat, there are not enough defenders to counter Lazarov's squad with effective fire and they soon reach a larger ruin, which offers high ground from where they could fall into the rear of the hostiles exchanging intense fire with the Stalkers below.

"Borys, can you hear me? Hey, Shrink!" Lazarov shouts into the radio.

"*Calm down, Major. Where are you?*"

"I am calm," he screams. "Reached high ground. I can see your position. Move forward!"

"*It was about time.*"

Rock by rock, Lazarov's squad purges the slope of the hill of enemies. Now the fight is all about close quarters; the time has come for Zlenko and the two Stalkers with shotguns. Lazarov switches to his Beretta and rushes forward to meet their enemies, who may be surprised and desperate but still act agile and sharp.

Zef, his head in the purple haze of pitched battle, leaps at a commando who is firing his pistol at him, throwing the adversary to the ground and finishing him off with his shotgun, only to be the perfect target for a rifle burst from another Chinese fighter leaning around the corner. Lazarov sees red stains broadening on the South African's sand-colored armor. *Reckless fool,* flashes through his mind as the Stalker steps back, re-charging his shotgun with disregard to his wound.

"Frag out!" Lazarov shouts, tossing a grenade around the wall where the shooter hides. The explosion covers the ruin with dust and sand. Skinner arrives from nowhere and blindly fires his shotgun into the dust cloud. Ilchenko's machine gun barks from somewhere above them.

"To the right! Hostiles to your three, Major!" Zlenko's scream is subdued by the sound of machine gun fire.

Shit, not another pillbox!

But it's a Stalker with a machine gun, followed by another one, firing his AK from his hip at an enemy that Lazarov is unable to see.

"Into the trenches! Let's clean the trenches!"

Zlenko and the machine gunner run through a dilapidated arch that may have been a palace gate once but now only hides more enemies. The sergeant tosses a grenade into a cavity among the rocks, the thunderous explosion throwing out dust and body parts as if the earth itself was spitting them out. Lazarov is about to follow them when an enemy appears before him. He pulls the trigger on his weapon but it doesn't fire. A knife flashes towards him through the dust. He skillfully evades the thrust, grabbing his weapon's barrel to use it as a club to defend himself, not having had time to change the magazine, but before he can strike the enemy who is about to jump at him again, knife ready to thrust into

Lazarov's neck, Skinner intervenes and fires two shots from his Remington.

"Close shave," he shouts, jumping over the body of the collapsed enemy fighter and rushing on towards the receding gunfire on the east side of the hill.

By the time Lazarov catches up with him, the noise of full-on battle has ceased, with only an occasional gunshot heard as the Stalkers' finish off the remaining enemies.

"Cease fire!" Lazarov shouts. His voice is hoarse and he can feel sand between his teeth. "Infil squad, on me! Everyone, cease your fire!"

One by one, dusty and exhausted, his fighters emerge. They all look unscathed except Zef, who has a big bloodstain on his side.

"You're wounded," Lazarov observes. "Next time don't try playing Rambo, okay?"

"Sorry, boss. But they got you too," the Stalker replies, pointing at Lazarov's arm. Looking down, he sees a cut on his left arm at the point where his exoskeleton's armor is weakest. Even now that he knows about his wound, he doesn't feel pain, just dumbness in his muscles.

I own Goryunov a crate of vodka for this suit.

Yet he feels weak and he has to sit down to relieve his trembling knees. An unknown feeling overwhelms him. The relief of having survived the pitched battle vanishes, making way for the desire that he could be far away from this place, where dozens of men have died fighting over a low hill covered with all but impressive ruins.

"Are you all right?"

"I'm fine, Viktor... I'm fine." He takes a deep breath, trying to forget the memory of deep green eyes. "Looks like we made it."

"Yep... even the negro did, although he got more than one bullet in his ugly hide."

The Stalkers look at Ilchenko.

"Actually, there were moments when I was thinking I should help the dushmans in finishing off this monkey."

"Shut the fuck up, soldier," Zlenko says. "What the hell is wrong with you?"

"Never mind, Sarge. We are all still running on adrenaline," Zef says opening his exoskeleton and applying a bandage over his wound. "Once I had a girlfriend..."

Lazarov cannot concentrate on the Stalker's anecdote. There is something in Ilchenko's manner that worries him, and it's not his offensiveness.

"Machine gunner," he says coldly. "Take Skinner with you and give the Stalkers a hand in mopping up the place. Move. Now!" As the former Guardian stands from the rock where he was resting, Lazarov stops him. "Keep an eye on Ilchenko. Something's wrong with him."

"Will do," Skinner replies, reloading his shotgun and following Ilchenko.

Lazarov turns back to the Stalker. "What about that girlfriend?"

"Nothing important, boss... she once told me, a woman can't take anything that men say after having sex seriously. I say, a man can't take what another man says after a battle like this seriously."

"I guess so."

"Are you all right, Major?" Zlenko sounds anxious. "You look... distracted."

"Do I?" Lazarov is not sure what to reply. "I told you, I'm fine. It's just... Suddenly I felt a desire to crush Ilchenko's head."

"There you are!" exclaims a cheerful voice. "We routed the bastards, didn't we, Major?"

Borys the Shrink climbs over a pile of mud bricks and sits down at Lazarov's side. As Shrink looks at him, an impending sense of dread moves over the Stalker's face, so quickly that Lazarov is not sure if what he saw was real or just a reflection of his own, adrenaline-soaked mind.

"Take some medicine," Shrink says, offering him a bottle of vodka with more seriousness in his voice than usual. The major gladly accepts. The bottle goes around among them. From around the ruins, they hear the conversations of the Stalkers, some of them crying out excitedly when they find some valuable loot on the fallen enemies' bodies.

"I could use some food." Zlenko opens a can of processed meat, but Lazarov shakes his head when the sergeant offers him a chunk of meat on the tip of his bayonet.

"I'm not hungry."

Zef shares a loaf of bread with the sergeant.

I should have accepted, Lazarov thinks. *What is this strange feeling in my stomach?*

To distract his attention from the weird feeling in his guts, he turns again to the South African Stalker.

"So brother, what's your story? You've come very far."

"My last stop was England, actually. Been to many places. Wherever there was money to earn."

"You have been a mercenary?"

"I tried to make a living from what I do best."

"What's that, giving first aid?"

"No. Using a shotgun." The black Stalker scowls. "Shot a man in Cape Town. They made me leave my home country."

"Nothing gives amnesty more openhandedly than the Zone."

"I did not need amnesty, boss. I was with a police SWAT team. One evening we moved into a township to round up a gang of robbers. I had to shoot one. He was one of my people."

Lazarov wants to reply, '*One can't meet anything here but fucked up lives*', but grasps his weapon instead as a short rifle burst comes from not so far away. Borys jumps up, keeping his rifle ready to shoot.

12 October 2014, 11:50:20 AFT

"What's going on there?"

Lazarov recognizes the sound of a Stalker's Kalashnikov, followed by the replying thumps of an automatic shotgun. "It's probably your men mopping up the place," he tells Borys.

"I better check that out, Major."

"And you better finish your lunch," Lazarov tells his men, "we still have some work to do... and I have a feeling that the shit was only up to our ankles until now. Once we get into the ruins, it'll be up to our waist."

"Are you sure we have to do this, boss?"

"Now's the time to opt out if you're going to, Zef. If you change your mind later, I'll shoot you."

"Okay, boss... chill out, man. I don't want to change my mind. I'll follow you."

"*Komandir*, we could rest a little more," Zlenko nervously suggests. "You're wound up like a spring."

"I'm fucking fine. How many times do I need to tell you, Sergeant Zlenko? Mind your own business."

Zlenko looks hurt and Lazarov is surprised at his own harshness. A headache has crept into his skull and his throat remains parched no matter how much water he drinks, but he has to put such things to the back of his mind when Shrink arrives, swearing and looking very concerned. His rifle's safety catch is off and he poises it ready to fire.

"Two damned Stalkers shot each other over a stash of worthless garbage. Never seen such a thing before. Not among my assistants!"

Time to resolve all this, comes to Lazarov's mind, without him knowing exactly what he has to resolve. Words, conversations, messages, everything he has learned since he arrived in the New Zone is swarming in his head, coalescing to construct a vague but dreadful conclusion.

"Shrink, take your men away from the ruins immediately. Form them into two groups and prepare ambush positions to the north-east and south of the hill. Just in case... can you manage that?"

"Sure. And I agree —" Borys cuts his words short.

"Spill the beans."

"I'm not easily scared but this place... there's something about it that gives me the creeps. The sooner we leave here, the better."

"What I am concerned about is why the mercs left in such a hurry. Zlenko, if you have finished your lunch, round up Ilchenko and that renegade."

"On my way, *komandir*."

Walking up to the hilltop the fate of his two squads weighs on Lazarov's heart like a heavy stone.

Twenty-two paratroopers, all dead... how I wish they were here now. All my fault.

Lazarov has to stop and sit down, his mind full of rage against himself. He covers his face with his hands, regardless of the pain caused by his fingers pressing his skull. He wipes the sweat from his face. The movement makes the Khan and his self-torturing spring to mind, especially when he had been talking about his son.

What determination, what willpower does one need to go through all this and still stay at least remotely sane, able to command others even while losing the strength to command oneself?

"The squad is assembled. We are ready to move in... Major, you are bleeding."

He looks up to Zlenko. "My arm is fine."

"It's not your arm... your chest."

He looks down at the place where his camouflage shirt juts out from under the exoskeleton's armored breastplate. Blood has seeped through the fabric from a wound that apparently no hemostats and collagen can heal.

"Did you find the entrance?" he says.

"We did."

The die is cast, then. I have my orders... it's all I have now.

He stands and looks into the eyes of his men. "I don't know what's lying in wait for us, but I am Major Mikhail Lazarov and I will lead you through whatever stands in our way. Sergeant Zlenko, Private Ilchenko, you have the honor to complete Operation Haystack. Let's prove that the sacrifice of our comrades was not in vain. Skinner and Zef, you are capable fighters but this is not a raid for loot and relics. If you are getting cold feet, tell me now."

He is unable to see Zef's face under the heavy tactical helmet's visor, but a bow of the Stalker's head signals his readiness. Skinner's features turn into a cruel and cynical grin, full of self-confidence as he readies his shotgun.

"All right Stalkers, let's go stalking. Ilchenko, take point. Lead us to the entrance. Zef, cover our rear. Let's go."

"God be with us," Skinner mutters behind the major's back as they march towards the rectangular gate hewn into the rocks and enter the darkness inside.

City of Screams. bunker level, 12 October 2014, 12:40:41 AFT

Zlenko's Geiger counter is reading normal values while the five men cautiously proceed further into the steeply descending tunnel, weakly lit by the emergency lights fastened to the wall.

"Put that thing away for now," Lazarov tells him. "You'll hear when it goes beyond normal. Just keep your eyes peeled."

The tunnel leads downwards and is reinforced with concrete beams, making Lazarov wonder how much work it took and, even more, what secrets lie hidden in the depths would justify these efforts.

They have been moving in for more than ten minutes now, descending all the way. The lack of opposition does not relax him. On the contrary, the eerie desolation in the dark tunnel puts his nerves on edge. He is almost relieved when the shaft at last leads into a room with crude concrete walls, looking like a storage room with fuel drums and shelves that still support tool boxes and maintenance gear, though their contents are dispersed on the ground in pools of gore. Blood is still flowing from the corpse of a commando, the remains lying there having been torn to pieces.

"No bullet killed him," Skinner says.

"How can you be so sure?" Lazarov steps closer, instinctively recoiling from the corpse as it seems to shift in the circle of light from his headlamp.

"Bullets usually don't tear out whole pieces from a body," the Stalker replies, "and this guy has everything missing that he once had between his chest and dick."

"More," Zlenko adds, swallowing thickly.

Lazarov scans the room with his headlight. "There's nothing of interest here. Let's move on."

"At least now we know what made the mercs run."

"Really, Ilchenko?" Lazarov asks. "If you have any clues, please tell me."

"Hunger."

"Keep your stupid jokes to yourself," Zlenko snorts.

"Hunger," Ilchenko repeats. "Hunger. *Hu-u-unger.*" His voice fades into a whisper.

"Private, take the lead," Lazarov snaps.

When Ilchenko steps by him, Lazarov exchanges a glance with Zlenko. He can't see the sergeant's face under the visor, but his gestures tell of increasing fear.

The tunnel bends and narrows. Moving in front of him, Ilchenko enters the pool of an emergency light and is then engulfed by darkness until he reaches the next one. Lazarov carefully moves through a section where the concrete beams are fractured, barely holding the ceiling up. His own light follows the nervous movements of his head, lighting up the wires and pipes on the wall, the concrete beams above, the hard-trodden ground under his feet. Up ahead, Ilchenko stops. The Geiger counter ticks slowly, its sound almost silenced by Lazarov's own breath and heartbeat.

"You hear that?"

All other senses fade away while Lazarov concentrates solely on his hearing, holding his breath. He is about to tell Ilchenko that he hears nothing when a faint noise comes from the deep darkness into which the tunnel leads, seizing his tongue. Nothing falls into view from the next lamp's light a few meters in front of the private, or the next after that. The third melts into darkness behind them. The other lights ahead are nothing but glowing points in the black tunnel – but, from the darkness beyond them, comes a sound that resembles a human voice screaming in fear, or something else roaring after finishing its hunt.

"How many times did you survive in the Zone?"

Lazarov looks up. The voice in his intercom sounds familiar, but he is not sure who is talking to him. He shakes his head, as if to rid himself of the voices as well as his worsening headache.

"Keep the channel clear." The message to his men was supposed to sound reassuring, but it emerges only as a whisper. "Move on, Ilchenko."

"This asshole didn't make it."

"What?"

"I mean that body there. I almost stepped on it." Ilchenko turns it over with his foot. "Looks like someone dragged him up here but then left him behind... must have been in a hurry."

The light from Lazarov's headlamp falls on an orange colored set of overalls with oxygen tanks on the back and a helmet covering the face with thick, darkened plexiglass. He kneels down next to the body and examines the protective suit.

"Judging by his suit, this was one of the scientists we were supposed to save," Zlenko says.

The belt containers are empty, but the scientist's dead hand clutches something that he had refused to let go.

"No, Sergeant... we were supposed to save this." Opening the rigid fingers, Lazarov takes a memory stick and carefully puts it away in his pocket.

"Let's move on, Stalkers... there's no loot on the body. Not even a dirty magazine." He grins at his own joke and pats Ilchenko's back with his rifle. "Move your ass, soldier."

"I don't like this tunnel," Zef says. "It's way too creepy down here."

"It's just dark," Skinner tells him. "Watch our backs and we'll be fine."

"But I see a spot where it is darker than anywhere else."

They all turn their heads in the direction the Stalker is pointing in. The light circles of their headlamps meet on the wall, showing nothing but a stretch of concrete and rocky earth no different to everywhere else around them.

Zef shrugs. "I must be hallucinating."

"Your strength will not be enough here."

"Who the hell said that?" Lazarov looks around at his startled comrades.

"Nobody spoke, sir," Zlenko quietly observes.

Fifty meters on, the tunnel leads to a metal door. It is open and a corpse lies at the entrance. The torso is still covered with the usual mercenary body armor, but the rest of his body is missing.

"Looks like he wanted to drag himself out," Skinner remarks, stepping over the corpse. "Even when mortally wounded."

Lazarov enters and looks around the room. "Looks like a guard room," he says, pointing with his rifle to the mattresses on the ground. The walls here are solid concrete with round holes housing the ventilators, one of which is still rotating. He checks his instruments. "Radiation normal... no anomalies detected. Should be safe to take off the gas masks."

The smell of earth, rot and damp floods his nostrils as soon as he removes his protective mask.

"Nothing here but debris," Skinner groans with dissatisfaction.

Ilchenko opens the next door and cautiously peeks out. "*Damn!* This is just where the bunker begins… and I was hoping this would be over with soon."

"Already missing the fresh air, Private?"

"No, Major… it's just damn tight in here with that monkey breathing on my neck." Ilchenko casts a glance of disdain towards Zef. "I hope he will not steal a Kalashnikov mag and eat it, thinking it's a banana."

Lazarov sees the black Stalker's eyes flinching. "Let's move on," he quickly says, "Viktor, come over here for a second."

"*Komandir?*"

Lazarov waits until Ilchenko and the two Stalkers leave the room. "What's wrong with Ilchenko, Sergeant?"

"I don't know… but I don't like his behavior any better than you."

They follow the Stalkers into the dark tunnel. After a few steps Lazarov sees Ilchenko signaling them to stop. He does not need to ask him for the reason. Beyond the next door, something heavy is stirring. Lazarov can even hear a slow, beastly rattle.

"Action time," Skinner grins and steps forward without waiting for orders. Before Lazarov can stop him, the Stalker opens the metal door by a couple of inches. In the next instant, a mass of malevolent force slams the door wide open and knocks Skinner off his feet. The rattling sound grows into a blood curdling howl and Skinner screams in fear and defiance as the mutant launches its attack.

"Mutant!" Ilchenko screams, firing his machine gun. Tracers and bullets pierce the darkness while Lazarov throws himself to the ground to give Zlenko a free line of fire.

"Shotguns! Blast it! Blast that beast!"

Now he recognizes the mutant: it's a bear, crawling over Skinner's body as it views the rest of its prey. Its thick hide absorbs every bullet, and the long claws are already reaching for Ilchenko when the bear rears up in pain, trying to stand erect on its hind legs. The narrow tunnel obstructs the creature, allowing it to rise only to the extent that Zef can fire a half dozen heavy bullets into its belly. Unnaturally strong muscles propel the dying mutant forward as Zlenko and Lazarov fire their rifles into its head. Eventually, its howling ceases. Panting, the men gasp for breath. Skinner's trembling voice breaks the sudden silence.

"Thank God for confined spaces," he says, standing up and cleaning matter from the massive, serrated combat knife he'd planted in the dead mutant's hide. The Stalker's face is bloody and his armor is in tatters, the upper layers torn into rags by the bear's claws.

My God, he knifed that beast even while it trampled him down!

"Sorry for letting you remove your gas mask, Stalker."

"What?"

"That beast must have stunk like hell so close in..." The men smile. "Awesome job, Skinner. Fit for a Guardian. And now let's see what's in the next room."

"Now you deserve Bone calling you assface," Zef jokes to Skinner, who is still wiping the blood from his face as the other man steps past him. "You had that bear's ass all over you, man. That sucks."

Entering the next room, Lazarov has a sense of déjà vu. The concrete walls with the pipes running below the low ceiling, the rusty machines, and the metal debris remind him strongly of the underground laboratories back in the old Zone. So do the dim emergency lights, one of them crackling as if its fitting was broken and lighting up a body in the corner for a second. It is wearing the long, dark green coat worn by scientists conducting research in the Zone. Skinner is already moving to check the body for loot, but Zlenko stops him.

"Chain of command, Stalker."

"You're nothing but a lap dog, *boyevoychik!*"

The Stalker looks unhappy but makes way for Lazarov, who examines the body. The dead man is still clutching at a heavy-duty laptop. Patting down the pockets of the coat, he also finds a small notebook, its pages filled with charts, calculations and hand-written notes.

"Maybe we should check that out," Zlenko says.

"Later… when we can allow ourselves a little break."

"There might be a map with hidden stashes on that shit," Skinner tells Lazarov with a greedy look in his eye. "Let's check it now!"

"Later, I said. Move on, Stalkers."

"Boss," Zef says from behind, "can't we fix these generators? This darkness…"

"At least you blend in, negro," Ilchenko says followed by a creepy laugh.

"Watch your tongue!"

"There's nothing in my job description about bearing the smell of monkeys, Major."

"What the hell is wrong with you?" Zlenko yells.

"It's OK, Sarge," the black Stalker calmly says. "I can put on my gas mask if this cheekyprawn is scared of my face."

"I do need a fucking gas mask to protect me from your smell!"

"Ilchenko, hold your tongue. Last warning. That's an order!" Lazarov snaps.

"Order, order… fuck this whole shit."

Lazarov sees Zlenko raising his shotgun. "Private Ilchenko," he says in a low voice, almost soft but barely able to contain his anger. "If you continue disrupting discipline I'll take that machine gun from you and let you take point empty-handed. Pray that a mutant saves you from court-martial!"

At last the machine gunner remains silent. Lazarov signals him to take point and follows him, closely watching his movements. Through a door at the end of the corridor, they enter a narrow staircase spiraling downwards. After two flights Lazarov cautiously opens another steel door. The dim light from his headlamp barely illuminates the large room, from where several corridors branch off.

"Maybe we should break into teams of two, scout those corridors and meet back here?"

"I don't think so, Viktor... there might be more mutants around. We only stand a chance if we stay together. Let the Stalkers check their ammo while I see what's left in this room."

"Yes, *komandir*."

The sergeant's obedient words relax his nerves.

At least he's retaining his sense of duty.

Lazarov watches Ilchenko and Skinner as they count their remaining shells and magazines.

If we start falling apart or have people going off for the loot, this mission is finished.

Empty soda and water bottles lay strewn around the ground among the debris of destroyed crates. A field table stands in the corner, turned onto its side. Lazarov almost stumbles over a wrecked chair when he steps closer to see if there's something behind it and is greeted by the sight of a headless corpse. He frowns and moves to where another body lies in the corner, still gripping a pistol in its hand.

That guy must have fought to his last bullet.

"Strange way to die." Lazarov stirs when he hears Ilchenko's voice behind him. "No blood on that one... he was smashed against the wall with such force that his neck broke... I mean, normally a neck isn't fully twisted to the side like that."

"How much ammo do you still have, Ilchenko?"

"Enough."

"What kind of reply is that, Private?"

"I said, enough. Enough to kill the world."

He's losing it.

Lazarov doesn't see the murderous light glimmering in the soldier's eye, but Ilchenko's hoarse voice is enough to make him more than concerned.

"Major, you better have a look at this."

"What is it, Viktor?"

"Zef found a map. It must have been torn from the wall."

Lazarov studies the sketchy blueprint. It is torn and heavy boots have trampled over it, but the layout of the bunker is still visible.

"Excellent… this long part is the entrance shaft… yes, then we crossed the guard's room and now we are in the former mess room… look, that tunnel leads to a chamber labeled *excavators' storage room*, whoever they are… the one in the middle leads to the laboratories."

"I love laboratories," Skinner cries out. "That must be where they keep all the relics for testing and stuff like that!"

"And from there?" Zef asks, ignoring the other Stalker's excitement.

"It says *excavation area* but the map ends there. There's only an arrow, directed downwards."

"To the labs, then?"

"No… first we check out the storage room. Maybe they have ammo there or first aid supplies… unless they used them all up when hell broke loose."

A growl comes from the darkness as if in response to the major's last words. But this time it is followed by a howl, with a third mutant joining the jarring chorus.

"Weapons at ready! Watch that tunnel to the left!"

For a moment, the major hopes that the light of their headlamps would blind the three jackals that leap out from the darkness, but the beasts don't hesitate to attack Zef, who stands closest to them. One jackal sinks his fangs into his arm, not leaving him a chance to shoot and, to Lazarov's horror, Ilchenko suffers the same fate. Perception or agility offer the soldier a better chance. He lets his machine gun fall with the two jackals still clinging to it with their teeth, and uses the moment gained to pull out his pistol. Lazarov, Skinner and Zlenko are firing like mad into the bundles of flesh, muscles and fangs while Zef, gathering all his enormous strength together, smashes the third mutant against the wall and pins it there while Skinner pumps three shells from his shotgun into its flesh. Even then, the mutant keeps growling as it falls to the ground and starts crawling towards them, oozing blood and gore. Ilchenko finally grabs his machine gun and fires a lengthy burst into the mutant, his voice roaring over the rattle.

"What the hell does it take to kill that fucking bastard?"

The mutant growls no more as the last casing falls to the ground from Ilchenko's weapon.

"What the fok!" Zef's eyes are wide enough to expose a ring of white around his corneas as he studies his arms. The mutant's fangs have bent his exoskeleton's reinforced metal frame like soft wire. "Those beasts just tore my shotty out of my hands and tried to bite them off…"

"Need a bandage?" Lazarov inquires.

The black Stalker shakes his head. A strange look appears in his eyes.

"They were after my… baby! But she is only mine!"

Lazarov scowls, but before he could ask Zef about what he meant, Skinner butts in.

"Had you worn anything other than an exo, you'd now have nothing to beat your dick with," the ex-Guardian sardonically retorts, reloading his shotgun. "It's your lucky day, brother."

"Let's move on, everyone… and keep your eyes peeled."

"There'd better be some loot in the storage room. I don't want to leave without a swag."

"You should be happy if you get out of here alive, and for that, luck is all you need hoping for."

"Major, are you soldiers not interested in loot at all? If the army pays so well, I'll sign up myself."

"We don't need money, Skinner. All we grunts want is vodka and stale bread... at least that's what some generals seem to think."

The corridor is narrow and the sickly smell of decaying bodies lingers in the damp air. The smell drives saliva into Lazarov's mouth. He swallows it. Skinner behind him spits.

"It stinks here!"

"Stop." Ilchenko signals a halt. "Can you hear that?"

A faint noise grows from the darkness, like someone rubbing their hard-skinned palms together. Beyond the light circle of Ilchenko's lamp, the darkness seems to move on the ground. Tiny, dim green spots evolve and move towards them.

"Back! Fall back!" Lazarov shouts. He sees two amber-colored lights appear high above him. "Holy shit! A snake!"

This time the major is not alone. The bullets riddle the mutant's erect body as it is about to strike. Obliterated by shotgun shells and rifle rounds, it collapses with a long, vanishing hiss. Lazarov gasps for breath.

Damn this place... and this is only the first level.

Beyond the steel door of the storage room they locate the origin of the smell. A pile of bodies lie on the ground, some of them missing limbs. Half digested chunks of flesh coat the concrete. Lazarov quickly puts on his gas mask, but the sickening smell is still in his nose. He quickly looks around the small room with uneven shelves on the wall.

"At least this was not for nothing," he grumbles. Fighting back his nausea, he picks up four heavy bundles from a crushed crate.

"What's in there?" Skinner asks curiously as they walk back into the large room, weapons ready to fire.

"Explosives."

"Getting angry, huh?"

"Not yet."

Back in the lobby's relative security, Lazarov orders a short rest. "Check weapons. Have something to eat. In ten minutes, we move into the laboratories. Ilchenko, you keep an eye on those corridors. Sergeant... come over here for a minute." He sits down on the ground and pulls out the notebook from his pocket. "Let's see what we have here."

His headlamp illuminates neat, old-fashioned handwriting. A name is written on the cover's inner page but the ink is smeared, leaving only *Korolev* legible.

"Hello, hello, Professor," the major mumbles, thumbing the pages. He reads the writing from the first legible page aloud so that Zlenko also knows what they are about to discover.

"According to researchers, the two statues were built by an ancient tribe called the Lokottaravadan. Ancient Sogdian manuscripts, discovered by Sir Aurel Stein's expedition and obtained by us from the British Library, tell that the female priests of this tribe possessed almost magical healing powers. However, this is dismissed by most historians as merely the stuff of legend. Anthropologists also agree that the Lokottaravadan are long extinct but Stein insisted that a few of them might still be found, scattered among the local Hazara tribes. We also learned from the manuscripts that the famous statues at Bamyan, called Samal and Shamama, did not only serve spirituality. The Lokottaravadan sculpted them to watch over a site where, according to their faith, a demon or object of destructive power was buried. In later centuries, long after this mysterious people were annihilated, the same site became known as the City of Screams, after Genghis Khan massacred every inhabitant of the city standing there in 1222."

"Don't tell me this was all about some stupid anthropologists getting a boner from superstition and legends... what is the meaning of all this?"

Lazarov struggles to find the right words. "Well... What concerns us now is that there's something very bad and evil down below... that is what the scientists were after... I should have guessed. Anyhow, it goes on: *From samples taken from the debris of the statues, we could establish a striking similarity between the molecular structure of local stone fragments and certain relics, found and known in the northern Zone for their health-restoring effects. However, the local samples don't emit any radiation, except at very low values which might be due to the nuclear fallout after the recent events. Another intriguing feature is that occasionally the fragments start to glow but without emitting heat of their own. Understanding the nature of these fragments would be a major scientific breakthrough."*

Lazarov looks at the Stalkers. Zef and Skinner are sharing a can of energy drink, while Ilchenko keeps his eyes fixed on the dark corridor and murmurs to himself as if in a delirium. Zlenko is pale and sweating. All look tired and winded.

"We'll get back to this later... now let's have a look at that laptop."

To his dismay, the drive is encrypted. He puts it into his rucksack and takes the pen drive recovered from the first body they encountered, hoping to have better luck with that one. Lazarov is relieved when after plugging it in his palmtop, a directory appears with files arranged in chronological order.

29 July, 2014
Moscow is not satisfied with our process. We offered extra payment to motivate the excavators. I hope they will dig faster. This place is a damn warren. To make things worse, someone before us destroyed the access to the lower levels. We have to make our way down by digging and explosives... I can ignore the Academy but my buyers are getting impatient too. They reduce my money each day until I find that relic, or whatever it is.

15 August
We had a setback today. An excavator started a fight. He screamed something about ruling the world and killed two others before the guards shot him. Again I had to double the excavators' money. They are becoming anxious.

28 August

Now it's really about time to enter the lowest level... I already lost tens of thousands of dollars due to the delay. Anyway, even if this goes wrong, they paid me enough for the Gauss gun blueprints before. I don't have to worry about my old age... I only wish this mission would be over either way, because this place is becoming eerier with every meter we dig deeper.

10 September
Shame on me. Couldn't bear the pressure. I wanted to bide time and told the buyers everything... two days later they were here. They shot the guards and took over command. Sakharov is so much lost in his research that he didn't even notice that our output now goes to Beijing instead of Moscow. But what I'm concerned about is that they made a pact with the dushmans... that wasn't part of the deal. That's a fucking betrayal. What the hell could I do? I'm powerless. How I wish it could be possible to get away from this cursed place and enjoy my earnings... I would give everything I got for this if I could just get away from here!

11 October
Holy shit! The test subjects broke free! The guards are panicking. What should I do, what should I do... We are holed up in the mess room. Those fucking howls from the depths! They drive me insane. I want to get out. They can't leave me here! I am their friend! They can't betray me like this!

Zlenko sighs. "Permission to..."

"Cut the crap, son... we're way beyond that, you and I. Speak your mind, for God's sake."

"Does it still make any sense to go deeper? There are no scientists to save here anymore."

"That's no excuse for us to leave this place... we need to search the laboratories and secure any research results we find. Those are our orders. As a matter of fact, the scientists are less important to the FSB than what they found out."

Zlenko doesn't look happy.

"Are you still with me, Viktor?"

"I am, *komandir*. But I'm worried about the Stalkers... I overheard Skinner talking to the black guy about leaving us and going to look for relics. We better watch our backs."

"Uh-hum."

"I'm even more worried about Ilchenko... he's on the edge. He was always a cocky sonofabitch but... not like this."

"Keep a close eye on him and don't let him get into a fight with Zef. With all the mutants around, the last thing I need is them shooting each other." Lazarov stands up and claps his hands. "All right, Stalkers... let's go down into the labs. Ilchenko, you're a good point man. Keep it up! Come on guys, look alive!"

"Can I take point for a change?" Skinner asks, taking his shotgun from his shoulder. "I don't want that machine gun guy grabbing all the relics."

"Suit yourself, Stalker. Ilchenko, stay with me."

The Khan's tower, Fire Base Alamo, 12 October 2014, 14:01:31 AFT

"Sir, we need to collect insane quantities of swags to pay for the new vehicles."

"Maybe the warriors shouldn't drive as recklessly as they do, Top."

"It's the terrain, sir. It takes a toll on the Hummvees. Someone should put in a word to make the drivers quit running over mutants and dushmans, too. After that Bagram operation..."

"It was fun."

"Yeah, maybe for you out there but it was me who had to remove all the gore from the chassis. That wasn't even remotely funny."

"I thought—"

The conversation between the Khan, Sergeant Major Hartman and Boxkicker is interrupted by three knocks on the door. Nooria enters the room without waiting for a reply.

"Top, Boxkicker, will you excuse us?" the big man asks.

"Top can stay," she says with a voice of authority.

Boxkicker rolls his eyes. He collects sheets of blueprints from the field table and leaves, grumbling something under his breath.

"You look troubled, child," the Khan says to Nooria.

"I am not troubled."

"Then why did you interrupt us?"

"We must help him."

"Don't tell me we should move out once more to help that man."

"We must."

The two men share a look of impatience, although the barely concealed smile on Hartman's face hints at his amusement over the tiny girl challenging the mighty commander of the Tribe.

His amusement vanishes when he looks in Nooria's eyes. He looks out of the window like one would do to check the skies just after having been warned of an impending storm.

"Did the Beghum sent you?" the Khan asks.

Nooria shakes her head.

"Do you think *you* can order *me* around, silly child?"

Another headshake, but this time she raises her hand and points to the window in a gesture of explanation or referring to a higher authority, though when Colonel too looks out to the wilderness all he and Hartman can see is the empty horizon. When they again look at Nooria, mystified, the light reflected in her eyes appears like gleaming shards of the merciless sun shining outside.

Several heartbeats of heavy silence. Then the Khan turns to his second in command.

"Have Lieutenants Ramirez and Collins assemble their squads immediately. Take them after her man."

Laboratory, 12 October 2014, 14:29:02 AFT

The corridor leading to the laboratories is short, with doors opening into small rooms. Looking inside as they move by, their headlights fall on destroyed field furniture and scattered documents. Lazarov takes a few sheets from the ground. Unsure if the long rows of numbers hold any valuable information, he lets them fall back to the ground.

A metal staircase winding down lies at the end of the corridor. A faint, bluish light glimmers beneath. If Lazarov had to choose between the darkness of the bunker level or the disconcerting light below, he would rather stay in darkness.

"Steady, Skinner... move quietly!"

The Stalker is halfway down the stairway when he suddenly stops. "Vaska," he shouts, "is that you?"

Lazarov cannot figure the reason for the Stalker's agitation, but leaps down the stairs to stop him from rushing forward into the large room where the stairs emerge. Wherever he looks, he sees devastated furniture and smashed cabinets, with broken computers and their blown out screens scattered around the floor. It is emergency lamps that spill the cold blue light over the devastated room, lending the room all the ambience of an operating theatre in Hell.

He hears the others descending the metal staircase, but the clunk of boots on metal cannot nullify the faint but discernible voice of a man crying in agony.

"Vaska!" Skinner shouts, his voice echoing in the room. "Where are you? Is that you over there?"

"Stalker! Stay here!"

Ignoring Lazarov's words, Skinner runs to the other end of the room, where a steel door swings open. Skinner cries out in despair and horror.

"Oh no! Vaska! What did they do to you?"

Cursing, Lazarov moves to pull him back. He has almost reached Skinner when he becomes aware of something that freezes the blood in his veins. As if the sound of a woman's desperate cry wouldn't be enough, his eyes widen in horror at what he sees.

"Nooria!" he utters upon the sight of her lying on the floor with blood covering her belly and limbs.

"*Fuck!*"

Skinner's voice and the gunshot following it bring Lazarov back to his senses. He grabs the Stalker's shoulder and drags him away from the door.

"Don't come closer," he shouts to the others. "Back up the stairs, move!"

"Let me fucking go," Skinner shouts, trying to wrestle himself free from Lazarov's grasp. "It's Vaska from the Asylum! I must help my friend!"

"It's just a fucking mutant trying to scare you away!"

The Stalker's heavy body suddenly becomes lighter as Zef joins Lazarov in his efforts.

"Hold him," Lazarov shouts when they reach the staircase, taking a grenade from his ammunition belt. Nooria's defiled corpse becomes clearer with each step he takes toward the door but, overcoming his horror, he leaps forward and tosses the grenade into the next room. A painful howl follows the explosion. Then all falls quiet. The apparitions disappear.

"I saw Vaska..." Skinner bemoans as Zef eases his choke-hold. "He was my best buddy... I believed him dead but I saw him... first he was in a fucking cage, and then bound to an operating table with fucking pipes and catheters screwed into his head..."

"It was just your imagination," Lazarov explains, but his own voice is trembling too. "The mutant wanted you to run away in fear. It's over. Vaska is fine!"

"How can you be sure of that? We must find him! Maybe he is still alive somewhere in here..."

"There's no one here except fucking mutants, you asshole," Ilchenko shouts and aims his machine gun at the Stalker. "Stop this moaning, you're making me nervous. Very nervous!"

"You haven't seen what I saw." The Stalker stands up and looks at Ilchenko, his eyes molten with rage. "You haven't seen those cages. I saw them, just a moment ago. They are for real. I'm through with you! I'm going to save my friend!"

"Skinner, if you want to live, stay here!"

"I'm a free Stalker, not a soldier you can order around. To Hell with you and your mission!"

Lazarov pushes Zlenko's rifle down as the sergeant aims it at the departing Stalker.

"Skinner! We're all together in this! Come back!" he calls.

"Fuck you," the Stalker shouts back as he disappears into the darkness beyond the steel door.

His three remaining men look at Lazarov.

"He's a dead man," Zef quietly observes.

"What was I supposed to do? Shoot him?"

Nobody replies.

"I couldn't bear his moaning about relics anyway," Ilchenko finally says. "I could have done you a favor, Major, if you still have the guts for things like that."

"The soldier has a point. We could have killed him and taken his ammo."

"I don't need you to agree with me, monkey-man."

"I'm with Ilchenko on this one too, Major. It was a mistake to let him go like that."

Zlenko's comments come as a surprise to Lazarov. This is the first time the sergeant has openly chastised him. Nor has he seen fear appear on the huge Stalker's face before, though it is present now.

"What's wrong with you men? Again: was I supposed to shoot him or what?"

"Yes," Ilchenko eagerly replies.

Lazarov notes the agreement on the other's faces. He places his finger on the rifle's trigger. "Forget about that Stalker. Ilchenko, Zlenko, we search the lab for intel. Zef, keep an eye on that steel door."

"If you say so, boss," the Stalker replies, reluctantly.

Keeping one eye on his soldiers and the other on the debris on the floor, Lazarov looks for anything that might hold a clue to the scientists' fate. With his curiosity prevailing, and not sensing any immediate danger, the major continues reading Professor Korolev's notebook.

Compared to the research output from the northern Zone, our own measurements indicated a strange connection between how the unfortunate events known to us affected the Zone of Alienation and the developments in Afghanistan after the nuclear accidents. It is a proven fact that massive nuclear contamination alone is not creating alienated environment. Now that we have learned that the relic hidden under Gholghola acts in a similar way to the entity in our Zone, we might get closer to the explanation. To better understand their similarity, we need to better know their differences.

The local phenomenon doesn't seem to follow a reasonable pattern. Instead, it appears to influence all creatures by multiplying their level of aggression. Our observations of mutated carnivorous species have proved that this influence develops motoric capabilities in a way to facilitate the success of aggression. In other words, it first turns aggression into the basic instinct, overruling all other behavioral patterns; then develops physical features that give the affected species more chance to succeed with their aggression. It is the strangest form of mutation we have ever observed. We don't know yet how humans as a highly intelligent species are affected. Probably individuals with a particular tendency of aggression and violence are more prone to be affected. However, appropriate psychological research needs to be conducted to clarify this. We were promised that in a few days the first test subjects will be delivered.

The excavators are still clearing the passages leading into the lower level. We cannot wait until they break through into the oldest catacombs. Currently we are set up in a room that we built between the former Taliban bunker complex and something that might once have been an underground fortification. The excavators are clearing it now. To facilitate our research, we constructed the test subjects' cages in such a way that they can be lowered below. All we have to do is to expose them to the psychotic influence for a certain period of time and take psi-measurements afterwards. I have no problem with using mutants for my experiments but do have reservations about using human beings, even if they are criminals taken captive by our guards. But for science, sacrifices have to be made.

Pages with long rows of numbers and scientific equations follow. The words on the last page were written by the same hand, but the writing is barely readable, as if put to paper by a gravely unsteady hand.

Our expedition has been betrayed! There was a traitor among us, selling us out to a hostile power. I am an old and weak man – what can I do now? The only way to prevent our research results falling into the wrong hands is by unleashing the research subjects on those who hijacked our expedition… God have mercy on our souls!

The writing ends abruptly.

He has barely put away the notebook when a muffled scream comes from the direction Skinner had disappeared in, followed by a quick succession of shotgun blasts. The sound that follows the shots is not something that Lazarov would have expected to hear, though: a bellowing laugh full of malice. Lazarov glances at Zef. The Stalker aims his weapon and takes a step back from the door. He is breathing heavily.

"Maybe he found his buddy after all," Ilchenko says with a grin.

Zlenko appears. "There's another room to the right. Should we check it?"

Lazarov nods and follows the sergeant. He keeps his weapon at the ready when opening the door, but the small room behind only holds two bunk beds, a table and bookshelves. A half-empty bottle of vodka and an open can of luncheon meat still remain on the table.

"Someone had his breakfast interrupted," Lazarov observes to Zlenko.

Stepping back to the computer room, he has to convince himself that what he sees is for real. It is not Ilchenko's sinister smile or the machine gun pointing at Zef's head that seems so surreal, but the sight of the Stalker sitting on the floor and weeping, bashing his head with his fists.

"What the —"

"I—I saw it all again..." Zef sobs. "When we entered the room it all came back to me. It's in my fokken head again!"

"Ilchenko, point that barrel elsewhere or I swear I'll shoot you... what the hell happened to you, Stalker?"

Zef reaches into his exoskeleton's ammunition compartment. What he pulls out makes everyone's eyes round with surprise: it is a tiny, blonde-headed doll.

"I can't bear this anymore. I tried to forget about her. And when that damned Stalker opened the door it suddenly all came back to me... I saw her lying there!"

"Hey Zef, relax," Zlenko tries to comfort him. "What's wrong?"

But the absurd scene is too much for Lazarov's temper.

"Pull yourself together!" he shouts and shakes the Stalker as if he was a malfunctioning machine. "What the hell are you talking about?"

"I felt that desire again. Oh God, I swear I tried to resist it, I tried so hard, but she was so sweet when I gagged her, it was only supposed to be a kidnapping, oh God the whole fokken thing went shit, and her body was soft like butter, her neck just melted away in my hands, I swear I tried to resist, Jesus how long I've tried to forget her but now she came back into my head, oh God—"

They listen to the Stalker's sobbing words in silence. Zef wipes his nose with the back of his gloved hand.

"That's why I went to the Zone. I wanted to pray to make her go away, but then during those nights when you hide in a hole in the earth and wish you'd be one with the dirt, she kept coming back to me... I tried to die by fighting all *kak* the Zone throw up against me but didn't. Then I came to this fokken land and for what? She came now back to me and fok all weapons and all bullshit, now I look at her again... she's fokken all I have and I'll never get rid of her, oh God, now I don't even want to... her long, blonde—"

"Enough of that shit, monkey-man." Ilchenko grasps the doll and tears it from the Stalker's hands before throwing it to the ground and stamping on it. "Killing little white girls, eh? You fucking savage, now I'll blast your head off!"

Ilchenko aims his weapon at the Stalker but Zef jumps up and throws his massive body against the soldier. Before Lazarov and the sergeant can intervene, the two men roll wrestling on the floor, the Stalker's immense strength against Ilchenko's willpower boosted by inhuman aggression.

The major realizes that Zlenko, the only man left with his sanity seemingly intact, would be no match for the Stalker's strength, so barks an order for him to apprehend Ilchenko while he grasps Zef's neck, putting the Stalker in a choke-hold. Even with his hand to hand combat training, Lazarov knows that, under normal conditions, he would stand no chance against the big South African, but the steel bones of his exoskeleton and the Emerald relic multiply his strength, making him more than a match for Zef.

"I'll fucking kill you!" Ilchenko swears, held tight by the sergeant. Zef tries to grapple Lazarov's arm off his throat, but his resolve is weak and his exoskeleton's power inferior to Lazarov's.

"That's enough. Enough!"

Feeling Zef's strength wane, the major slowly loosens the grip around his neck. Ilchenko has also run out of steam, and is now on his hands and knees, coughing heavily.

Lazarov takes the doll from the dirty floor and gives it to the Stalker, though now Zef is nothing more to him than a carrier for the Stalker's shotgun: an ugly but lethal tool needed to help him survive. He reaches into his backpack.

"Take a shot of vodka. Calm down. Once we're back on the surface you can kill each other, I don't care. But while we're down here, you keep killing mutants. Is that clear?"

Lazarov knows his hoarse voice fails to hold the power to impress the two men.

The big man was right... I'm about to fail. I can't control my men anymore. Maybe I should have just let them kill each other.

He glances at Zlenko, afraid of him drawing the same conclusion. The sergeant doesn't return his glance. Lazarov too draws a gulp from the bottle, taking a swig during a mission for the first time in his life. The warmth of the spirit relaxes his guts, which feel like they have turned into painful knots during the past few minutes.

"Let's move on."

The fighters pick up their weapons, avoiding each other's eyes. Zlenko watches carefully over them. Lazarov removes the magazine from his rifle and replaces it with armor-piercing bullets.

I hope it will not come down to me shooting my own men.

The sound of the magazine sliding into place sounds like a warning.

"Ilchenko, take point. I'll follow you. Zef, fall in line. Sergeant, watch our six."

They enter the room where the djinn's corpse lays, riddled and burnt by the grenade's countless metal fragments.

"Good riddance," Lazarov says, stepping over it. Another tunnel opens to their left. From the emergency lights glows a warm orange light that is a relief after the eerie blue haze of the computer room.

Driscoll, the brothers, the Khan... how I hated them in the beginning. How I wish they were here with me now. But if they could make it through here, we can make it too.

The tunnel descends for a few meters and leads to yet another steel door, this one standing wide open. Ilchenko quickly looks around before entering the room beyond, and then moves on with the precision of a machine between a row of cages and desks loaded with computers, stopping at a corpse that lies on the ground.

One lamp is turning around on the ceiling with a whining noise that reminds Lazarov of a knife scratching a plate. The noise makes him shudder.

"Another Chinese bit the dust here."

"And a scientist too," Lazarov says, checking the body but finding nothing. He looks around, hoping to see something that provides him with a clue.

What were these cages for?

There is an opening in the wall at the other end of the corridor, covered by a gritty plastic curtain.

"Maybe this room was a zoo where they kept monkeys like that son of a..." Turning back to look at the major, Ilchenko finds himself facing the barrel of the major's rifle. "Okay, okay... just guessing."

The walls of the long, narrow room are dark and shiny. Lazarov sees the reflection of himself and his men moving along the row of cages, all fastened to the ceiling with heavy chains. One place is empty, the chains leading through two holes in a mechanical trapdoor. *They must have lowered that one into the abyss beneath,* Lazarov thinks. Then the light of his headlamp falls on another body, poised on his knees and still clinging to the lever of a device fastened to the wall.

"Major... Mikhail, you are bleeding."

He looks down at his armor where blood has soaked through all the protective layers. Zlenko's words making him aware of the pain. Lazarov feels an unsettling sensation, as if the stone sewn into his flesh by Nooria had become animated,

413

but it is not his body rejecting it; the stone seems to move of its own accord. Two seams of cord fixing the neat cut have already burst. He closes the armor.

"Looks like an old wound," the sergeant says.

"Not the first if its kind," he replies without any intention of telling more. "And now… let's see what this switch does."

He moves the lever upwards. The device clicks to his reassurance. Suddenly a bright light beams up.

"What the hell? Where are we?"

Lazarov is dumbstruck as he sees a huge cavern just an arm's length from him. The walls reflecting their images are windows through which he now looks down into an abyss. He wants to reply to Zlenko but only manages to utter a surprised gasp as he sees a human form taking shape at the other end of the room. Its mouth arches into a cruel sneer. In the next second the same terrifying laugh booms that they had heard in the level above.

"Screw you, motherfok!"

Zef steps forward, his shotgun spitting lead into the apparition while Ilchenko's machine gun joins in. The bullets' impact shakes the humanoid, but it keeps moving closer with each step. It strikes Zlenko in the head, sending him to the floor with a scream, then grabs Ilchenko's machine gun and, ignoring the pain from the hot barrel, tears it from the soldier's hands and turns the weapon towards Lazarov. He tries to dodge it but a long, brawny arm arrests him and slings him against the glass wall. Horror overwhelms him as he slams into the glass between himself and the dark abyss outside. Fortunately, the glass does not break, leaving Lazarov merely winded. Zef watches the major slowly slump to the ground, his eyes glowing with rage as he turns towards the mutant.

"You are one ugly motherfok. Come to me, get some!"

Lying on the ground and wheezing from pain, Lazarov watches the Stalker wrestling with the mutant. Zef's face is distorted from pain and his brutal effort to match the monster's power as they grapple face to face, the dreadful arms in the Stalker's hold, a desperate human aided by an obsolete exoskeleton fighting something that was once human, but is now two hundred pounds of muscle obeying the sole instinct to kill.

Lazarov's rifle has been kicked away, so he reaches for his pistol and switches to automatic mode, dragging himself closer until he is able to fire the full magazine into the mutant's skull.

Wounded, it gradually falls to its knees with Zef towering over it, still holding its arms, then the Stalker raises his foot and kicks the mutant in the head, breaking its neck.

"*Fuck!*" Lazarov grunts, panting heavily and spitting out sour saliva.

"That's my thank-you for giving me back my baby, boss."

Zef's mouth gapes open but only a hoarse rattle leaves his lips as the tip of a knife appears in his mouth. He coughs, then blood starts streaming from his throat. Ilchenko's grinning face emerges behind him.

"The Moor has done his duty... the Moor can go. It's an urban legend that Shakespeare wrote it but now it's a perfect time to quote!"

In trepidation, Lazarov watches Ilchenko pulling his bayonet from the Stalker's head. Ilchenko licks the blood from the blade.

"I hate racists. All the blood in the world tastes the same. Like... salty oil."

Lazarov is helpless with his handgun empty and Ilchenko now aiming his weapon at him. "What have you done?"

"I have finished the mission. No more *yes, sir* to idiots like you. I am smarter than you, better educated than you, and aiming a fully loaded machine gun at you. I am free now. In other words, I am the king of this fucking universe!"

"You are pathetic."

"If so, why are you the one on his knees? An officer, a fucking major, falls to a private!" Ilchenko leans so close that he can feel the spit the private ejects with every word he scowls. "This is the moment of truth, *komandir*."

A shadow falls on Ilchenko from behind.

"Indeed it is, Private... could you take a step back?"

"Last wish granted," Ilchenko laughs as he retreats, "and what's in that for you?"

"I'll have less of your educated brains on my face when Zlenko fires his shotgun."

Surprise is the last expression on Ilchenko's face before his head is blown to pieces and his massive body collapses. Smoke still trickles from the barrel of Zlenko's Benelli as he quickly reloads it.

"I couldn't make it earlier," the sergeant says, pointing to his badly wounded face. "The punch was one thing... but that beast threw me against something sharp."

"Thanks, Viktor... I won't forget this."

"I never liked him," Zlenko replies with an indifferent shrug.

The light is stabbing into the major's eyes as he stretches out on the metal floor. He carefully touches the wound on his chest. When he removes his hand from under the armor, it is covered with blood.

Which drop will be the last one?

The sergeant sits at his side, his eyes like two black holes. Slowly, Lazarov sits up.

"Now there's only you and I left, son."

Lazarov is glad that his visor hides his eyes from the sergeant. He realizes how fond he has become of him and now, in this moment, how he would gladly give his own life if that would help Zlenko survive. He takes some bandages and a first aid kit from his pack and tends to the sergeant's wound.

"Do you think I'm a coward, Mikhail?"

"On the contrary... I will turn every damned stone upside down to get you a promotion to lieutenant."

"Being a lieutenant... that's much better than being a sergeant, yes."

Lazarov realizes how shallow his words sound. "You are right... I should have just said that no, I do not think you are a coward."

"So you won't take it for cowardice if I say: let's turn back. I am actually begging you to turn back. It will only get worse if we cross this bridge!"

Lazarov seeks the words to explain all the pieces of the puzzle that just keep falling into place within his own perception, things he feels rather than knows.

"Have you seen Ilchenko's madness?" He asks, having finished bandaging the sergeant's wound. "How Skinner ran to help an already dead friend? How Zef's wits fell apart?"

"I do."

"Did you have a close look at the sand and rocks in this land, the ruins, the wrecks of tanks once driven by our father's generation? Have you seen the killing machines that people turned into, people who once had more freedom and earned more money than we could ever dream about?"

"I did."

"Then listen... all this shit comes from that damned thing." Lazarov beats the floor with his fist. "Or so I read the clues... but it clearly radiates evil—look how it had turned us against each other! It creeps into our mind at our weakest point... We have to destroy it if we can. The FSB wanted to have it. Our enemies tried to snatch it from our scientists. Who knows what powers are still queuing up to take it? At least we should try to end this madness. This is our mission now, son!"

Lazarov is almost begging. Zlenko gives his hands a thousand-yard stare. He is opening and closing his fist, as if checking that his hands still obey his will.

"All the things we saw... it's beyond human influence, Mikhail. I don't think we can change anything here, or anywhere in this screwed up world for that matter. Frankly, I think we should leave and let this cursed place keep its secrets." He stretches his back, like a man preparing for heavy work. "But if you go, I'll follow you."

Lazarov removes his helmet and rubs his hand over his sweaty hair and grimy face. "Why?"

"Because I'm supposed to follow my orders."

Lazarov had been hoping for a reply that would have proved to him that the almost fatherly feelings he developed for the young sergeant had not been in vain. He wipes the dust off of his helmet, then slowly puts it back on his head and fixes the neck strap under his chin.

"Well then... if you still follow your orders, take Ilchenko's machine gun and ammunition." He staggers to his feet and reloads his pistol. "Then, if you are ready... let's go below."

Zlenko stares at the darkness beyond. "I don't like the look of this."

"Neither do I."

Catacombs, 12 October 2014, 15:58:16 AFT

Holes in the wall mark the places where timbers once held a wooden staircase, now replaced by a steel ladder. His headlamp is too weak to illuminate the lower end. For a moment he considers tossing a grenade into the depths to clear the ground, should anyone or anything be laying in wait for them below. His cautiousness prevails.

The less noise we make, the better.

The ladder seems endless. Dust rises from the ground and gathers in the beam of his headlamp when, at last, his heavy boots touch the bottom of the pit with a muted thud. He steps ahead, so that Zlenko too can descend from the ladder.

Their weapons at the ready, the two soldiers proceed cautiously. The tunnel walls are made of crudely hewn rock, the small light circle of the headlamps casting dark shadows on the stones as they move. It is pitch black. The generators illuminating the laboratory either have no power to operate the emergency lights wired to the tunnel's ceiling, or the wires had been sabotaged. After a few steps, huge shadows loom in the light of their headlamps. Two corridors sprout from the tunnel.

Lazarov decides to take the descending corridor to the south. Zlenko follows him without question.

Pain burns his chest. Touching his wound, his fingers tell him that another stitch has torn.

That stone is moving out of my flesh… what is happening to me?

In one place, where the tunnel curves and continues downward in a steeper descent, the walls bear the marks of heavy tools.

"They used enough effort to dig a metro," Zlenko whispers. "Someone must have been really keen to clear these catacombs."

"Halt," Lazarov whispers back to the sergeant, "I see a light ahead. Switch to night vision."

He kneels down. The faint hum of his night vision is the only sound he can hear. The low, greenish contrast strengthens enough for him to make out a brawny figure standing in the darkness.

"Steady," he whispers, and aims his weapon. The reticule slides towards the mutant's face. It seems to be just an arm's length away. Whatever happened to it, Lazarov can still see human features, wishing recoil would be the only thing he felt when he pulls the trigger. Despite the silencer, the rifle shots sound like thunder in the narrow tunnel. For a second, the mutant's head jolts with impact as the bullets hit it, then it turns in the direction of the shots. Lazarov fires again. The mutant roars, its heavy steps pounding on the ground towards him. Zlenko fires the machine gun.

What the hell does it take to kill this beast?

Gritting his teeth, Lazarov fires burst after burst. The mutant collapses but still manages to crawl towards them.

"Can't you understand you're fucking dead?" Zlenko screams, firing the M27 directly into the mutant's head. "Die at last! *Die!*"

The mutant lies sprawled on the ground, motionless but for its fingers, which are still twitching. Its nails have grown into inch-long claws. Zlenko draws his combat knife, kneels down and cuts the mutant's throat. The claws dig into the ground and move no longer.

"At least I could use my bayonet again," he says, coldly. "Now it's dead enough."

For a minute, Lazarov suspiciously studies his last remaining companion's face. "Good job, Viktor," he says.

"I know."

Turning his back to Zlenko, Lazarov is dogged by a persistent feeling of uneasiness. Reaching a wide cavern with a campfire in the middle, he puts the fire between himself and Zlenko so that he can watch his movements.

"Looks like we interrupted its dinner," he says, looking at the half dozen corpses lying on the ground, some of them revealing bite marks. Even so, the still-human face of the mutant makes him feel uneasy.

Zlenko shrugs. "It's done for. No place for remorse. It was not human anymore, just pure evil turned into brawn and claws."

Lazarov frowns.

He was not supposed to know what I think.

"How much ammo you've got left?"

"Only two mags."

"Keep your pistol ready... just in case."

"It won't be necessary. We won't get much further." Zlenko's words sound pessimistic but there is a strange, detached resolve in his voice.

"We will, Sergeant."

Zlenko doesn't reply. He checks the corpses. "Civilians mostly... technicians, I believe."

So these were the excavators.

Lazarov moves to take a closer look at them, to find a map or something else that might be useful, but as he looks back at the mutant one last time, the light of his headlamp is reflected by something metallic. He turns the corpse over. Fastened on a metal chain like a dog-tag, a note hangs from its neck in a small plastic case.

Psychological test subject Number 3. Origin: Ghorband area. Personal notes: Vasilyev. Species: homo sapiens. Nature of test: ~~voluntary~~ – involuntary. Exposure time: 12 hours (estimated).

"You know, Viktor… actually, I am relieved that we don't have to rescue these scientists."

"I disagree. We came to rescue them. We have orders. And I will not go beyond or ignore my orders."

The major frowns. He looks at the sergeant's heavy body armor and, for a moment, is tempted to reload his rifle with armor-piercing ammunition once more.

Not Viktor. Not him. Please.

Before they go on, Lazarov looks around the cavern. Heavy rocks and debris still lie on the ground where they had entered, and the walls of the cavern are smoother than in the tunnels. He can even see the faint traces of stone ornaments on the walls, and closer examination even reveals faded paintings. Parts of human figures are still visible, but their faces have been scratched away and huge bullet holes have otherwise rendered their remains unrecognizable. The tunnel continues as a row of stairs, leading deeper into the darkness.

"Have you realized we didn't stumble into Skinner's corpse?" Lazarov inquires. "Maybe that tough bastard is still alive and lurking about somewhere here."

"Yeah. Maybe," Zlenko replies, again with an insubordinate shrug.

After a few meters, the tunnel broadens. The stairs are broken, and a narrow wooden plank runs through. Zlenko moves straight forward. He is barely half a meter away from the ruined steps when Lazarov sees a little hole in the ground, like those he had seen at Hellgate.

"Stop!" he screams, but is too late. Columns of burning steam thrust from the ground, filling the tunnel with noxious fumes and flames. He grasps the sergeant's shoulder and yanks him back to safety.

"A Geyser! Watch your step!"

The anomaly burns for a minute before extinguishing itself as quickly as it had appeared. Zlenko's suit is badly burnt and Lazarov can see seared flesh through the torn leggings. He quickly takes a roll of bandages and is about to apply it on the sergeant's wounds when Zlenko shakes him off.

"It's nothing," he says calmly and stands up. "Let's move."

"You have burns all over your legs," Lazarov shouts at him.

"Stop being such a father figure."

He watches Zlenko move on with determined steps. Cursing himself, he runs to catch up with the sergeant. Lazarov can barely halt himself when he finally reaches Zlenko. Under the arched tunnel ceiling, his faintly outlined silhouette stands still against inky darkness.

Another yawning chasm opens before them. One ramshackle rope bridge stretches out from where Zlenko stands, its other end invisible in the gloom beyond.

"I suppose you want to take point, Major."

The sergeant's words strike home like an order and Lazarov bites his lip. Deep inside him, all his instincts scream *Danger.*

He steps onto the bridge. The ancient ropes creak as the shaky bridge accommodates his weight. The chasm below could be ten or ten thousand meters deep, but soon the other side appears, where an elaborately carved stone arch leads into another tunnel.

"You can follow... it's safe," he shouts back to Zlenko the from the middle of the rope bridge. When he has almost reached the other side, he repeats, "Viktor, you can—"

"I will not."

With his weapon ready but his finger off the trigger, Lazarov slowly turns back towards his last remaining comrade.

"Come again?"

"I said I will not. I *can* not follow you any longer."

Lazarov's eyes glaze over with fear as he looks back at him. The sergeant has removed his helmet and, where the face of a young, carefree man once was, the deadly features of a killer now appear. The light of Lazarov's headlamp reflects in his eyes as a fiery red tone.

"Viktor," Lazarov desperately shouts, "you are still under my command, for God's sake!"

"There is no god here. Nor was there any command on the way here. I always had my doubts about listening to you. It was through your mistake that we got shot down. I saw you spending all the money we had for the team on personal weapons. It was you who left us to go and fuck some dirty tribal bitch while we were fighting for our lives at Bagram. It was you who led us down there where all the others died. I am a loyal soldier. But you don't deserve my loyalty — you were supposed to lead us, instead the New Zone kicked you around like an empty vodka bottle!"

Lazarov's instincts try to move his rifle so he can shoot Zlenko but his will does not obey. The wound on his chest becomes more unbearable with pain. He drops to one knee, grasping the ropes on the bridge that is wobbling under his weight.

"You know that all of this is not true!"

"I don't care because I no longer need you. It is the City of Screams that has tested you and found you wanting." The bayonet glints in Zlenko's hand as he starts cutting the rope. Lazarov needs both hands to prevent himself from falling into the depths. His rifle falls into the abyss.

"Viktor!" Lazarov screams in despair. "My brother... my son, this is not you talking!"

"I am not your son."

Zlenko cuts the other ropes. The bridge swings violently and thrashes against the rocks on the other side while Lazarov clings to the rope and planks with all his might, spitting blood as he meets impacts against the sharp stones. A bullet whizzes by close to his head and hits the rock wall. Putting all his strength into his left hand he clings on, pulling out his pistol with the other.

"Viktor! Don't make me do this!"

More bullets come by way of reply, chipping sharp pieces of stone from the rocks. Lazarov's eyes are blurred by pain and tears as he aims and pulls the trigger. Zlenko recoils, blood gushing from his forehead. Then he falls to his knees, and his body, losing its balance, plummets headlong into the chasm below.

The rope has almost frayed right through. Climbing up plank by plank, with some breaking beneath his hands, he finally reaches up and pulls himself to the safety of the entrance above, where he stays on the dusty ground, fighting for breath and using the most terrible cusswords he knows.

Lazarov's heartbeat at last returns to normal, but he feels as if all the blood had vanished from his veins, leaving only adrenaline in his muscles and a growing rage within his heart.

12 October 2014, 16:30:27 AFT

Whatever Lazarov has been through during the past few hours, the only pain he is aware of is in his chest, where the wound has by now almost fully opened again.

Maybe without my relics and the exo I would just collapse like an empty sack.

He reloads his pistol. With his Beretta drawn in one hand and holding the combat knife in the other, he proceeds into the shaft with determined steps. The walls are made of neatly cut stone, just like the dust-covered stairs that had led down here. Another anomaly lurks up ahead but he walks through the fire columns thrusting up from the ground, ignoring the pain when the flames sear through his damaged armor and painfully lick his skin. From a corner unlit by his headlamp, a shadow detaches itself from the deeper darkness.

He doesn't even pause as he fires his weapon, now even hoping to witness the pain in the once human eyes as the bullets hit the brawny torso. Throwing his empty pistol away, he leaps at the mutant with a screaming battle cry and thrusts his knife into its chest, driving it around in the flesh before pulling it out and striking again. Then he marches on, not even looking at the dying creature now wriggling on the ground in death throes of violent, agonizing spasms.

The shaft runs straight and leads towards a red glow that permeates from the distance. Reaching it, Lazarov steps into a cavernous room with four earthen braziers in the corners. A grey stone slab lies in the center of the room, undecorated and plain apart from a shallow niche in its middle section. It holds a small stone exactly like the one Nooria had inserted into his flesh.

A sense of devotion possesses him. As he looks around, the light of the fires makes the faded paintings on the wall come to life. They resemble a long line of figures, all looking towards the stone slab with foreboding faces, like a religious procession devoted to the stone — or watching over it.

No more doors to open. Nowhere to descend. I have arrived.

He remembers the faces of all the comrades who died at his side, soldiers and Stalkers alike.

Yet I am here. No one could stop me. I truly am the chosen one.

He watches the stone darkening to deep black, as if it was a mass of pure darkness itself. His body feels like a freshly forged blade after tempering: pure, cold, its edge ready to kill. Only the pain in his chest reminds him of his human nature.

Nobody and nothing could stop me on my way here. If I leave, I will be unstoppable wherever I go, whatever I want to take.

By now the slab looks like a pool filled by a black void. The room starts moving around him, but he doesn't feel any drowsiness. The ceiling and floor eventually disappear and he sees himself standing at the center of a rotating, black orb.

A voice echoes from far above. *"Why are you here?"*

Fearfully, Lazarov looks up. The shape of a humanoid figure towers above him like an angel of darkness. Its face is the ultimate conclusion of all the horrors Lazarov has ever experienced in life and also in nightmares.

"I followed my orders."

"What are you orders?"

"I don't know anymore."

"From now on, it is me who will give you orders."

"Who are you?"

"I am your essence. I am the essence of the fate of all living souls."

"Are you… the devil?"

"How foolish! I only make living souls aware of their potential. I give you the means to destroy yourselves. Everyone according to what he does best. I was always here to do that."

"Whatever you are, the ancients built those statues to keep your power at bay… and the fanatics set your influence free when they destroyed them!"

"I see your time here was not wasted. I have always been here, I have always been everywhere. Waiting to erupt, waiting to take over. You have a choice now. Yield to your most primordial instinct of destruction. Each second you spend with me, your body will grow stronger to follow this instinct. You will be the mightiest of humans."

With every word echoing in his mind, Lazarov's rage grows.

"Only two others were offered this choice. Only two understood. One ruled the world known to him. The other was a failure. My partial failure. He had power over his men who were supposed to follow my will and prevent him from reaching me. He himself was supposed to kill those who were with him but he was shielded from my will. I still have time to come to him, and I will. You should make your choice now."

"And if I don't yield?"

"Then you will be of no use to me anymore and vanish. What is your choice?"

Lazarov steps closer, instinctively looking up at something glistening on the wall. A small, red precious stone reflects the light of his headlamp. A female shape appears in the light circle, faded, scratched and worn, but he can recognize the tattoo on her forehead. Half-forgotten words resound in his mind with such clarity as if he had heard them just a second ago. *'You will shed blood and last drop will be yours. If you want me to live, you will have to make a sacrifice.'* The burning pain in his chest intensifies. *'One part protects you. Two parts bond darkness.'*

For a moment, he hesitates between the rage engulfing him and the only humane feeling left in his heart.

"What is your choice, human? Power or oblivion?"

Closing his eyes, he takes a deep breath and raises his combat knife. "I yield to your power. Without you, I could not do what I have to do!"

Lazarov yields to rage—and unleashes it upon himself to overcome his own fear and pain.

He dips the blade deep into his wound, cutting it open and removing the stone. His body suddenly becomes aware of its exhaustion and injuries. Crying out in pain he falls onto the slab. With trembling, bloody fingers, he places Nooria's stone next to the other into the slot.

When the two parts join, the fires blaze up and a deep, humming noise drones from beneath as if the earth itself was sighing in relief.

Pain and fear captivate Lazarov as he realizes that he is in the depths of a labyrinth, armed only with a knife and bearing wounds all over his body.

But his knees do not tremble now. A sudden feeling of freedom invigorates his exhausted limbs as he runs from the chamber and soon he reaches the exit of the shaft. The depth beneath his feet seems bottomless. Seeing no other way of escape, he starts descending the ruined rope ladder. Reaching the end, he looks warily into the abyss.

There's no other way than into the chasm.

Hoping that his exoskeleton still offers enough impact protection to save him from breaking his bones, he lets himself fall. After what seems an eternity, he hits the ground, the titanium alloy body frame of his armor creaking from the impact. He doesn't need to check the exoskeleton thoroughly to know that this was the last time it had saved his life.

Getting up, he sees broken planks from the bridge on the rocky ground. Without anything to guide him, Lazarov follows his instincts. He gives a start as the light from his headlamp falls on a corpse.

Such a waste, he thinks and closes Zlenko's lifeless eyes. He takes his pistol from its holster.

Not far ahead, the lights of the cage room glow high above. Lazarov recalls that one of the cages was lowered. Hoping that it will offer him a chance to get out from the abyss, he moves forward. It doesn't occur to him that the cage was not empty when lowered until he hears a howl.

Oh no… this isn't even remotely fair.

Two red dots emerge in the darkness above. Prepared to be attacked by more than one enemy, Lazarov recoils and desperately looks around to find a position to defend. The dots grow into a pair of luminescent eyes. It is not two mutants but one, the hugest he has ever seen, blocking his way.

He has nowhere to hide, so Lazarov turns around and runs, hoping to find a way out from the cavern where the mutant would be unable to follow. He stumbles and tries to get up but his muscles begin to seize up in terror. It was not a stone that had made him fall. Phosphorescent light glows an arm's length away from him. He rolls to his side and recoils, still on the ground. The snake is faster. Reaching him, its fang-filled jaws open to tear into him. Then the snake turns its head away. For a moment, the humanoid mutant and the snake face each other — and then the snake strikes down upon the mutant. With lightning-quick reflexes, the enormous hands grasp the scaly body. Panting heavily, Lazarov watches them wrestling for life and death over a prey that would be him. He removes the Jumpy relic from the container.

I need fire.

Meanwhile it is the roaring humanoid that is gaining the upper hand. The snake's jaw opens wide in agony from the suffocating stranglehold. Lazarov only has a few moments left before the humanoid turns on him. He throws the relic to hit the mutants and, aiming as best as he can, plunges the fire-alloyed combat knife into it. He has only one second to be surprised about his own accuracy when the enhanced blade hits the relic, triggering a thunderous explosion of fire and acid. Blood and shreds of ripped flesh splash around him as he huddles on the ground.

Climbing to his feet, he realizes that the half-ruined exoskeleton, until now perfectly fitting his size, seems to have shrunk, become much too tight in places.

I better get out of here before I become a mutant myself.

For a long moment, he studies the dead, humanoid mutant. Then he pulls the laptop from his backpack, which most probably contains descriptions of experiments leading to the creation of such abominations, and smashes it on the ground. He tears the research notes into tiny pieces too.

Removing his knife from the carnage, he moves on towards the dim light from the bridge above. To his relief, the cage is there but without any device or switch to operate its elevating mechanism. He starts climbing up the cable, holding himself with all his strength on the slippery, greasy steel and kicks the metal trapdoor open.

Climbing into the long room spanning over the cavernous abyss, he feels as if he has arrived in the safest place on earth until the sight of the two corpses brings him back to reality.

Both of them deserved a better grave than this.

Lazarov takes one pack of explosives from his backpack and positions it in the middle of the room.

No one will go beyond anymore.

He has climbed only a few steps on the ladder leading into the laboratory level when the detonation occurs, followed by the deafening shriek of metal bending as the bridge implodes into the abyss. The choking dust vomited up by the shock waves still covers him when he gouges out a rock from the wall with his knife and replaces it with another pack of explosives.

The timer is broken. Can't adjust it to more than ten seconds.

He attempts to climb again, as fast as his exhausted muscles will permit, but the detonation almost throws him out of the shaft. Heat scorches him once more. The shaft collapses, sealing the way to the lower levels.

Where should I place the last charge?

The entry level comes to mind, where the ceiling was close to collapsing under its own weight.

Lazarov runs. He passes by the ruined computer room and climbs the stairs leading to the bunker, driven by a compulsive urge to see the sunlight again. He stumbles. Lying on the ground with his face in the dust, a tempting desire seduces him to remain there and deny his willpower the right to torture his worn-out muscles any longer. For a moment, he wants to allow himself to succumb to his pain and spend his last minute trying to recall the best moments of his life, before the tunnel collapses and buries him forever.

I must stay alive. It's the big man's order!

Digging his fingers into the dust, he heaves himself forward and gets to his feet. Out of breath and holding a hand over his bleeding wound, he keeps running.

When he reaches the long shaft leading outside and the passage with the insecure ceiling, he plants his last explosive charge. His movements freeze when he hears an unexpected but familiar noise from above.

Could it be helicopters? Could it be a rescue squad? Could it be that everything gets straight in the end?

By now he is positive that the noise is that of helicopters hovering above. All he has to do is to set the last charge, make the catacombs inaccessible, and depart.

With fingers twitching from exhaustion and impatience, he adjusts the timer and makes a last dash for the exit. When the charge goes off and the tunnel disappears behind him in massive plumes of smoke, he falls to the ground, once more crawling towards the light shining ahead, his fingernails breaking on rocks and stones, until suddenly daylight greets his sore, blinking eyes.

He wallows in the dust exhausted, bruised and panting for breath, enjoying the sound of Mi-24 Hinds hovering over the City of Screams, their guns and missiles blasting away at an unseen enemy.

12 October 2014, 17:21:45 AFT

A pair of heavy boots appears in front of his face. As he wearily raises his head, looking up at a man in a now-familiar Guardian exoskeleton but this time without the helmet, Lazarov's heart sinks. A pale, hard face looks down on him with a cynical grin in the grey eyes.

"You're a real die-hard, Lazarov, I give you that."

"General Voronov?"

"Yes, it's bad to see you too, Major. Now give me that relic we're all here for."

He laughs triumphantly as he stands over Lazarov with his helmet in his hand and surrounded by his guards from Bagram. None of them offer any help while Lazarov gets up, slowly and painfully.

"I don't have it."

"What did you just say?"

"It was not a relic, you greedy, ignorant bastard! It is something beyond your understanding!"

"Now you're really pissing me off, and my mood was already bad." His face reddening from sudden anger, Voronov waves to his guards. "Captain, handcuff this piece of shit."

Lazarov looks at the dozen assault rifles that are trained at him. He gets to his knees, bows his head and pulls the gloves from his hands, throwing them to the ground as a sign of surrender. "How could you betray your own men like this, General?"

"I was paid a hundred times more for those damned suits than I had earned in a century, even after giving Zarubin his share. And I don't have a century left to live. Do you think I want to die living on state pension in a cockroach-infested apartment block? But that money would have been nothing compared to the relic you have left down there!"

"You have no idea what lies below… and I made sure that nobody enters its chamber again."

"You are such an idiot, Lazarov, but at least you have been a useful idiot. You helped me a lot, you know? You made those exos walk directly to me, self-propelled! Including this one that you somehow managed to steal back from me… damn, it's all ruined. Then you took care of the air defenses of the Chinese so that my choppers could fly in. You saved my skin when they bribed the dushmans into attacking my base. You opened the way to the undergrounds. All this, and now you crawl out half-dead and say you don't have the mother of all relics! Did you at least find the research results?"

"It was not a relic, and no one will ever get the research results either."

"Damn you! Do you have any idea how much… You were ordered to secure them, that's all your bloody mission was about! You disobeyed direct orders!"

A horrible thought visits Lazarov's mind. "How do you know about my orders?"

Voronov grins widely. "This is not your lucky day, huh?"

The major looks at Voronov while the guard handcuffs him. Collecting all the saliva remaining in his dry mouth, he spits into Voronov's face. "You are a traitor and a disgrace to your country, General!"

"You're naivety explains why you are just a major," Voronov replies, wiping his face in disgust. "But yes, let's not forget that you were an officer before you turned into an animal... at least you'll get your court-martial for disobeying your orders, and I will have the honor to be presiding over it."

At last, now I know I'm dead. So this is how it comes to me. Well, at least I made death work hard.

A voice comes from the radio receiver fixed to Voronov's armor.

"Falcon One reporting. The Stalkers are clustered. Landing a team now to intercept them. Requesting permission to return to base once done. Over."

"Falcon One, proceed." Voronov turns to his gunmen. "Let's get out of here. Off to my chopper with this walking corpse!"

Someone kicks him in the back and he falls directly at Voronov's feet, who kicks Lazarov in the face.

"Your soldiers dead, the Stalkers routed... call it a day, Major!"

The general's men grab and manhandle him towards the transport helicopter that is waiting nearby.

Red Idol Gorge, 12 October 2014, 17:25:54 AFT

To the Stalkers manning the perimeter of the ruined city, it all happened too fast.

Their turned their anxious faces to the skies when the sound of helicopters came. Then the rockets started to pound them, followed by the murderous bursts of 12,7mm Gatling machine guns. Shrink had no chance to give any command for his Stalkers to take cover, neither was it necessary with the small group scattered within seconds. When the two helicopters moved by and prepared to turn back for another strafing attack, Shrink did the only thing he could to rally the rest of his decimated fighters.

"Fall back, fall back!"

Hoping that they would be safer in the narrow gorge leading back to the east, he waved his hands to everyone to follow him.

"What about Lazarov?" Mac shouts.

"We can't help him if we're all dead!"

More Stalkers fall in the hail of heavy bullets. What had meant doom for the dead helps those still alive to escape: the dust clouds stirred up by machine gun fire is the only cover shielding Shrink, Mac and the dozen survivors running away with them from the death raining on them from above.

Probably knowing that the Stalkers are all but eliminated, one helicopter turns away. The other one disappears from the Stalkers' sight among the ragged hills flanking the gorge, only to re-appear after a minute and strafing them one last time before it too turns away towards the ruins.

"Shrink!" Mac shouts as loud as her exhausted lungs allow. "We might be running into a trap!"

Her warning is in vain. Cursing and panting, Shrink leads the Stalkers towards the entry of the gorge where they finally flop down behind the nearest boulders.

"Who's still alive?"

Hearing the beaten and exhausted Stalkers reporting one by one, Shrink curses. Barely more than a dozen are still capable to fight from the group that was so defiant and self-confident until just a few minutes ago.

He is about to ask his men to share any medical supplies they might have with the wounded when Mac's jackal begins to bark. Mac opens her mouth to shout a warning but before the words could come to her lips their position is already under heavy rifle fire, coming from the hillside above them.

"I told you it's a trap," she says in despair and loads a grenade into the integrated launcher of her rifle.

"Yes you did," Shrinks shouts back. "Now you can die happily, you arrogant tart!"

"Fuck death! I don't want to die and will not die!"

"Machine gun!" shouts a Stalker, crouching behind a rock and spitting dust from the impacting bullets close by. "Machine gun at nine!"

Peeking out just long enough for aiming the grenade launcher, Mac releases a grenade in the direction her comrade has pointed out. The projectile misses but the machine gun crew sees it better to relocate. While doing so, one of the attackers makes the mistake of sticking his head out from behind the rocks for a second — long enough time for a young Stalker to score a hit from his Dragunov. He is about to emit a satisfied shout but it freezes on his lips as he is mowed down almost immediately.

The hostile fire suddenly ceases.

"Hey, Stalkers!"

Hearing the voice, the pinned down defenders know it is not a call to surrender. It is mocking them as part of a cruel cat-and-mouse game.

"Did you stash some nice relics? Tell us where and maybe we kill you quickly!"

"May all mercenaries burn in hell," Shrink says and spits.

"I have a Heartstone up my ass," Mac shouts. "Come and dig it out!"

The attackers renew their fire with even more force, apparently angered by the remaining Stalkers' laughter that followed Mac's defiant shout. The defenders return fire as best as they can, but they begin to falter as their inevitable doom looms closer.

"Diagnosis: our condition is terminal," Shrink says slamming his last magazine into his rifle.

Almost completely wasted, with her ammunition deduced to a half-empty magazine and two grenades, Mac releases the cords fastening the little jackal's bag to her assault vest.

"You don't have to be part of this, my friend," she says with tears in her eyes. "This is not a mutant thing... it's a human thing. Go, find a jackal girl and show her what you've got!...."

"Out of ammo!" a Stalker shouts.

"Grab some from the fallen," Shrink replies, "and keep your head down!"

All hopes for a vain but valiant last stand are shattered when more heavy machine guns start barking. Mac and Shrink share a tortured look.

"We will not die here like sitting ducks," a Stalker with a battered AK-74 shouts. "Let's charge and die standing!"

"Brothers, it's been an honor treating you," Shrink grimly replies. "At my count, we charge."

Mac, who has almost released Billy by now, looks up.

"Five. Four," she hears Shrink counting.

The heavy weapons which have joined the onslaught a minute ago are either manned by terrible shooters or firing blank, because no matter how deafening their fire is in the narrow gorge, their bursts don't impact around the defenders. It even appears to her that the hostile fire from above is directed away from them, though still enough bullets fly around their position to make peeking out and assessing the situation unwise.

"Three—"

"To the mother of the Zone, to the father of mutants and my bottle of vodka," a Stalker murmurs as if saying a prayer, "we'll be brothers forever!"

"Two—"

Then Mac realizes what's happening.

"Stop!" she cries out. "Shrink, stop! It's .50 cals! The Tribe! It's the Tribe firing!"

"Excellent!" replies the Stalker who was praying. "I'll keep my last bullet for them!"

The hillside is being pounded by machine guns and automatic grenade launchers. Now it's the veritable avalanche of dust and rocks released by the impact that rains on the beaten Stalkers. This danger, however, is far less lethal than the fire directed at them till a minute ago, which is now reduced to sporadic shots and then ceases permanently.

Mac puts her face mask on and runs through suffocating clouds of dust to the jeep track leading through the gorge. Shrink shouts after her.

"Mac, come back! What the hell are you doing?"

Waving her hands enthusiastically, she greets the first Humvee of a small column that has to brake hard to avoid running her through. The bulletproof window goes down and a Lieutenant's dusty, helmeted face appears.

"Thank you!" Mac shouts overtaken by joy and relief. "Thank you! *Spasiba! Gracias!*"

"*De nada,*" replies the Lieutenant. Before Mac could recollect herself from the surprise, Sergeant Major Hartman cuts in from the passenger's seat.

"Get out of our way, scavenger. We have urgent business!" He waves to the Lieutenant. "Let's move on, Ramirez."

Encrypted transmission between Moscow, the New Zone and the Old Zone, 12 October 2014, 17:35:08 AFT

#Eagle Eye, this is Diver, do you copy?#

#Eagle Eye to Diver. Loud and clear. #

#Did you receive the voice transmission?#

#Good job, Diver. We have it on tape. Do you have a visual on the target?#

Positive. He is entering a helicopter.#

#Eagle Eye to Diver. You are cleared to execute.#

#Eagle Eye, the friendly element is on board. Call sign Condor. Advise. Repeat: advise on Condor.#

#[static noise]#

#Diver to Kilo One. I know you're listening in. Make up your mind.#

#Diver, this is Kilo One. Bring him back. We need his intel about the American renegades.#

#This is Eagle Eye. Affirmative to Kilo One.#

#It was about time! Team is moving in. Over and out.#

Aboard General Voronov's helicopter, 12 October 2014, 17:40:58 AFT

Lazarov feels nothing but fatigue and pain in his limbs. With his hands shackled behind his back, he looks up at Voronov who returns his gaze with pure disdain. As the rotor blades turn quicker and the helicopter prepares for take-off, Voronov draws his pistol.

"This will be a very short flight for you."

"Why don't you finish me off right now, General?"

"To cherish the moment, I guess," Voronov replies lighting up a cigarette.

The helicopter takes off. The moment of parting from the land where he fought, suffered and loved during the last days of his life fills Lazarov's soul with sadness. He looks at the jagged hills through the open hatch.

I would have happily died in battle... but to live would have been better.

"Disappointed to leave, huh?" Fumbling with his pistol, Voronov chuckles above him. "Imagine how many times I was disappointed to see you live! But now —"

Suddenly, Lazarov's ears detect a muted *bang-bang*, coming from the ground. Almost immediately, the helicopter shakes as if hit by several blows from a giant's sledgehammer. The engine loses power and thick, oily smoke fills the compartment.

"What the —"

Another heavy blow sends Voronov to the floor he desperately grabs for something to hold. He drops his pistol and, as the helicopter tilts, it slides through the open hatch.

"We are under fire!" The pilot's voice turns into a scream amidst the shattering noise of breaking cabin glass. More bullets riddle the cockpit and the helicopter crashes to the

ground with a huge deafening, grinding thud, tossing Voronov and his men around in the compartment, screaming in despair. Something hard hits Lazarov, sending a sharp pain into his already spinning head. The engine dies out.

Groans of wounded men mix with the black smoke. The major coughs up when the fumes bite into his respiratory tract.

"Take up defensive positions!" the general cries out. "*Davay!*"

One of the guards gets up, but is hit by several bullets from an automatic rifle as soon as he reaches the hatch. He sinks to the floor with a curse having turned into a moan.

"To the windows, men! Move, move you idiots!"

Voronov's voice is full of pain, but his orders still have an effect on his men. The few guards who have not been incapacitated from the crash jerk themselves to the compartment windows and try to return the fire that is now directed at the wreck from all sides, while Lazarov takes advantage of the confusion to move closer to the hatch, from where he can see who is responsible for the assault. Peering between the guards' feet as they frantically try to assume firing positions, he has clear view to the rocky ground outside.

From behind the cover of the boulders and rocks dotting the shallow defile where the helicopter had fallen, several commandos are engaging the men inside.

But Voronov's men are not easily beaten. One of them stumbles over Lazarov's body, curses, and even takes the time to kick the major before kneeling to open fire through one of the shattered windows. The same *bang* sounds outside that Lazarov had heard before the engine was hit, and a split second later the head of the general's man is blown off by a heavy bullet, drenching the agonized defenders next to him with blood and brain matter. The guard's body remains in a kneeling position and his fingers pull the trigger for a last time, executing the last order of a mind that had ceased to exist a second ago.

Lazarov embraces the floor, keeping his head as low as he can while the bullets keep raining on the wreck like hailstones, tearing more and more holes into the thin metal of the fuselage and allowing the light to fall in and pierce the smoke and blood vapor inside, right until the last firing weapon of the defenders falls silent.

With his ears still ringing, Lazarov barely hears the commands coming from outside, but he sees a shadow approaching.

The red beam of a laser aiming device pierces through the darkness, then a Stalker's silhouette appears. He aims a pistol as he enters the compartment. The red dot of the aiming device moves from body to body. Lazarov cannot see the face but the hood and the heavy rifle on the Stalker's shoulder look familiar, just like the exoskeleton he is wearing.

"*Pomogi*... help me." Voronov's voice is barely more than a whisper. He lifts his left hand. The other is broken, with a bloody chunk of bone poking out from his forearm.

"That must be painful, Captain Bone," the Stalker says, "but at least it gives meaning to your call sign."

"You can't leave me here... I am an army general!"

"No longer."

Dread is the last expression on General Voronov's face before two bullets hit his head and chest.

Lazarov is too weak to warn the Stalker of the wounded guard who is reaching for his weapon, and before he can gather enough strength to shout out, a rifle fires. Hit, the guard slowly sinks down to the compartment floor and moves no more.

Another silhouette appears in the hatch, pointing his assault rifle inside. By now Lazarov recognizes his gear: the rifleman is wearing the heavy combat kit of Russian special forces.

And I thought there could be no more surprises.

The Stalker turns to Lazarov. "I told you I could take down a chopper with that rifle. Now we're quits for good!"

"Crow?"

"At last it's time for that proper introduction, Major." The Stalker pulls his hood back and takes off his balaclava. A round face under blond hair appears, the expression almost jovial, though the gray eyes remain cold. "Captain Igor Sokolov, Spetsnaz Alpha Group."

Noticing Lazarov's surprise with a grin, he kneels down and cuts the plastic handcuffs from the major's wrists with a combat knife. "Sorry if you expected Oksana Fedorova."

"It's time for some explanation too, Captain."

"A few months ago, the Guardians learned that a rogue officer appeared at Bagram. They weren't sure whether it was a renegade or someone posing as one of their officers, but they couldn't let either happen. Their brass wanted to find out, but you know how the Guardians are: *Boom, bang, kill everyone!* They have no talent for clandestine jobs. So, they called in some old favor with the army, the army asked the FSB, and here I was... Here, have more water!"

Crow, or better Captain Sokolov puts the tube of his camelback to Lazarov's lips.

"Then I found out about the arms smuggling. When it became clear that Voronov was not only an impostor and an arms dealer, but was also killing soldiers to get at their precious gear he was declared fair game. A trap was set to have all this proofed—with you as bait, sorry—and once it snapped shut..."

Sokolov draws the tip of his thumb across his throat.

"I could have guessed it," Lazarov says sitting up and rubbing his raw wrists.

"Our mission is complete with you secured. Almost, that is." Sokolov turns to one of his men. "You know the drill."

"*Yest, komandir,*" sounds the operator's reply.

"Come, let's get out of this wreck!"

Lazarov groans as he grasps Sokolov's hand and gets to his feet. Leaning on his shoulder, the major has barely stepped out from the compartment when a shot is fired inside.

Half dozen heavily armed operators wait for them outside, one of them running up to give his commander a helping hand. Together, they move Lazarov and carefully place him to the ground, letting him lean with his back against a boulder.

"With or without that exo, you're heavy," the Spetsnaz commander tells him. He wipes sweat from his face. "What are you on? Steroids?"

"What about the Stalkers?" Lazarov asks back, ignoring the question.

"Voronov's choppers beat them into flight but I saw Shrink and a few others making it into the gorge."

"Why didn't you help them?"

"Getting to that bastard was our priority and taking on two gunships would have been too dicey anyway. You're lucky that Voronov was flying in this tin can."

Two more shots are fired inside the helicopter, followed by a faint scream. Sokolov doesn't bother to look there. "Medic!" he shouts, waving at one of his commandos. "Over here!"

The squad medic scowls when he arrives and sees Lazarov's condition. He starts tending to Lazarov's many bruises and wounds, first of all putting a bandage on the major's chest. More bandages and painkillers follow.

"You are in a dreadful shape," Sokolov anxiously says, holding the camelback once more to the major's lips. "Drink. There will be better stuff back home."

Slowly regaining his strength from the cool water and the painkillers administered by the medic, Lazarov looks around. Beyond the defile, the ruins of the City of Screams loom in the sunset. The snow on the far mountains appears pure and the sky is clear to the east where the Tribe's hidden valley lies.

"Home?"

Lazarov stretches out his arms, as if he wanted to embrace the landscape. The captain frowns.

"Hope you don't plan to stay here... I'm not sure if the army will approve of your idea of deserting."

"Deserting? Who is a deserter in this place, where everyone betrayed everyone else?"

Sokolov nods and sighs at length. "Does the call sign Kilo One mean anything to you?"

"It does," says Lazarov with the ghost of a smile on his face, "but I don't want to talk to him for a while... he could send me on another mission to a place worse than this."

"I doubt there's any place worse than a Zone of Alienation, be it this one or ours."

"Any place is bad where they are not."

Sokolov does not reply, but a barely noticeable bow of his head suggests his accord, or at least consideration.

The Spetsnaz ordered to finish off Bone's surviving guards appears.

"The chopper is clean," he reports and presents a bag. "I found this inside."

"Is that your gear?" Sokolov asks.

Lazarov peeks inside. Eagerly, he retrieves his belongings that were taken from him by Voronov's men. Sokolov whistles when he sees the relics appear. Lazarov carefully puts them into the containers on his belt. Closing his eyes, the major takes a deep breath as he feels the relics radiating their benevolent powers into his body again.

Another Spetsnaz arrives with bulky communication gear on his back. "HQ is calling for a sit-rep."

Strider takes the speaker. "Mission accomplished. No casualties to report. The friendly is secured... Understood. Standing by." He listens to the reply and gives the speaker to the major. "Colonel Goryunov."

Lazarov waves the speaker away. "I don't care anymore. Just tell him... tell him that I've gone on a long raid. No, wait... Here. Take this." Lazarov removes his most valuable relic from its container. The warmth in his body diminishes and a slight ache creeps back into his head, but he has been through much worse. "Take this to Goryunov and mention to him an old lady in Moscow. He will know what to do."

444

Captain Sokolov studies the relic with pensive eyes. "Is this what I think it is?"

"Yes."

"Are you sure about this?"

Lazarov nods. The captain shrugs but takes the relic and transmits his words.

"Understood. Moving to the extraction site. Diver out." He gives the speaker back to the radio man. "Goryunov wants you to know that, soon, that old lady will be a very rich lady. He also wants you to know that you'll be missing Zarubin's court-martial."

Lazarov shakes his head. "I've had enough of court-martials."

"What will you do now?"

"I will see the only healer who can give me comfort and cure my wounds. They are deeper than your medic could treat. And then… I'll have to visit a friend's son in America."

Sokolov and the medic exchange a puzzled gaze.

"Come on, let's go home. Just think of all the vodka we'll have tonight. It's not something you can have with the Tribe, can you?"

"Hostiles! Hostiles approaching from the east!"

It is the sentry shouting from edge of the defile.

Captain Sokolov barks quick commands to his operators. It takes only a minute for the well-trained squad to take up a defensive position around the helicopter's wreck. By that time the noise of heavy vehicles approaching can be clearly heard.

Speak of the devil, Lazarov thinks.

"I don't think we're about to be attacked, Captain," he says.

"How do you know?"

A voice from a loudspeaker proves Lazarov right.

"This is Sergeant Major Hartman. We have no hostile intentions. If you don't open fire, we won't fire. If you do, we'll blast your sorry asses back to Russia. We are here for Major Lazarov!"

Hartman's voice comes from about two hundred meters away, from beyond the edge of the defile. The distance doesn't prevent Captain Sokolov from shouting back defiantly.

"Come and get him, Yankee!"

Lazarov rises to his feet. "If you don't mind, Captain, let me do the talking."

Followed by Sokolov and two Spetsnaz with their weapons at ready, Lazarov climbs the low slope out of the defile.

"I agree," Sokolov says noticing the Humvees surrounding the crash site and their machine guns pointed at them, "it's better if you do the talking."

Hartman leaves the lead vehicle and walks up to Lazarov and the three Spetsnaz. Two Lieutenants follow him. When they stand face to face, the sergeant major gives Sokolov and his men an inquisitive look from under his bushy eyebrows. Concluding that Sokolov must be an officer, he salutes. Captain Sokolov returns the salute but no handshakes are exchanged.

"Glad to see you still in one piece," Hartman greets Lazarov.

"Sorry to say but you missed hell of a show, Sergeant Major."

"We had a little trouble on our way that had us delayed."

The faint noise of a helicopter comes from far away. "That's our bird," Sokolov says. "You can still change your mind and leave this land."

Lazarov looks him deep in the eyes. "Would any real Stalker?"

"What, you're a free Stalker now?" Sokolov asks.

"You are here on the big man's orders, aren't you?" Lazarov asks Hartman. "I'm not supposed to leave with all the knowledge about your secrets, right?"

"*Slushaite, Maior!*[1] There's a reason for me insisting on you coming back with us," Sokolov hisses in Russian, apparently

---

[1] Listen, Major!

hoping that the Americans can't understand. He cocks an eye to Hartman's two Lieutenants standing there motionlessly, keeping their fingers on their machine guns' trigger guards. From under the dark visors of their helmets they must be giving Sokolov the same look of suspicion. The two Spetsnaz behind their captain raise their weapons.

"We aren't here on Colonel Leighley's orders," Hartman says, calmly, but drawing his hand over to his holstered pistol. The Lieutenants immediately aim their weapons at the three Spetsnaz. Lazarov however, no matter the growing tension, notices that the Sergeant Major has called the man who would be Khan by his real rank and name. He cannot think of anything else but a bond between the two warriors going back for a very long time. "He only approved of *her* wish."

Looking around, Lazarov lets his eyes wander over Sokolov and his Spetsnaz, the sergeant major, the Lieutenants and fighters, all these heavily armed men set to get at each other's throats over him, and beyond them the desolate hills of the New Zone that appear so deceitfully tranquil from the distance.

Eventually he steps to the renegade Marines, turns round to face Sokolov and gives him a bitter smile.

"The worst enemies are my best friends now. I have to see how far this takes me."

Sokolov sighs and bows his head.

"I see."

His Spetsnaz relax their hold on their rifles. The sergeant major removes his hand from his pistol but the Lieutenants still don't relax their threatening stance.

The two Russian officers exchange a salute. "Time for us to get out of here, Stalker," Sokolov says, "but don't hope that we will just forget about you!"

"I won't," Lazarov replies.

Sokolov gives Hartman only a nod this time.

Lazarov watches the captain rejoining his men squad and move out of the defile, making their way westwards through the rocky terrain where the setting sun has by now turned the shades of ochre into pale red.

"Wise choice," the sergeant major observes.

"They were heavily outgunned", Lazarov says. "Sokolov is not crazy to put up a fight against such odds."

"I didn't mean him."

"Me then? After all I've been through it wasn't hard to make."

"I wasn't talking about your choice either, Major, but *hers*."

"Nooria?"

Hartman looks down at the ground where the wind-blown sand is swirling like a delicate veil.

"Is the sand flying on its own, or is it the wind blowing it?"

Lazarov walks to the nearest Humvee, still thinking about the sergeant major's enigmatic words. Before entering the vehicle, though, he halts for a moment.

"Does this mean I belong to you now?" he asks.

"No," replies Hartman. "You don't belong to us, just like we don't belong to anyone but her."

Now Lazarov understands. He smiles as he climbs inside through the door courteously held open by Lieutenant Ramirez. "Then let's go home at last!"

Slowly gaining speed, the small convoy sets out towards the Tribe's hidden stronghold where desperate men from all over the world flock to live a life according to a code of honor that not even the greatest evil could overcome, and where Mikhail Lazarov, now a free man belonging only to the Zones, has found the solace without which not even the strongest men can live.

END

Author's acknowlegdements

I pay my respect and express my biggest thanks to all those who supported my endeavor to produce this book:

Rok Nardin, Martin Snooks, Chad Beauregard, Ville Vuorela, Tim Wells, Sonny Burnett, Matthew Dippel, Jas A. Devlin, Joe Coleman, Alex Kane, Kristopher Haessler, Steel Thunder, Noah Stacey, Nick Wheeler, Alex Bobl, Andrew Kegley, Nicholas Gutcheck, Víctor Ocampo, Penille Andersen, Joe Mullin, Mary Elizabeth Klimkosz, Erica Coluccio, Lee Prindle, Christian Diaz, Desi Ivanova Zmiicheto, Ivan Piper, Jonas Oxbøll, Marshall Stone, Drew C. Gaona, Dies Irae, Георги Георгиев, Aimee Gill, Pytor Malenchenko, Rick Braat, Ruben Figueiredo, Kevin D. Nantel, Cem Topal, James Ward, Martin Heteš, Jonathan Roos, Andrew Stone, Dalton Reid, Артур Даун, Felix Pütit, Nils Berends, Jack Burton, Kit Tonkin,Val Klimov, Alfredo Sandoval Ruezga, Rae Celta Nikolai, Pratap Singh, Alexandra Walker-Kinnear, Karl Relf, Justin Lister, Владислав Ліщук, Nicholas Walker, Чебурашка Сергей, Jason Francis Colwell, Todd Curcuru, Sebastien Ranger, Brando Currarini, Cristian Castro, Alexander Mead, Eduardo Becker da Rosa, Vincenzo Travaglini, Andrew C Hasfjord, Aaran Dignard, Iestyn Ap Daffyd, Ian Cleary, Humberto Gonzalez, Sajjad Marandi, Adalbert Greenbert Hrinchenko, Ben Wilson, Kalle Toukonen, Zack Gabbert, Matthew French, Matt Bonomo, Daz Gurney, Jed Palmer, Ивайло Иванов, Kuze Hideo, Austin Nicholson, Charles Calleja, Vincent DiStefano, Patterson Brown, Dustin Leroux, Olivier Brault, Karlo Kaštelan, Benjamin Bailey Waddington, Mike Lee, Nikolai Thomas, Maximilian Payne, Dawran Dllan Dmghb, Al Rivera, Skeletor Jopko, Cristian Ramos, Pascal Meunier, Ryan Riley, Burnaby North Secondary, Grant Warkentin, Juri Freiberg, Nikhil Vyas, John Siegmund, Ramapo Chutipong Jimmy Sutawan Ruangrit, Brian Frank, Gustavo Sosa, Sean Sheehan, Brian J Harrison, Guy Bélanger, Fredrik Patrickson, Douglas Gibbons, Fabian Flores, Jayme McDonald, J.p. de Bas, Xi Yang, Arek Snow Glowacki, Miro Bobik Neuman, Ian Slutzky, Edwin Zavala, Richard Krawczyk, Alec Blewett, Kevin Welsh, Sergej Koroliovas, Kurt Sengstock, Linus Borgström, Bryan Pacheco, Tommy Gilbert,

Leandro Quintana, Caleb Green, Nick Rebain, Geoffrey L. Bunn, Mateusz Prętki, Matthew Drummond, Skrotiz Widén, Benjaman Pollhein, Igor Yagolnitser, Pratab Singh, Sascha Bogdanov, Matthias Hoffmann, Milán Szabó, Ernestas Vaščenka, Typhoon Mc Enteggart, Harrison Cauley – and many others.

"If the toughest sons of the Zone will keep together – who can stand against us, brothers?"

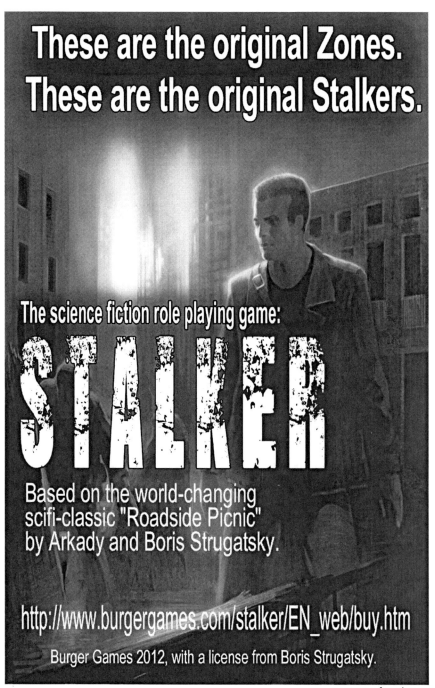
- courtesy advertisement

CPSIA information can be obtained at www.ICGtesting.com
Printed in the USA
LVOW07s0145090913

351550LV00017B/433/P